Jane Costello was a newspaper journalist before she became an author, working on the *Liverpool Echo*, the *Daily Mail*, and the *Liverpool Daily Post*, where she was Editor. Jane's first novel, *Bridesmaids*, was an instant bestseller. *The Nearly-Weds* won Romantic Comedy of the Year 2010, *Girl on the Run* was shortlisted for the Melissa Nathan Award for Romantic Comedy 2012, and her latest novel, *All The Single Ladies* is yet another bestseller. Jane lives in Liverpool with her boyfriend Mark and three young sons. Find out more at www.janecostello.com, and follow her on Twitter @janecostello

Also by Jane Costello

Bridesmaids
The Nearly-Weds
My Single Friend
Girl on the Run
All the Single Ladies

The
Wish
List

Jane
COSTELLO

SIMON &
SCHUSTER

London · New York · Sydney · Toronto · New Delhi

A CBS COMPANY

First published in Great Britain by Simon & Schuster UK Ltd, 2013
A CBS COMPANY
This paperback edition published 2013

1 3 5 7 9 10 8 6 4 2

Simon & Schuster UK Ltd
1st Floor
222 Gray's Inn Road
London WC1X 8HB

www.simonandschuster.co.uk

Simon & Schuster Australia, Sydney
Simon & Schuster India, New Delhi

A CIP catalogue record for this book
is available from the British Library

PB ISBN: 978-0-85720-556-8
EBOOK ISBN: 978-0-85720-557-5

Typeset by M Rules

Printed and bound by CPI Group (UK) Ltd, Croydon, CR0 4YY

For my brother Stephen

Acknowledgments

There are so many talented people at Simon & Schuster working behind the scenes on my books that I could easily fill more than a page with their names. But I'd like to say a special thanks to just a few of those – Suzanne Baboneau, Ian Chapman, Kerr MacRae, Clare Hey, Maxine Hitchcock, Emma Harrow, Dawn Burnett, Sara-Jade Virtue, Alice Murphy, Ally Grant and Lizzie Gardiner. I'm so grateful to you all.

Thank you, as ever, to my brilliant agent Darley Anderson and his Angels – Clare Wallace, Rosanna Bellingham, Camilla Wray and Andrea Messant.

Finally, thanks to my parents Jean and Phil Wolstenholme, my lovely children, and my boyfriend Mark O'Hanlon.

Twenty years from now, you will be more disappointed by the things you did not do than by the things you did do. So throw off the bowlines. Sail away from the safe harbour. Catch the trade winds in your sails. Explore. Dream. Discover.

Mark Twain

Prologue

Opening my eyes has never been so excruciating. I can manage but a tiny slit, one that involves a degree of movement as painful as it is infinitesimal.

Don't let me give you the impression it's only my optic system that's troubling me, though. I've been awake but immobile for several minutes wondering what hideous torture device has been used to peel the lining from my guts. I'm cheek down on a pillow, contemplating why my tongue feels three times its usual size and is holding what can be no more than a quarter of its normal water content.

'Urghhh . . .'

My fetid groan sounds like that of a recently exhumed corpse attempting to come back to life. Then I feel it beside me. Movement.

My eyes spring open, sending a slice of pain through my frontal cortex. I take in my surroundings and two horrible facts become instantly apparent:

1

Jane Costello

I am in a bedroom.

And it's not mine.

I squint through evil shafts of sunlight that stream through grubby vertical blinds and bounce off a snowstorm of dust particles.

The floor boasts the sort of swirly carpet fashionable in public houses of the 1970s – only this one doesn't have the benefit of the dirty ash of several thousand discarded fags trodden into it. It is psychedelic to a nauseating degree: an angry clash of paisley patterns in orange-brown shades that range from tartrazine to dog poo.

In the corner is a greying Formica dressing table with intermittent gilt edging, next to it is a faux-teak chest of drawers, and the main door looks as though the only possible thing it can lead to is a basement full of dead bodies.

The flicker of a red LED drags my attention to the bedside table, where a solitary item sits entirely out of place: an Alessi alarm clock, straight out of the design pages in GQ. It reads 08.26.

I feel the quilt slide slowly across my back, as if someone's pulling it sleepily towards them. I freeze again, my chest hammering.

There is a living, breathing person next to me, of that there is no doubt. Who that person is, is quite another question.

My mind starts whirring while I attempt to piece together the events of our girls' night out. I remember chatting to the barman ... then the guy who looked like Ryan Gosling ... then there was that paramedic – oh God, I've come home with the

2

paramedic! He was supposed to be helping that poor woman in labour in the restaurant above the bar. The swine! She could've been stuck there, swimming in her recently broken waters, while that guy was downstairs picking *me* up!

Then it hits me. There was someone *after* the paramedic. I think.

There's only one thing for this.

Painfully slowly, I attempt to move my head to the other side so I can get a look at exactly who I'm sharing these bedclothes with.

It takes several seconds, not only because I don't want to wake him up, but also because my mouth appears to be stuck to the pillow with an adhesive of similar quality to No More Nails.

My bed partner has his back to me.

A broad, muscular back with a small mole on his shoulder and a faint tan line round the neck. I carefully push myself up, freezing each time he stirs, until I have a side view of his face.

He has long, dark eyelashes with a tiny blob of sleep in the corner, a straight nose and soft, parted lips from which he's snoring lightly. He's handsome, if dishevelled, and I'd put him in his early thirties, though he could be younger. Then it comes back to me. *It's the guy who looks a bit like Tom Hardy!* The guy with the lovely ... I breathe in his smell and have my first and only positive experience of the day.

He moves again, pulling the duvet over himself. Adrenalin rushes through me as my immediate priority slaps me in the face: I've got to get out of here.

I manoeuvre myself to a sitting position, making absolutely sure that the bedding touching him doesn't move, and realise I'm wearing my clothes from the night before. I'm torn between revulsion and relief.

I slowly swing my legs out of bed, fully expecting to see my Karen Millen jeans, but I am confronted instead by something that makes me gasp. My legs. Not my jean-clad legs, you understand. *Just* my legs.

Struggling to breathe, I manage to stand and at that point spot something that confirms categorically that I did something very, very bad last night. My knickers. Only, they're a long way from the piece of anatomy they're supposed to cover – and are caught around the toes of my right foot.

'Oh. My. God,' I whisper.

The implications of this engulf and appal me.

Not only have I breached my no-more-than-four-drinks rule – the one that's remained unbreached since 2001 – but I have had *a one-night stand.* The thought sends a wave of nausea through me. The closest I've ever got to recklessness before this was leaving my antibacterial hand gel at home.

With my heart racing, I drag my tangled underwear up my legs, silently tug on the jeans – which I locate on the other side of the room – and, after three or four minutes of silent but hysterical surveillance, throw on my high heels, one of which had somehow made its way behind a maroon velour curtain.

I creep to the door from hell, not risking a backwards glance, and step out of the room into a hallway. Then I realise I'm in a

4

flat, not a house, although that doesn't alter the decor, which is even more retina-burning here than in the bedroom.

I am feet from the front door when I career into something large and hurtle to the floor, generating a noise comparable in volume to that of a runaway boulder smashing into the side of a mountain.

I blearily register that it's one of those inflatable space hoppers with ears for handles and a smiley face painted on the front. Then I register something else. The bedroom door is opening ...

I scramble to the front door, open it and throw myself out. Then I sprint down the street as fast as is possible in two strappy sandals with only one heel between them.

Chapter 1

One week earlier ...

Have you ever stumbled across something you completely forgot existed, but the second it's in your hand, your head floods with memories?

That's what happens when I discover the list.

It was the picture of my mum blowing out candles at her thirtieth-birthday party that tumbled out of the photo box first. It's not the best image of her. It has that slightly blurry quality of most pre-digital snaps – from the days when you could count on only two pictures in a film of twenty-four not to have decapitated the subject matter.

But you can see this much: she's laughing. Her face is full of joy, her eyes sparkling with life. She looks so carefree. And she was. The date on the back is 17 January 1988. Just a few weeks before everything changed.

The picture belongs in an album that fell out of my photo

box – the one I had to wrestle from the cupboard to reach my overnight bag. It's not the only thing that puts a momentary halt to packing for my forthcoming weekend away.

The list is written on a folded piece of A4 paper tucked in the back of the album. The handwriting is neat and distinctively teenaged, embellished enthusiastically with biro hearts and several declarations that 'Cally luvs Johnny'.

I instantly recall when we composed it.

It was during one of the revision sessions I had with Cally and Asha, probably during a break – we had at least four per hour to minimise the risk of 'burning out', as I remember.

It also must have been during a temporary ceasefire in the constant war between my older sister, Marianne, and me; that's the only explanation for her inclusion.

I can picture every one of us, although whether the uniform 'Rachel' haircuts, Doc Marten boots and blue mascara are real detail or my imagination at work, I couldn't tell you.

It is dated 1997 – the year Tony Blair came to power, the world was introduced to Harry Potter, and I broke my ankle dancing to 'Groove is in the Heart' by Deee-Lite at Mark Blackman's party.

We were fifteen years old. Underneath are four signatures – Marianne Reiss, Emma Reiss, Asha Safaya and Cally Jordan. And finally there's the hilariously grand declaration that we will 'undertake to do our utmost to perform the above achievements to the best of our abilities within the agreed and specified timescale'.

It sounds terribly serious.

As I take a last look at the picture of my mum, something occurs to me. Fifteen years on, perhaps we didn't take that list seriously enough.

Chapter 2

I've always been unconvinced by the concept of a fish pedicure. Don't get me wrong: I'm all for spa days. I simply fail to comprehend how shoving your feet in tank of marine life so the tiny vertebrates can banquet on your blisters is a better alternative to a pumice stone from Boots.

'Emma, it's lovely,' declares Cally, wiggling her toes. 'Just get your feet in.'

I peer into the bowl, where the fish are swarming round her toes, battling for space like the stars of a sex-education video.

'These fish are illegal in America,' I inform her.

'I don't think they carry the death penalty.'

I'm in Edinburgh with Cally and Asha after being invited by my sister, Marianne, five months after she relocated here. She promised a 'lovely, relaxing weekend' for my friends and me. Only, it didn't start well.

The four-and-a-half-hour journey from Liverpool – which involved wrong turns, Cally flinging the satnav out of the window and a set-to with an HGV driver at Westmorland Services after she squirted his Cornish pasty while cleaning the windscreen – was far from serene.

But by the time we'd arrived at the spa, swathed ourselves in fluffy white robes and proceeded with our lavender oil massages (which admittedly has left me smelling Shake 'n' Vac-ed), we were well on our way to chilling out.

Cally is taking that mission very seriously. And I can't blame her.

My best friend's two-year-old son, Zachary, might look gorgeous, with a smile that makes that kid from *Jerry McGuire* look as cute as Les Dawson. But even his devoted mother admits he's redefined the term 'terrible twos' and has a similar effect on passers-by as a rampaging velociraptor.

Despite my efforts to get Cally out more, her childcare is limited. She already relies on her mum a lot and Zachary's dad is not on the scene to help out. Which means this weekend is the most excitement she's had in a while. Especially since becoming a mum had a more fundamental effect on Cally than any of us could have imagined.

It's not that she looks any different from before. If anything, she's more attractive, with generous *Mad Men* curves, lustrous strawberry-blonde hair and bright green eyes that no sleep deprivation dulls.

But she is different, at least in one way.

'So, Cally, do you think you might *meet someone* this weekend?'

She looks at me like I've escaped from somewhere that serves antipsychotic drugs for breakfast.

'I've got a bed all to myself – with lovely white sheets, no small child and no prospect of being woken at three thirty in the morning with a request to watch *Toy Story* for the fourth time. There's no way anyone else is getting in it with me.'

There was a time, not so long ago, when this statement could never have been attributed to my best friend.

When she was fifteen, Cally was boy mad (even if her experience was theory-based and derived from a combination of bonkbuster novels and Brook Advisory Centre leaflets). When she was twenty-five, she was man mad (in the three years we lived together the rare Sunday mornings were those when I *didn't* bump into a strange man in the kitchen).

These days, she isn't *anything* mad. Instead, she is celibate. Defiantly, unapologetically so.

On the day Cally became pregnant as the result of a one-night stand she lost interest in the opposite sex and never regained it. I thought this might change when she returned to work at a big accountancy firm after maternity leave. I was wrong.

'Emma – seriously – this is only a half-hour session. You need to get your feet in.'

The door opens and in walks Asha.

'How was your massage?' I ask.

'Utter bliss,' she smiles, sitting next to me and fixing her robe. I can't help but notice that the spa technician, supposedly just sipping sparkling water on the opposite side of the room, is sizing her up. Not in a bad way – it's just that Asha has incredibly striking looks and people of both genders find it impossible not to look twice.

12

Her grandparents were from northern India and, although her mum was Lancastrian through and through, and her dad grew up in Liverpool, she has the dainty, almost doll-like features of a Bollywood princess.

But don't let that, or the dulcet voice, fool you. Asha is the most passionate and principled person I know – a teenage feminist who grew into a woman determined to make a difference.

'I feel as though I've earned this after the week I've had,' she tells me, taking off her slippers and sliding her feet into the water.

'Heavy week?' I ask.

'They all seem to be, lately, Em.'

Asha's work crises put everyone else's in perspective. For six years, she's worked at a domestic-violence refuge at a location in Liverpool that's secret to all but the staff and its residents. For the last three, she's been in charge of the place, a position that's involved tears and frustration but for which Asha couldn't be more perfect. Her empathy is seemingly endless, as I discovered at first hand in the immediate aftermath of my recent – and very messy – break-up.

I don't know why spa days, like dieting and Jennifer Aniston films, are better suited to life when you're not seeing anyone. I suppose that's one advantage of my current lack of romantic action. Though I must admit that I'm not entirely happy with this state of affairs.

It's not being single *as such* that disagrees with me. I'm independent enough, so I've enjoyed the post-relationship Saturday nights with the girls – and the prospect of never again watching

Jane Costello

a programme presented by Jeremy Clarkson fills my heart with unrestrained joy.

But I *am* missing something from my life – and his name is Rob. Sweet, handsome, devoted Rob, who I think about all the time. So why are we no longer together? That would be because I dumped him. And *why* did I dump him? Oh. Don't ask difficult questions …

'Aren't you partaking?' Asha asks, gesturing at the fish.

'Of course,' I shrug.

'Go on, then,' urges Cally.

'I *will*.'

I lower my legs slowly towards the water.

'This is *supposed* to be enjoyable,' Cally pipes up – completely putting me off.

'I nearly did it then!' I bluster.

Cally and Asha exchange looks. And I know it's time to get on with this.

So I straighten my back, take a deep breath, and carefully sink my feet into the water as the fish dive towards them. It's not unpleasant. But it's not pleasant either.

In fact, there is only one, single overwhelming adjective I can use to describe it.

Ticklish.

Within the split second it takes for this to register, I am literally shaking with it, gasping like a four-year-old with a feather duster under each armpit.

'I wonder if we've put too many fish in your tank?' muses the spa technician helpfully.

This is all it takes to know I simply have to remove my feet. *Now.*

They emerge, Neptune-like, as I catch my breath, paying little attention to the suckers attached to them. Fortunately, most of the fish make a last-minute escape. That's . . . *most* of them.

The exception is the one poor creature that's happily nibbling my big toe one minute, and, the next, is flying across the room as if it's been inadvertently caught in a pancake-tossing competition.

The scene is like a maniacal cross between *Finding Nemo* and *The Dam Busters* as the room is brought to a standstill and the fish is propelled in a perfect arch . . . into the spa technician's sparkling water.

She screeches, picks up the glass, completes several hysterical circuits of the room then chucks the fish – complete with ice – back into the tank, before turning to me, Estée-Laudered lips contorted into the grimace of a serial killer.

'Well, that was nice,' I say brightly. 'Now I'm off to the bar to ask a man to make me something cold with a slice of lemon. And I don't mean a fruit salad.'

Chapter 3

Marianne has always had an eye for cool places. And the Hotel Missoni on Edinburgh's Royal Mile is *dripping* in coolness – from the sexy dreadlocked doormen in designer kilts to the fact that Cally bumped into the Kings of Leon in the lift. Literally. She got a high heel caught in the hem of her wide-legged trousers and launched herself head first into the hairy one with the beard. Which *wasn't* cool. Neither was the look on his security guard's face.

Still, this place is enough to make anyone regret trying to get away with two extra weeks between highlights.

Apart from that, I'm as comfortable with my appearance tonight as you can be in the presence of a professional model – although, given she's my sister, that's something I've got used to. And I'm proud to say that I am exactly the same weight as Marianne, give or take a pound.

Of course, she's five foot eleven and I'm five foot four, but let's not dwell on that. Plus, we look alike in some ways, with the same blue-grey eyes, fair hair and generous mouth. The difference is that Marianne has cheekbones you could stand your drink on and her last zit appeared on a camping trip in 1994 and turned out to be a mosquito bite.

This is only the second time I've visited Marianne since she moved here five months ago – although she is planning several trips back to Liverpool in the next few months to pick up various bits of furniture she's got stored at Dad's. Even though my sister and I haven't lived in the same city for years, I never really stop missing her.

I can't pinpoint exactly when I ceased thinking she'd been put on earth specifically to ruin my life. I suppose when you've grown up without your mum around, having another female in your life goes a long way. Dad did an amazing job of raising us, but he isn't the sort of man in whom you'd confide about the issues that vex girls when growing up. Marianne and I preferred to maintain the illusion we were the only women on the planet to never experience a period, kiss or underarm hair. I suspect we were all happier with that set-up.

'I can't wait to show you round the city,' my sister tells us, crossing her ludicrously long legs. 'We'll do the castle in the morning, then climb up Arthur's Seat, then we'll go shopping in Princes Street. I only wish Brian wasn't away this weekend too.' He'd had to take his mum to visit relatives in Aberdeen last time I was in Edinburgh. 'Emma, I'm dying for you to meet him.'

Brian is Marianne's new boyfriend and, although I haven't met him yet, I already know this much: I can't quite understand her enthusiasm for him.

Obviously, I'm happy that she's happy – if she *is* happy. But my worry is that living here with Brian is the complete antithesis of the life she had in London. A life she adored – and who wouldn't? Two years ago, Marianne had a glamorous career, a devoted man and a trendy Primrose Hill apartment. She was like Gwyneth Paltrow without the pro-biotic jumpers and cabbage crisps.

Her fabulous lifestyle was unrecognisable from the world she'd left behind as a gawky teenager when she was spotted, aged seventeen, by a scout at the *Clothes Show Live*. But she seemed to slot in effortlessly – and retained one obvious reminder that she'd never forgotten her roots.

'Do you ever hear from Johnny these days, Marianne?' asks Asha.

Cally glances at my sister to see if our friend has put her foot in it, but Marianne shrugs, only slightly awkward. 'He's still a Facebook friend. He's doing well, from what I hear.'

Marianne was twenty-two when she started dating Johnny Farndon, on whom I, Asha and Cally, especially Cally, had a crush while we were at school. Marianne had never actually spoken to Johnny in those days, but she bumped into him while home at Christmas in 2003 and quickly discovered he'd lost none of the self-effacing charm that had made girls' knees buckle when he was sixteen.

He adored her from the start of their romance – it was obvious. Within months he'd left Liverpool and followed her to London, where, over the next few years, he became involved in various bar and restaurant businesses. He was an unfeasibly young and dynamic entrepreneur, successful but modest too.

In case you can't tell, I thought Johnny was great. Johnny *is* great.

The only person who can apparently no longer see it is Marianne. She left him for Brian, an aspiring television scriptwriter – who, while he's in the process of aspiring, works full-time in a car wash.

She and Brian had been friends for years in London before they became an item and moved to Edinburgh together. And, although he seems nice enough – he must be, because the move was to enable him to be closer to his elderly mother – I remain confounded. The city is fantastic, but Marianne's modelling work hasn't been as easy to come by here as in London. And I'll never understand how she knowingly let someone like Johnny slip through her fingers.

'Didn't you say you had something to show us, Emma?' Cally asks, sipping her drink.

'I can't believe I forgot.' I open my bag and take out the A4 paper, unable to suppress a smile as I unfold it. 'Anyone remember this? "Things to do before we are 30 – by Marianne Reiss, Emma Reiss, Asha Safaya and Cally Jordan".'

Asha gasps. 'I do!'

'Me too . . . vaguely,' says Marianne, clearly dredging the inner recesses of her brain. 'We did it in your bedroom, didn't we, Em? While you were revising.'

Cally and Asha both lived in our street in those days, which was why I was such close friends with them, despite my birthday – a few months after theirs – putting me in the year below them. I distinctly remember enjoying the kudos of having friends in the year above – particularly as they didn't mind me revising with them during their GCSEs.

'I have no recollection of this whatsoever,' says Cally, shaking her head vacantly. 'How depressing. I never realised baby brain could be so acute.'

'Read it out,' Asha says with a grin. 'Let's see if we've managed them all.'

'I suggest you lower your expectations,' I say, clearing my throat. 'Number one . . .'

1 Sleep under the stars.
2 Gain jobs as:-

- Nursery nurse (Marianne)
- Head of the Equality and Human Rights Commission (Asha)
- Carol Vorderman's replacement on Countdown (Cally)
- Internationally renowned interior designer (Emma)

3 Own a cottage in a picturesque Rutshire village (or other location in Riders by Jilly Cooper) and/or learn to play polo.
4 See the Northern Lights.
5 Have a one-night stand.
6 Learn to play the guitar.

7 Find the man you're going to marry.
8 Grow hair long.
9 Eat at a Michelin-starred restaurant.
10 Fit perfectly into a size ten dress.
11 Snog somebody famous.
12 Jump out of a plane.

'I don't know what's more shocking,' Cally says, as I pass the paper to Asha. 'The fact that I've achieved only one – or that we thought Rutshire was a real place.'

Chapter 4

'It's an eclectic mix,' Asha says, smiling. 'I'll give our fifteen-year-old selves that.'

'What was behind some of these?' I say, scrutinising the list.

'An obsession with *Riders*,' offers Cally. 'That bit I *do* remember. We all read that book after I'd pinched it from my mum. It was pure filth – absolutely brilliant.'

'That's where the cottage and the polo came from,' adds Marianne. 'But the one-night stand? That's terrible!'

'I added that,' confesses Cally. 'I'll have been trying to guarantee I'd manage at least one of them. Which I did. More than once.'

'"Learn to play the guitar" was because we loved the Stone Roses,' I continue. 'Getting good jobs ... requires no explanation.'

'What about the Northern Lights?' asks Asha.

'Emma and I had this lovely picture book about them when we were little,' Marianne says. 'Do you remember, Em?'

'Yeah ... it was about a girl who lived in Norway, wasn't it?' I reply. 'We *loved* it.'

Asha frowns at the list. 'Snog somebody famous ... I remember that. We'd originally said: "Snog Leonardo DiCaprio, Kelly from the Stereophonics or Keanu Reeves." But we decided we weren't being realistic, so opened it up to *anybody* famous.'

'So, technically, snogging Ed Miliband would count,' Marianne points out.

'Yes. Why, have you?' I ask.

'Ed Miliband, no. Though I did have a smooch with the face of Abercrombie and Fitch once.'

'No!' say Cally and Asha in unison.

'This was pre-Johnny, obviously,' Marianne continues. 'His breath smelled of peanuts.'

'There are worse things,' I say.

'Not when you find one stuck in your teeth afterwards.'

The list launches a frenzy of reminiscing that takes us through half the bars in the Grassmarket and is disrupted only when Cally and I find ourselves being chatted up.

'I need to tell you now,' she says, clutching the lapels of her tall stranger, 'I have absolutely no interest in having sex with you. Don't get me wrong ... you're not bad-looking. Although I've had several mojitos so that probably helps. It's just that nobody goes near my lady bits these days. They've probably got rust on.'

'I see,' he murmurs, shifting uncomfortably. 'Shall I just leave when my friend gets back, then?'

'I'm not saying that! We need someone to pair up with Emma here and your friend Barry—'

'Larry.'

'He'll definitely do. Though admittedly Em's always been fussier than me and—'

'Actually,' I interrupt, 'I'm not in the market for this sort of thing either.'

'Of course you are!' Cally protests. 'You've been moping about Rob for a month; it's time to get your act together. You dumped him for a reason, remember?'

'Yes,' I say solemnly, draining my drink.

'Oh?' Cally's man perks up. 'What was the reason?'

I'm about to tell him to mind his own business, when Cally steps in. 'He asked her to marry him.'

Our admirers last about forty-seven seconds after that. Part of me thinks that's a shame. Not because I was particularly enamoured with them. But I undoubtedly need something to take my mind off Rob – a fact underlined when I glance at my phone in the taxi on the way to Marianne's flat and discover a text he sent three hours ago.

Hope you're having a fantastic time in Scotland – you deserve it. Love, Rob xxx

'Why does he have to be so bloody *nice*? And *perfect*? And *lovely*?' I sigh. 'I broke his heart. He should despise me. Yet he's still sweet enough to send texts like that – just to show me there are no hard feelings.'

'He can't be *perfect* or you wouldn't have split up with him,' argues Marianne.

'He *is*,' I insist. 'Which is what makes this so worrying. I strongly suspect it's *me* who's got the problem.'

'Subconsciously, perhaps you're attracted to men who treat you badly,' Asha suggests sympathetically. She's obviously been reading *Vagenda* today. 'Lots of women are. You need to train yourself to fall in love with *good men*.'

Cally looks at her incredulously and shakes her head. For the past few months, she's been firmly of the opinion that Asha isn't qualified to determine what is *a good man* – a viewpoint she hasn't been afraid to vocalise.

Toby, the man with whom Asha is hopelessly, irrevocably in love, has everything going for him. He's intelligent, caring, has an amazing career as a paediatrician and constantly declares his undying love for her.

Everything would be wonderful if it wasn't for one matter: he's married to someone else. He might have the marriage from hell – with constant rows, daily conflict and no affection right from the beginning. But it *is* a marriage.

Asha met him after a bruised woman and her terrified and injured little girl arrived at the refuge and she drove them to the children's hospital, where Toby was on duty.

Asha watched as he gently reassured her, even coaxing a smile as he treated her injuries, which fortunately turned out to be minor. Their paths crossed several times again through work, and it wasn't long before they found it impossible to stay apart.

'Cally, it isn't that Toby isn't … *good*,' Asha insists. Her words might be defiant but, as ever when she discusses this, shame burns unmistakably in her eyes. 'He's just in an impossible situation.'

'He's *taken*, Asha,' Cally replies firmly. 'And he has two kids. He's not yours. It's as simple as that.'

Asha sighs. 'You're right. And it can't go on. One way or another, it can't go on.'

We're silent for a moment after that – and as I reread the text from Rob, I experience a wave of clarity. I pull up his number and go to press Call.

'What are you doing?' asks Marianne.

'I'm going to get back with Rob,' I tell her.

'It's three in the morning!' protests Cally as my sister grabs my arm, ends the call, and places the phone firmly back on my lap.

'Emma, you weren't in love with Rob. You were sure about that at the time,' Marianne argues.

'Maybe I've changed my mind. I mean, look at that list. I haven't achieved a single item. Not one.'

'What's Rob got to do with the list?' asks Cally.

'Maybe I *did* find someone to marry – someone wonderful, worthy and gorgeous. But I chose to tell him he was getting too intense ... I chose to boot him out of my life and carry on as before.'

Marianne rolls her eyes.

'Don't you ever think you haven't been *brave* enough in life?' I put to them all. 'Because I do. I mean, why *didn't* I become an interior designer? Why haven't I slept under the stars? Why didn't I move to the countryside?'

'Hay fever?' offers Cally.

Asha smiles. 'Oh Emma, it's just a silly list.'

'I know,' I concede. 'And I'm not saying I feel a burning desire to do all of those things *specifically*. It's more what they represent.'

They're all too tired or too tipsy to respond. And I know when to shut up. So I simply stare at my phone screen and register that the date is Saturday 30 June. There are less than six months until I turn thirty.

And I wonder if anything will have changed by then at all.

Chapter 5

There are some jobs for which the Monday-morning blues are perfectly acceptable. If I was employed at a call centre, for example, facing a hard day of interrupting *Jeremy Kyle* viewers to ask them to review their broadband package. Or if I worked in IT and had eight hours of hard toil ahead, suggesting that callers switch off their computer, then on again.

Anyone would understand if you were a bit on the grumpy side then.

But mine isn't that sort of job. My job requires a disposition that never deviates from happy-pill cheeriness and that's the case whether your house has burned down, your car has been clamped or your cat has vomited in your new shoes.

I walk along Rodney Street with a warm morning breeze in my hair until I reach the door of Little Blue Bus Productions. It doesn't look bad from outside. If you didn't know any better, you might be quite impressed. Rodney Street is one of the grandest roads in Liverpool, home to businesses ranging from financial planning institutions to upmarket cosmetic surgery clinics.

Even when you open the distinctive dark-blue door into reception, you'd be forgiven for thinking this place was kind of swish. They've got an Illy coffee maker. A Conran sofa. Abstract-looking canvases on the walls – stills from the show that made its name.

It's only when I've said hi to Carolyn, the receptionist, and reached the room I call my office, four flights up, that things take a turn for the worse.

The once-plush carpet is now held together with bits of gungy masking tape. There is mouldy coffee in cups abandoned over the weekend, a damp patch on the ceiling and a creaky stationery cupboard that nobody opens for fear of being flattened by a mountain of unfiled paper.

This room was once lovely, bright, conducive to creative thought. Now, like the business itself, it shows all the signs of neglect and chaos.

'You will not believe what that interminable tosser has done to my storyline.' My colleague Giles is staring with characteristic fury at his computer screen and I'm convinced he's trying to blow it up through the power of thought alone.

Despite being otherwise brilliant at his job, Giles has some way to go before he masters that disposition I mentioned. I like to think of him as misunderstood largely because I genuinely like him – and the alternative is to think of him as the grumpiest bastard on the planet.

'I had a lovely weekend, thank you,' I say, smiling as I sit at my desk.

Giles looks up. 'Oh … uh … sorry, Em. Bad morning.' He scratches his chin sheepishly and I notice he's growing a beard again, as if he wasn't hirsute enough. I saw his chest once when he got his jumper caught in the photocopier and he's like a woolly mammoth.

Apart from that – and his ubiquitous heavy-metal T-shirts – Giles isn't bad-looking. I've seen women eye him up on the odd occasion, though that inevitably stops as soon as he opens his mouth. Because, while *I* know that Giles is a pussycat, he has a terrible tendency to give the wrong impression.

It's his favoured method of communication – grunting – that does it. In Giles's world, the grunt is still as *à la mode* as it was in the days when men dragged their knuckles on the ground. It also doesn't help that ninety per cent of what he says is about how shit work is, how screwed up the world is and how stupid his colleagues are.

'You know I don't mean you, don't you, Em?' he said to me once. 'Nor Denise in accounts – she's lovely. And the blokes in studio are sound. Apart from that, they're all unremitting wankers.'

'So,' he says, 'did you take my advice and go to that bar in Edinburgh I recommended?'

'Thanks, but it didn't look like my kind of place. We stuck to white wine and Cosmopolitans in the Hotel Missoni.'

He looks appalled. 'You're not into that poncey crap these days, are you? You were drinking bitter at the Christmas party.'

'I had half a pint, Giles, and only because you persuaded me to try it.'

'*You* persuaded me to do karaoke. I'll never forgive you for that.'

'I barely had to ask twice.'

'Bollocks. And switching the song to "Hey Frankie" by Sister Sledge was unforgivable. I was expecting a classic.'

'"It's Raining Men" by the Weather Girls?'

He grunts.

'So what happened to your script?' I ask.

His face turns a shade somewhere between red and green, before he necks his coffee – it's gone eight thirty so it'll be at least his fifth – and says, 'It's been butchered. I'm incandescent. I won't rest until I've ripped someone's head off.'

'You're taking it well, then?'

Of course, by the time Giles's script actually appears on screen, our viewers won't have any clue about the blood, sweat and politics that go on behind the scenes. Not least because all they'll see is a highly edited, beautifully produced, tightly scripted piece of film-making.

And because the average age of our viewers is three.

Little Blue Bus Productions is a highly successful children's programming company, responsible for what was once – only a few years ago – the UK's number one pre-school kids' show.

The appeal of *Bingbah* is simple. It's gentle enough for parents to approve of, and weird enough for kids to love. There have been comparisons with *Teletubbies* and *In the Night Garden*, yet its creator – Perry Ryder Senior – came up with the concept long before Iggle Piggle picked up his red blanket.

He'd been writing and producing successful, nay legendary, children's television since the 1970s, and, although the other shows exist solely in the archives these days, *Bingbah* continues.

The stars of the show are the three Bingbahs: friendly, overgrown kitten-type creatures with big eyes, sing-song voices and a penchant for marshmallows, which – in the land of Bibblybobbly (where they live) – conveniently grow on trees. They are gentle souls, whose adventures in each episode usually involve fending off the evil squirrels who want to spice up their diet of nuts by stealing the marshmallows.

I have been writing this stuff for eight years now. Don't ask me how. All I know is, it comes naturally, not because I have any great understanding of children – from whom I generally try to stay as far away as possible – but because ... God, I *just* don't know.

By ten o'clock, the office is a hive of activity. Raj, our producer, is downing Natracalm like Smarties – but still looks like his head is about to explode when he glances at the pile of schedules on his desk. Jo, the assistant producer, is firing instructions to James, an animator, who's scribbling as if the end of his pen is on fire; Harry, our editor, is splicing together scenes; Jill, the administrator, is dishing out mail, and everyone is more creatively fired-up (and frantic) than you'd think possible for a Monday morning. The only exception is Jez, the music producer, who doesn't do frantic – even when Raj pushes his feet off the desk, grabs him by the shoulders and screams: 'Don't you understand the word *deadline*?'

They're a brilliant team, one I'm proud to be a part of. Which makes the fact that success doesn't come as easily to us as it once did a fairly bitter pill to swallow. There's little doubt in people's minds about who is the reason for that.

'You're back!' My boss, the venerable chief executive officer, proprietor and son of the genius that was Perry Ryder Senior, storms over to my desk.

Perry Junior is the only member of staff not wearing jeans and a T-shirt, which makes him an anomaly in our industry. Though Perry would be an anomaly in any industry. Today, he is suited and booted in a Sherlock Holmesian three-piece, his shock of curly hair even wilder than last week.

'How's our world traveller?' he booms. The gap in Perry's front teeth sometimes looks wide enough to drive a four-by-four through. 'Have fun in Wales?'

'It was Scotla—'

'I had a cracking holiday in Portmeirion when I was your age. I'll never forget sitting overlooking the sea with a large Piña Colada in my hand. Mind you, anywhere'd look good after a couple of those!'

Perry perches on the edge of the desk and crosses his arms tightly, swaying back and forth hyperactively. He seems to have been forever perched on this desk since Sarah McIntyre, the creative director, left three months ago. Sarah, who was my immediate boss, kept us sane – she seemed to be the only person capable of protecting us from Perry's insanity.

When she left to emigrate to Australia with her husband, we all hoped whoever was appointed as her successor would be as good. Which made one big assumption: that there would be a successor. So far, Perry hasn't got round to advertising, deciding to hold the fort himself so he can indulge in some 'hands-on' creative work with Giles and me. You can imagine how well that went down.

'So. Are we both fired up to our creative bests this Monday morning?' Perry's face is round, waxy, permanently cheerful and resembles one of those potato Smiley Faces you get in the freezer sections of supermarkets.

'I'm not doing badly,' I say brightly, to deflect attention from Giles, who's staring at Perry as if he's flown in on a spaceship direct from the Planet Arsehole.

'That's what I like to hear. I want to talk to you when you've got a min, Emma. I'll get Carolyn to bring us both a nice cuppa char and we'll have a good old brainstorm, eh?' He winks, before bouncing out of the door.

'If he tries to get me to work on one of his shit ideas, I'll have something to say about it,' mutters Giles as the door closes.

'He hasn't said anything yet.'

'Yeah, but you know what he's going to try to make you do, don't you?'

Sadly, the answer is: yes, I probably do.

*

The big problem with having a history that boasts some of the UK's most successful children's programmes is finding ways to follow them. And, frankly, we haven't. Little Blue Bus Productions – to the disbelief of the industry – has failed abysmally to capitalise on the success of *Bingbah* and produce our Next Big Thing, despite Perry's perennial attempts at rooting it out since his father retired five years ago.

The team – not least Giles and I – have come up with a million ideas. But Perry doesn't want to produce a TV programme from one of *our* ideas. He wants to come up with the idea all by himself.

Which I can partly understand, given that his dad is considered to be one of the world's most inspirational children's writers, a man lauded globally for his ingenuity, talent and ability to tap into young minds.

The problem is, every one of Perry's ideas is worthy of only one description – a word favoured by Giles but so perfectly suitable in this context I can't bring myself to use anything else: shite.

'I've come up with a humdinger overnight,' Perry tells me. 'And I want *you* to work on it!'

'Oh . . . great!'

'You're going to *love* this, Emma. This is going to make your career. Sit down. Go on – I'll clear a space.'

He pushes a compost heap of paperwork onto the floor and pats the chair enthusiastically.

'Here's the pitch.' He claps his hands as I sit down. 'We've got a mouse. A damn clever mouse. He's the main character.'

'Right.'

'He's got friends too – I don't know, a duck ... and a dog, hell, maybe we'll even throw in a mouse girlfriend. We'll work on that bit. So this mouse, our hero – he can talk and dance and has *crrr-aaazy* adventures with his pals.'

I sigh. 'Does he have red shorts and yellow shoes, perhaps?'

'How did you guess?'

'And a squeaky voice?'

'Great minds!'

I put down my pen and paper and look at Perry. Really look at him. As if to *plead* with him to recognise the problem with this idea before I have to spell it out. He gazes at me like an eager puppy waiting for a pat on the head.

'You're not worried that people might think *our* mouse is a bit similar to ... *Mickey* Mouse?'

His face drops. 'Hmm. There *are* some potential areas of crossover there, aren't there?'

Chapter 6

In the absence of an opportunity to purchase a cottage in Rutshire – with wisteria round the door, a millionaire neighbour and an adorable Labrador to lick my cheeks when I come home – I rent a flat in south Liverpool instead.

I was ludicrously house-proud too, until I was reminded by that list of what the alternative was. Still, it's not bad. In fact, it's not bad at all.

I live in Grassendale Park, which sits in isolated splendour on the banks of the River Mersey and consists of a cluster of tree-lined avenues, a grand esplanade and some jaw-droppingly elegant nineteenth-century mansions. The place is overflowing with charm and grace, which, obviously, is me all over (ahem).

I never dreamed I'd be able to live somewhere like this. I'd look at these houses in the property section of the local paper and the experience was nothing less than pornographic. I'd be flushed at the decorative coving, frothing over at the original features, groaning with pleasure at the prominent positions within mature landscaped gardens.

My neighbours are a mixed bunch. Next door, in the seven-bedroomed stucco building, is Charles Cavendish QC, a barrister, and his (fifth) wife Stacey. Directly opposite is Vlady Simeonova, a Bulgarian striker who plays for Liverpool FC and owns more flashy cars than I own matching lingerie.

My building is an elegant Victorian villa with a buttermilk exterior and a coach house in the grounds. It's been converted into five apartments, ranging from the gorgeous four-bed penthouse with huge bay windows and dark wood floors – to the teeny, tiny, minuscule one-bedroom broom cupboard on the ground floor.

That one would be mine.

It's fair to say that when I moved into the flat two years ago I fell in love with the area and the house as a whole, rather than being bowled over by any generosity of floor space.

Despite the size, though, the apartment is lovely – recently refurbished, with a wood-burning stove in the living room and a trendy fitted kitchen. Courtesy of my addiction to interiors magazines, I've put as much of my own stamp on it as I'm allowed to – playing at being the interior designer I was desperate to become when I was a teenager.

I've almost got used to the fact that I have to turn sideways to squeeze into my bathroom, that I bang my head on the sloping ceiling in my bedroom and that it's the only apartment in the building that doesn't have a window overlooking the communal gardens.

Instead, my kitchen overlooks the house next door – the bottom floor of which was the home of Rita Harvey-Esteves, a former dancer and actress who appeared in a string of television dramas of the 1970s and who refused to let the fact that she had reached the autumn of her years ruin her fun. Friday afternoon wasn't Friday afternoon if I didn't bump into her with a glass of champagne in one hand and a young man in the other. She died of lung cancer in February after a six-month battle, the irony being that smoking was the one vice in which she never indulged.

I loved Rita and I still miss her. Whenever I look out of that window, I still expect to see her there, teetering down the road in last night's clothes or assuring the postman that there must be a mistake whenever he tried to deliver promotional material from Saga.

Tonight, my car crunches up the gravel driveway and I step out with the shopping I picked up on the way home in preparation for Cally coming for dinner with Zachary. It's long overdue, and is something I've been putting off while I looked into ways of bomb-proofing my flat so that it would be able to withstand the force of this particular two-year-old.

'Emma! Pssst!'

I know this is Stacey before I even turn to face her because she always addresses me with a 'pssst'. The first time she did this, I spun round expecting to be confronted by Inspector Gadget.

'Hi, there, how are you?' I say. Stacey looks as though she's in her mid-forties, but I suspect you could throw a few years on top in reality. She has gleaming red hair, freckled, dewy skin and Madonna-esque arms.

'I haven't stopped today,' she sighs. 'It's been *all go.*'

'What have you been up to?'

'Gym. Lunch. Hair. Nails. Scrutinising the Dow Jones index for potential investments. *Ha – joking!*' She barely pauses for breath. 'Anyway, they've found a buyer for Rita's place.'

'Really?' I suddenly feel a bit sad. 'It doesn't feel right without her around any more, does it?'

Stacey screws up her face. 'Not to speak ill of the dead, but Charles thought she lowered the tone.'

I tut spontaneously.

'Oh, don't get me wrong, he *liked* her,' she leaps in. 'We all did. But you know what I mean. There comes a time when every woman needs to give up topless sunbathing.'

'Well, I thought she was fantastic and funny and I miss her.'

'Oh yes, me too,' she says hastily. 'But it's good that the apartment isn't going to be left empty, don't you think?'

'Of course. When are they moving in?'

'Very soon, I gather. And ... it's a *man.*' The second part of the sentence is loaded with implication, as if this man creature is a strange and mysterious phenomenon, to be subjected to serious in-depth anthropological research.

'A man,' I repeat.

She purses her lips mischievously, her pupils dilating wildly. 'Mmm-hmm. And he's good-looking, apparently. Marjory on the second floor saw him with the estate agent. She said he's very, *very* handsome.'

I put my key in the door. 'Stacey, Marjory thinks Cliff Richard is a great big stud.'

'True. I just thought, seeing as you are single these days, there might be some ... *po-ten-tial.*'

I open my mouth to protest that it's not quite that straighforward. That I might be single now but I'm considering being attached again soon, because Rob is lovely and gorgeous and maybe I *do* love him after all ... when I stop myself.

Not least because my frontal cortex feels like it's going to melt every time I think about this.

'I don't think so, Stacey,' I say simply. 'Listen, I'd better run. I've got a dinner to cook.'

'Ooh – for anyone exciting?'

'Well, yes, actually.' A little too exciting if the truth be told.

Chapter 7

'Oh – sweetie, don't do that. Come on, darling. Angel. Ow ... that *hurts!*'

Zachary is trampolining on Cally's knee as she attempts to conduct a conversation that's been cut short several times amid cries of: '*Mummy! Pay me some detention!*'

I spent far longer organising Zachary's dinner tonight than my own, having sourced a recipe for Fussy Eaters' Pasta on the internet and arranged it with carrot and cucumber crudités in the shape of a smiley face. The website in question seems certain this will impress any two-year-old. But they haven't met Zachary.

Cally finally grapples him into a standing position and ushers him to his chair at the kitchen table, where he narrows his eyes at my culinary offering.

'Go ahead and dish up while I go to the loo,' Cally tells me. 'You'll be all right with Zachary, won't you?'

He takes several sharp sucks of his dummy as I wonder when the two Dobermanns are going to arrive at the door.

To be absolutely fair to Zachary, he's not the only child to elicit this increase in my anxiety levels. They all do. As a breed, I find them terrifying. I have no idea why – it's not as if I was bitten by one in my youth. I just find children, particularly the little ones, terribly ... unpredictable. And loud. And messy. God Almighty, they're messy.

'Are you hungry, Zachary?' I can hear the strain in my voice, like there's a fork impaled in my tonsils. 'I hope you like this because Auntie Emma tried very hard to find something that would appeal to you.'

Even I know this is a ridiculous thing to say to a two-year-old. I deserve the resultant look of disdain he throws me before turning his gaze to the fresh, puréed sauce, the special pasta shapes and the lovingly arranged crudités. Then he looks back at me, giving nothing away. It's like catering for A. A. Gill.

'Tuck in!' I add, handing him a fork. He stares at the dish, assessing it suspiciously as his lip starts to curl.

'Is everything all right?' I whimper, but he flings down his fork, crosses his arms, and blurts out a single, loaded word.

'*Yuck!*'

'I made friends with Abigail Daes on Facebook last night,' Cally tells me after she's spent an hour trying to coerce Zachary into consuming six pieces of pasta and a cucumber eyebrow, before finally skipping to the cupcakes.

He's in the living room now, engrossed in a *Bingbah* DVD and probably smearing the cake on the sofa, but I'm beyond caring.

'Wasn't she the quiet one in 4R?'

'Yes – glasses and a funny twitch.'

'What's she up to these days?'

'Pan Asian Marketing Director for a global software company. She's based in Singapore.'

I nearly spit out my tea.

'I was shocked too,' Cally says. 'She never really had much about her, did she?'

'Wow.'

'You should see the pictures of her apartment on Facebook. It's stunning. The size of a football pitch.'

I stand up, banging my head on the space-saving recess next to my back door.

'She'd have to be work-obsessed to get to a position like that,' I venture, placing the dishes in the sink.

'Actually, she seems to be up to quite a lot. She's getting married next year, to a guy that looks like Olivier Martinez. And she's climbing Kilimanjaro in October, to raise funds for a charity she's on the committee of. Oh, and she was voted Woman of the Year by her colleagues in April.'

I take a deep breath. 'Please tell me she's fat.'

'Size eight. Tops.'

'That's settled, then. I hate her.'

Obviously, I'm joking. Clearly. I wouldn't begrudge anyone their fabulous lifestyle and achievements and I have absolutely no doubt she's had to work extremely hard to get to where she is today.

But while I'm certain I don't feel resentful, I definitely feel *something*.

Something that is still lingering as I'm clearing up the devastation after Cally and Zachary have left. I go to open the freezer to put away the litre and a half of hidden vegetable pasta sauce I might get around to eating myself one day. And when I close the door, I'm confronted by something stuck to it with a magnet: the list.

I pick it up and stare at it, reading each line.

I don't know what it is *exactly* that persuades me to make the decision there and then.

Maybe it's because the countdown to turning thirty has well and truly begun. Maybe Abigail Daes and her luxury Singaporean apartment have brought out my competitive side. Or maybe it's that picture of my mum on her thirtieth birthday, taken less than a year before she died. Since it tumbled out of my photo box, I haven't been able shake the feeling that I should be treating every second of my life as precious – grasping every opportunity, no matter how mad or scary.

It could be all those things, or none. But once the decision is in my head, there's no going back. So I clutch the list and head to the living room, where I fire up my laptop and type two words into Google.

Polo lessons.

Chapter 8

'Are you serious?' Asha splutters into her tea.

'Actually, I am.' I'm at her flat on Thursday after work, trying to ignore the implication that I must've suffered a severe blow to the head.

'But, Em,' she says gently, 'how are you going to buy a cottage in Rutshire?'

'I can do half of that one – the polo lessons. Besides, I didn't say I'm necessarily going to do *everything*. There's got to be flexibility or it'd become a full-time occupation and I've already got one of those. But by the time I hit thirty, I want to have achieved ... I don't know ... seventy-five per cent. Enough to make the point.'

Asha's flat is at the top of an enormous Victorian terrace off Lark Lane. It's an Aladdin's cave of a place, courtesy of the travelling she's done over the years, with rugs from Turkey, batiks from Swaziland, tea caddies from Hong Kong and a dozen other far-flung places.

She examines the list and raises an eyebrow. 'Have a one-night stand. When are you going to do that, then?'

'That's in the twenty-five per cent I won't bother with. I haven't got the bottle to even try it.'

'But you have to *jump out of a plane*,' Asha points out. 'Remind me how many people you've slept with, Emma?'

I suck in my teeth and start counting on my fingers until I've used up both hands twice over. Then I look up. 'Three.'

I'm no prude; at least, I don't think so. I've simply never found myself in a position to have sex with someone who isn't a long-term boyfriend. Of whom, there have been only three.

'Surely picking and choosing things on your list destroys the object,' Asha muses. 'Shouldn't it be all or nothing?'

'Two minutes ago, you thought I was deranged to even consider this!'

She laughs. 'Maybe I'm coming round to the idea. You could spend six months ticking things off your list, then have a party to celebrate.'

'I'd like a thirtieth-birthday party,' I confess. 'I've never done anything before because my birthday's so close to Christmas. I think I'm due one.'

'Well, if you're going to have a one-night stand, it's Cally's birthday night out on Saturday – that's the ideal opportunity.'

I squirm, really wanting to drop the subject. She notices. 'You're still not sure you did the right thing with Rob, are you?'

Asha knows the story of my relationship with Rob inside out; she and I have dissected the whole thing, like a frog in a school biology class. She always has been a brilliant listener – patient and generous, never far from the end of a phone. If only that made things any clearer.

Rob and I met last year after he walked into the offices of Little Blue Bus Productions for a meeting with Perry about a fundraising dinner for Alder Hey children's hospital.

Rob's company is big on 'corporate social responsibility' so he's often charged by his boss with generating cash for worthy causes – something he enjoys almost as much as his day job as a 'wealth manager'. Which, as far as I can tell, means making rich people even richer by investing their money. To great effect, as I understand.

He turned up at our office at eleven thirty that day like the Diet Coke man, leaving the womenfolk of the parish so overcome with lust most of us could barely walk straight. He and I got chatting in the lobby as I was leaving to grab some lunch – then carried on as we realised we were both heading into the city centre. He asked me if I would join him for lunch and, two Pret sandwiches and a couple of lattes later, our relationship had begun.

To call Rob eye candy would do him a disservice. He's a feast of gorgeousness – all tanned biceps, dark blond curls and a smile so dazzling it could alert passing ships to hazardous rocks.

But there's more to him than looks. He's sweet, charming, clever, my dad loves him and, basically, he's as close to perfection as it's possible for anyone who isn't Matthew McConaughey to be. If I wrote a list of things that were right about Rob and a list of things that were wrong, there would be virtually nothing in the second column. He does own a Craig David album, but that's a minor misdemeanour in an otherwise overwhelmingly positive list of attributes.

I miss him so badly it sometimes makes my insides ache. Which begs one almost constant question.

Why wasn't it love?

No. Let me rephrase that ... why wasn't I *sure* it was love?

There have been so many times since we broke up that his absence has been so aching, so cold, that it *must've* been. Yet, something stopped me from saying yes when he asked those big, beautiful and destructive words back in the spring.

He'd booked us in for a couple's spa day at a hotel in Cheshire and we'd spent many hours being massaged, pampered and steaming up the Jacuzzi well beyond its highest setting.

Afterwards, we went for a walk along the Roman Walls in Chester and paused to sit under a tree by the River Dee as the sun glittered on the water. He'd never looked more fanciable. The day had been perfect. The evening had been perfect. Then it all went wrong when he said something that turned the blood in my veins to stone.

There was a long prequel in which he declared me to be the most 'awesome, sexy and wonderful woman' he'd ever met. How I'd made him happier in eight months than he'd been in his life. How he'd been keeping a lid on his feelings but could do so no longer.

All the time I was thinking: God, I think he might be about to suggest something really outlandish, like going on holiday together.

As he continued talking, I'll tell you what was going through my head: *A week's a bit long, but I'd consider three days in Rome. Or maybe Barcelona, because you can get an easyJet flight there—*

'Emma, did you hear me?'

'Of course! Where were you thinking?'

He looked taken aback – and unnervingly happy.

'Well, we'd have to take a look at a few venues but ... does that mean it's a yes?'

Then something clicked. Nobody could be *that* happy about the prospect of a dirty weekend, even if I promised to go on a spending spree at Agent Provocateur and take a course of pole-dancing lessons in advance.

With my heart hammering, I shoved my hands in my pockets and found a packet of mints Dad had left in my car at the weekend, feeling a sudden urge to put one in my mouth. 'You're not talking about going away, are you?' I mumbled.

'Emma, I don't care *where* we do it, I only care *that* we do it.'

'Do ... what?' I asked, praying his answer would be 'snowboarding'.

He sank to one knee and uttered four words that killed my blissful notion that what we had together was frivolous, thoroughly enjoyable and just a bit of fun.

'Will you marry me?'

I nearly choked on my Fox's Glacier mint.

Chapter 9

My bid to tackle the list gets off to a flying start.

By Saturday, the day of Cally's thirtieth birthday, I have a polo taster lesson booked, although it's not until the end of September. I cancelled this morning's hair appointment so that I can 'grow hair long', as the list puts it, despite my awareness that aspiring to look like Daryl Hannah in *Splash* by December might be ambitious. And I Googled various Michelin-starred restaurants – even though, as I did so, something hit home.

Completing a list that features everything from the Northern Lights to jumping out of a plane (although I'll need a personality transplant to go through with that one) will not be cheap.

I sit at the kitchen table with my laptop and log on to my bank, flicking onto the second account that's been virtually untouched since it was set up when I was a little girl.

It contains five hundred and seventy-five pounds, money I've never considered actually spending before. You might think that's odd. Except this was money left to me by my mum when she died – the rest of her estate was put in trust with Dad – and I've never really had a clue what she would've wanted me to do with it.

But now has to be as good a time as any to use it – even if that sum alone probably won't be enough. Some of my aspirations are seriously expensive and going into my thirties with a bankruptcy under my belt isn't part of the plan.

My immediate priority needs to be to cut back – even if I'm not one of life's natural cutter-backers.

That Money Saving Expert bloke leaves me cold: if I spent all the recommended time switching energy suppliers, swapping 0% credit card deals and researching ISAs, I wouldn't have time for full-time employment – and that'd be *terrible* for my finances.

Still, I hit the supermarket in the afternoon and fill my trolley with own-brand goods, trying not to think about what a £1.49 washing powder called Supasoapa might do to my skin, or the fact that the Cheddar-style cheese looks capable of removing chalk from a blackboard.

The evening's festivities, however, don't do a great deal for my economy drive.

Cally has decided to mark her thirtieth birthday in Alma de Cuba, a place overflowing with atmosphere, where Latin dancers whirl under Gothic chandeliers, petals are strewn from a balcony and two-hundred-year-old frescoes can be seen above enormous palm trees.

It is a fantastic evening – even if, four hours into the celebrations, something has happened to Cally. *Something* being two rounds of cocktails, a couple of G&Ts and an unspecified amount of rum and Coke.

'Do you think we ought to wake her up?' Asha asks, nodding at Cally.

Not so long ago, Cally would've been surrounded by admirers and batting her eyelids like she was trying to give them a blow dry.

Today, she is propped up on a bench in her chic sage-green dress, with her face slumped on the table in front of her, her mouth contorted into a concave polygon. She looks like a shooting victim in *The Sopranos*.

'I don't think she'd forgive us,' I reply. 'She was up at five thirty with Zachary and will welcome all the sleep she can get.' I suddenly realise I'm slurring my words – and have hit the four-drink limit I've stuck to since a hideous vomiting incident at a bus stop in my first year at university. People often ask me if I find it difficult to stick to, but the memory of my guts emptying in front of an audience of commuter traffic has meant it genuinely has not been a challenge.

'Does it count as sleep?' Marianne asks, frowning at Cally. 'I'm not sure she's conscious.'

My sister is home for the weekend to retrieve some of her effects from Dad's loft – which is why she's out with my friends and me again. Her own circle of friends, although large, has spread far wider than mine over the years, so she's always happy to have a drink or two with us when she's back. Judging by how she looks tonight, I can't deny Edinburgh life agrees with her. Her skin is luminous and the couple of pounds she's gained since leaving London suit her.

I'm about to tell her as much when Asha's phone rings. She takes it out of her bag, sees Toby's number and gestures that she's taking it outside.

'What's all this about a one-night stand?' Marianne asks when we're alone.

'Oh ... did they mention that?' I mumble.

'You're not going through with it, I hope.'

'I wasn't, no.' The truth is, I've thought a lot about that particular item on the list and, despite the fact that I have for the first time in my life put a Durex in my clutch bag, it *isn't* going to happen. It's just not me.

'Good.' Her expression is somewhere between smug and matronly.

I frown. 'Why *good?*'

'I don't want any little sister of mine throwing herself around like the last tart in the bordello.'

Indignation rises up in me. 'As if you've been an angel!'

'I'm serious. If you'd said yes, I'd have dragged you out of here and bundled you into a taxi.'

I cross my arms. 'Marianne, I am twenty-nine years old. If I choose to hone my fellatio skills on half the British athletics squad, that's up to me.'

'You'd regret it.'

'I may or may not. That's up to me.'

She shakes her head, prompting a reminder – a small but

perfectly vivid one – of the fury she would arouse in me when we were teenagers.

'Maybe the more I think about that one, the more I think it epitomises my failure to have done most of the things on that list,' I continue casually, enjoying winding her up. 'Or indeed *anything* on that list.'

'What are you talking about?'

'I've been risk averse.'

'You're not a pension fund,' she tuts.

'I've spent my entire life firmly within my comfort zone.'

She puts her hands on her hips. 'Emma, don't you *dare* have a one-night stand. I mean it.'

Suddenly, this is about more than winding her up. 'Marianne, I am a grown woman and I can think for myself.'

'Don't be so pathetic. Honestly.'

I hesitate, thinking of a retort.

'Well, guess what?' A smile twitches at my lips. 'I'm doing it.'

I suddenly feel outrageously confident; outrageously clear. I am free from the shackles of my constant over-thinking and have a moment of clarity that removes any doubt from my mind.

'Why?' she shrieks. 'Because I told you *not* to?'

'No, Marianne. Because I am twenty-nine years old and counting,' I reply, spinning on my heels. 'And I'm about to do some *living*.'

Chapter 10

Simply saying those words makes me feel fabulously worldly-wise, a sensation that's tripled when I make a conscious decision that this is one occasion that absolutely *requires* a fifth drink. So I buy one, before slipping through the crowd like a Bond girl, pretending I'm a woman who lives on cocktails of danger and passion, not M&S ready meals.

If I'm going to go to the trouble of *doing some living*, it goes without saying it needs to be with someone gorgeous. I wouldn't usually approve of putting looks ahead of personality, but in these circumstances I'd have to make an exception.

The only way I can reconcile myself with unleashing my inner trollop is if it's with someone so jaw-droppingly bootilicious that anyone could be forgiven for doing the same.

Plus, although I'm now seriously feeling the effects of the fifth drink, I'm vaguely aware that Marianne is right and there's every chance I might regret this. So I need to mitigate it in the most effective way possible: by thoroughly enjoying it.

Problem is, there's no one here better-looking than Rob, who set the benchmark depressingly high. I look down and realise my glass is empty – so plump for one more cocktail in the perverse hope that I develop beer goggles.

'A French martini, please,' I ask the barman, and, as I focus through my spirit-induced haze, I realise that he isn't bad-looking. In fact, the further I lean in to examine him, the more twinkly eyed, cheeky-smiled and adorably dimpled he is.

'How are you?' he winks, flashing me a smile that could drop knickers from ten paces.

I grin. 'Fine, thanks.'

Flirting isn't one of my natural skills; I'm better at Scrabble and cracking my knuckles. But as I force myself to pout and run my tongue subtly across my lips – noting how well it goes down with the barman – it's easier than usual tonight.

'Having a good evening?' He shakes the cocktail, dropping his eyes to my cleavage.

'Ab-so-*lute*-ly,' I breathe, handing over a note.

He scrunches up his nose. 'I'm afraid we don't take those.' I glance down and realise I've handed over three Tesco Clubcard vouchers.

'Whoops!' I mumble woozily, rustling in my purse for valid currency. *Dimples* is still smiling when I find some and he gives me my change.

Over the course of the next half-hour – which I spend chatting intermittently to Chris, the barman – it becomes apparent that I am *definitely in*. His flirting becomes so suggestive, I feel as though we're in the first forty-five seconds of one of those special DVDs you can get in Ann Summers.

I can't be certain of how much sense I'm making. The French martini had a fairly drastic effect on my ability to think straight and the subsequent Piña Colada finished it off altogether.

He looks only vaguely impressed when I tell him I'm an air hostess, having suddenly convinced myself it'd be more of a turn-on than what I really do for a living. But I'm pretty sure that the button I undo on my top doesn't go unnoticed, nor does the hair flicking – especially the flicking, which I employ so enthusiastically I almost fall off my stool.

I snatch pieces of information about him and learn that by day he's studying medicine at Liverpool University, but I need to get down to business. I'm now so squiffy I'm seriously concerned that if I get him into bed, I'll lose consciousness before I've removed my shoes.

'What are you doing later?' he asks finally.

I smile sweetly. 'Sleeping with you.'

I'm instantly astonished at the fact that these words came out of *my* mouth. Still, this is no time for subtlety, and the effect on him is astounding. He's stunned into silence, but one thing's absolutely clear – he looks perfectly chuffed.

'She *isn't* – she's coming home. Come on, Emma. Everyone's in a taxi outside. We're waiting for you.'

I spin round and narrow my eyes at Marianne. 'Look, Mother Superior, could you leave me in peace?'

I won't bore you with the ensuing conversation, except to say that it is a word for word repeat of the earlier one – with a few slurrier words – and culminates in a 'FINE!' from Marianne that's so loud and furious it nearly singes the salsa dancers' feathers.

Still, at least I get rid of her, and spin back to Chris. 'What time do you finish?' I purr.

He leans over and brushes my hair away from my face. 'In two and a half hours.'

I sit bolt upright. 'You're kidding?' Keeping my eyes open for two-and-a-half minutes is a challenging enough prospect.

'I'm on the late shift,' he explains.

'But that's no good *at all*.'

'I'll make it worth your while,' he adds with an air of desperation.

Dejectedly, but with no better offers, I order a double Red Bull, followed by another. I am about to go for a third, but spot myself in the mirror behind the bar.

I am not the vision of grooming I thought I was – unless you're comparing me to an Afghan hound on the way to getting its fur washed after jumping in a puddle. One thing's for sure: I can't wait around for – I glance at my watch – two hours and twelve minutes. I need to find someone else. Quickly.

Chapter 11

Some chat-up lines are corny. Some are classy. Some are memorable, earth-shattering or stop-in-your-tracks offensive. But, even for someone who is no great authority on the art form, I'm aware that mine is unusual.

'Hello, I'm Emma. Do you think you're likely to want to leave in the next hour or so?'

He's the fifth person to whom I've put this question and I'm not sure why I'm persevering. Not that my opening line is the only problem – in three cases I realised instantly that, close up, they didn't look remotely like they did from the other side of the room. One transformed from Ryan Gosling to Tom Jones at close range, and it was a similar story with the other two. The fourth turned out to be a paramedic on his way to a woman who'd gone into labour in the restaurant upstairs.

I've decided that if I don't get talking to a serious prospect within ten minutes, I'm going home. Only ... well, the fifth one ... he has potential.

'Probably. Why do you ask?'

He looked like Tom Hardy from a distance and while, as with the others, he's nothing like him up close – he's still gorgeous. Very good-looking, with dark, cropped hair, a lovely physique and stubble that's strangely alluring, even if it looks capable of removing the make-up from my chin with one snog.

The other physical feature that can't go without mention is his smell; it's nothing less than knee-trembling. They say physical attraction is a chemical thing, influenced by the mingling of pheromones and stuff (clearly, I am paraphrasing the relevant articles in the *New Scientist* here).

If you buy that, all I can say is his pheromones and my pheromones are getting on like a house on fire. I could sit here and sniff this man all day, if that were considered in any way socially acceptable.

'I need someone to share a taxi with.'

He frowns, amused. 'We might live in totally opposite directions.' His voice is accentless, erring towards posh.

'Where do you live?'

'At the moment, Crosby.'

In totally the opposite direction. 'That's on the way!'

He eyes me suspiciously. 'Are you okay? You seem a little . . .'

Flirtatious?

'. . . drunk.'

I straighten my back. 'I am *not* drunk. What a cheek!'

'Sorry,' he concedes, looking naively guilty. 'Aren't you here with friends?'

'I was, but they had to leave. I decided to stay a little longer. There's no stopping me! Aren't *you* here with friends?' In a conversation I'm aware is less than stimulating, this is the best I can do.

He gestures to the corner, where a guy with red hair has his tongue down the throat of a tall blonde in a barely there skirt and earrings that look like they belong on the Trafalgar Square Christmas tree.

'They look like they're having fun,' I say.

He laughs. 'Whether Jeremy will be as enthusiastic in the morning has yet to be found out.'

There's something about the way he says this that alarms me. A tone that isn't disapproving exactly . . . but hints that this isn't the sort of thing you'd catch him doing.

The second this doubt enters my mind, it takes on a life of its own. What makes me assume he's single anyway? Or straight? Or – most fundamentally – interested?

I take a deep breath. If I'm going to go through with this, I need to get down to business and come on to him, at least a little. But, suddenly, I feel stupidly self-conscious, and the lack of inhibition that's required for this endeavour deserts me.

'Are you all right?' he asks.

I'm about to respond when I get a waft of his aftershave and it sends a flash of heat across my chest that nearly sets my bra straps on fire.

I reach out and put my hand behind his neck, pulling him into me as I stand on my tiptoes. Then I place my lips languorously on his cheek, noting how much softer than expected his stubble is. 'I feel great,' I whisper. 'But I can think of something that'd make me feel even better.'

Chapter 12

Waking up after my first ever one-night stand is an experience that I will never, ever forget. From the painful shafts of sunlight to every swirl in that heinous orange and brown carpet – it'll be there with me until the day I die.

Nor will I forget running from the flat. Or rather, attempting to run – with one broken shoe and every tiny, rancid cell in my body pleading for mercy. I hobble down a set of stairs, down a strange street and don't stop until I've turned several corners and am certain I'm not being followed. At that point, I pause, breathless, aching and on the verge of vomiting, as I scan the street for any landmarks.

It's then that I spot Crosby Cinema and know exactly where I am – miles from home.

Deep breaths.

A taxi will cost a fortune from here but I don't care. Only, as I look in my purse and realise I have precisely four pounds twenty-seven and a handful of Tesco Clubcard vouchers to my name, it becomes apparent that the train's the only option, unless I find a cashpoint. Which, in the event, I don't.

The trek to the station takes approximately eight minutes, but it's one of the most unremittingly miserable experiences of my life. Not a single car is capable of whizzing past without its passengers rubbernecking at this heap of a human being, its broken heels, tangle of hair and asbestos eyes.

I arrive at the station, pay for my ticket and head for a bench on the platform, desperate to take the weight off my feet. The only available seat is next to a handsome, straight-backed woman in her early sixties, who is wearing a chic cashmere throw and taupe wide-legged trousers. She is reading the *Mail on Sunday*, from which she pauses, looks up briefly, then sniffs and returns to the article.

My eyes surreptitiously dart to the page, which boasts the headline:

BRITAIN: CAPITAL OF CASUAL SEX

Next to it, with a nice blue border, there is a panel about genital warts; apparently these have reached epidemic proportions among eighteen-to-thirty-year-olds – a category I remain part of – just.

She looks up again and catches my eye. I glance away and straighten my back, as if sitting up nicely is going to alter the fact that, currently, I could be mistaken for someone heading home to pay her pimp then breakfast on a crack pipe.

I board the train and avoid sitting near her, not because I resent her disapproving looks, but because I deserve them. The headline flashes into my brain and my throat goes dry, before I open the clasp on my clutch bag and carefully unzip the side pocket. I pull out a small cardboard packet marked 'Durex' and my stomach turns over.

It is unopened.

And I want to cry.

Chapter 13

When you earn your living conjuring up heart-warming stories to make small children smile, it can be difficult to focus when you're convinced you've contracted chlamydia – or worse.

'Would it breach the brand guidelines to make a Bingbah ride a bicycle?' Giles muses, knocking back an espresso the colour of Marmite.

'Not sure,' I reply distractedly.

'Can you check while you've got it open?'

'What open?' I barely register his voice.

'The brand book. You said you had it open, twenty seconds ago.'

I shift in my seat. 'Oh. Sorry, I shut it down.'

Giles scratches his head. 'Forget it, I'll look. Though I don't know why I'm bothering. Our new unofficial creative director will no doubt take one look at the script and suggest I turn it into a frigging solar-panelled spaceship.'

Giles's knickers have been in a terrible twist over the issue of

Sarah's replacement – and the fact that Perry is showing no urgency to appoint anyone. Nevertheless, he's slightly calmer today for a reason I can't put my finger on, but it could be something to do with him consuming only twelve cups of coffee by two p.m. instead of the usual fifteen.

Yesterday was a different story.

Having presented a script to Perry – seeing as there's nobody else to present it to – Giles was advised by our esteemed boss that he should inject a little more 'oomph' into his dialogue. At which point I was convinced the veins in Giles's neck would burst, as if someone had attached him to a 12-volt tyre inflator and forgotten to turn it off.

'What are we going to do, Emma?' he howls. 'About Perry, I mean. It can't go on like this. The place is . . . Em?'

'Hmm?'

'What are you working on?' He leans over curiously.

I shut down my browser so rapidly I almost sprain my wrist, although I don't know what I'm worried about; the only time Giles actually gets up and walks to my desk is when I've got Hobnobs.

'The usual,' I grin.

I haven't produced a jot of work since I sat in this seat at a quarter to eight this morning, having arrived early to try to make up for the work I failed to produce yesterday.

I have instead spent the day Googling sexually transmitted diseases, trying to work out the odds of me having contracted one – or, more likely, a suite of them – and, as a result, how rapidly this will result in symptoms ranging from mild itching to certain death. And that is not something for which you can go to Boots and get the morning-after pill, as I did. Twice.

'I thought you weren't even sure you'd had sex with him?' Cally says on the phone as I pace up and down Rodney Street later that afternoon, attempting to hear her over the hum of traffic.

'I'm now ninety-nine per cent certain that I did,' I tell her despairingly. 'I'm now itching. Plus, I've been on this medical website and—'

'Oh *Emma*,' she interrupts. 'Steer clear of those websites.'

'Why?'

'Because you type in "mouth ulcer" and three clicks later you are convinced you've got throat cancer with six weeks to live.'

'Did you know that incidences of chlamydia have more than doubled since 1999?'

'That doesn't mean *you've* got it!'

'I'm bound to now, aren't I?' I huff. 'Even you at the height of your sexual escapades never went out without a handbag bursting with prophylactics, did you?'

'Well, that's true. The time that led to Zachary was my one and only misdemeanour.'

Cally's little boy was the result of the briefest of liaisons (four hours from start to finish) that she had with a guy called Pete, whom she met in a bar nearly three years ago when she and I were on a night out in Manchester.

He was tall but otherwise unremarkable, with blond hair, a

faint Mancunian accent and, presumably, a soft spot for redheads with generous curves. Cally last set eyes on him the same night she met him. She has no idea where he is, and he has no idea that Zachary exists.

'Let me ask an indelicate question,' Cally continues. 'Did you *feel* like you'd had sex? *Down there*, I mean. You know ... gynae-cologically speaking.'

For a reformed nymphomaniac, Cally can be surprisingly coy.

I take a deep breath. 'I don't know. I was asking myself the same on the way to the station and ... sometimes I convinced myself I couldn't feel anything ... other times I definitely could.'

'Do you know who this person is?'

'The man I slept with? No idea. His name was Mike. No – Matt.'

Marianne, clearly, does not have a clue about all this. As far as my sister's concerned, I got in a taxi immediately after she did; there's no way I'm prepared to discuss this with her. It was bad enough when I was half cut and convinced I was right.

'You didn't get his number?' Cally asks.

'No – and there's no way I'd contact him anyway.'

'So knocking at his door is out of the question?'

'I'm not turning up on his doorstep, like a double-glazing sales-man, to say, "Why, hello again. Could you possibly disclose whether you and I exchanged bodily fluids at the weekend?"'

'Then all you can do is try to relax – and get yourself checked out.'

'The incubation period for HIV is three months, chlamydia is

70

three weeks and gonorrhoea a month. So, basically, I'll be in purgatory for the foreseeable future.'

She sighs. 'Emma – I need to run. I was due to be in a monthly forecast meeting with my boss three minutes ago. But do me a favour and stay off those websites, won't you?'

I head back into the office, unable to focus on anything except how utterly rubbish *being reckless* is, when I bump into Perry on the stairs.

'Just the gal! I've got a brilliant idea I want you to work up. You'll love it. It's about a bunch of kids and a dog who travel round in an old van trying to solve spooky mysteries. What do you think?'

Chapter 14

I'm opening the door to Asha that night when I spot somebody coming out of Rita's old flat with a clipboard. Stacey mentioned she'd heard a survey was being done today. I watch the man, who's in his fifties and balding, head to his Micra and get in, and I feel a shudder of resentment. To me, that apartment will always be Rita's, and I feel inexplicably apprehensive about her replacement.

I close the door and go to the kitchen, where Asha has flicked on the kettle. 'How are you?' she asks.

'Apart from itchy?'

'You could be imagining it,' she offers. 'Don't give yourself too much of a hard time, Emma. Nobody can blame you for wanting a bit of action with the opposite sex. I was single for over a year before I met Toby and I was nearly climbing the walls.'

We both pause, taking in her last sentence and the fact that Asha clearly doesn't consider herself 'single' any longer, despite the circumstances.

'Do you think he'll leave his wife?' I ask tentatively.

'We've discussed it, but I'm trying not to even think about that at the moment,' Asha says, lowering her head, 'as certain as I am that I'm a symptom, rather than a cause, of the marriage breakdown.'

Toby and his wife married after she accidentally fell pregnant at university only four months after they'd met. From what Asha's told me, it was a match made in hell at the beginning and hasn't improved much since.

'I still feel *terrible* about this situation, though,' she adds, closing her eyes. 'That's despite knowing their marriage can't continue while they're at each other's throats. And despite knowing it's surely better for the children to live with two separated but happy parents – rather than two who are together and at war.'

'What do you think is stopping him?'

'He's got to work things out before he takes a step like that – money matters, who's going to get the house, how it would work with the kids. He wants to do the right thing by all of them, not just disappear into the sunset. I'm not taking any of this lightly, Emma. But I love him. And I can't live without him. It's as simple as that.'

'I know,' I reassure her, clutching her hand.

'You know, part of me thinks Cally's right. At the end of the day, I've been a mistress for the last six months. What sort of bitch does that make me? This goes against all my principles.'

'You're not a bitch,' I insist. 'Some relationships in life just aren't very straightforward, that's all.'

She sighs. 'Have I ever shown you a picture of Christina?'

'You've got a picture of his wife?' I ask, incredulous.

'I mean on Facebook. Is your computer on?'

Reluctantly, I bring out my laptop. Asha logs onto her Facebook account and clicks onto to Toby's profile. He hasn't got many Facebook friends – only twenty-nine – and it's clear from the lack of any photos – of his family or anyone else – that he's joined only recently and is no avid user.

Asha scrolls down his Friends list and clicks on the profile of a woman by the name of Christina Gregory.

I finally put a face to a woman we've heard so much about over the last half-year. It strikes me, as I take in her glossy black hair, slightly over-done lipstick and oval eyes, that she knows nothing about me – but I know dozens more things about her than I ought to.

I know about her sex life. I know about her children. And I know that her husband is sleeping with another woman. It's not a thought I feel at all comfortable with, certain as I am that it's an unworkable marriage.

Asha leans across and moves the cursor, stretching awkwardly as she navigates the site. 'Some of her pictures are public . . .' she begins, but I don't want to see any more.

I'm about to object when she emits the sort of gasp that you'd expect from someone who's been underwater for two-and-a-half minutes.

'What is it?'

'Oh my God. Oh my God Almighty! *What the hell am I going to do?*'

Asha's face blanches and she stands up, then sits down, then stands up again, her mind clearly racing about something, and there are several minutes of hysteria and panic before I find out what it is.

'I've sent her a "friend request",' she shrieks. 'I've sent a woman whose husband I'm having an affair with a bloody *friend request!*'

Chapter 15

When entering the Genito-Urinary Medicine clinic at the Royal Liverpool University Hospital, it is impossible to shake the feeling that you've got an enormous neon sign over your head reading: '*I'M A GREAT BIG DIRTY SHAGGER!*'

I'm torn between walking into the department with feigned nonchalance, in the hope that people think I'm an off-duty nurse, or with a severe limp, to give the impression I've taken a wrong turn after having my ankle X-rayed.

I arrive and sit before a smiley middle-aged receptionist who has obviously attended some sort of School for Non-Judgemental Grannies.

'Hello, lovely, pop yourself down there,' she beams, as if she's about to serve me a cream tea. 'I'm going to take some details.'

After reluctantly parting with my particulars, I am invited into a further reception room, which is literally packed with patients, but at least has the benefit of being women only. Men – aka the horrible swines who got us into this mess – use another entrance.

I don't know what I expected from the clientele here, but I must say none of them look especially reckless or stupid or – the word on everyone's tongue – slutty.

The wait is interminable, but my mind is occupied in flipping between several issues. First, Asha: who was at my flat until midnight last night trying, between frenzied sobs, to get hold of Toby to confess her mistake. He was at a black-tie event – with Christina – and simply reassured her to leave it with him. She was unreassured.

Then there's my itching, which I'd almost convinced myself I was imagining until I walked through the door here, since when it's increased tenfold.

And that brings me to the final issue. How I'd never be in this mess if I hadn't dumped Rob. There's no way Rob would've given me something that made me feel like I'm wearing a wire-wool G-string, that's for certain.

How I crave being part of a couple again, without having to deal with this crap. I keep thinking about his arms round me, how warm and loved I felt and what the hell possessed me to do what I did.

I'm hit by a flashback of the night I introduced him to Cally and Asha at our local pub quiz – and how impressive and lovely they thought he was, without being remotely showy. They warmed to him instantly – everyone does. I close my eyes at the thought of it. What the hell is wrong with me?

I take out my mobile and scroll down to his number, for a split second considering calling it. I remind myself that phoning from the clap clinic probably wouldn't make for the most romantic of reunions.

The doctor I finally see is a skinny, soft-spoken man with an African surname and the same smiley manner as the receptionist. He confirms all my details, before asking me what the problem is.

'Right. Well. I had this, um ...' I lean in and whisper, '*encounter* ...'

'You had unprotected sex.'

'Yes,' I croak. I clear my throat. 'I wouldn't normally. I wouldn't *dream* of it. I'm not that sort of girl.'

I half expect him to grab me by the shoulders and shout: 'You had *unprotected sex*? Are you *insane*? In this day and age? *You idiot!* Haven't you heard that incidences of chlamydia have gone up by *fifty per cent* since 1999?'

But he doesn't. He looks at me as if to say: 'It happens. Now let's deal with it.'

'Have you experienced any symptoms you're worried about?'

'Hmm. I think I could be ... possibly ... maybe ... itchy. But I might be wrong.'

'We'll perform a full screen, shall we?'

'That'd be lovely,' I reply, as if he's offered me a cut and blow-dry.

After a few more relatively painless questions, the doctor leaves and is replaced by a nurse in her late thirties who could win an Olympic medal in talking.

'Have you *seen* the queue out there?' She snaps a strap on my arm and starts prodding around for a juicy vein. 'It's always like this in summer. Everyone's back from their hols. I'm just back from Benidorm. Been anywhere nice yourself?'

'Italy,' I reply, because, even though the answer is France with Marianne for two days in March – we both adore the place – I am hit by an incomprehensible desire to not reveal anything personal in here. Apart from my genitalia, obviously.

I am instructed to undress behind a curtain, then have to grapple with a hospital gown, which has approximately seventeen tabs and is clearly designed for a person with a humpback and five arms. The doctor arrives ten minutes later, as I am pacing up and down, having now read and memorised the medical abbreviations on the wall for everything from Cardiovascular Syphilis to Sex Worker, and applied enough hand gel to my palms to peel off a layer of skin.

'Would you mind if we allowed a medical student to be present?'

I hesitate, then reply breezily: 'Not at all!' I don't want anyone to think I'd be daft enough to let my hang-ups hold back the next generation of medical professionals; the only sensible, grown-up option is to say yes.

As he goes to the door to invite in the student, I am instructed by the nurse to leap onto a reclining bed and place my legs into two stirrups underneath a spotlight, enabling an optimum view.

I stare at the ceiling, counting polystyrene tiles in an attempt to take my mind off the stranger who's prising open my knees and peering between my legs.

After a short rummage around, he senses my tension and says reassuringly: 'I can't see anything untoward.'

'Really?' I gasp gratefully, flipping up my head.

Only, it's not the top of the doctor's head that catches my attention.

It's the medical student at his shoulder.

And the reason he catches my attention is not because he's nodding studiously as if having a guided tour of the Elgin Marbles, or because his mentor is gaily pointing out notable features of my vagina.

It's because this is not the first time we've met.

I freeze and turn a violent shade of crimson as I'm assaulted with a flashback of Saturday night, when I last saw this student – who apparently doubles as Chris the barman from Alma de Cuba. The one I *almost* slept with. The one I *would* have slept with, had his shift finished two-and-a-half hours earlier.

'The patient is concerned about previous sexual contact and has been experiencing abnormal irritation,' the doctor tells him.

It's at that point that he glances up and makes eye contact with me, a split-second occurrence in which his expression shifts dramatically – and five words are screamed internally by us both: *'Get me out of here!'*

He doesn't move – he can't. And neither can I, given that I'm in the sort of position into which you'd manoeuvre a turkey, pre-stuffing.

Clearly at a loss as to what to do, the student bends down hastily to pretend to scrutinise the most intimate part of my anatomy. He doesn't look up, but I can recognise one thing after the doctor's commentary about my health concerns.

Never in his life has he been as grateful as he is now for having been stuck with Saturday night's late shift.

Chapter 16

Asha phones that afternoon to confirm she's in the clear after what's obviously been a torturous morning.

'Toby got home from the event and, while Christina was getting changed, he logged onto her Facebook profile in their study. Hers is the default account on their PC and all her passwords are saved on there.'

'So he rejected the friend request?'

'Exactly, then deleted the notification she was sent.'

'So – panic over?'

'Yep,' she says flatly. 'I guess so.'

Then there's a silence. Because it doesn't feel like much of a triumph somehow.

Asha's roller-coaster romantic life is a long way from that of my sister. Marianne is so firmly in the couple-zone these days, I'm worried she's a step away from his 'n' hers undies.

'Brian and I are thinking of going away to Devon,' she announces, when I Skype her later that night.

'Really?' I love Devon myself but I'm wondering when this became exciting to a woman who used to pop to New York for a weekend.

'It's meant to be lovely – he has family there. And things are a bit tight for him at the moment so going abroad is out.'

'It'll be nice.'

'I think so. I spent years travelling to places like Ibiza and Paris and never really discovered half of the UK. Hey, Brian's just come in! Why don't you say hello?'

Marianne disappears and after a short background conversation, followed by shaky webcam adjustment, I am confronted by a gargantuan brown jumper, a tent of an item, underneath which is a man I recognise – just about – to be Brian. I say *just about* because, since the last picture Marianne showed me on Facebook, he has grown enough facial hair to knit a matching hat.

'Emma, we meet at last!' he grins. At least, I think he grins. The beard moves, certainly.

'Hi Brian – how are you? I've heard a lot about you.'

'Not too much, I hope! So, is your job keeping you busy? I'd love to have a good chat to you about it.'

According to Marianne, Brian is fascinated by my job because of his own aspirations to be a television writer. I'm really trying not to be too sceptical – I mean, *I* manage to make a living as a scriptwriter despite it being notoriously competitive.

The difference is that I have a steady job working for an established company, and I've learned the ropes over the course of eight years. Brian's on-the-job experience is limited to operating the jet wash at Gleamers.

Despite that, I can't deny he seems nice; he's funny and unassuming and he obviously adores Marianne.

If I hadn't ever met Johnny – dynamic, entrepreneurial, charismatic Johnny – I probably wouldn't think twice about her new boyfriend. But I have. And the stark, glaring contrast between them means it's impossible to conclude anything other than that Brian is punching above his weight with my sister.

When I end the Skype call, the rest of my evening becomes dominated by one other very pressing matter: what's going on – to use Cally's phrase – 'down there'. I will spare you the detail, but say simply this: there is not a shadow of a doubt that something is wrong. Very wrong.

As I grimly open the fridge, I spot the list and gaze at Cally's teenaged handwriting.

After almost two weeks, I've managed to cross off only one 'achievement' – a one-night stand – and add another unexpected one: I've contracted my very first sexually transmitted disease. What a proud moment. I wonder if I get a certificate?

The only thing I've got in for dinner is a ready meal that claims to be 'beef hotpot' but actually contains so little meat I'm convinced the Vegetarian Society would approve it. After my three-and-a-half-minute dinner, I log onto my laptop in front of the TV for another fun-packed session of Googling medical conditions.

I flick onto Facebook first. Only, my usual unquenchable desire to look through the wedding photos of people I have never met and never will meet is diverted by the notification of a friend request. As I scrutinise the name and picture, a tight knot develops in my stomach that I know has nothing to do with the hotpot.

Matt Taylor.

My mouth widens enough to swallow a whole mango. It's *him*. My one-night stand. I click the link to a message.

Hello Emma,

I hope you don't mind me contacting you – you suggested when we met that I should either phone or look you up on Facebook. The number you left had seventeen digits, several of which I could recognise only as Ancient Sanskrit, so that was out.

I just wanted to say that it was nice to meet you. I thoroughly enjoyed the brief time we spent together and your job as an air hostess sounds fantastic – I've never seen anyone so passionate about what they do for a living.

Sorry I missed you on Sunday morning. Despite my battered ego struggling to come to terms with the possibility that you never want to set eyes on me again, the born optimist in me thought I'd drop you a line in case you were interested in getting together again.

If not, fair enough. But I couldn't let you go without saying I think you're a fantastic woman with an amazing sense of humour and, given the choice, I'd love to get to know you.

If not, I feel duty bound to say anyway that you do the best
in-flight safety demonstration I've ever seen.
Take care and best wishes,
Matt
xxx
PS I *really* hope you didn't wake up with regrets about
Saturday night. If you did, rest assured that I'm a model of
discretion.

Regrets? Re-bloody-grets? Well, yes, I've got a few, thank you very much, Mr Matt Itchypants Taylor. And that's without knowing the full details of my in-flight demonstration.

I storm into the kitchen and make myself a Horlicks to try to calm myself down. It doesn't work. So I return to my computer and begin hammering a response into the keyboard with such force that the F pings off and lands in my mug.

Mr Taylor,
You're very perceptive. Yes, I never want to set eyes on you
again and, yes, I am consumed with regrets.
I realise that I was coming on strong. But nobody except
the most morally bankrupt would've gone ahead with what
you and I did – in the full knowledge that your little
'affliction' was guaranteed to be passed on to me.
So, thanks for that – the 'gift' you left me with. It's an
unpleasant reminder of our time together that, for my part, has
resulted in a two-hour wait in a clinic I never want to enter again

in my life, and symptoms that are getting worse and worse. Please don't bother to reply as I'm going to block you, which I hope you'll interpret as a clear indication of just how much I don't want you in my life.

I pause for breath, suddenly stuck for ideas on how to end this rant.

Thank you and goodnight.

I hit Send and am about to block him, when I'm compelled to snoop around his page. The man's given me a venereal disease – I've at least got a right to appraise the old school pictures he's tagged in.

There are photos of him with a woman – an attractive woman – and three little boys ranging from about three to seven, who, it appears from the captions, are his sons.

Aside from that, he's tagged in pictures of his university days, and a holiday in Mexico with the same woman. He's an intermittent Facebooker, and the last thing he posted was a photo of his littlest son in 3D glasses.

Trip to the cinema ended four hours ago, but Josh thinks this is a snappy new look.

It's just as I'm blocking him that I spot the killer line in his personal info. He's *married*. It's there in black and white. I suddenly feel very queasy.

Chapter 17

'It's not a sexually transmitted disease,' the doctor tells me as I sit before him the following week in the seventh circle of hell (aka the GUM clinic).

'What? But it must be . . . I'm in agony . . . that's why I've come back. I'm not making this up . . . I want a second opin—'

'It's an allergy.'

I frown. 'I don't get allergies.'

He throws me a look that I imagine he thinks is sympathetic. 'You do now.'

'But I thought the results all took at least two weeks to come back.'

'They take two weeks for us to *send* them to you – at the outside. I've got them on my computer here. They're all negative. Of course, you'll need to return in a couple of months to repeat some of them, as we've discussed. But the only actual symptoms you have are those of a skin allergy. Have you experienced itching anywhere else? Or changed your washing powder?'

'No, I . . . Oh . . .' My voice trails off as I remember how much Supasoapa I've lavished upon my laundry recently. I glance at my arms and realise I've been scratching at my wrists too. I'd barely noticed.

'So I didn't get this from my . . .' I lean in and whisper, '*liaison*?'

'I would say not. This kind of sensitivity is very common.'

I traipse to the office recalling every word of that Facebook message. If it were possible to die from cringing I'd be midway through the embalming process right now.

I'm turning down Rodney Street when a text arrives that instantly makes my heart twist. It's from Rob.

How are things, Emma? xx

I still can't get over the fact that he sends me these texts inter-mittently, despite what I did to him. Cally thinks it's because he wants to get back with me, but I genuinely don't think that's the case – he is simply an incredibly nice person. Oh God, if only I was still with him!

I text him back immediately.

Good, thanks – not much to report.

Which I know is technically not the case, but the particular details of what's been vexing me are not for sharing.

What are you up to? Xx

His response arrives as I'm pushing open the door to the office.

Day off today so I'm just chilling with my guitar.

I hesitate over the handset, reading those words, as a thought occurs to me. But I'm ambushed before I can process it fully.

'Emma! Into my office!' instructs Perry with a manic spring in his step that indicates that what follows isn't going to be good.

'I was talking to one of the bods over at Kidsplay TV last night,' he says, wide-eyed. 'Nice chap. Lovely shoes.'

I fail to come up with a response to this.

'He was telling me that there's a grant knocking about from some European disability rights doodah. He reckons there're pots of cash to be made if you come up with a storyline that fits their agenda.'

'Right.' My head starts spinning with dreadful possibilities about where this is going.

He sits on the sofa and crosses his legs exuberantly. 'So I thought, *we're* a right-on company! *We* should be the guys taking advantage of this!' He leaps up again and starts pacing the room.

'What did you have in mind?'

'What do you think of this idea . . .' He holds up his arms like Spielberg pitching this to his very first producer. 'We have a cat. And a mouse. By golly, they can't stand the sight of each other. The cat is forever trying to catch the mouse in a variety of outlandish and totally wacky ways. Except the mouse . . . well, he's a clever little chap. He manages to get away, time and time again –

by doing things like ... ooh, I don't know, smashing a frying pan over the cat's head ... or snapping his tail in a mousetrap!'

'This is sounding very like Tom and Jerry, Perry.'

'I *knew* you were going to say that!' He clicks his fingers in front of my face. 'But I'm a step ahead of you. Several steps, in fact.'

'Oh?'

'My cat and mouse have a twist.'

I raise an eyebrow.

'They're in *wheelchairs*!' he says triumphantly. 'Kids'll love it! The BBC'll love it! The European disability rights doodah will love it! I *adore* political correctness, don't you, Emma?'

Perry's 'blue sky thinking' proceeds to turn every shade of the rainbow. I try to pitch an idea to him that I thought of a few weeks ago – about a clothes shop in which all the garments come to life when it's shut. But he barely hears me.

'I don't know why I bother,' I tell Giles as I slump in the seat in front of my computer, mentally fatigued.

'Let me guess: you got his idea about Tom and Jerry on Stannah Stairlifts. Honestly, this place is going to the dogs, Emma,' he says, leaning over and pinching a Hobnob.

I open my *World of Interiors* magazine and start flicking through it for want of a distraction. 'To be absolutely fair, you've never been a glass-half-full person, have you, Giles?'

'I don't think there *is* a glass at the moment. It's a polystyrene cup with cracks in the side and penicillin at the bottom.'

I take a deep breath. 'Do you enjoy this job, Giles? I mean, really? I know you grumble a lot. But what do you think about it, deep down?'

Giles looks slightly scared. He and I don't do heart to hearts; the only time I've ever asked about his feelings was when he got his finger trapped in his desk drawer.

'A few years ago, you wouldn't have needed to ask,' he says, serious all of a sudden. 'We *all* loved it, didn't we?'

I pause and think about this. Even in those days, Giles didn't exactly walk in every morning, throw his arms open to the world and declare himself glad to be alive. But he's right: he loved it, I loved it, we all loved it. Which makes the present situation all the more frustrating.

'Deep down, Emma, I know there aren't many people who get paid to dream up stuff like this every day. Deep down, I know I'm good at it ... almost as good as you. I was born to do this stuff and I'd hate to do anything else. But I'm not sure how long this can go on before the whole place sinks into the shithole that's Perry's twisted mind.'

'You think he's messing things up that badly?'

'You've heard the rumours?'

I frown. 'No.'

'Perry's trying to sell the business.'

I put my hand over my mouth. You don't need to be an expert in industrial relations to work out that this doesn't sound good. Still, I try to look on the bright side. 'Maybe that wouldn't be *such* a bad thing. Maybe someone great would buy it and start running the company as it should be.'

'Or they could just take the copyright for *Bingbah* . . . and start making it themselves.'

Giles is not what you'd call one of life's optimists, but this doesn't sound unrealistic.

His words eat me up for the rest of the day, interspersed with flashbacks to the loopy concepts dribbling out of Perry's mouth all morning. I eventually reach an inescapable question, one that stems from a declaration I made fifteen years ago.

Am I really in the right job?

The fact that I'm rubbish with kids is an irony not lost on me. What on earth is it that compels me to come in every day and start attempting to entertain three-year-olds? There are a dozen other professions to which I'd be better suited, a dozen others from which I'd gain satisfaction – top of the list being the same job to which I aspired as a teenager: interior designer.

When did I put my true career aspirations in the 'too difficult' drawer and stumble into a job that's patently wrong for me? When did my dream become something I lived out only via the pages of *House Beautiful*?

Obviously, it's difficult to escape the fact that I have no experience in interior design and it's been nothing but a hobby for ten years. But if I'm ever going to go for this, it's got to be now. Because the grim alternative is reaching the *end* of my thirties in exactly the same position.

I open up my latest script and read what I've written so far.

Then I take a deep breath.

The problem is, it's not *only* a lack of courage that's stopping me.

I'd miss this job, there's no doubt about that. I'd miss writing *Bingbah*. I'd miss the energy and creativity. And I'd miss the people – even on Giles's darkest days he's never anything other than entertaining.

As I look up at my colleague's furrowed brow and think about his words, though, it strikes me that I might not get a choice. The way Perry's going, the place could be sold to an American consortium by the end of the year.

Not for the first time this week, I surreptitiously log onto a website I shouldn't be on, although this one isn't about venereal diseases. There's no escaping it. It's time to start exploring my employment options.

Chapter 18

Job hunting, it turns out, can be a dispiriting affair.

I never expected my dream career as an interior designer to leap out from the pages of the *Liverpool Echo* and tap me on the shoulder, but I also wasn't prepared for opportunities to be *this* threadbare. It becomes apparent after hours of flicking through websites that my experience and qualifications in this field have equipped me for little more than painting the windowsill in McDonald's.

My only option would be to start at the bottom, a prospect that could be exhilarating if it wasn't for one thing: I really would be *broke*. I've been in full-time employment for eight years and have steadily and unapologetically accrued a half-decent salary. One I've got used to.

I don't want my sole retail experience of Ted Baker to return to that of a miserable window-shopper. I don't want to retune my taste buds to the gastronomic delights of Batchelors Super Noodles and HP Sauce, like when I was a student. And I don't want to relinquish my gym membership in favour of a Davina DVD, particularly since kick-boxing moves in my living room would shatter the window. Yet, the alternative is looking increasingly grim.

I can't be bothered making anything more exciting than pasta with pesto tonight, and while I wait for it to cook, I pause and review the list.

Even the ones that are technically easy – such as growing my hair long – are proving a ball ache. I'm normally meticulous about visiting the hairdresser; if I leave it longer than eight weeks, I look like Frank Gallagher after a sheep dip. I was due for a cut last month and, while I'd love to say my locks are delightfully thick and lustrous, the reality is that my new hobby is counting split ends.

Still, *if* I can pull off this list, there will be some undeniable pleasure involved. I'm hopeful of achieving 'sleep under the stars' and 'see the Northern Lights' – even if how and when isn't entirely clear.

I don't really want to head off to Norway or Iceland or wherever by myself, which leaves the question of who to go with. The longest Cally's spent away from Zachary was the two nights in Edinburgh and she vowed not to repeat it until he's eighteen because she missed him so much. Asha has already got this year's holiday planned, and Marianne will *obviously* be away with Brian. Even more pressing is the money issue. My savings won't go far if I blow it on a break to that part of the world, which is far from cheap.

Despite that, I'm keeping a blindly optimistic eye on Groupon, in case the stories about people scooping a five-star luxury holiday for £16 are true. So far, the only things that have caught my attention are a desktop yoghurt maker, a one-night stay in the Outer Hebrides and hot-stone massages in forty-three separate beauty establishments.

I also make a mental note to look again into skydiving – and not shut down the website the second my palpitations start.

It's when I read the bit that says 'Learn to play the guitar' that I remember I haven't texted Rob back. I pull out my phone and the thought that occurred to me earlier returns. And makes me squirm, again.

The thought is this: I *really* want Rob to teach me to play the guitar ... even though I know I shouldn't. Splitting up with someone should involve a clean break. The problem is, this break already isn't clean. Not for him and not for me.

So, before I can stop myself, I'm composing a text that says:

Hope you had a great day off. Funny you should mention the guitar, actually – I may have a favour to ask xx

The thought of seeing him again gives me a small surge of happiness. I stick the list back on the fridge and glance out of the window as a silver car pulls up onto Rita's drive. The rain I got caught in earlier has eased off and a milky sun is pushing through the clouds as the car door opens and a man steps out.

Facing away from me, he walks to the back to open a door, out of which a small boy leaps onto the gravel and begins collecting twigs. He's sweet-looking, blond, with curly hair, a gap in his teeth . . . and is strangely familiar.

Two older boys pile out of the car after him, and then the man turns round. And every thought in my head rushes away like water slipping down a plughole as I stand, gasping, at my kitchen window.

'You have got to be joking.' I realise I've tipped my pasta into a bowl of Domestos.

Matt Taylor, welcome to the neighbourhood.

Chapter 19

Fifteen years ago, when I declared my ambition to 'learn to play the guitar', I assumed I'd be a natural. Even until recently, by which I mean thirty-five minutes ago, that belief remained unchallenged. I had a *feeling*, nay a certainty, that I was a born musician. I love music – and wipe the floor with everyone else in the pop round of our local pub quiz.

'When do I get to play a proper song?' I ask Rob, strumming the guitar. Every time, in the second before I do this, I expect the resulting melody to be something Tracy Chapmanesque – soulful and romantic. The reality is that it sounds like a chimpanzee attempting to riff with an empty Flora tub and four elastic bands. But I'm not perturbed – we've only just started.

'Normally after half a dozen lessons or so, although' – he winces as I strum – 'let's say a dozen. To be on the safe side.'

He looks outrageously hot today – even hotter than I remember from when we were together, and, believe me, I never took that for granted. I simply couldn't. All he'd have to do was gaze at me with those glittering green eyes, or smile one of his devastating smiles, and I stood no chance.

I have literally never found a man as physically attractive as I find Rob. My two previous long-term relationships – with Mike, who I was with for the three years at university, and Will, for four years in my early twenties – were more like friendships, with hindsight. And certainly never involved lust-levels comparable to these.

'I was hoping this would be a crash-course. But, okay – as long as I can play something *good* by my birthday party. Like the Stone Roses or KT Tunstall. Oh and Adele's "Whenever I'm Alone with You" has a guitar bit.'

He looks alarmed. 'It has *two*. That's ambitious, Em. I was thinking more along the lines of . . .' he hesitates. '"Kumbaya".'

I give a feistier-than-intended strum, only for my plectrum to disappear completely into the hole in the guitar. A frustrating ten-minute break follows, during which I'm forced to tip the instrument upside down, peer into the hole and shake it over my head repeatedly until the small piece of plastic plops out and almost harpoons my retina.

I can't deny it feels odd being at Rob's on a Saturday morning now we're no longer an item. He lives in a two-bedroom apartment overlooking Sefton Park, which is lovely, or at least, *could* be lovely. Rob is one of those men who have never quite got used to their mum not being around to clear up after them, and labour under the misapprehension that the only cleaning a lavatory requires is flushing it.

I don't want to overstate this; the place isn't hideous. But you can tell a twenty-eight-year-old bloke lives here and not *me*, for example, whose instinctive urge to bleach his dishcloths on walking through the door is as unstoppable as a category five hurricane.

'You don't look very relaxed, Em – let me show you the best position to sit.' He gently takes the guitar from me, sending a shiver of electricity up my arm as our fingers touch. Then he sits back and launches into the Verve's 'Bittersweet Symphony'. I find myself mesmerised by his hands, his fingers . . . his biceps. 'Do you see what I'm doing?' he asks, finishing the song and handing the guitar back to me.

The muscles in his arms flex again as I take it from him and I'm suddenly struggling to respond. Oh God! I really *must* stop fancying Rob so much. It's not good for anybody.

'I can do that,' I say confidently, gripping the guitar and focusing on the task at hand. I picture myself as Laura Marling . . . Courtney Love . . . Susanna Hoffs. I imagine how amazing it'd feel if I could play in a way that even *approaches* that by my birthday. I could cavort round the stage, *owning* it, lapping up applause as I swing my hips and—

'Emma?'

'Oh. Sorry.'

I play only four notes, but my efforts are perfectly horrible. I've never felt like such an underachiever. The lesson lasts half an hour after that and Rob looks mentally exhausted when he shows me out.

'Are you sure you don't mind doing this?' I ask, as I drink in one last look of his face. 'You know, getting together when we're not still ... together.'

He hesitates then nods. 'I'm sure we can both be grown-up about it, can't we? It's absolutely fine,' he smiles, holding my gaze. My heart skips a beat.

'Well, I'm really grateful,' I whisper.

He nods again, failing to remove his eyes from my face. I suddenly want to kiss him, to hold his face in my hands and press my lips against his. But I know how catastrophic submitting to my temporary lust for him would be when, ultimately, I can't give him what he wants.

'Enjoy the rest of your weekend,' I manage, forcing myself to turn and head down the stairs.

'You too. And keep practising, won't you?'

Chapter 20

I stop at the supermarket to pick up supplies for lunch with Dad. He offered take me out, go for a drive in the country, but as I know this would involve a Little Chef and a technicolour array of money-off coupons, I take matters into my own hands.

The house hasn't altered much since Marianne and I moved out, and even then the only bits that were updated after Mum died were the bedroom walls and the posters on them, which we once revised bi-monthly.

I've offered to redecorate for him, to put my tendency to mentally interior-design everyone else's house into practice, but he declined. It's not that Dad's incapable of DIY; in truth, it's one of his few obsessions, but all he does is repaint the walls in variations of the same shade (Dulux, Nutmeg) that Mum chose twenty-five years ago.

Technically, it's not 'my kind of house'; I love period properties, anything pre-twentieth century, with history and charm. This house has no history pre-us to speak of, no original features or listed status. It's simply a quiet, mid-sized semi with achingly suburban brickwork and equidistant bedding plants in the front garden.

That doesn't change the fact that it's home and always will be. I always knew that wherever I ended up in life – five minutes away or close to the Arctic Circle – this was my shelter, a place of memories, happiness and excellent biscuits.

'That you, Emma?' Dad cries from upstairs as I enter the hall and am assaulted by a waft of Air Wick.

'Hi, Dad,' I reply, heading to the kitchen to unpack my bags.

'Won't be a sec!'

I'm preparing a chicken salad, with Classic FM in the background, when I hear Dad in the doorway.

'*Ta-da!*' I turn round. 'What do you think?'

It is immediately evident that my father has been clothes shopping. This I know because every time he does so – on average once every two years – he does the '*Ta-da!*' thing. At which point, Marianne or I tell him that he mustn't, simply *mustn't*, leave the house in daylight.

What I'm confronted with today, however, is different from the usual terrible jumper/too-big slacks combo. It's different and it scares me. The problem with this outfit is not that it's unfashionable. It's so *on trend*, I start hiccuping in shock.

'What in God's name are you wearing?' I splutter.

He frowns. 'Do you think it's a bit groovy for my age?'

I look him up and down, taking in the Superdry T-shirt straining across his generous belly. He looks like Father Christmas going surfing. I take in the jeans – the *twisted* jeans, no less – and, just before my head spins round, I focus on the bag. It's ... it's ... a man bag! My father owns a *man bag*!

This situation could not be more wrong if it had a giant 'F' and 'See me after class' stamped on it.

'It's definitely erring on the groovy side, Dad.'

'How did your guitar lesson go?' he asks gaily.

'Hmm ... I've got some way to go, but it was only my first lesson. I'm determined that by my birthday I'll be playing "I Am the Resurrection" by the Stone Roses, or something of that standard.'

'I've got great faith,' he grins. 'Anyway, come and sit down. There's something I'd like to talk to you about. I need your advice.'

I was six when we lost my mum. I wish I could say I remember her vividly but, to my enduring frustration, I don't. Marianne, being a little older, has something I don't: memories. Rich, plentiful reflections of the past.

I can recall only fragmented bits and pieces, a scrapbook of thoughts collected from anecdotes and photographs. Such as the one in which she's painting my toenails pink, or laughing on the beach – or drawing pictures with Marianne at the kitchen table.

There's one particular photo I love of all three of us, the women in the family. She's wearing a silk shirt and a diamond necklace that I apparently loved to borrow, convinced that simply wearing it qualified me as a princess. I've no idea what happened to the necklace; it went missing somewhere along the way, like most of my memories.

You get different reactions when you tell people your mum passed away from cervical cancer at the age of thirty. Some are horrified to have asked, fearful that the mere mention will reduce me to tears. Others are awkward, some emotional, some just plain sad.

Except I've lived without a mum for seventy-five per cent of my life and my sense of loss isn't acute; it's not furious or all-encompassing. On some days, it barely feels like a loss. I hardly had her in the first place. But therein lies my sadness in those moments when I do think about her. A quiet, underlying sorrow for something – someone – I've been denied.

Mum was the love of Dad's life, a woman who defined him as much as he defined himself. She was seven years younger than him and they couldn't have been more different. She was soft-spoken, clever and beautiful; he was the outgoing but gentle soul who quietly adored her. Which was about the only thing Dad did quietly.

'So, Emma,' he says, twiddling with a Bourbon biscuit. 'Have you heard of a thing called . . . Match. Dot. Com?'

'Yes. Why?'

'Well . . . you might not believe this. But I've got a date.'

No, no, no, no. And no.

Coping with the idea of my father in a skinny-fit T-shirt is one thing. Supplying him with dating advice is quite another.

What the hell does he want me to say – 'Make sure you use protection'?

'It all stemmed from me joining that Facebook whatnot,' he explains, filling the kettle. 'It's smashing that – isn't it?'

I can't bring myself to respond. I hyperventilated enough when I got the friend request from him. I couldn't believe it. My father. On Facebook. With one hundred per cent access to every hen-night picture I've been tagged in, including my old university friend Sarah's Amsterdam jaunt with the six-foot penis (and I'm not referring to the waiter).

'Well, I told Deb and she started saying that now I'd gone all digital I should do some *internet dating*.' He whispers the last two words behind his hand, as if he's sharing his pin number with me at a football match.

Deb is assistant manageress at the shop my dad established thirty years ago. It's a mobility shop, with every brand of scooter, stairlift and walking aid known to man. My dad can say more about battery charging and off-road capabilities than any unsuspecting customer thought they wanted to hear. Deb has been his sidekick for sixteen years, an outspoken redhead he refers to as a 'girl', despite her being fifty-six.

'She met her new man, Barry, on it,' he continues. 'I don't think much of him, personally. A flashy sort – he goes line-dancing. Still, the principle obviously works. She's been banging on about it for months and I finally thought: why not? I'm going to Doodle it.'

'You mean Google.'

'Absolutely.' He puts down two teas and carefully tears off the lid of one of those little milk portions you get on flights. Given that it's been two years since he last went abroad, I try not to think about this. 'I've been a member for a month. I wasn't impressed until I met Suzie – the lady I'm going out with.'

'Why?'

'Well, she's got all her own hair and teeth and—'

'No, I mean, why weren't you impressed with the others?'

'Oh.' He squirms. 'Lots weren't my type. They were a bit too . . .'

'What?'

'I hate to use the word floozy—'

'I hope you avoided *them*,' I interrupt, horrified.

'Of course. Suzie's nothing like that. We've been emailing for three weeks.'

My mind is awash with thoughts. I know I should be full of encouragement; after all, it's twenty-three years since Mum died and Dad's never gone out with anyone since, not properly.

He did have one 'friendship' a few years ago with a woman who ran the Neighbourhood Watch in the next road, but that ended abruptly when she suggested that all the photos of Mum should be put away as they were hurting her feelings.

Obviously, I don't want Dad to grow old by himself. Obviously, I'd love him to hook up with a lovely woman who adores him and could persuade him to paint the hall a different colour.

At the same time, I feel an instinctive unease. Especially as one obvious question is nagging at me.

'This Suzie isn't eighteen, is she?'

He looks appalled. 'Why on earth would you think that?'

'Because you're dressed like one of the Inbetweeners.'

He rolls his eyes. 'She's fifty-eight. And the reason I've bought new clothes is simply because Suzie's *with it*. She's chic. At least, she looks it on Facebook. She used to be a dancer.'

'She sounds nice,' I reply, hoping that *dancer* doesn't mean *stripper*. 'So when's your date?'

'Lunchtime next Saturday. So: your advice. Where's cool in town these days?'

I cross my arms. 'Dad, you don't need somewhere *cool*. You're sixty-one years old. You need somewhere *nice*.'

'If you say so,' he mutters, clearly deciding to change the subject. 'I believe you spoke to Brian on that Sky whatnot.'

'*Skype*.' Any technology created post-Sinclair Spectrum blows my dad's brains. 'I did, yes.'

'Marianne seems very happy with him,' he continues brightly. 'What did you think?'

I hesitate. 'Nice. And as you say, she's happy.'

He stirs his tea as it becomes obvious we're both thinking the same thing. 'Not like Johnny, is he?' Dad says quietly.

'No, Dad,' I reply, unable to deny it. 'He's not like Johnny at all.'

Chapter 21

My economy drive – despite the hiccup with the washing powder – is going surprisingly well. That's the bright side of spending Saturday night in, the one benefit on which I'm trying to focus.

The downside is that I'm consumed by what Rob might be doing tonight; by whether he's having a quiet night in, venturing out with friends, at a work event or – and I'm going to *have* to recognise this possibility – spending the night with another woman.

The thought makes me feel queasy and is followed by a wave of frustration. Do I just simply want what I can't have? Why has he become so unbelievably desirable now we're no longer an item?

The reality is, desire – in its simplest, physical form – was never a problem when it came to my feelings for Rob. It was (and is) absolutely clear that I fancied the pants off him. But there's a big difference between wanting to constantly tear someone's clothes off them and wanting to marry them.

Maybe, with time, I'd have wanted to do both.

It wasn't as if it was *only* about sex with him. I genuinely enjoyed Rob's company – whether it was during a simple trip to the cinema or one of the glitzy fund-raising events he was involved in.

I loved going to those with him. Part of that was about the razzle-dazzle – the champagne, the celebrity guests, the posh dresses. But they were also a reminder of how hard Rob must have worked to be as successful as he was; he didn't just hover around the edges of that world like I did – he was right at the centre of it.

Sometimes I think that the only problem with the idea of getting married to Rob was that it came far too soon. Before the thought had ever even occurred to me – after only months together. Even he'd have to admit that was way too quick. Only, he never did admit that. I suspect, as far as Rob's concerned, *weeks* wouldn't have been too quick.

I drive home from Dad's determined to put such thoughts out of my mind and focus on my evening of pure – albeit thrifty – indulgence. I'm going to have a Jo Malone bubble bath (a Christmas present, your honour), a box of Maltesers (they were on offer) and an evening of cinematic pleasure in front of *The Notebook* on DVD. I don't know why weeping in front of a film cheers me up quite so much, but this one does it every time.

As I turn into my drive, I spot a removal van outside Rita's old apartment.

'Shit!' I mutter, as my heartbeat triples in speed and I slam on the brakes and duck my head under the dashboard.

I *cannot* let my new neighbour see me. Not just because he has a detailed knowledge of my gynaecological bothers. Or because seeing him again would breach the terms of my one-night stand (which involve sleeping with someone *you never see again*, not someone with whom you share a council tax band). But also because I'm very aware that he has a wife. And I want to see her even less than I want to see him.

With my head in a brace position, I attempt to roll the car the final few feet into the drive, assuming that after two years of living here I can do it with my eyes shut.

It's apparent this is an optimistic assumption when I smash a potted azalea and come alarmingly close to scraping the car against the wall in the manner of someone taking a potato peeler to it.

I turn off the engine and listen. There are voices outside Rita's old flat, instructions to removal men about where to put pieces of furniture. I refuse to move until they die down, and even then it's only to cautiously pop up my head to check the coast is clear.

Then I fling open the door, swing out my legs, slam it shut, and am about to race to the house, when I realise I've trapped my cardi. I manage one large stride before being catapulted, Laurel and Hardy-style, onto the side panel and almost rupturing a kidney on my wing mirror. Muttering expletives, I stumble up the five steps to the main door, then I hear something that nearly melts my brain.

'Hey!'

Matt Taylor, my One-Night Stand, is walking towards me – waving, smiling, clearly counting on a pleasant introduction to his new neighbour.

Well, screw that.

Stacey might have been straight round there with a basket of her home-made satsuma jam, but not me. I stumble up the steps, holding my hand against my face, like Lady Gaga avoiding the paps, before racing into the house and slamming the door.

I storm along the hall, feeling stress fall away from me the second I'm in the refuge of my flat. I open the Maltesers immediately, the ready meal now surplus to requirements.

For the remainder of the night, I feel like a prisoner in my own home. No matter how many Maltesers I pop, how many times I rewind the snog-on-the-lake bit in *The Notebook*, my mind is firmly focused on two issues.

The first is the unsustainability of this. No matter how much I try to convince myself that perhaps he's only renting and might move out in a week, I know that meeting Matt Taylor – and his wife and children – is inevitable.

The removal van doesn't leave until gone eight and, for an hour afterwards, my new neighbour is striding between his car and the house. Not that I'm looking. Oh, okay, yes I am. And thinking about the night we spent together, and my knickers, and my hangover, and Marianne's warnings – basically, my kaleidoscope of regrets.

Which brings me to the second object of tonight's obsession. Rob. And how I wish with all of my heart that he was here with me tonight.

Chapter 22

Despite my determination to have a restorative lie-in, I wake the next morning at 7.05 a.m. with an odd combination of grogginess and agitation. I throw off the covers, slip on my flip-flops and pad to the kitchen to make tea and tidy up a bit.

I don't know when de-cluttering became fashionable. I suspect it was courtesy of those *House Doctor* programmes that advocate removing all evidence of human life, leaving all the ambience of a Travelodge room.

I open one of the cupboards in the kitchen and am shocked to discover a recyclables crate I completely forgot to empty after a girls' night in a few weeks ago. I pick it up, avoiding stale dregs of booze dribbling on the Cookie Monster PJs Dad bought me for Christmas, and stagger to the door.

I head straight to the back of the house, but when I reach the recycling bins I realise that something's amiss. My wheelie bin isn't there. *Somebody* has nicked it.

As soon as this thought flashes into my head I dismiss it. It's hardly high value and wouldn't be easy to pinch, even for a career criminal.

I tiptoe round the house, surveying the area – then glance next door and narrow my eyes. I don't *know* that my new neighbour is responsible for this wrong-doing – but I do know that it never happened before he moved in.

Stealthily, I make my way to the three-foot wall that separates the houses. I put down the crate, then jump over, dart underneath Rita's old kitchen window and creep to the back. The bin is outside his patio door. It's unmistakably mine – I'd recognise the angle of the Bank Holiday Collection sticker anywhere.

I silently begin dragging it to its rightful home, wincing as it creaks. When I reach the three-foot wall again, I have a choice. I can either take it all the way to the front of the house and pull it up the driveway in full view of . . . *anyone*. Or I can try to get it over the wall quickly.

Speed is the only option.

I attempt to heave it over the wall, contorting myself into a variety of positions that culminate in one that makes me resemble a constipated sumo wrestler. It's when I'm convinced this ungainly squat will allow me to pull the bin over on my back, that I am interrupted.

'Need a hand?'

The bin slips from my grasp and I fall to my knees – arse in the air, pyjama bottoms shredded and a hideous sense of dread running through me.

It is not even seven thirty. I seriously hope today gets better.

Chapter 23

He recognises me the instant I stand and look him defiantly in the eye.

It's the only option. Trying to make my getaway is pointless. I'm going to have to face the man I shagged and ran from. With that horrible fact emblazoned on my brain I decide the only tactic is to do as Scooby Doo would do: create a diversion.

'This wheelie bin belongs to me.'

'Does it? Sorry – it must have been the—'

'Having to search for it at this time on a Sunday morning isn't my idea of fun.' Even as I'm saying it, my reaction feels over the top. I sound like a lunatic. But I don't care. Because the more I keep talking, the more he'll be prevented from raising our liaison, email exchange, or the fact that I've been caught breaking and entering his patio.

'I'm sure. But you see—'

'I don't mean to be petty,' I continue, contrary to evidence, 'but you *have* misappropriated my property.'

He frowns, focusing on my pursed lips and the hands I appear to have placed on my hips as if I'm about to start doing 'The Time Warp'. It's then that I notice the smell again. The irresistible, delicious scent literally oozing from this man. I take a step back from him.

'I think you'll find it belongs to the council,' he replies calmly. His lip twitches and I can't work out if he's about to burst out laughing or tell me off. I am now crimson. Even my ears are blushing.

'And the council have assigned this wheelie bin to *my* flat.'

He looks over my shoulder to the overflowing crate of wine bottles. 'Heavy night?'

I don't rise to the bait. 'I should stress that, had you wanted to borrow the wheelie bin, or even deposit your own recyclable goods in there, I'd have had no problem at all if you'd asked.'

'I see.'

'As it is, not only have you removed my wheelie bin, you've also filled it with non-recyclable items.'

'Right.'

'Which means that if it'd gone out on a Tuesday, the bin men would've put a big sticker on it, announcing to the world that I was the sort of woman who placed non-recyclable items in a bin designed solely for recyclable ones. And I am not that irresponsible.'

He stands staring, as if waiting for me to finish. Which I wish I'd done after the first sentence.

'That's all,' I conclude.

'Thank you. Well, first of all, I apologise that your wheelie bin ended up in my garden – it must have been a removal man, because it wasn't me. But I'm genuinely sorry for the inconvenience. Second, may I say that of all the welcomes I've received since moving in – the cards, the friendly hellos, the bottles of wine – yours is, without doubt, the most … memorable. And I say that as someone who received four jars of satsuma jam.'

I open my mouth to speak, but he gets there before me.

'As for you being reckless, irresponsible or anything remotely negative, I would never be so presumptuous about someone I hardly know.' He holds my gaze meaningfully at the last words.

'Good.'

He looks at me again and an awkward silence hovers in the air.

I go to turn away, when he says something that makes my stomach flip over. 'You know we spent the night together, don't you?'

'Yes,' I hiss. 'I also know you have children and are married and—'

'Separated.'

'What?'

'I'm separated. My wife and I aren't together.'

I straighten my back. 'I see.' This does alter things – and I'm relieved. But not enough to make me proud of having a one-night stand with my new neighbour. 'Fine. Good. But I'd still rather you didn't mention … you know, to anyone.'

'"You know"?'

I narrow my eyes and focus on him so hard I could be about to fire lasers from them. '*You. Know,*' I repeat, then spin on my heels and march away, dragging my wheelie bin back to its rightful home.

Chapter 24

I'm almost overjoyed to get to work on Monday morning. 'Almost' because, while I'm sick of hiding in my flat and relieved to escape from it, being at Little Blue Bus Productions today only underlines my growing suspicion of one thing: I really should get out of this job.

The irony is that Giles and I have a brilliant morning.

We've finished the script on a new series and had a meeting with the animators, who were effervescing with enthusiasm as they started sketching out ideas. As Giles and I stood over the shoulder of one, James, we smiled at each other like proud, but dysfunctional, parents.

We achieved loads, were bursting with ideas and laughed so much – about everything from Giles's comedy coffee spill when Denise from accounts walked in, to the slip of James's pencil that left a Bingbah looking like the bastard love child of a My Little Pony and Chewbacca from *Star Wars*.

It was one of those mornings that reminded me why I've loved this job for so many years – the creativity, the buzz, the energy you get from talented people doing what they do best.

Then I got back to my desk.

Perry had embarked on an emailing frenzy, something that sends ripples of terror round the office each time it happens.

He goes underground for weeks, resulting in urgent and repeated requests going totally unanswered. Then you'll log on and suddenly nineteen of the buggers will be sitting there in bold type, sprinkled with random punctuation marks – Perry's approach to exclamation marks can be compared only with that of a toddler with a tub of hundreds of thousands.

The first in my inbox is a response to an email I sent in December 2010 asking if it'd be possible to leave early on Friday for a dental appointment.

**Course, no problem Emma! Not dentures, is it?!!!!! ;-) !!!
:-/**

The second, third, fourth, fifth, sixth and seventh take me to the present day, authorising payments for stationery that's been long recycled, holidays from which my tan faded months ago – and issuing feedback on scripts that have not just been produced in the interim, but have also been aired, watched by millions, and are now repeated on Boomerang.

The rest consist of a variety of increasingly certifiable sugges-tions for changes to a script that he'd signed off weeks ago and on which the animators are well advanced. One of them includes the suggestion that we kill off several Bingbahs in a variety of unpleasant ways – a concept apparently inspired by a leaflet entitled *Telling Your Child About Bereavement* that he read in his GP surgery on Thursday.

When I get home, I feel a weird mixture of emotions. A deep concern that with no alternative openings in the interior-design industry, I'm destined to spend my life in the asylum that is Little Blue Bus Productions.

A fear that, even if my 'dream job' did leap up and bite me on the nose, nothing would ever compare to the incredible buzz that we once experienced every minute of the day, the taste of which I could clearly recall today.

And a sadness that, with Perry at the helm, those days are unlikely to return.

Chapter 25

I see Matt Taylor three times over the course of the week and, on every occasion, I wish I owned one of Harry Potter's invisibility cloaks.

The first is on the way to work on Tuesday, when he's walking down the steps of Rita's flat and gives a little wave I can't help but interpret as sarcastic. I pretend not to notice, feigning concentration as I press random buttons on my satnav, despite the journey to work being one I've now completed approximately two-and-a-half thousand times.

The second is on Thursday, on my return from a dispiriting guitar lesson at Rob's during which I tortured myself about him no longer being my boyfriend, and tortured *him* with my musical skills. Despite my efforts, I am reluctantly coming to the conclusion that I have all the melodic flair of Jedward.

There's no avoiding Matt this time and he actually says hello. I say hello back. It's all perfectly civil and grown-up – but I'd still rather it wasn't happening.

The third is this morning, Saturday, just after Asha has phoned to say she can't make it out tonight as Toby is whisking her off to the Lake District for two nights – a big thing given that they never usually get to spend that sort of time together. I step out of the car and then bump into Stacey, who regales me with every tiny detail she's uncovered about Matt's life, including his impending divorce, three children, super-duper jet-setting job as a top photographer and the fact that he wears Vera Wang after-shave, which she's identified with the detection skills of a Customs and Excise sniffer dog.

I say nothing, refusing to be impressed, as his car pulls into the drive and I make my excuses.

I'm inside my flat before the need to engage in conversation arises, and I watch from the kitchen window as Matt lifts out his little boy from the seat in the back of the car and the other two follow. The two bigger boys are play-fighting, while the little one is giggling as his father tickles him. He finally puts him on the ground, grinning as he follows them all to the garden behind the house.

'Do you think it still counts as a one-night stand, given that I keep bumping into this man?' I ask Cally that night. We're at a Comedy Club and I've taken the opportunity to put this to her while my sister is at the bar.

'*If* you slept with him, then . . . why not? It'd be churlish otherwise—'

'*Yes!* My guitar lessons are going *brilliantly*, thanks!' I hoot, changing the subject as Marianne returns.

The Comedy Club is in the basement of a trendy converted warehouse in the Albert Dock and, having attended before, this time I've chosen the table with absolute precision. On my last visit – with Rob – I made the error of sitting within picking-on distance of the stage and was subjected to a barrage of repartee that culminated in the compere speculating on what our children would look like (Gonzo from *The Muppet Show*). Personally, I felt we'd got off lightly, but I could tell that Rob was a little upset. I don't know why that thought makes me feel a swell of affection for him, but it does.

'When do we get to hear your new-found musical genius?' asks Marianne.

'My birthday party. I'm still gripping to the probably misplaced hope that my talent will be unleashed when Rob lets me play something more ambitious.'

'I thought you said you'd progressed to something more complicated?' Marianne replies.

'Yes. "Jingle Bells".'

'Ahh, Zachary's favourite.' Cally grins. 'Hey – I've got to show you this.'

She reaches into her bag for her phone and plays a video shot in her kitchen today – of Zachary singing the Black Eyed Peas' 'I Gotta Feeling'. It is undeniably hilarious and he's very cute – a description that only ever seems clear to me when he's at a safe distance. I look up at Marianne and can't help noticing she looks more subdued than I'd expect.

I've had a feeling for a couple of years that my sister's getting broody. It happens to me too every so often – though it usually passes, a bit like wind. Marianne has always been a more obvious candidate for motherhood than me – she's a natural with stuff like that.

Although, try as I might, I just can't imagine her new boyfriend as the father of her child.

'Brian really wanted to come with me this weekend, but his mum's not been very well,' she tells me during the interval. We're in one of those trendy unisex loos, something I've never approved of. It's fine if you've only got to wash your hands and apply lipstick. But it's very difficult to sustain a healthy degree of mystique when members of the opposite sex witness you buying Tampax or applying concealer to unsightly zits.

'Really? Is it anything serious?' I ask.

'Oh I don't think so, but she's old and he worries about her. He's such a caring person – honestly, he always puts others before himself. Which is one of the reasons I love him. That and the fact that he makes me laugh more than anyone I've ever met. He's great, Emma. He really is.'

I can't help but smile. There's no doubt about it, Brian – as unlikely a love interest as he is for Marianne – is clearly making her very happy. I don't quite *get* it – but I can't argue with it.

We're about to head back, when she freezes.

'Are you okay?' I frown.

She nods and gestures to the other side of the room, where a figure is drying his hands as women sashay past, desperate for his attention.

And it's no wonder why.

Johnny is the best-looking man in the place; he radiates charisma without even saying anything.

'Bloody hell . . . I haven't seen Johnny for ages. Are you going to go over and say hi?' I ask.

'I suppose I'd better.' But Marianne doesn't move.

'Come on, then,' I insist, dragging her by the arm.

He is overwhelmingly pleased to see us.

'Emma!' He sweeps me up in a rib-shattering hug. 'Wow! You look amazing! How are things?'

'Um . . . great,' I reply, slightly taken aback at this deluge of enthusiasm. Johnny and I have always got on well, but you'd think I'd told him I'd won the lottery and was giving the proceeds to his St Tropez yacht fund. 'Are you back for the weekend?'

'Yep! Here to see my folks. I'm home a few times a year still. Just on my way out of here, actually. To think, I might never have seen you!' He claps his hands gleefully, then takes a deep breath and turns to my sister. 'Marianne!' He laughs as he leans in and kisses her on the cheek, squeezing her into him. She shifts away awkwardly.

'I need to get to the bar before it shuts for the next act,' I announce, deciding to leave them to it. 'It's my round.'

Then I slip off, leaving my sister – clearly torn between unease and elation – with her ex-boyfriend.

When I return to the table, I'm spilling over with the news. 'Marianne's talking to him now,' I tell Cally.

Her eyes widen. 'Is he coming over?'

'No, he's on his way out. He was a bit drunk. He clearly still adores her, you know.'

She takes a sip of her drink. 'Hey, did I tell you I've started reading *Riders* again?' I'd rather still discuss my sister's love life – but am aware that it's probably not as interesting to everyone else.

'Is it as good as it was when we were fifteen?' I ask.

'It's *great*. Can see exactly what we saw in it.'

'It was called sex, wasn't it?' quips Marianne, sitting down again.

'That was quick. So how was he?' I ask.

She shrugs and glances at Cally. 'Completely off his head.'

'He *was* drunk, no doubt about that,' I concede.

The next performance is about to start, when someone pulls up a chair next to me.

'Thought I'd join you after all,' says Asha sheepishly.

'What happened to the Lake District?' I whisper as the lights dim.

She shakes her head, clearly upset. 'Domestic emergency. It's not a big deal. It's just one of those things.'

'Asha, it *is* a big deal,' Cally insists. 'I'm *worried* about you.'

Asha doesn't know how to respond. And before she can, her phone rings and she picks it up to look at the number.

'It's the man himself,' she tells us, hitting the Answer button. 'Yes?'

Her voice is slightly cold and it sounds alien coming from Asha. She says nothing, simply listens as he talks, frowning every so often. Eventually, she takes a deep breath.

'Toby,' she whispers, her voice heavy with hurt and anger. 'I understand why you don't want to leave your family in the lurch, I really do. I understand how painful the prospect of leaving must be. But I can't go on like this. I can't be a *mistress* for the rest of my life. I cannot be a *mistress*, full stop.'

Cally leans over and clutches her hand.

Asha swallows. 'It's this simple: if you're a single man, I will be with you. If you remain married, if you don't *do* anything . . . then I can't. I can't be a part of this any longer.'

He says something to her and she ends the call with tears in her eyes. 'I need a drink.'

Chapter 26

Asha insists we stay for the final act, determined to take her mind off things. It turns out to be a good decision. The comedienne is brilliant, although whether the male section of the audience found her graphic description of bikini waxing as enjoyable as us is questionable.

'Do we always think the last act is the best because we're usually drunk by then?' Marianne muses.

'Absolutely not,' Cally replies. 'Hic!'

There's no doubt that most people in the room are better-lubricated now than at the start of the night. And none more so than those in the VIP section of the bar on the other side of the room; they've been whooping and hollering as if emulating the mating call of migrating swans.

It's been the source of some consternation over the years that, despite the fact that I 'work in television, *don't-cha-know*', entry to VIP areas of bars and restaurants eludes me. The only ones I've been in are in London, where I was hanging on Marianne's coat tails.

'Is there anyone famous over there?' Asha asks, screwing up her nose.

'The actors on that soap – you know ... *Hilly Oaks*,' Marianne informs her. 'I went to a couple of events with one or two, back in the day.'

'Hey, Emma,' Cally says with a worrying twinkle in her eye, 'wasn't one of your challenges to *snog somebody famous?*'

'I decided against that one,' I reply, before she gets any ideas.

'Why, because you're so brilliant at the guitar?' Marianne asks.

'Because the only one I've achieved wholeheartedly so far is the—'

'One-night stand. Yes, I know,' Marianne says, pursing her lips.

'Well, I'm determined that the next thing I do will be something worthwhile. Noble. Not *snog somebody famous*,' I scoff.

'We'll twist your arm,' Cally grins.

'You won't.'

'Bet we will,' Asha adds, managing a smile for the first time.

I throw her an indignant look. 'You *won't*.'

'Have another drink,' Cally says, topping up my glass.

I sit up straight. 'My sister wouldn't allow it.'

'I wouldn't say that,' she shrugs, clearly enjoying this. 'It's not the same as sleeping with someone, and for a woman who's done that much ...' I open my mouth in horror – she obviously thinks this is a half-arsed way of proving her original point. 'How about we agree to a peck on the lips?'

I cross my arms. 'I am absolutely, one hundred per cent not going to be persuaded.'

'I thought you wanted to be braver?' says Cally. 'Come on, Emma – where's your backbone?'

I have no idea whether this gentle but persistent winding up is because (a) they're drunk; (b) it's entertaining; or (c) both. But there's only one thing more irritating than my friends doing it. The fact that it works.

Every cast member of *Hilly Oaks* is gorgeous. You're not allowed to appear in it if you've had even a tickle with the ugly stick. There's the tall, dark one with the unbeatable six-pack. The tall, fair one with the to-die-for bum. The tall, redhead with the granite-toned upper arms. And that's just the women.

The men are perfection personified: six foot two inches (on average) of delectability. Although it isn't a particularly edgy look – if they were five-and-a-half feet shorter, they'd be driving round in a pink jeep keeping Barbie company.

I have a terrible suspicion that between the ears of each and every one of them there is little to speak of, but that doesn't matter. After half an hour of being dared, goaded and – finally – accused of being a Grade A wimp if I don't give this a go, I've agreed to take the challenge.

I'm determined that, by the time I'm thirty, nobody will be

able to accuse me of being a wimp. An appalling guitar player maybe, but not a wimp.

So I straighten my back and attempt to walk brazenly into the VIP section, confident that if I look the part, nobody will challenge me.

'Where d'you think you're going?' asks a security guard.

I open my mouth, trying to think of an answer – but someone gets there first.

'She's with me.'

He is, without question, one of the best-known characters in *Hilly Oaks*. I can't deny it; this guy is famous, close to a household name. And from the way he ushers me past the security guard and invites me to sit next to him, every indication is that he'd be prepared to snog me.

The problem is, when my fifteen-year-old self signed up to that list, I had someone in mind other than Bruce McNulty – who plays the *father* of one of the main characters.

He's wearing a toupeé that looks like something six grey-hounds would chase round a racetrack. He's as old as Jagger but doesn't move like him, not unless the Stones frontman ever finds himself recovering from a hip replacement. And while none of this would disqualify him from being either famous or a potential snogee, I'm not sure I can go through with this without bringing up my dinner. I grin, hold up my hand and wave like a maniac, despite him being a foot away.

'*Hi!*'

'Enjoy the show?' He licks his lips and smiles, revealing dental work that outshines the disco ball.

'Yup! You?'

'Great.'

I try to think of something else to say, but it's torturous. I glance at my friends, noting that they're in fits of hysteria, on the verge of bursting vital organs.

I turn back to my suitor. 'So . . . you're in *Hilly Oaks*.'

'That's right.' He knocks back a bright blue cocktail that looks as though it's been scooped up from the shallow end of a swimming pool. 'Watch it?'

The answer is no, never have, never will, not unless I lose several billion brain cells in a terrible accident with a disorientated asteroid. 'Doesn't everyone?'

'It appears so. I hate to get straight to the point, but would you like to get outta here?'

My overwhelming desire is to run, run a thousand million miles – but I need to take decisive action.

'I'll be honest, I'm not sure. I wouldn't mind a snog, though.'

He looks at me, undecided about whether he's shocked to the core or totally dispirited by the fact that I'm only prepared to invest my lips in any amorous action.

I take a fortifying slug of wine, glance at my friends – who are clearly determined not to believe I can do this – and smile. 'Oh go on, pucker up.'

I lean in, close my eyes and press my lips hard against his before the antiseptic effect of the wine wears off. For the sake of doing things properly, I stick out my tongue – withdrawing it sharply – then I pull away and straighten up.

'Thanks very much!'

Then I leap up and march away in the direction of my friends, each of whom is strangely incapable of removing her chin from the floor.

Chapter 27

I'm not nearly as hungover as a woman who snogged Bruce McNulty the night before should be.

I'm up far too early the following morning – at ten – after a text arrives from Rob.

> You left your sunglasses here the other day. Shall I pop over
> or do you want to collect them at your next lesson? xxxxxxx

I would love to arrange to meet Rob today, but daren't go ahead – that would be a mixed message too far and I'm already uneasy about the guitar lessons. I groan and scrub my mouth with the back of my hand for the sixtieth time in twelve hours – the comparison with my ex-boyfriend's beautiful, luscious lips does Bruce McNulty's horrible mush no favours.

An hour later, I'm on my way to meeting Asha for brunch at a café on Allerton Road when Marianne phones – before she heads back to Edinburgh – to tell me about Dad's date.

Apparently, they had lots in common. She is attractive, funny and loves *Midsomer Murders* as much as he does. Sadly, she's getting back with her ex-husband and moving to Weston-super-Mare. I feel suddenly very sorry for him – until Marianne tells me he's got another date on Wednesday.

I arrive at the café at the same time as Asha and we find a seat by the window.

'How are you, sweetheart? Have you spoken to Toby again?'

'Sorry you had to hear all that last night. Things are just … tricky.'

'What did he say?'

'We've had a chat this morning on the phone. He's mortified about letting me down. It's a long, convoluted story, but the upshot is, he's desperately sorry.'

I frown. She's nothing like as defiant as she was last night. 'So you've made friends?' I ask.

She's unable to meet my eyes. 'I meant what I said to Toby last night, Emma. When I said it can't go on.'

'What does that mean?' I ask.

She looks at me with an expression that betrays a million emotions: happiness, fear, guilt – and endless others in between.

'It means he's finally doing it. He's going to leave his wife.'

Chapter 28

Matt Taylor has proved impossible to evade, even with my sophisticated avoidance tactics – including parking on the far side of the drive, ducking behind the bush by the porch and only emerging from the passenger door of my car.

I have resisted the temptation to purchase a balaclava, break in via one of the flats at the back of the main house and – an idea brilliant in its simplicity – never, ever return home.

But this time, carrying enough heavy bags of shopping to tear a ligament in my neck, my guard is down.

'Emma!'

One handle of the heaviest bag slips from my hand – and out rolls one of my purchases. Not any purchase, mind you. Not the sophisticated, flavoured olive oil. Not the inoffensive cauliflower or bunch of coriander.

No, this is a two-pack of Odor-Eaters, the one I bought because it was on special offer. And, okay, because my trainers whiff a bit – a fact I'd really rather keep to myself. I freeze, drawing breath like the turbine on a Dyson, and think fast – before wellying the pack into the bushes with a kick Pele would be proud of.

Only, instead of landing conveniently underneath the foliage, as I'd hoped, the pack wedges itself on top, giving the appearance that it sprouted from there. With no time to stop, I increase my pace, pumping my legs hard and fast to get to the steps before he catches up. But he's quicker than me – significantly – even with a small child on his back.

'Emma,' he repeats, as I slow down, blowing a sweaty clump of hair off my face. 'Anyone would think you were avoiding me.'

I look up and he smiles. Only, it's not a nice smile. Not a 'lovely weather isn't it?' type smile. This is an unashamedly cocky smile, one that says: 'Yup, you and I have done the biz ... walked the walk ... reached parts no other neighbours have ...'

'I can't imagine why you'd think that,' I say coolly.

A ripple flickers across his forehead as if interpreting this response, then he turns round, momentarily distracted.

'Look, I know we got off on the wrong foot, but Joshua *really* wanted to meet you. He absolutely insisted.'

He crouches down to allow the little boy to jump off his back as I wonder why on earth he'd want to meet me.

'Are you the Bingbahs' mummy?' he asks, giving me my answer.

Matt smiles. 'Stacey told us you worked on that show. Obviously, in conjunction with your career as an air hostess.'

I cringe. 'Oh ... dear.'

He laughs. 'Well, I personally think *Bingbah* is more impressive. It's Joshua's favourite programme.'

'But I don't like the squirrels,' he adds. He's incredibly sweet-looking, with huge eyes, soft blond hair and an impossibly cute gap between his teeth.

'No, they're not nice, are they?' I agree.

'Where do they live?' he asks.

I could respond with: 'In my head, until a sociopathic heavy-metal fan and I turn them into a television programme.' But I don't. 'Bibblybobbly.'

'Is that a real place?' he asks sceptically.

'Of course. I visit every day.'

His mouth opens wide and he looks at me as if not only am I the luckiest woman in the world, but also he has a million more questions, to which I probably don't have the answer.

'Ollie! Jack!' Matt calls over to the two other boys – but they're too busy sword-fighting with large bits of foliage. 'Sorry,' he says, turning back to me. 'Those two clearly have far more important matters to attend to.'

'Oh, that's okay,' I reply. 'I'd hate to interrupt.'

Matt smiles. 'Well, that's Ollie, anyway – he's seven. And Jack, who's five.'

Joshua suddenly steps forward and holds up his hand like kids used to do when playing cowboys and Indians in the days before political correctness.

'Erm . . .' I lower my voice an octave and hold up a hand opposite his. '*How!*'

Matt suppresses a laugh. 'He wants you to give him a high five.'

'Oh.' I was obviously being optimistic when I thought it was impossible to feel any more stupid in this man's presence. 'I see. Um ... right.'

I hold up my hand again and he slaps it so hard I wince.

'Gently,' Matt says, holding Joshua's hand. 'Like Daddy showed you.'

'Sorry,' he says sheepishly.

'So what does the Bingbahs' mummy do at weekends?' Matt asks.

'Oh ... depends,' I say casually, feeling myself redden. My discomfort is because the question *sounds* like a prelude to him asking me out, a prospect that makes my heart race, and not in a good way. I don't want strange men, neighbours or otherwise, asking me out – even if I have danced the sideways lambada with them. I want *Rob* asking me out. Even though I wouldn't say yes. Maybe.

'Well, what are you doing *next* weekend?'

'I'm not sure yet.'

'If you're free, I'm having a few people over for a house-warming. I'm going to have a barbecue in the communal garden, a bit of bubbly, that sort of thing. You'd be very welcome. It starts at two.'

'I'll see what I'm up to.' I shrug so awkwardly I nearly dislocate my shoulder. 'So, Stacey said you're a photographer. Is it landscape photography you specialise in?'

Jane Costello

'Mainly, but I do all sorts. My main clients are travel companies – I take photos for brochures and magazines.'

'Wow.'

'It's fun. I've worked everywhere from Sydney to South Africa, but these days I get withdrawal symptoms if I'm away from the boys for more than a few days.'

'You don't ever go to Norway, do you? I've got a budget of about three hundred quid and absolutely need to see the Northern Lights this year – so if you know anywhere insanely cheap, I'd be grateful for the tip.'

He laughs. 'I've never done Norway, although I've photographed the Northern Lights in Iceland a few times. Sadly, I don't think you'd get out of Liverpool Airport for three hundred quid.'

I become aware that Joshua looks bored.

'Joshua, do you like your daddy's new flat?' I ask.

'Hmm . . . not really.'

Matt looks concerned. 'Why not, sweetheart? We're going to get your room sorted next weekend so it'll feel more like home.'

He looks up. 'I liked it better when we all lived at Mummy's house.'

Matt bends down and squeezes him tightly. I suddenly feel as if I shouldn't be here. 'So did I, Josh. So did I.'

Chapter 29

Friday night and another of my friends has hit the Big 3-Oh.

'Do you feel different?' I ask Asha.

'Yes. I feel drunk. Very drunk.'

Asha spent ages deliberating on what to do for her thirtieth and considered everything from paintballing to skiing at one of those indoor slopes. Given that I never mastered a snowplough turn that didn't look like I was squatting over a bidet, I'm happy with the alternative – a table for ten in the Malmaison hotel on the waterfront.

I love this place. It's glitzy and Gothic, with opulent velvets in the bar and a dramatic centrepiece flame in the lobby. It is also the place where Rob and I spent our first naughty weekend.

Actually, it wasn't quite a weekend – it was one night, a Sunday, because it was on offer. And it wasn't that naughty, as both of us were streaming with cold. Snotty snogging is nothing like as enjoyable as the conventional kind, but we managed to have a good time somehow.

Tonight, our group is all girls: Asha's neighbours, work colleagues and old school friends – including Cally and me. Some of us have never met before, although it hasn't taken long for everyone to mingle, judging by the fine detail with which Cally's now regaling some of them about chapter forty-six in *Riders*.

'You're entitled to be drunk, Asha,' I decide, shortly after our main courses arrive. 'It's not every day a girl says hello to a new decade.'

'This is true,' she replies. 'But in answer to your question, I do feel a little different. I'm looking forward to my thirties. They're going to be good, I know it.'

I grin. 'Why so optimistic, as a matter of interest?'

She thinks for a second. 'Because I know more than I did when I was twenty – but still not enough to spoil my fun in trying to find out the rest.'

I laugh and it strikes me how much more than me Asha has achieved in her twenties.

'Besides,' she continues, 'all that pressure on women to look eternally youthful doesn't wash with me. I won't be sitting here in another decade comparing Botox with you, Emma – I promise you that.'

'I'll have to talk to Cally about it, then.'

She shakes her head, laughing.

'How long till your birthday now?' she asks.

'Five months. And, while I've managed to snog a pensioner, risk a life-threatening STD and learn the opening bars of two Christmas carols on the guitar, all the exciting things on my list elude me. I have no new job – and no impending Northern Lights trip.'

'You've booked the polo, though.'

'I have,' I concede. 'And my hair has grown at least half a millimetre. Admittedly, the ends look like the bristles on a twenty-year-old toothbrush.'

There is a pause, then she puts down her fork and leans into me. 'I haven't mentioned anything to the others,' she whispers, 'but Toby's doing it tonight.'

I stiffen.

'He's leaving Christina.'

'Oh God,' I whisper back, unable to think of anything else. 'How do you feel?'

She rolls her eyes as if she doesn't know where to start. 'Nervous. Guilty. Elated. I want it over and done with. I last spoke to him on the way here – and he was heading home to do it right then. He told me not to expect a phone call until late tonight, though.'

'Why?'

She bites her lip. 'There's going to be . . . fallout.'

I clutch her hand, processing my thoughts. The marriage can't go on in the horrific state it's in. And there's no doubt it will be for the best in the long term, for everyone. But that doesn't mean tonight isn't going to be horrible. I might not know Toby's wife, or his children. But the thought of what could be happening now to a family on the other side of the city makes my stomach twist.

Chapter 30

The rest of the evening involves a reasonable amount of wine – and a lot of fun. We're torn between going on somewhere else and simply relaxing in the bar. In the end, the fact that we're all talking like it's going out of fashion, turns out to be decisive – so we stay.

It's nearly eleven when I go to the loo and take out my phone. Rob has had a habit of texting me when I've been out lately and I get a twinge of concern that he hasn't tonight. I pull up his number and find myself composing a message.

Guess where I am? x

He texts back seconds after I've pressed Send.

Put me out of my misery! Xxx

Malmaison. It's nicer without a runny nose! x

I'm returning to the bar when another text arrives.

Coincidence – Jimmy and I are in Albert Dock. xxx

I know this is a hint. I also know I'm delighted to an inappropriate degree about it. The angel on my shoulder might be telling me I should stick to my guns, let Rob get on with the rest of his life and continue his search for 'The One' who isn't me.

But she isn't as persuasive as her evil twin, the one on my other shoulder. It's she who's calling the shots when I dart back to the loo to check my lips are moist but my underarms are not. She's the one in charge when I text Rob to say:

Pop over for a drink if you get a chance x

– and is still in charge when he arrives about seven minutes later, so fast I can only conclude that he either water-skied here or broke the thousand-metres sprint record.

'You look gorgeous,' he declares, slightly out of breath.

'So do you,' I reply. And, God, he really does. He's wearing my favourite shirt – otherwise known as the Sexiest Shirt Known To Man, an item of clothing that emphasises every contour of his torso. When he smiles tonight, his whole face is luminous – quite an achievement, given it's so dark I nearly asked if they had the cocktail menu in Braille.

'Where's Jimmy?'

'He was chatting someone up. I think I may have lost him.'

I take a sip of my drink. 'So you're all mine?'

He hesitates, then smiles. 'I'm all yours.'

The girls greet Rob like their long-lost friend, and it's impossible not to feel happy that he's here. He gives Asha a birthday kiss on the cheek – making her blush in the process – before insisting on buying everyone drinks.

While I become vaguely aware that I'm behaving badly by lapping up his attention, I convince myself that the flirting is light-hearted and not to be taken seriously. Until I feel his hand on mine.

He clutches it and leans in to whisper in my ear: 'Get back with me.'

I pull away gently, even though I feel an overwhelming desire to grab him by the collar and kiss him passionately, before agreeing to what he wants. Because he's a great person, because I miss him and, most compellingly, because he looks as hot as hell in that shirt.

'Then we'd be back to where we started. And I can't ... I don't want to ... *you know.*'

He stares at me with hard eyes and the spell is broken. 'Yep, I did something really awful when I asked you to marry me, didn't I?' He doesn't say it bitterly, not really. He's trying to hide how upset he is.

'I'm sorry, Rob.'

'Me too,' he replies, swallowing a large mouthful of his drink.

I become aware of someone standing over us and look up to see Asha. She has a strange expression on her face.

'What's up?' I ask, but she suddenly looks so distressed I don't wait for her to answer before apologising to Rob and taking her into the loo.

She leans on the sink and crosses her arms. 'He's changed his mind.'

'What? He didn't do it?'

She struggles to find her voice. 'He didn't do it.'

'But . . . did he say why?'

'He didn't get a chance. I didn't want to speak to him.'

I lean in to hug her. 'Oh, Asha . . . I'm sorry you have to go through all this. You don't deserve it.'

'Maybe I do,' she sniffs, as tears flood down her cheeks. 'I mean, I'm the mistress, aren't I? I'm the bad guy. I deserve all the punishment I get.'

It suddenly seems like a good time to go home. So, after we've touched up Asha's make-up – enough to hide her tears – we head out.

'Where's Rob?' Asha asks, scanning the bar.

And it seems she's not the only one going home alone tonight.

Chapter 31

What exactly does one wear to a house-warming barbecue? Or rather, to Matt Taylor's house-warming barbecue? There is a difference. Cally had a house-warming barbecue and that was easy – I wore jeans and a vest top because I knew I'd end up playing Twister, downing dubious vodka-based cocktails and reeking of the smoke from cremated sausages.

Matt Taylor's house-warming barbecue will be a more sophisticated affair, I'm certain of it. It's not just the fact that Matt's what Cally would term 'a classy kind of guy'. I've also seen a catering company van outside the house this morning – *and* there's going to be champagne! You don't sip champagne in the same outfit you'd wear to clean your step. Not that I have a step. I can only aspire to accommodation sizable enough for a luxury like that.

Every item in my wardrobe is catapulted to the floor as I become increasingly worked up about the dearth of suitable items. My wardrobe is suddenly – officially – a fashion desert.

'If you could go to the shops now and get your dream outfit, what would it be?' Cally asks when I phone her in desperation.

I consider ball gowns, combat pants, jodhpurs, a tutu. 'I have absolutely *no idea*! I can't go splurging on new clothes anyway – I'm economising. What are you wearing?'

'I hadn't really thought about it.'

'Cally, it starts in three hours,' I point out, hiding my exasperation.

'Jeans and flip-flops, then, I guess. Or maybe shorts – it's going to be roasting later.' I sit down to stop blood rushing to my head.

After convincing my best friend that this'll be more than a shorts and flip-flops affair, I try on about sixteen outfits – but find everything too low-key, too high-key or just plain wrong. I end up in the silk dress I wore to Rob's cousin's wedding, despite it prompting an explosion of memories, including one of Rob dedicating 'Always On My Mind' by Elvis to me, before he swept me up to dance and whispered, for the first time, that he loved me.

The dress is a floaty, raspberry-coloured number, and I decide that, as long as I don't embellish it with too many accessories, it'll be perfect.

Only, when I slip on my ballet pumps, it's not just the shoes that are flat – the whole outfit is. Seven pairs of heels later I settle on the nude ones that *Grazia* promised would elongate my calves. This, I feel, would be a good thing for someone who has the sort of legs that could appear in panto alongside Snow White.

It still doesn't look right. So I add earrings. Then a bracelet.

Then a necklace. And a ring. I'm poised with the same fascinator that I wore when I last donned this outfit, when I restrain myself and take several deep breaths.

When Cally turns up later with Zachary, I am pleased to see that she's taken my advice on the dress code.

'Isn't that the outfit you wore for the races?' I ask.

'Yes,' she mutters, as Zachary dives into my flat. 'It fits me even less now than then.'

'You look lovely,' I say, as she clumps in. Cally has never felt comfortable in heels. Anything higher than two inches and she takes on that 'I wish I was in wellies' gait Camilla Parker Bowles boasts during royal visits.

'I hate these heels. I've never mastered walking in them.'

'You'll be fine,' I reassure her. 'They suit you.'

'You once told me I walked like Camilla Parker Bowles.'

I wince. 'I'm sure it was a compliment.'

Asha arrives five minutes later, looking stunning in one of those outfits that is understated but stylish enough to work anywhere. And I suspect – or at least hope – that it's only me who'll be able to tell she's been crying.

'Hi, honey,' says Cally, appearing from the kitchen and kissing her on the cheek.

'Hi. Where's my favourite boy?'

Zachary runs up to her and kisses her on the mouth, then gives her an enormous hug.

'I'm only coming for an hour or so – is that okay, Emma?'

'Of course.'

'Have you spoken to Toby?' Cally asks.

Asha shakes her head. 'I told him not to phone me. And he hasn't.'

Cally looks as surprised as I am. 'Really?'

'Not once.'

'Maybe something's ... going on at home,' I suggest tentatively.

She sighs. 'I must admit, I'd kill to know what's going through his mind.'

I look at my watch. 'We should probably head next door.'

Cally looks down at her outfit. 'Are you *sure* we're not going to be overdressed? I've never worn anything like this to a barbecue before.'

'It's not just a barbecue, not with those *caterers*. This is going to be like a wedding.'

'I hope not,' she replies. 'At the last wedding I took Zachary to, his nose bled on the bride's dress, his remote-control plane crash-landed in the cake and he kept referring to the groom's mother as "that man". It was almost a perfect day.'

Chapter 32

It becomes apparent within a millisecond of setting foot in Matt's garden that my interpretation of the dress code is catastrophically at odds with everyone else's.

I know this before I've focused on the casual attire of scores of couples and their kids – hipster jeans, Converse pumps and checked shirts. And before I've tortured myself over the absence of heels, clutch bags or blingy hair pins.

I know this because Cally grips my arm with the force of a gorilla who's ten centimetres dilated and in the late stages of labour. '*What* is everyone wearing?'

'Er . . .'

We are poised to turn on our heels when Matt waves from the other side of the sun-drenched garden, then heads towards us.

'Lovely to see you,' he smiles, giving me an unexpected hug, one that brings my neck out in blotches.

'Thanks for the invitation. This is Cally and Asha, my two best friends.'

Cally tugs at her dress and they shake hands. 'You've got a lovely place.'

'Yeah, I like it,' says Matt. 'There's a lot of work still to do inside, but I always wanted a project.'

'You haven't got rid of the tiles in the living room, have you?' I blurt out.

'No, they're staying. I'll show you round later, if you like.' He spots Zachary and bends down. 'And what's your name?'

Zachary glares back, saying nothing. 'He's called Zachary,' Cally says with a smile, helping him out.

'Cool name. And how old are you, Zachary? Let me guess. Are you . . . eight?'

Zachary splutters with laughter. 'No!'

'Hmm . . . twenty-three?'

'I'm *two*!'

Matt has an unmistakable natural chemistry with children – one that's always eluded me. 'Well, then,' he continues, 'I know some boys you might like to play with. Would you like me to go and get them?'

Zachary shakes his head and grips Cally's leg.

'Maybe later, then,' Matt shrugs. 'They *have* got pick 'n' mix, though.'

Zachary releases Cally's leg, clearly not having anticipated sweets in the equation.

'I'll go and find them,' Matt grins. 'Ladies, can I get you some champagne?'

We spend the next half-hour stopping Zachary from ripping

sugar teeth from the hands of other children, listening to Stacey regale us with how *frantic* life is now she does Zumba on a Thursday, and pondering how we can duck out to get changed.

The dress issue really *is* an issue – one that becomes no less intensely embarrassing post-champagne. Nobody says anything, but only because they're too polite to ask why two women look like they're waiting to put a bet on the third race at Ascot.

The other guests are a nice bunch. Most have travelled from Manchester or Cheshire, where, it turns out, Matt is from, and are work contacts, old friends or family. His mum in particular seems to be having a whale of a time with the children. She's attractive and energetic, the sort of woman you'd see modelling Fendi tops in the *Guardian*.

Matt is a cool host, flitting between the drinks tent and the barbecue, the chefs in charge of which are from his cousin's catering company. He taps me on the shoulder a short while after we arrived, as Asha and I are talking to his friend Richard, a property surveyor from Didsbury.

'Do you fancy that tour? It's an improvement on the last place of mine you saw.' My face reddens as a question that has persistently vexed me re-emerges: what the hell *did* we get up to that night?

If I had sex with him, I want to have been good at it. Not necessarily ten A stars, but certainly passable. Given that I could barely remember my own name by the time I awoke the next morning, I'm gravely concerned that my performance wouldn't scrape me a Brownie badge.

I leave Asha talking to Richard and follow Matt.

'So why *were* you staying in that grotty flat in Crosby?' I ask.

'A friend of mine is a landlord – he buys places like that, does them up, then lets them. I needed somewhere to stay until I got the keys to this place, so he offered. *Different*, wasn't it?'

As he pushes open the kitchen door, I have mixed feelings about seeing Rita's old flat in the process of reinvention. Part of me wants to remember the living room as her haven of demented decadence: the velvets, the animal prints, the crusty books. But, obviously, I can't resist a look at its new incarnation.

'The kitchen and living room are the only rooms finished so far,' he tells me.

The kitchen is now completely different. He's painted the walls pale green, adding light into what was previously a dark room. The style is quirky-traditional, with wood surfaces, slate tiles and dozens of cool finishing touches like a giant blackboard and a birdcage filled with plants.

'You've done so much already! It's gorgeous. I'm stupidly jealous.'

He laughs. 'I'm glad you approve.'

The living room is equally stunning – and I love it all, from the floor-to-ceiling bookshelves to the tree-stump side table.

'The rest you've seen. It's my predecessor's decor. Like I said, this is a project.'

'She'd have liked this.'

'I'm glad. So when do I get a tour of your place?'

'It'll take about four seconds. It's not as big as this.'

'Ah well, size isn't everything – is it, Josh?' he says, as his little boy scurries in carrying a ball.

'Grandma says, when is it time to play rounders?'

Matt turns to me. 'Don't suppose you were on the school team?'

'For rounders? I was, actually. Although I'm not dressed for it,' I point out, holding out my skirt.

'Emma – have you got a minute?'

I spin round and see Asha, with an urgent look on her face.

I make my excuses to Matt and we step outside to speak privately.

'I need to go,' she says.

'What's happened?'

She takes a deep breath. 'I've spoken to Toby.'

'Has he ... done it?' I ask anxiously.

She shakes her head. 'No. But there's a reason.'

'Go on.'

'Christina's father had a massive heart attack yesterday. Toby was on his way home to tell her ... then events overtook themselves.'

'So ... is her dad okay?'

She looks at me, distraught. 'He died.'

I hold up my hand to my mouth. 'Asha, I don't know what to say.'

Asha throws her eyes to heaven. 'No, Em. Neither do I.'

Chapter 33

'You're in demand,' Cally grins, thrusting a rounders bat in my hand.

'How did you get changed, you traitor?' I gasp, looking her up and down.

'We slipped home. I felt like I was in fancy dress.'

I glance at the bat. 'Why have you given me this, as if I'm first up?'

'Cally assures me you were *brilliant* at rounders when you were thirteen,' Matt says, appearing from nowhere.

'I was brilliant at squeezing spots then too – it doesn't mean I want to do it now.'

'No excuses!' Cally drags me by the arm towards the centre of the garden. 'Em – you're on my team.'

'I haven't played it for fifteen years,' I protest, ripping up half the lawn with my heels as I stumble across the grass.

'Zachary'll be disappointed if you don't do this. I've told him you're a champion.'

Logic tells me that Zachary's about as likely to have a view on this as he is on the Greek debt crisis. Nevertheless, part of me thinks that it'd be nice to win some credibility, from him and everyone else.

'Let me go to the loo first.'

'Be quick!' she urges.

The toilet is as it was in the days when I'd pop over for a cup of herbal tea – and end up being plied with pastis that, even when diluted, was potent enough to remove nail varnish. The only difference now is that there are plush Egyptian cotton towels, two framed, retro comic book covers and a beautiful hand-wash and cream set. I rinse my hands, give them a cursory dry, and, never capable of leaving an upmarket moisturiser alone, apply it liberally, before heading outside.

My eyes haven't even adjusted to the sunlight before I'm flung into the batting area, barely having time to slip off my heels. 'We're relying on you,' Cally grins as I take the bat.

Matt is bowling. His mum is on first base. A teenage girl in vintage cut-offs is in second. And Matt's friend Richard is on third, putting on the worst display of nonchalance I've ever seen. Kids of all ages are dotted around the garden, their mildly tanked-up parents eager to join in.

Suddenly, I'm determined to show everyone what I've got.

I'm transported back to 1995 and I'm facing St Hardknocks School (or something) in the rounders finals – the day I smacked the ball so far across the field I almost tripped over my Green Flash trainers in shock.

My eyes focus and Matt grins as he steps back, swings his arm and releases the ball.

It's as it is hurtling towards me that a piercing alarm registers in my brain, alerting me to an issue with my grip. Or lack of it.

My still-damp hands might now be delightfully scented with Lime Basil and Mandarin, but the hand cream with which they're smothered has the lubricating qualities of WD40.

The implications of this become apparent when the ball is a metre away, and, by then, instinct has taken over. The only option is to go for it. With legs astride, I swing hard and fast, the thrill of potential victory running up and down my spine.

I'm convinced this will be a four baser. My aim is impeccable ... my stance is faultless ... and as the ball makes contact with the end of my bat, everything is perfect.

Except for one thing.

I can *see* the bat slip from my fingers before I feel it, then I watch it hurtling out of my hand and spinning erratically through the air like a shot-down helicopter.

The normally innocuous two-foot piece of solid wood becomes a lethal weapon, soaring towards the horizon as small children wail, elderly ladies hobble for cover and the barbecue chefs dive away from their sausages.

The fact that it clouts nobody on the head is a miracle for which I will remain grateful for all eternity.

But I get off far from scot-free, as is clear from the devastating smash of the kitchen window, its thunderous reverberation across the garden and, judging by the shock on everyone's faces, the near-cardiac arrest of all those over the age of thirty-five.

The glass shatters like we're in a scene from *Die Hard*, each tiny piece raining down onto the patio. It never seems to stop. It simply continues falling like coins in a Las Vegas slot machine until, finally, eventually, there's nothing left of the window except one or two jagged edges that hang precariously over the potted gerberas.

The silence that follows is so deafening I think my ears are bleeding. Slowly, incredulously, each guest turns to me, open-jawed.

Cally raises her eyebrows. 'Maybe someone else should go next.'

Chapter 34

'Emma, please.' Matt looks at me sternly as I throw an empty Fruit Shoot bottle in the recycling bin. 'You know what I'm going to say, don't you?'

I wipe my hands on my jeans. Ah, yes, my jeans. I have never felt so glad to be in them. 'I know, but I really am so—'

'Don't!'

'But I'm—' He throws me a warning look and I back down until the pressure becomes too much. '*I'm sorry!*'

He shakes his head. 'It is *not* an issue. It was an accident. I'd intended to replace the window anyway.'

'Why do I not believe you?'

'You must be a cynic.'

It is nearly midnight, the final guests left half an hour ago, and if you didn't know any better, you'd never believe there'd been a huge party here today, particularly one involving the damage I generated.

Six hours ago this was a scene of chaos, especially with adults trying to keep small children away while the same-day glazier (whose bill I've insisted comes to me) got to work.

'You don't have to do this,' Matt tells me. 'I'm fine clearing up by myself.'

Paranoia prickles through me. 'Would you rather I left?'

He prises the recycling bin from me. 'I'd rather you sat down and had a beer. Or at least a cup of tea.'

Matt returns five minutes later with two steaming mugs and, after placing them on the cast-iron table, he brings over five tea lights. My shoulders are warm with sunburn, although when darkness fell the temperature dropped. I take a sip of tea and a welcome flood of heat sweeps through me.

'So which exotic location will you be flying to next?' I ask.

'My favourite – the Greek Islands. I go tomorrow night. It's only for four days.'

'And this is work?'

As he laughs, my eyes are momentarily drawn to his Adam's apple. 'There are some people who'd like the idea of making up children's stories all day, you know.'

'Oh, I've never claimed mine was real work,' I say dismissively. 'Although – and you'll think I'm a diva for saying this – it *can* be harder than it looks.'

'I don't doubt it. I've got a friend who tried to write children's books and got nowhere. Turns out that getting into the mind of a three-year-old can be tricky. You must have a gift.'

'I don't know about that. I don't entirely understand it myself. It was never my dream job, put it that way.'

He looks surprised. 'What's your dream job?'

'I wanted to be an interior designer when I was younger. I've always loved beautiful homes, *unusual* ones, something with character and personality. I approve of yours.'

'Glad to hear it.' He's pretending to be flippant but it's obvious he's pleased. 'So what stopped you?'

I shrug. 'I stumbled into kids' TV. Which *nobody* does, by the way – jobs like mine are stupidly competitive. While I was at university doing my history degree, I had arranged to do my work placement at an interior-design agency in Manchester, but it fell through at the last minute. My dad's neighbour was the brother of someone who worked at Little Blue Bus Productions, and he got me in to spend two weeks with the scriptwriters. To my surprise, I loved it. And, not to sound immodest, I turned out to be good at it. So I never left. It's easy to stay in a job when that happens, isn't it?'

'You could leave if you wanted to.'

'I have no experience in interior design and couldn't get a job unless I started at the bottom.'

'That doesn't sound like it would pay well.'

'Quite. Only, I'm thirty soon and part of me thinks it's now or never.'

'A watershed year.'

I nod. 'It's made me think hard about my life, my achievements and, well, what I want to have done by thirty.'

'When's your birthday?'

'Twenty-second of December.'

'Plenty of time,' he grins.

'You haven't seen my list.'

'What list's that?'

I look at my mug and wonder why I blurted that out. I think about offering to go and make more tea as a diversion, but something stops me.

'It all started fifteen years ago ...'

I spill the beans about the list, my ambitions, and why – fifteen years later – I felt compelled to take notice of it. Part of me is embarrassed. Except, the way he's listening ... well, it makes me want to tell all. *Almost* all.

'I think it's a great idea,' he says when I conclude. 'Honestly, I do. Everyone feels the same when they turn thirty, though. I don't think you should worry about that.'

'How old are you?'

'Thirty-two.'

'Ah, well, do me a favour and tell me your thirties are *so* much better than your twenties and that I'll love it. That'd be some consolation for getting older.' I grin.

He looks at his empty mug. 'Actually, my thirties haven't been great. But I'm not holding it against the decade. It was ... circumstances, that's all.' He shifts in his seat, keen to change the subject. 'Hang on a minute, what's on your list again?'

I reel them off.

'You said there were twelve.'

'Oh ... did I?'

'You listed only eleven.'

'Who are you – Poirot?'

He grins. 'Come on, what's number twelve?'

'It's one I ... it wasn't a good idea,' I bluster. 'No offence, but ... it's not really me, that kind of thing. I'm not that sort of girl and—'

'You've already done it?'

'Hmm ... yes.' I'm trying to think of a plausible non-X-rated alternative, but my mind is blank.

'Let me guess,' he says, amused. 'It's obviously something racy if you say you're not that sort of girl. I've got it! You streaked at a sporting event?'

'God, no! With my cellulite?'

'You had webcam sex?'

'*No!*' I shriek.

'You did burlesque?'

I tut and shake my head.

'You posed topless in a lads' mag?'

I roll my eyes. 'As if they'd have me.'

'I'm sure they'd be delighted. Come on, don't be shy. I'm very non-judgemental.'

'Clearly,' I say, my mouth engaging before my brain again.

He frowns.

I decide there's only one way to deal with this, painful as it is. 'It was ... the one-night stand.'

He says nothing.

'I'm partly telling you this because I want you to know that

167

I've honestly never done that before. When I said I'm not that sort of girl, I meant it. And, whatever it was like – and I genuinely have no idea – I regretted it instantly. Not because I'm sure you weren't very competent,' I add reassuringly. He doesn't seem that reassured. 'It's just ... all these "achievements" were meant to make me feel good about myself. They were meant to make me *braver*. Which is a noble cause, isn't it, only—'

'Emma,' he interrupts.

I sigh, having run out of things to say. 'Yes?'

'Do you think you and I had a one-night stand?'

I swallow. 'Didn't we?'

'I don't know the dictionary definition, but I'm sure you have to have sex for it to constitute that.'

'You mean ... we never ...'

'No.'

I look away, my mind whirring with relief, gratitude, and a dozen questions followed by the sudden realisation that I said something in our Facebook exchange that I need to clear up immediately.

'I haven't got an STD!' I blurt out. 'And I've never had one!'

He looks taken aback. 'Okay.'

'I know it might have sounded like I had one, but I didn't. I have firm medical proof that I didn't.'

'You really don't have to explain. These things happen.'

'But not to me! Honestly, Matt, I'm one hundred per cent ... healthy. In that department.'

'Good for you.'

I sigh. 'Are you finding this funny?'

'Not at all,' he claims, failing to suppress a smile.

'Now you mention it, I didn't *feel* like we'd done anything,' I continue. 'Problem was, there was physical evidence to the contrary.'

'I see.'

'My knickers weren't where they were supposed to be.'

'I know.'

My mouth drops. 'So how . . .'

'Emma,' he begins coolly, 'you put on a bit of a . . . performance when you got to my flat. I tried to stop you, but you were determined and—'

'What sort of performance?' I croak.

'It began with the in-flight demonstration. Then it progressed to . . .'

'What?' I ask grimly.

He suppresses another smile. 'It's a shame burlesque *wasn't* on your list. You could've ticked off another one.'

Chapter 35

I see Matt the following afternoon while I'm washing dishes in the kitchen. Only, it's not just him I see.

A huge white Audi pulls up in front of the flat and the driver – an exceptionally good-looking man with a slender build and dark hair, leans over to kiss the female passenger. And I mean kiss. He can hardly bear to let her go, doing so eventually when she steps out, the engine still running.

I recognise her from Facebook, but in the flesh – even from a distance – Matt's wife is more attractive: a goddess in skinny jeans and cowboy boots, with glossy auburn hair in a high ponytail.

She waits uncomfortably by the door after ringing the bell, her demeanour changing only when it opens and her three children rush out. Matt follows, kissing each goodbye, before they leap into the car and drive away. He stands for a second, gazing after them with hard eyes, before returning to the house and slamming the door.

Part of me is glad he won't be around for a few days.

He found the whole burlesque thing hilarious, but I'm afraid I'm struggling to do so. I laughed, of course, in the absence of a convenient spaceship to beam me to an adjacent galaxy.

I thought I'd hidden my mortification well, until he paused and said, suddenly serious: 'Emma, it's *fine*. We all do daft things every so often. And I got you into bed before I saw anything. Honestly, I didn't even peek.'

At that point, I suppressed the urge to wail as if alerting the neighbourhood to an air raid – and simply made my excuses and left.

For four days afterwards I feel, for the first time since he moved in, that I can relax in my own home – an issue I'm pondering on Wednesday, the day before he's due back, as I'm driving home from work.

The beep of my phone alerts me to an email and I pull in and check it, my heart fluttering with hope that it's from Rob.

We've exchanged a few texts this week. Polite ones, sweet – but noticeably unflirtatious and largely dominated by guitar prac-tice updates. I'm still struggling to gauge what's going through his mind – or indeed my own mind.

The email is from mattdwtaylor@hotmail.co.uk and is sent from his phone.

Given that my revelations meant you had to strike the one-night stand off your list, could I help with another? My friend Anna – whom you met at the barbecue – owns

a restaurant in Cheshire. It has a Michelin star. They have
a three-month waiting list but she's invited me over at the
weekend to sample the new menu. Would you like to
come?

I gasp audibly. Is he inviting me on a date? Because I don't
want to go on a date with Matt, for a multitude of reasons. He's
attractive, I can't deny it, but there's no way I'm leaping into
something with my feelings about Rob still far from clear – and
especially not with my neighbour.

I decide to play it cool, essential in the light of the revelations
about my burlesque performance – even if I am sure I looked
more like John Cleese than Dita Von Teese.

I set about composing a response that sounds casual – something that looks like I've hit the Reply button without giving
it a second thought. I complete nine drafts before it's right.

Sure, that'd be great – where and when?

Okay, it's not Tolstoy, but it's important to get these things
right. I tell myself that if he's talking about Saturday night then
that has serious implications. Saturday night means a date. I
couldn't even consider that. His response doesn't arrive until the
following morning.

Saturday lunchtime okay? About 12.30?

A flicker of disappointment runs through me and I tell myself not to be ridiculous. I grab my work jacket and briefly scan my wardrobe for an outfit suitable for my non-date. One thing I am sure of is that it isn't going to involve floaty dresses.

Chapter 36

Despite this being a non-date, despite the fact that my brain is still tangled with thoughts of Rob, despite the fact that I've spent a week *partly* dreading seeing my neighbour, I feel odd on Saturday morning.

I can't eat – and that *never* happens.

Even when I had severe gastroenteritis after eating dodgy chicken liver pâté at my cousin Tara's wedding, I soldiered on heroically and managed a banana muffin and latte from Starbucks the next day.

I potter round the flat doing my usual Saturday morning chores – hoovering the lounge and waxing my bikini line (not simultaneously). In the meantime, I am trying to work out whether the loss of appetite is because I read *Heat* last night and noted that my thighs are at least two and a half times the size of Paris Hilton's.

Then I realise they always have been – and am forced to ask: am I *nervous?*

I push the thought out of my mind as a text arrives from Rob.

> No problem about moving your guitar lesson to tomorrow.
> I'm free all day, so whenever you like. Have you been
> practising 'Mary had a Little Lamb'? xxxxxxxx

> Of course! xx

It's a lie.

Matt knocks on my door at twelve thirty and my heart is racing as I open it. The phenomenon is instantly exacerbated when I see what he's wearing: a black shirt. I should stress that this does not beat the Sexiest Shirt Known To Man. Nothing beats that. But it's rolled up his arms to display the outline of toned biceps and undone at the top to reveal a tanned, muscular chest, and a terrible thought hits me: Emma Reiss, do you *want* this to be a date?

I dig my nails into my hands. Of course I don't.

'It obviously didn't rain in the Greek Islands.'

He grins and moves aside as I step out. 'Not much.'

Whenever a man challenges my love of shoes, I throw one word right back at them. Cars. I don't *get* men and their attitude to cars. I don't get it at all.

As anyone with half a brain knows, a car is a large metal object that gets you from A to B. It is not a piece of art, or a fine wine and, patently, it is not a beautifully crafted Louboutin (which, for the record, costs approximately one per cent of a Skoda).

I would rather watch facial hair grow than *Top Gear*.

Consequently, most of the cars I've owned have been little flashier than a large baked bean can on wheels. The two-door Fiat I drive now is as extravagant as it gets. And I'd be the first to admit I don't treat it with the respect it deserves: something has to physically drop off for me to even consider acting on a light on the dashboard.

Still, I can't deny that there's something special about whirling through the Cheshire countryside in Matt's BMW; about the blur of hedgerows, the scent of lavender and the bluest of skies above. Even with the baby seats in the back, it reeks of luxury – although possibly that could be the Magic Tree.

The restaurant is smaller than I'd imagined of somewhere with a Michelin star. It's a converted white-stone cottage, and decorated inside with coir carpets, striking wallpaper and plush furniture.

'Matt! Thank you so much for coming!'

I remember Anna from the barbecue. It's not that I spoke to her directly, but she performed one of the more spectacular moves to escape my rounders bat – a forward-roll-type affair that, had the circumstances been different, I'd have congratulated her on wholeheartedly.

She kisses Matt on the cheek, pushing her dark wavy hair back from an elfin face. 'It's Emma, isn't it? I couldn't forget you after last week, could I?' she giggles.

I'm immediately hit by a severe bout of motion sickness, despite standing totally still.

'She's just kidding,' Matt murmurs as we're shown to the table. 'Honestly, Anna's great.'

'How do you know her?' I ask.

'She's my wife's second cousin.'

I try to think of a response to this. 'Oh,' I manage, failing miserably, and scan the menu instead.

He gauges my unease. 'Don't worry – Anna's in touch with me more than Allison these days. Plus, she knows you and I are just friends. And even if we weren't ... I mean, Allison and I aren't together any more so ...' For the first time, Matt looks uncomfortable.

I suddenly feel an urgent need to know more about him and his ex-wife, but say nothing.

At least, I say nothing *about that*. Throughout lunch, Matt and I generally talk and talk and don't stop, covering everything from his children to my mum – and whether I should've included 'Learn to bobsleigh' on my list. Which was his idea, incidentally.

The flowing conversation *may* have something to do with the flowing Sancerre, of course, although I register that only well after the damage has been done.

The problem is this: the staff here are so attentive to a diner's every need that you never have anything approaching an empty glass. You take a sip of wine, and before you've noticed, it's full again. You do it again, and the same thing happens.

It's like playing What's the Time, Mr Wolf? – you never catch anyone moving, but there's no doubt it's happening, a fact confirmed when, for the first time since we got here, I spot the waiter filling up my glass – and nearly rugby tackle him.

'No more, thanks!' I blurt out, aware that I'm precariously close to my four-glass limit – something I can't remember happening on a Saturday afternoon before.

Then I lean in and peer at Matt's glass. 'Please tell me you've drunk more than one glass.'

'I've drunk more than one glass,' he replies firmly.

'Oh, thank God.' I narrow my eyes. 'Are you sure?'

'Well, no.' He suppresses a smile. 'I just wanted to make you feel better.'

I take a sip of water in an attempt to dilute the liquid currently going through my renal system. 'Well, now I'm tipsy I might as well ask you what I wasn't going to ask you.'

'Which is?'

I look into his eyes, suddenly serious. 'What happened with your wife?'

He looks shocked, more than I'd expected. I instantly regret my insensitivity.

'Sorry – I didn't mean to—'

'It's fine.'

'Matt, that was a stupid thing to—'

'Emma. *It's fine.*'

I swallow as he pauses to gather his thoughts.

'She left me. She left me for another man.'

178

'I'm sorry,' I whisper.

He looks up. 'Me too.' He presses his lips together, clearly not used to opening up about this. 'She was the love of my life.' He says this without any sense of drama; it's simply a statement of fact. And I don't know what to say in reply.

'I'm trying to get over things ... to get over *her*. But it's difficult to imagine ever feeling the same way about someone.'

I note the present tense.

'When did you split up?'

'Six months ago, back in February. I'd suspected the affair for a while before she confessed to it. We separated almost immediately afterwards – or rather, she left. With the kids. The hardest part is that ... she isn't a bad person, my wife. Not at all. She just fell out of love with me.'

'That must have been so hard. Especially with the children.'

'I don't think any of us imagine the fairy tale will end that way, do we? Not when we fall in love.'

I sigh. 'I'm not sure I've ever been in love,' I confess.

'Really?'

'Maybe I'm doing Darren Jones a disservice.'

'Who was he?'

'We went out together in sixth form for a month. He was a teenage animal-rights enthusiast. I was besotted, for a couple of days at least.'

'What happened?'

'I dumped him.'

He shakes his head and suppresses a smile. 'Callous.'

179

'He never, ever removed his Parka. Never. I went round one lunchtime and caught him asleep in bed with it on.'

He laughs. 'So nobody else has come close?'

I hesitate. 'Somebody *did* come close.'

'Recently?'

I nod. 'He asked me to marry him.'

'What did you say?'

I squirm. 'I dumped him too.'

'Oh God!' he laughs again and, despite the fact that I generally find *nothing* funny about that particular situation, the sound is infectious.

I put my hands over my face. 'I'm not a man-eater, I promise,' I plead, shaking my head.

'I'll take your word for it,' he grins.

For some reason, I feel the need to drag the conversation back to the question I started with.

'So, your wife ... or is it ex-wife?'

'Technically, she's still my wife. We're not divorced yet – although proceedings have begun.'

'Did you have a happy marriage before this other guy came along?'

He takes a sip of coffee and thinks. 'I'd say so, overall. I can't pretend it was perfect, obviously.'

'Hmm.'

'The worst thing about modern relationships is our expectations,' he continues. 'We *expect* way too much. It's easy to have fireworks at the beginning. It's easy to *fall* in love. But we have

180

this unrealistic notion that it'll always be like that, without hiccups or hard work.'

'You don't think fireworks are necessary?'

'I don't think love needs to race at a hundred miles an hour all the time,' he insists. 'I don't think there's anything wrong with it being quieter and low-key. That's what I thought I had with Allison.' He narrows his eyes. 'Why do you ask?'

I shrug. 'I suppose I'm thinking about my ex-boyfriend. There weren't fireworks every minute of the day. My heart didn't race every time I saw him. And yet, I can't deny I find him *very* attractive. I'm punching above my weight with him.'

Matt raises his eyebrows and smiles. 'He's a looker, then?'

'Hell, yes!' I admit. 'It's not just that, though. I *love* being with him. If I stand back and look at the situation, he's everything I could want and he'd do anything for me. I miss him and spend an unnatural amount of time thinking I should get back with him.'

Matt sits back in his chair. 'You know what I think? I think that sometimes the answer is so obvious it's staring you in the face.'

'What do you mean?'

'People like that don't come along every day, Emma. You should make the most of it when they do.'

Chapter 37

Monday is frazzling. I'm not sure if that's even a word, but nobody could witness the day I'm enduring and challenge me on it.

The latest series is in the can, and in my humble opinion it's some of the best work we've produced. Even Giles is excited – at least he was last week – and that never happens unless I bring in Hobnobs *chocolate* (the culinary equivalent of gold plating).

All that remains is for Perry to give it the nod and for us to deliver it to Channel 6. Which is fine, except for one thing.

He isn't here.

Our esteemed leader announced on Friday that he was considering taking a 'holistic sabbatical' for four weeks in Austria, where he hopes to not only discover himself, but also find the next big thing in children's programming.

He promised to return *brimming* with ideas – a word he virtually shrieked, as if hearing it didn't hurt enough. I walked away from his desk wondering what I'd have to eat to induce a violent bout of food poisoning on the day he's due back, just so I can phone in sick.

What I failed to realise – at that point – was that the semi-spiritual experience he was embarking on was due to happen now. As in *right now. Tout de suite*. Without him having signed off *anything*.

The result is a series of irate phone calls from everyone from the animators to Channel 6 themselves, who quite reasonably would like to get their hands on the programme they've paid for.

The only option is for Giles and me to attempt to track him down, which isn't easy because he's apparently switched off his phone so as not to disturb any potential epiphany.

'This. Isn't. My. Sodding. Job.' Giles slams down the phone so hard it nearly cracks the handset. 'Exactly how can tracking down our bum-wipe of a boss when he's on holiday yodelling or praying, or whatever the hell he's doing, be considered *my* job?'

I open my mouth to answer, but he beats me to it.

'I make up stories for a living. If I'd wanted a job dealing with *people* I'd have become a sodding salesman.' The word 'people' is pronounced as if directly interchangeable with the term 'kitten torturers'.

'Giles,' I sigh, 'I know all this. I know all this *and it's not my job either*. But we have no choice. What did that woman in the spa say when you phoned her last?'

'That he was busy having a hot-stone massage. I hope they singe his nuts.'

We finally receive a call from Perry – in response to my thirty or so messages – at ten past five. His massage has clearly had an effect similar to that of inhaling a potent strain of marijuana all day.

'What's all the fuss?' Perry chortles as I grit my teeth and thank the Lord that he got through to me instead of Giles. 'I sent you an email on Friday saying yes – to everything!'

'It never arrived, Perry. Did you remember to press Send?'

There's a short silence. 'Shoot. I'm always forgetting that bit. Never mind, consider it signed off. Great work, team! Right, I'm off to Reiki. I've already come up with an idea you'll adore and—'

'Ooh, Perry – the line's going. Bye!' I slam down the phone.

When I leave work two hours later, I'm convinced there's a volcanic outbreak between Giles's ears – there's so much steam coming out of them.

'Giles,' I hear myself saying, 'I don't mean to sound flippant or play down what a nightmare Perry can be . . . but I'm worried that you're letting this get to you too much.'

He grunts.

'It gets to me too but . . .' I pause, thinking about how to handle this diplomatically. He gets there first.

'Well, I'm afraid Perry is winding me up way too much these days.'

'Can't you switch off at home?'

'No.'

'Maybe you need a hobby.'

He flashes me a look. 'Do I look like a knitter?'

'I suppose not.' I turn to go to the door. 'Bye, then.'

'Bye,' he says. Then, after a moment, he calls after me. 'Emma?'

I turn back and look at him. He shrugs. 'You know.'

I frown.

'Thanks,' he mumbles. 'For giving a shit.'

Giles and I are not the only ones to have had a bad day. I phone Dad as I'm walking to my car because I know he had a date today – at the Cathedral. I was sceptical the second I heard that that was the venue. They might have a perfectly nice refectory, but can you really concentrate on whether you've got the hots for someone in the presence of the Lord Almighty?

'It wasn't a *dream* first date,' he says reluctantly.

'What was the problem?'

'I'm going to sound uncharitable.'

'Dad, be brutal. You have to be.'

'She was very nice in lots of ways. Divorced. Two children. Nice. I think.'

'Come on, now. What was wrong with her?'

He hesitates. 'Her feet, mainly.'

'What?'

'We barely talked of anything else. She's got terrible bunions; she showed them to me. And verrucas. She caught those from her grandchildren – they'd been using her bath after swimming club. And apparently she's got awful dry skin that cracks and—'

'Oh stop!'

'I'd have liked just to get to know a bit more about *her* – from the ankle up. And I must admit all the talk about ingrowing toe-nails did put me off my cream tea.'

I get a text from Cally on the way home saying that Asha's coming over and I should pop in if I get the chance. When I arrive, Cally looks both hyperactive and dead-dog exhausted – a combination only the working mothers of small children seem to master.

'I can't even offer you a glass of wine,' she sighs, holding up one of the few things in her fridge. 'Strawberry Nesquik, anyone?'

'I'll pass.' I put an arm round her. 'Have you been put through your paces today?'

'I have had the day from hell. I forgot to process our managing director's expenses, which meant his company credit card got knocked back at Manchester Airport this morning. I was stalked by an irate client over a mix-up with payments – not my fault this time. I was dragged into plotting the restructure of the entire finance department. I spilled a skinny latte on my computer keyboard. And I was almost late to pick up Zachary from nursery. Not so late, unfortunately, to avoid signing an entry in the Accident Book detailing how he developed a humungous bruise on his forehead.'

'Aw, poor Zachary,' I say. 'How *did* he get it?'

'By head-butting another kid.'

'Ah.'

'At least he's asleep before eight thirty. Though, admittedly, that might be concussion.'

'I don't know how you do it sometimes, Cally,' Asha says, flicking on the kettle to make some tea.

'Well, he's worth it. And so is the job – most of the time. Besides, I can live vicariously,' she grins, holding up *Riders*. 'I'm loving it. Enough to make me wish I had someone to play naked tennis with.'

'Let me get this straight,' I say. 'Are you saying you're on the *lookout* for someone to play naked tennis with?'

'Oh God, no,' Cally says, then hesitates as Asha puts a cup of tea in front of her. 'Well . . .'

'You're ready to get back in the saddle!' Asha laughs.

'The theory and the practice are different,' Cally replies. 'I'm happy *reading* about men. How are things with you, more to the point?'

Asha looks down at her cup. 'I'm not entirely sure how things are with me, Cally, because I haven't seen Toby once – literally – in over two weeks.' Her expression softens. 'Oh, I'm being unreasonable, aren't I? Christina's dad's died. There's no way he could have left her in the light of that.'

Asha glances from one to the other of us. 'He will do it, you know. It's just a question of when.'

I stay at Cally's for another half-hour, before heading home. I'm almost back when I get a text from Marianne suggesting a Skype chat.

I log on just as Brian is leaving the flat.

'Give me a min,' she says, standing up to kiss him briefly.

When I hear the door shut, Marianne turns to me and grins.

'He's off to meet a friend. They're collaborating on a new screen-play. I've got a really good feeling about this one – from what I've read so far, it's just fantastic. So ... how's it going with you? Getting any better at the guitar?'

'My skills are a work in progress.'

She laughs. 'Isn't it weird seeing Rob all the time still?'

'A bit.'

'You're sure he's okay with it?' she asks, raising an eyebrow.

I frown. 'I don't know what to do about Rob, Marianne.'

'Why ... are you thinking about getting back with him?'

'I miss him more than I ever imagined. I think about him all the time.'

'Do you think you would've split up with him if he hadn't asked you to marry him?'

'No,' I say truthfully.

'So what made you anti-marriage?'

'I'm not anti-marriage! I'm just not ready to decide whether I want to marry someone after only a few months together.'

'That's not unreasonable.'

'The other day I was talking about this issue with ... a friend. Do you think relationships need to be passionate and all-consuming? For it to count as love, I mean?'

She thinks for a second. 'I think they should certainly be fairly passionate and all-consuming in the beginning.'

'Hmm. I always think about you and Johnny – the way you were in the beginning. How mad you were about each other. That's the benchmark, surely.'

Then I look up and take in her expression.

'Johnny and I aren't a good example, Emma,' she says stiffly. 'In the beginning, it was amazing, certainly. But that elation ... the buzz ... it was all just hedonism. It wasn't real. I don't think that could last for anyone.'

'But you adored each other.'

She looks irritated. 'Emma, Johnny and I weren't perfect.'

'You *seemed* to be. Look, I know how much you feel for Brian now, but ... well, it came out of the blue when you split up.'

'Not entirely – we'd had a three-month break a year and a half before we went our separate ways for good.'

'You said that was only because you'd been so young when you first got together. Look, I'm just using it as an example, that's all. If I get married to someone, I want to feel about them how you felt about Johnny. You'd walk into a room together and everyone could see it in your eyes. You can't deny it – no matter how much you feel about Brian these days.'

'I ... no, I can't,' she says. 'It was like that, once.'

I pause for a second. 'What happened between you two, Marianne?'

'I fell out of love with him, Emma.'

I bite my lip, realising I've gone too far. 'Sorry. I didn't mean to upset you.'

'You didn't. Listen, I need to go.' And after cursory goodbyes, she signs off, leaving me alone and contemplating another end to another less than perfect day.

Chapter 38

Isn't it weird how you can tootle through life wondering if anything is ever going to change then something amazing happens that blows everything out of the water?

Amazing something number one happens on a rainy Thursday afternoon, when Giles and I have spent much of the day debating the merits of dark chocolate versus milk chocolate. I firmly believe the former to be the spawn of the devil, whereas he will happily eat it for breakfast, in between his numerous fag breaks.

In some ways, it is a modern miracle, a fairy tale born out of the alchemy of technology and marketing. In other ways, it's just bloody good news.

I'm talking about a pop-up advert – something that's ordinarily about as welcome on my computer screen as the message 'This machine will self-destruct'. Usually, I despise them. You know how it is – you're working on a truly urgent document when you can't actually get to it because you're too busy chasing a Bingo scratch card ad round the screen, like Benny Hill pursuing a dolly bird.

But this time it's different; it's an advert for a jobs website I've never stumbled across before. Which is surprising, given that I've redoubled my job-hunting efforts after Perry's idea for a show based inside the human digestive system (main character: Percy the Prune, whose adventures in the lining of the duodenum are potentially limitless).

I idly click on the link and put in the details I've repeatedly typed over the last few weeks, expecting to be confronted with the same, familiar words: 0 results.

Only, something so unexpected happens that I launch into a coughing fit that prompts Giles – terrifyingly – to leap round the desk and start walloping me on the back as if trying to beat the dust out of an antique rug.

When I finally prise him off and he slopes back to his desk, I have a proper look.

Interior Designer – Apprenticeship

The advert is beautifully designed, a veritable work of art. I don't know why this impresses me so much; I've always been a sucker for a good font. And the job sounds amazing. The salary is less than I'm earning now, of course. But the position would involve working hand-in-hand with the managing director for six months, after which a promotion and a pay rise are virtually guaranteed.

My heart is throbbing as I flick through the company's website. Their client list is to die for, featuring upmarket boutique hotels

191

in Chester and luxury offices in Manchester. They specialise in a look that's both contemporary and classic – and their preference for the traditional is underlined by the fact that all correspondence with them is to be delivered the old-fashioned way, by letter. Candidates have to send off their CV and a covering note, as well as something else designed to test natural ability. A link on their website features a picture of a stylistically challenged room. I have to give it a makeover – theoretically transforming it within a specified budget, while demonstrating flair, taste and originality.

My mind starts whizzing with ideas of fabrics, textures, paints as I begin to compose my application. And for the first time since I found my fifteen-year-old list, I feel something approaching optimism.

The second amazing thing happens twenty-four hours later. And it takes my breath away.

I arrive at Rob's flat for my guitar lesson, have my coat off and am trying to remember the opening bars to 'Mary had a Little Lamb', when I realise he's looking strange. I don't mean he's wearing a false moustache and glasses or anything – more that he's on edge, as if he wants to tell me something.

'Everything okay?' I ask, taking a seat on his leather sofa as he paces in front of me. He nods and sits down. Then he stands up again.

He walks towards me slowly and gently takes the guitar from my hands, returning to the chair on the other side of the room.

He looks supremely handsome, in a plain grey T-shirt and those jeans that I've seen women actually dribble over when he walks past them in the street. He flicks back his hair and starts to strum.

'I want to play something for you.' His voice is husky and strangled at first. He looks self-conscious.

'Okay,' I say cautiously, somehow knowing this won't be a tune from my copy of *Very Easy Guitar Songs for Simpletons*.

'Ohhhh ... Emmahhh ...'

Ohhhh ... God.

Rob's smart enough to realise that this could go either way. On the one hand, writing and performing a song for me could be the most romantic gesture on the planet. On the other – more likely – hand, it could be cataclysmically naff.

At first, I'm not entirely sure into which camp it falls.

There are moments as he sings my name when his expression is torn between euphoria and torture and, perhaps because of this, it's far from a comfortable experience, at least at first.

The references to my *deep blue eyes*, and particularly to my *succulent thighs* (a description I last heard applied to a Bernard Matthews turkey), don't help.

But then he gets into it, really into it ... and, I've got to admit, so do I. The tune is genuinely beautiful, stunningly so. I knew Rob was good at *playing* the guitar, but I had no idea he could compose so well. And okay, the lyrics are never going to give Andrew Lloyd Webber a run for his money, but that's not the point.

The point is this: I am sitting in front of this amazing man and he is singing his heart out. To me. A song he has written. For me.

The room is suddenly silent and he can't look up.

So I ease myself off the sofa, and as I cross the room he meets my eyes. Then I kneel in front of him and I don't stop to think about whether what happens next is the right thing to do. I just know that I can do nothing else.

I take his face in my hands and draw him into me, until our lips touch. It's a soft kiss, brief. But loving enough to make it entirely clear that this is more than us making friends. This is something else altogether.

It's Rob who pulls back first.

'Emma,' he whispers. 'I'm sorry I asked you to marry me.'

The words feel like a rock thrown at my heart as I gaze into his eyes, which are now glistening with tears. 'Rob, don't apologise, that's ridiculous. You can't help how you feel and—'

'I feel differently now,' he interrupts.

'How?'

He takes a deep breath. 'I feel a lot for you, Emma. I can't pretend I don't. But what I can do – if you'll let me – is forget the idea of getting married or anything full-on like that. I can just be your boyfriend, exactly how it was.'

'Yes but—'

'Let me ask you a question, Emma. Have you missed me?'

I bite my lip. Then I nod.

'Well, I've missed you too. So it's this simple. I want you back in my life. If that means taking things slower, not thinking about the future and just enjoying what we have now, then . . . I've got my head around that.'

'Really?'

The question is a pointless one. Part of me suspects that once you have feelings for someone you can't just rein them in. Part of me knows that there's a real possibility that he still wants what he said – the M word – and is feigning this new easy-going Rob.

But another part of me thinks . . . so what? I'm here with a man with whom I love spending time, who I miss every day. And he wants to be with me.

'Really.' He squeezes my hands. 'Let's get back together.' It is neither a plea nor an instruction. It's four simple words. Let's get back together. It's how things should be.

I close my eyes and know that – right or wrong – there is only one thing to do. I put my arms round him and breathe in his familiar smell. 'Okay, Rob,' I whisper. 'I'm all yours.'

Chapter 39

I can't tell you how great it is having sex again. Even if I'm aware that, for Rob, it isn't quite the recreational experience it is for me.

Rob doesn't have sex, he *makes love*.

He hugs and caresses and holds, his eyes burning with passion and love. Which is so sweet – lovely, in fact – but does puts paid to any aspirations I might have to experiment with the techniques on Tracey Cox's website.

Not that I'm complaining – how could I? I have somehow managed to gain the adoration of a bloke with whom every woman he comes into contact with falls in love. God knows how. I am so aware of how undeserving I am that I tell him this every time I see him over the next two weeks.

'You know your problem, Emma? You feel uncomfortable with being happy.' He laughs.

I frown. He's got this from one of his self-help books. Rob reads them all the time and will psychoanalyse you into oblivion, given half the chance.

'I don't think it's that, Rob. That would make me certifiably nuts.'

'Come here, you beautiful woman,' he whispers, pulling me back to bed with a muscular arm. I fall into his embrace instantly, revelling in his sexiness, in how glad I am to be back with him.

I don't know why, but it's at that moment that I feel a swell of relief that, on the day we got back together, I remembered to remove the list from my fridge door and hide it in the kitchen drawer. It's not that I'm abandoning it – there's no way I'd do that at this stage – but explaining the *one-night stand* and *snog somebody famous* to Rob is something I'd really rather avoid.

'I've got to go, sweetheart,' I say, kissing him on the neck.

He nods and I wait for him to let go.

'I mean I've got to go *now*,' I clarify.

'Oh.' He releases his grip and I gather my belongings.

'You could stay tonight. You haven't stayed over for ages.'

'I need to get back to the flat to see if I've heard anything about my job application. Plus, I've got loads of washing.'

'I'll do your washing,' he offers.

I tut. 'Rob, I'm not having you washing my dirty socks.'

'I wouldn't mind,' he says. And the worrying thing is, I know he wouldn't.

It's gone nine when I arrive home and I am all of a quiver as I open my letter box. I flick through the post, which consists of two letters for my flat's previous occupant and a money-off coupon for the installation of a hot tub.

'*Emma!*'

I spin round to see Matt wearing the same blue T-shirt he wore for the barbecue, showing off his tanned arms and complementing his eyes. He looks delicious. To deny it would be like claiming tiramisu is no more pleasurable to the palate than a stale Ryvita. Yet the thought still sends a shot of guilt through me.

'I've been at my boyfriend's flat,' I feel compelled to announce.

He looks at me blankly, entirely unmoved. 'Um ... good. Ohhh ...' he says, with a flicker of recognition. 'This is the guy you were telling me about when we went to lunch?'

I nod. 'Rob.'

'Ah, that's great. I'm glad you gave him a second chance. He sounds like a lovely guy.'

'He is. He plays the guitar.'

He raises an eyebrow as if wondering why I'm imparting this information. As am I. 'He also has an amazing job as a wealth manager and can speak a bit of Cantonese and ... well, he's wonderful. You were right about me and him. Thank you.'

'I'm not sure what I did but ... well done. Oh, I've brought this over,' he adds, handing me an envelope. 'It was delivered to me by mistake.'

'Thanks.' I take it from him. 'Well. Goodnight, then.'

He holds up his hand and flashes me a smile. 'Have a good one.'

As he walks away, I push open my door, unfolding the letter

and barely thinking about its contents, which I half suspect will be an offer for a new conservatory. But it's something else entirely.

It's from the interior-design agency. I've got an interview.

Chapter 40

Matt makes amazing coffee. Which I know is a random fact, except this is so supremely delicious that I can't let it go without passing comment.

'The trick is using coffee that's really fresh – keep it in the fridge.' He pours Arabica grains into the espresso maker I bought a few years ago. It's one of those traditional Italian stove-top ones that are like mini versions of how 1950s comic-strip illustrators imagined spaceships would look.

I bought it for its chicness, although I'd heard that the coffee in Italy is universally glorious so was convinced I'd never set foot in Starbucks again. Unfortunately, the espresso I make manages to taste as if it's been brewed in pig swill.

'And it's got to be full-fat milk,' he continues.

'Full-fat milk is for babies and builders.'

He tuts. 'You don't know what you're missing.'

'Oh, I do. About an extra stone and a half.'

If you were to ask me why Matt is here I couldn't give you an answer, except that it feels like the same reason I see Cally or Asha. There's a difference in this friendship, of course – we haven't tried on each other's shoes, debated the merits of a hairy chest or agreed once and for all *how much* is *too much* when purchasing handbags.

But a friendship – albeit a fledgling one – it undoubtedly is.

He hands me a cup. 'How's that?'

I take a sip. '*How* do you do that?'

'What?'

'Use exactly the same ingredients as me but make it taste like *that*.'

He grins. 'Didn't I tell you I was a trained barista?'

I fling a tea towel at him. 'Very funny, Pinocchio. Are the boys with their mum today?'

'Yes, they've all gone to Splashy World.'

'That sounds . . . wet.'

He laughs. 'Wet it most definitely is. How are you feeling about your interview?'

I'm about to tell him I'm so wound up about it that I'm unreassurable, when the doorbell rings. I excuse myself to answer it and as I open the door I am surprised to see that it's Rob. Actually, surprised isn't the word. Flummoxed is.

'Hello! What are you doing here? I'm not due over for the lesson until two.'

'I couldn't wait,' he breathes, stepping over the threshold and pulling me into him, kissing me on the lips. It's a strong, passionate kiss, the type I've come to expect from him. Rob is one of nature's great kissers and always has been. Under normal circumstances, I'd get right into it.

Except, with his lips now on my neck, I'm suddenly very aware of the presence of another person in the flat. I wriggle away and take him by the hand. 'Listen, my neighbour's in the kitchen. Why don't you come and say hello?'

'Oh.' He fails to hide his disappointment. 'Okay.'

In the three seconds it takes for Rob and me to walk to the kitchen, I remember a fact that makes my spine prickle with discomfort.

I have never mentioned Matt to Rob before. Not once. He has never seen him, nor heard of him, nor indeed – until now – been made aware of his very existence.

There is every possibility that when he walks into my kitchen he is expecting to see a sixty-five-year-old woman, like Rita.

I turn to look at Rob and he smiles as we enter the kitchen, where Matt is sipping his coffee and flicking through my *Marie Claire*.

'Matt, I'd like you to meet someone,' I say breezily.

Only, when I turn to Rob this time, his expression is different from three seconds ago.

'Um ... this is Rob!'

I don't know what it is about the situation that prompts me to smile so widely you'd think I'd swallowed something hallucinogenic. Actually, I do know. It's the curl of Rob's upper lip, the flicker of something in his eyes that's very dark indeed.

'Hi!' Rob grins and I do a double take.

Oh thank God – I imagined it. Because soon my gorgeous neighbour is shaking hands with my gorgeous boyfriend and I find myself the filling in an eye-candy sandwich.

'Hi!' Matt grins.

They continue shaking hands. And grinning. Then do a bit more of it. So much more in fact that the situation becomes distinctly uncomfortable – something that can't be attributed just to the fact that when three people stand in my kitchen it's like being in a lift.

'Soooo,' I say, clapping my hands together in the manner of a primary-school teacher about to suggest finger-painting. 'Rob, would you like some coffee? Matt makes it brilliantly.'

Rob glances at me and I wonder if I ought to explain why Matt has made the coffee at my flat and not me. Then I think that if I explain it'll look like I've got something to hide and, patently, I haven't. Although it'd be best for all concerned if I never disclosed that we once spent the night together and I thought he'd given me a venereal disease.

Matt opens the kitchen cupboard and takes out a cup.

At this point I also start to wonder if I should explain why Matt knows where my cups are kept, and from the look on Rob's face I'd guess that's an issue he'd very much like to address later on too.

'I've heard a lot about you, Rob,' Matt offers.

Rob stiffens.

'All good, of course.'

Rob shifts onto the other foot.

'Emma tells me you can speak Cantonese,' Matt adds, and I try to stop myself from visibly wincing.

'I know about three sentences,' Rob mumbles. Now I wonder if I need to explain the fact that I *wasn't* trying to make him sound more impressive than he is. Honestly. 'My old girlfriend was Chinese,' he explains.

I have no idea why the reference to the old girlfriend is yet another little pancake to throw into this frying pan of awkwardness, but it is. We all bite our lips.

'So … what do you think of Emma's list?' Matt asks. I hold my breath.

He's saying it to change the subject and, in the words of my dad, *he means well*. It should be a welcome relief, a light-hearted diversion in a conversation that's already stuttering so badly it needs therapy.

Should is the operative word.

'What list?' He scrunches up his nose as Matt glances anxiously at the fridge – where the list was once displayed, until I hid it in the kitchen drawer precisely to avoid alerting my boyfriend to it.

The reason for the move – its two slightly risqué entries – clearly hasn't occurred to Matt. Perhaps he thinks Rob wouldn't care about those items, or perhaps he assumes that I've already given Rob the full details, or at least the edited highlights. The reality is that I haven't given him the highlights, lowlights or *any* lights.

'Oh … it's not a big deal,' I mutter. 'I was actually going to mention it this week. Just a daft thing that I'm doing. With the girls.'

'What daft thing?' Rob asks flatly.

I take a deep breath. Matt is looking at me stiffly, wide-eyed, as if trying to convey the words 'Whoops, sorry!' telepathically.

'Well, when the girls and I were teenagers we drew up this list of things that we wanted to do by the time we hit thirty. I found it a couple of months ago. So I decided that it was a good idea to give some of them a go, given that I'm thirty this year.' *Why do I sound so guilty?* 'So that's what I'm doing.'

He nods. 'What's on the list?'

My mind is suddenly blank and the *only* things I can think of are the one-night stand and the snogging.

'Polo!' Matt blurts out.

Rob frowns.

'That's it!' I add, as if I've discovered the theory of relativity. 'I'm going to learn to play polo. You can come, if you like. Oh, and the guitar . . . learning the guitar is one of them too. So you see – you've been helping me already. Thanks!' He looks entirely unmoved.

Matt makes his excuses and leaves shortly after that. And, call me inhospitable, but I'm glad to see him go.

Chapter 41

When I was at school, my careers advisor was fond of saying, 'Fail to prepare, prepare to fail.' So, having spent most of last week and all last night researching everything that's hip, happening and hot in the world of interior design, I couldn't feel more clued up if I was Jasper Conran himself.

While my mental preparation is second to none, the same cannot be said of my physical state. I wake on Friday morning – the day of the interview – with a zit on my forehead that I'm convinced is visible from the International Space Station.

I spend most of the morning employing a combination of attack techniques, with the aid of an elaborate, quasi-pharma-ceutical list of preparations – everything from tea tree oil to toothpaste.

I am, of course, totally determined not to do the one thing I'm desperate to do – but that all the books tell you *never* to do. Squeeze it. Listen to the beauty editor of any magazine and you'd be convinced there's only one certain consequence of squeezing a spot: your head will cave in. So, obviously, it is a no-no. For about three-and-a-half minutes.

The zero efficacy of the tea tree/Colgate combo means that, before I can even think about what I'm doing, I'm poised with a piece of loo roll on either side, assaulting the offending carbuncle until my eyes water. All of which does precisely nothing but make my horrendous red protrusion even more horrendous, red and protruding.

I won't bore you with the other minor disasters that the morning throws at me, except to say that they involve two pairs of laddered tights, a splattering of jam on my dress and, courtesy of having to run for the Manchester train, blisters on each little toe that could double for airbags on a Land Rover Discovery.

By the time I arrive at the office of Loop Interior Design, I'm feeling far from calm and collected.

Still, as I press the buzzer and am led into the entrance of the chic King Street office block, I take a deep breath, check for stray mascara in the lift mirror and compose myself. Then I check for anything stuck in my teeth. Or more jam stains. Or splits in the skirt of my dress, ladders in tights, bird poo in my hair or any other stray miscellany that might scupper my success.

It is just when I've decided to pull out my neckline and have a subtle sniff to make certain my Sure is firing on all cylinders that I glance up and realise that the door is open and that I've been enthusiastically inhaling my armpit in full view of someone.

'You must be Emma,' the woman says, shaking my hand as I step out. She's in her mid-fifties and dressed impeccably. I note a chic silver bob, smooth, papery skin and an elegant smile. She speaks with the tone of a voiceover artist for a luxury brand of chocolate: refined, deep. 'I'm Lulu McMasters. Come on in.'

The office of Loop is as you'd expect from an interior-design company: glorious. There's no other word for it. It's airy and beautiful, with soft grey sofas, white floors, splashes of colour on Moorish jacquard cushions and – I physically gasp when I see this – *a harp*. This office has a genuine real-life *harp* right there in the corner. I couldn't be more impressed if Enya herself was sitting at it, giving us a turn.

'Like it?' Lulu grins, clearly proud. And why wouldn't she be? I'd run to work every day if I were employed here.

'It's gorgeous. Exactly the sort of thing I love,' I say, wondering if this counts as arse-licking, given that it's actually true. There are five work stations in the office, only one of which is currently occupied, by an ice-cool blonde who appears to have survived on no-bread cucumber sandwiches for most of her life.

We end up in Lulu's office and I'm invited to take a seat on the other side of an imposing desk.

She flicks through my CV, and glances up. 'I'm glad you like what we've done in here. Although we're in the middle of a rebranding so I'll probably update the office area too.' Frankly, the office area couldn't look more updated if it'd been painted yesterday. 'Ooh. Let me show you the new logo designs.'

With a modest smile, she removes a folder from her bottom drawer. 'Have a look at how it compares with the old one,' she says, placing the two logos next to each other. 'I was never happy with that. It's just not right, is it? My old partner chose it and we never got on. It was a mistake going along with him, to be honest.'

She pushes the two logos in front of me.

'Oh, it's stunning!' I gush. 'This new one fulfils *everything* you're trying to achieve. It's contemporary but traditional, it's chic, it's sophisticated. I love the sage colour on the company name, the way the L curls round. It's a million times better than the old one. I mean, gosh ... I don't know what your partner was thinking but you're so right. It doesn't work at all, does it? *Not at all.* You were totally right going for this new one.'

She stares at me and then glances at the logo I have in my hand. If I'd gushed any more over it, I'd be in a big pool on the carpet.

'*That's* the old one,' she says flatly.

And I sink back in my seat, wondering if she'd consider a bribe.

Chapter 42

I'm all for the idea of being happy and contented when you're single. But there are some unquestionable benefits of having a boyfriend, one of which I am experiencing this Saturday night.

'This is so romantic,' I tell Rob, as we gaze over the city lights from Panoramic, the UK's highest restaurant. 'Thank you so much for booking it.'

He grins. 'I'm glad you like it. You deserve it.'

I don't argue with him. Not because I think I *do* deserve it, but because it'll just prompt another wave of him telling me how wonderful I am and me objecting because this perfect vision of Emma that Rob believes in is a long way from the real me.

I've started doing the odd thing in front of him lately to remind him that I am not the princess he thinks I am. I filed my feet with a pumice stone in his presence, inspired by my dad's awful date and certain that bits of flaky foot skin are a reality check *par excellence*. It had no effect.

Cally suggested I fart in front of him while we're watching telly, but I'm reserving that one in case things get really bad and it looks like he's in danger of proposing again.

'Well, I want to pay for this tonight,' I tell him.

'No way!' he laughs.

'I'm serious, Rob. I do. I want you to know how much I'm enjoying being back together.'

He shakes his head. 'That's all I need to know. Now, what are you going for?'

I opt for the fish dish, kidding myself that it's the healthy option, before taking enough bread to spark a gluten overdose and smothering it in butter. The evening is lovely. We eat, we drink Prosecco, we hold hands – and basically all is as it should be when a girl's on a romantic night out with her boyfriend.

Then things go awry.

'So you know my list,' I say, as we're finishing the main course. 'I thought it'd be nice if you could maybe help me out on one of the other items. Apart from the guitar, that is.'

Rob hesitates and puts down his knife and fork. 'Was there a reason you didn't tell me about the list?'

'I hadn't thought it was a big deal.'

'What else is on it?'

I take a deep breath. 'I'll show you it, if you like,' I say, making a mental note to edit it first. 'But it's stuff like go and see the Northern Lights, jump out of a plane, that kind of thing. Oh, and win a job as an interior designer – although I'm pretty sure I've got a long way to go before that happens.'

'You never know about the interview – I'm sure it wasn't as bad as you think.'

'Some of it was okay,' I concede. 'Some of it I was pleased with. And she really liked the room design I'd done for my application. I don't fancy my chances after my beautifully tactful assessment of the new branding, though.'

He frowns. 'So . . . the list.'

'Yes?'

'There's nothing *weird* on it, is there?'

I stiffen. 'Like join a cult? No.'

He isn't reassured by the joke. 'There *is*, isn't there?'

I shake my head. And keep shaking it. Over and over again. Then I stop and cave into pressure. 'Yes.'

'Well, come on, what is it? It can't be that bad.'

'It's not.'

'Then tell me.'

'I can't.'

'Well, I'm going to think it's *really* bad, then.'

'It's not *really* bad.'

'It must be.'

'It *isn't*,' I hiss.

He pauses and thinks, before leaning over the table. 'Have you experimented with a *same-sex liaison*? You know, done a Katy Perry – kissed a girl?'

I roll my eyes. 'No.'

He looks terribly disappointed. Then he folds his arms and glares at me. The list has obviously become a bigger issue in Rob's mind than it's worthy of being. Whether that's due to the fact that Matt knew about it when he didn't – or simply that his mind is running wild with what the 'weird' bits are – I don't know. Either way, I don't like the way he says the next sentence.

'Emma, I need to know what's on that list.'

I breathe out defiantly. 'Have a one-night stand,' I say, with a shrug.

His mouth drops open. 'You *didn't*.'

'No, I *didn't*,' I say – and despite the fact that it's the truth I still blush.

'What else? Come on, the dodgy ones, please.'

I purse my lips and look out of the window. 'Snog somebody famous.'

He sniffs. 'I know you wouldn't have done that.'

Now my mouth drops open. 'What makes you say that?'

'How would you get to snog somebody famous? It's not as though you spend every night at the Ivy.'

I cross my arms. 'I might surprise you on that one.' He looks shocked. 'But in this particular case, I'm not going to,' I add hastily.

'Any more?'

'It's just stuff like jump out of a plane—'

'You'll never do that either.'

'Why not?'

'You were nearly hysterical on half the rides at Alton Towers. You're scared of spiders. You even said that when you were in Edinburgh you weren't keen on those fish things that eat your feet.'

'Okay!'

'Any more *weird* ones?'

'They're all totally above board, I promise you,' I tell him. 'Come on, are you up for it?'

'Up for what?'

'The next thing on my list – polo. I'm taking a taster lesson.'

He sips his Prosecco. 'I'll sit that one out, Em, if you don't mind.'

'Fine,' I say.

'Fine,' he replies.

We stare at each other for a while, wondering how the evening has taken this turn.

'Look, let's get onto something a little less controversial, shall we?' He reaches over to touch my hand. The movement of his fingertips warms my skin and makes me smile.

'I'll drink to that.'

Chapter 43

The impending polo lesson is exactly what I need to take my mind off my less than perfect performance at the job interview. And because I'm now so convinced I can't go through with the skydiving, I cut it off the bottom of the list and stuff it down my waste disposal unit.

With Rob refusing to even consider joining me for the polo, I'd assumed it would be just me and Cally, whose mum has offered to babysit. Until, that is, my doorbell rings the weekend before we're due to go – as I'm midway through dyeing my eyebrows and have two large brown caterpillars crawling across my forehead.

I hesitate, but decide eyebrow-dyeing is not a good reason to turn someone away, so instead answer the door holding my hand to my head, as if swooning in an amateur dramatic society's production of *Pride and Prejudice*.

'I've brought you this,' Matt grins, thrusting something into my free hand. It's a bag of posh-looking coffee.

'Thanks,' I say, unsure whether or not to invite him in.

'Is now not a good time?'

I hesitate, before opening the door. 'It's fine, come in.' I direct him to the kitchen while I dive into the bathroom to rinse off the dye, about six minutes after I was supposed to, then emerge looking like Bert from *Sesame Street*.

I don't know how we get onto the subject of my polo lesson, in between Ollie's piano lessons, the fact that Joshua has suddenly started wetting the bed, my interview – which I still haven't heard about – and Stacey's satsuma jam (which just keeps coming, according to Matt). But I do know that his reaction was startlingly similar to Cally's.

'Polo? Hey, I'll come with you!' he announces, as if Christmas Day is happening twice this year. 'If you want, that is.'

'Of course,' I reply, even though my first thought is that if Rob finds out, it'd be a disaster. 'It's not like it's a date or anything.'

He scrunches up his nose, and I pray for a giant golden eagle to swoop down, grab me by the shoulders and whisk me off somewhere a long, long way away. *Of course* it's not like it's a bloody date, you idiot! He clearly never thought that for a second.

'Have you ever played polo before?' I ask, leaping at the chance to change the subject.

'No, but I love the idea of it. I can ride – just about – but that's it.'

I narrow my eyes. 'Are we talking Cheltenham Gold Cup contender or Blackpool donkey aficionado?'

He laughs. 'Somewhere in between.'

'Hmm. Me too. Although it's closer to the latter, so you're no doubt going to see me make a complete buffoon of myself.'

'You? Surely not.'

I decide to ignore him.

In some ways it isn't a surprise that Matt is up for something like this. It's definitely not a surprise that Cally is, although for different reasons. Unless her instruction is personally delivered by a bona fide Rupert Campbell-Black lookalike, complete with rakish smile, plummy vowels and possibly a whip, she'll be distinctly disappointed.

What is a surprise is how our little trio of novice polo players becomes a quartet. Actually, surprise isn't the word. I could not be more shocked if I stuck three fingers in an electric socket and sneezed on them.

'Polo? Oh, it's been years,' says Giles casually, while we're midway through conjuring up a script about a storm in Bibblybobbly that makes the Bingbahs' marshmallows explode.

I narrow my eyes, wondering if I've heard right. '*What's* been years?'

He scratches his beard and goes to take another Hobnob, before realising that the pack's empty. 'It's been years since I played.'

I am momentarily silenced by these words, for Giles does not and never has looked like my idea of a polo player.

Today he's wearing his over-washed black Metallica T-shirt, the one he interchanges with his over-washed Judas Priest,

Motorhead and Black Sabbath T-shirts. The fact that his style bible is non-existent is but one issue, however; for Giles's physique is a long way from that of Prince Harry. He's a behemoth of a man, a big, hairy, muscular chunk of human being which, with my admittedly limited expertise, strikes me as rather different from that on show at the average Cartier polo event.

I narrow my eyes. 'You?'

'You what?'

'*You* have played polo?'

He knocks back his espresso. 'A while ago. I played it with a couple of people at school.'

I sit back in my chair, lost for words. Then I shake my head. 'Giles, my school friends and I played rounders. Or hockey. Occasionally, there'd be a spontaneous conkers tournament. What sort of school did you go to where your mates played *polo?*'

He shrugs. 'Just a school. You know, with teachers . . . pupils . . . dinners capable of causing dysentery.'

I open my mouth in disbelief, unable to stop the smile spreading across my face. 'Are you telling me, Giles, that in all the years I've known you, I've never even realised . . .'

He frowns. 'What?'

'You're *posh?*'

He opens his drawer, removes a packet of fags, and raises his eyebrows. 'Couldn't you tell?'

Chapter 44

Our taster lesson is taking place at the Rose Polo Club in Cheshire. I've spent days looking at its website, at the fresh-faced horsey types that adorn its home page, and wondering if everyone's vowels will be as long as their jodhpur-clad legs.

The journey from Liverpool takes an hour, which means leaving at eight thirty on a Sunday morning. Getting up this early at the weekend feels deeply unnatural to Giles and me, but not to Cally and Matt, for whom, as parents, this apparently constitutes a lie-in.

Disloyal as it feels to say it, I'll confess to some concerns about unleashing Giles on Matt and Cally, who's only ever been introduced to him fleetingly, and years ago – usually when our respective work nights out ended up colliding (messily) at two in the morning. It's not that Cally doesn't get on with everyone, nor indeed that I suspect the same of Matt.

But while I've had years to get to know and love the real Giles, you'd forgive anyone for failing to spot his charms instantly. This isn't helped by his tendency to dismiss anyone with whom he comes into contact as a prat (or worse), until they prove otherwise.

In the event, I needn't have worried. Giles and Matt hit it off perfectly.

'Did you ever go to see Guns N' Roses live?' Matt asks, as we hurtle through the countryside.

'I'd have loved to,' Giles replies, before they launch into another discussion of some obscure heavy-metal event.

'I didn't know you were into that sort of music, Matt,' I point out.

'I'm into *all* sorts of music. I went through a metal phase when I was a teenager.'

'Me too. I never grew out of it.' Giles laughs, which makes his face do a weird and rarely seen thing: it makes him stop frowning.

'So are you going to show us all up with your polo-playing, Giles?' smiles Cally, leaning forward between the seats. 'I believe you're an expert.'

Giles freezes. 'Um ... not really,' he mumbles, then he bends down and rustles around in his rucksack, cutting short the conversation. Cally looks at me – and I shake my head, baffled by what she's done to offend him.

When we arrive, the presence of a small private plane on the edge of a vast green field – which turns out to be the pitch – makes me glad we're not in my car. It would look about as at home here as a can of Special Brew in the Royal Box at Ascot.

We're greeted by Katie, who runs the polo school, an effervescent South African with long blonde hair and an irrepressible passion for the sport.

'There are sixty members of the club and they range in age from eleven to seventy-two,' she tells us. 'This is a sport for everyone. You're going to be *hooked*.'

'I hope not,' I mutter to Matt, 'or I may have to organise a bank robbery to fund this hobby.'

'Hmm, I did hear that you can only be a member of a club if you own not one, but two, ponies,' Matt whispers. 'But don't worry, we'll buy a lottery ticket on the way home. We're *bound* to win.'

Because Giles has played polo before, he joins a group of advanced learners. The rest of us are with the beginners, taught by a Kiwi instructor called Nick. There are seven of us in total, which at first gives me a sense of safety in numbers. Until a quick vox pop makes it apparent that, of all the attendees, it's *me* who's the least experienced rider.

'Don't worry about it,' shrugs Cally. 'Polo ponies are meant to be easy to ride.' She turns to the instructor. 'It doesn't matter that she's not an expert rider, does it?'

He considers this for a second. 'Being good at riding obviously helps.'

'But your website said you took *absolute* beginners,' I say, my voice rippling with panic. '*Ab-so-lute*. *That's* what it said.'

'Yeah, we do, very occasionally. Why ... is that about your level?'

I stiffen, suddenly conscious I'm surrounded by people who are very clearly more competent than me. 'Not *exactly*,' I reply cagily. I accompanied Zachary on a horse in Center Parcs only a few months ago. 'I have *some* equine experience.'

'You'll be fine,' he smiles unreassuringly as he marches to the stables. 'Besides, I love a challenge.'

The first part of our instruction involves perching on a wooden horse – nicknamed 'Woody' – to learn to hit the ball with mallets. Nick performs a demo that's so effortless you'd be convinced that learning to use a knife and fork was more challenging.

'Bring the arm forward, then back . . . and, in a nice smooth movement, forward again . . . and make contact. Like so.'

The mallet hits the ball with a sharp, gratifying pop, propelling it across the field in a quasi-supersonic arch. He does it again, and again, smashing balls one after the other as far as the eye can see.

Cally nudges me. 'Piece of cake, eh?'

'Right, let's go in height order, shortest first. That's you,' he grins, pointing at me.

Marvellous.

I step forward obediently, my knees trembling so much I'm barely able to walk over to Woody, let alone perform all the moves that Nick has just demonstrated.

With seven sets of eyes scrutinising me, I hope to scale the wooden horse with grace and elegance, using the approach those women in *The Tudors* take when mounting (horses, not Jonathan Rhys Meyers).

Sadly, despite the presence of steps, my ascent is distinguished only by its spectacular ungainliness. I scramble on breathlessly, with all the finesse of Widow Twanky, pulling out tufts of nylon mane and apparently unable to prevent my arse from protruding comically in the air.

It's only when my bum cheeks have finally made contact with Woody that I realise how high up I am. I'm literally nowhere near the ground or indeed the balls I'm supposed to hit. You might as well ask me to play swing ball around the top of the Eiffel Tower.

'Your position should be like you're doing a snow plough in skiing,' says Nick, as if this helps in any way. 'Up on your stirrups, knees and toes pointing in, leaning down to the right.'

What he really means – as I discover when he positions me correctly – is that I am to perform the most accomplished impression I can of a knock-kneed ostrich suffering from excruciating constipation.

'Now, *swing!*'

The instruction is so forceful that all I can do is take a deep breath, focus, and, with utter determination, follow it.

I do everything as instructed. I don't put a foot wrong. By rights, I should smash that ball to the other end of the field in a move that'd make Princess Anne want me as her god-daughter.

There's just one problem, a matter that becomes apparent as I sit up, put my hand above my eyes and gaze into the distance to locate the ball.

'Nice attempt,' Nick smiles.

'Thanks!' I beam, pleased with myself.

'You do realise you missed, don't you?'

I've come to learn that determination only gets you so far in life when you're completely devoid of ability.

This becomes painfully clear in the latter half of the lesson, during the 'chukka' – that's a game to you and me.

A chukka is supposed to last for only seven-and-a-half minutes, but I find it impossible to believe that this is anything less than seven-and-a-half hours.

There are four of us playing: Cally and Matt, who are paired together, and Nick and I, who, despite being at opposite ends of the talent spectrum, are going head to head with my friends.

If I exaggerated my riding experience slightly, it is immediately obvious that they played down theirs, as if anyone is going to thank them for modesty in these circumstances.

While I perch stiffly on my pony, Begonia, struggling to get her to even think about moving, Cally and Matt scamper up and down the training yard as if this is the most natural thing in the world, hitting balls, scoring goals, riding each other off (which I promise isn't as rude as it sounds).

I'm not saying they're anything close to perfect – both repeatedly miss the ball and Cally almost falls off twice. But they are managing to *play*. I, on the other hand, am not managing to play. I am not even managing to move. I don't remember a single scene in *Riders* being like this.

While this action-packed game is going on around me,

Begonia displays only slightly more inclination to join in than Woody did. Part of the problem is that the last thing I want to do is encourage this animal to do anything hasty, like trot.

It strikes me that the most difficult thing about polo is that your brain has to engage in not one but *two* exceedingly difficult endeavours. The first is riding a horse; the second is trying to score goals. You might as well attempt to iron a linen shirt during a snowboarding session.

'Come on, Emma, get stuck in – get this ball off Matt,' Nick shouts encouragingly as he spots me hovering behind the others, who are clearly having a thoroughly enjoyable time.

Matt turns round and flashes me a grin. 'Fancy it?'

'Right,' I huff, determined to pull myself together.

I squeeze my feet against Begonia's ribs, hoping to get her moving. Not too fast, obviously, but some sort of forward motion would be a clear benefit. She shakes her mane but barely stirs. If I didn't know any better, I'd guess she was rolling her eyes and doing a mock yawn.

I take another deep breath. 'Come on, Begonia,' I say, digging my feet in harder.

Begonia doesn't need to be asked twice. Begonia, in fact, acts as though she has a rocket up her backside, shooting across the yard until I'm next to Matt, gripping on for dear life.

'That's right, Emma! Push him out of the way!' shouts Nick.

'What? With my horse?' I whimper, as the ball disappears under our feet.

'*Yes!*'

I edge to Matt's side as he inches away from the ball, our mallets knotting between us. Matt's horse pushes into Begonia and he wins control of the ball, only metres from the goal.

'Get it back! Go on, Emma!' Nick yells.

With my heart pounding, I head back as Matt is positioning himself in front of the goal.

'*Push him, Emma!*' Nick shouts.

I pull Begonia's reins and tap her sides with my feet, this time hoping to add a little more oomph. My wish is granted. However, instead of just edging Matt out of the way and winning control of the ball, Begonia moves so fast that I realise I haven't only pushed the horse out of the way – I've pushed its rider too.

I watch in horror as Matt is unsaddled and topples off like he's the top prize on a coconut shy.

'*Jesus!*' Matt yells, as he slams into the ground and Nick and Cally ride over.

'Oh God! I'm so sorry!' I splutter.

'Hey, don't worry,' Matt says, wincing in pain as he stands and brushes himself down.

'Is anything broken?' I offer.

He flashes me a look. 'Yes, my pride has suffered several fractures and could be in plaster until February.'

Chapter 45

By the time the session is over, I'm exhausted and sweaty – and wishing that the odds on us winning the lottery were anything like Matt predicted. Rubbish as I was, it was undeniably great. And that rush of adrenalin – the one I usually hate – has left me nothing but exhilarated. For a woman who freaks at the sight of a spider in the bath, as Rob pointed out, this is quite a step forward.

We spend the final twenty minutes watching in wonder as Giles trounces the team he was pitted against. He scores four goals and is a phenomenon – athletic, almost – which is something so at odds with the view I have of him most days (i.e. reaching for the biscuit packet) it's like looking at a different person.

'I'm pleased with some of the photos I took,' Matt tells me as we trudge to the car. 'The light was perfect today. There are some lovely ones of you in your first practice go.'

'Tell me you made me look like I knew what I was doing,' I groan.

'I'll show you while we wait for the others.' He throws his bag into the boot of the car, before climbing into the driver's seat.

I slide in next to him, feeling less than enthusiastic. I am the least photogenic person I know. The mere presence of a camera seems to make me gurn spontaneously so that, when someone says they've taken a 'natural shot', it generally means I look like Goofy having his glands emptied.

'You'll have to delete that one,' I begin. 'Oh, and that. And ... oh that's awful!'

He snatches away the camera. 'Emma, you look *lovely*. I thought they were great.'

I roll my eyes. 'I don't doubt that from a purely artistic point of view you've captured wonderful aspects of light and shade. Matt, you could probably win awards with these. Nevertheless, any artistic talent is entirely negated by one crucial, overriding fact.'

'Which is?'

'My bum looks big.'

Before he has a chance to respond, the back doors spring open and Giles and Cally tumble in.

'*Oooh*, stop it! My sides are hurting,' Cally hoots, as she slams the door. 'Oh, Giles – you are *terrible*.'

I glance at Giles, but his eyes are fixed on Cally. He's smiling, providing a full view of several incisors I never knew existed.

The pair of them spend the rest of the journey giggling like sixth formers on the back of a bus while Matt and I drop into their conversation only intermittently. When we approach south Liverpool, he offers to drop them both at home.

'That'd be fantastic, if you don't mind,' Cally says. 'Although, Mum's just texted to say she doesn't mind baby-sitting if I want to go for a drink tonight. I need to get back to see Zachary first and put him to bed but . . . anyone fancy joining me later?'

'Sorry, but I've got to get back for the kids. Their mum will be dropping them off soon,' Matt replies. 'Plus, I've got a few work trips in the next few weeks, then I'm off to Iceland in November, so I want to spend as much time as possible with them when I can.'

'Em?' she asks.

'Rob's making Sunday dinner for me.'

Cally hesitates, glancing at Giles.

'I'll join you for one.' And from the look on his face, this doesn't represent much of a hardship.

By the time I've showered, pulled on jeans and a T-shirt and made it over to Rob's, it's gone six thirty. He's made a delicious roast dinner for me, as if his credentials as the world's most perfect boyfriend could be any greater.

His roast potatoes are crispy and light, his chicken is as succulent as can be. It's all home-cooked and comforting and exactly as I'd fancied. We *make love* afterwards; at least, Rob makes love. I'm so stiff after my session on Woody I manage only the most basic of positions, the sort that tend to prelude a smear test.

229

He tries to persuade me to stay, but I always crave my own bed on a Sunday – Monday mornings are challenging enough even when I have all my personal possessions about me. Still, it's late before I get home and the crunch of gravel on my drive breaks the twilight silence in Grassendale Park.

The living-room light is still on in Matt's house, and I imagine him on the sofa, editing photos on his laptop after putting the kids to bed.

I go into the kitchen to flick on the kettle and make a chocolate drink, before taking out the list and crossing off another item. Then I approach the window to close the blinds. At that exact moment, I look up and see Matt drawing his curtains. He stops and catches my eye. We both laugh at the coincidence.

Then we stop laughing.

As I gaze through his window across the night air, his expression softens, but he doesn't move and neither do I.

He looks away first, glancing down at the windowsill. He bites his lip, looks up again and waves. I wave back.

Then we both turn away and are gone.

Chapter 46

I get to work early the next day so I can send some emails to check the availability of bars on my birthday. The inconvenience of being born in the peak Christmas party season means this necessitates getting in there in good time.

My heart is set on one venue – Leaf, a tea shop that serves food, drinks of the alcoholic and non-alcoholic variety and, if you fancy it (although I rarely do on a Saturday night), hundreds of varieties of tea. As well as hosting art and vintage markets, music and club nights, it's available for private hire – which my dad, God love him, is insisting on paying for me.

I also have to prepare for a meeting Giles and I are having with the animation studio. Usually, the creative director would be joining us, but in the absence of one – and with Perry still doing whatever he's doing in Austria – it's just us.

Giles hates meetings even more than he hates everything else in life that isn't real ale, heavy metal and technology, but even that doesn't account for how fine he's cutting it today.

He's normally the first in to work and the last to leave, an obsessive perfectionist who would never contemplate submitting a script that wasn't honed and polished until you could see your face in it. Only, today, it's 9.28 before he stumbles through the door.

'Hello, Sir Lancelot – did all that time on a horse yesterday tire you out too much to get up on time?'

He plonks himself behind his desk with *Night of the Living Dead* eyes. 'Hmm?'

'You're later than usual, that's all.'

He shakes his head. 'Am I? Shit!'

He fires up his computer and starts flinging bits of stationery and biscuit wrappers around the desk like Miss Piggy looking for her false eyelashes.

I hand him a printout of the script. 'Here.'

'Oh? Oh. Thanks!'

He's odd at the meeting too. I can't put my finger on why, except that he doesn't use a single word that begins with an f, he doesn't grunt, and he doesn't slag off Perry – which is astonishing in the light of his latest email from Austria assuring us he'll be home next week with 'a raft of sensational concepts'.

It's more than positivity, though. Giles is also vacant. Ponderous. His mind is clearly elsewhere. Which raises one question.

'Did you and Cally stay out late last night? I haven't managed to catch up with her this morning,' I say casually, not mentioning the fact that I've exchanged several texts with my best friend but failed to pin her down on what happened.

Giles shifts in his seat. 'Um ... depends what you'd call late.'

I try to think of a subtle way to quiz him without his head caving in. Before I can open my mouth, a text beeps on his phone and he dives to read it, juggling it like he's picked something off a barbecue with his bare hands.

His expression changes as he scans it, and that weird thing happens again – he smiles. It's an excited, wistful, *Seven Brides for Seven Brothers*-type smile.

I try not to scrutinise him too obviously as he types in a response, then deletes it and looks out of the window. Then he types in another response, deletes it, drums his fingers against the desk and looks out of the window again. It takes four goes before he's happy enough to press Send, and for the next twenty minutes you'd think he was awaiting the results of a life-or-death blood test.

This goes on for most of the day, interspersed with a series of unsubtle questions culminating in: 'Does Cally like tennis? She keeps asking me if I'm any good.'

I don't tell him that the particular sporting event she has in mind will probably involve removing his Metallica T-shirt.

I finally manage a conversation with Cally when I pop round the corner to the Quarter for takeaway coffees.

'What happened between you and Giles?' I ask, expecting to hear the ubiquitous speech about how sex is the last thing on her mind since she had Zachary and she can't understand how she was ever that into it and she finds it impossible to believe she'll ever feel an urge to indulge in anything remotely sexy again.

'I've been at it *all night*!' she announces triumphantly, as I almost drop both coffees on my shoes.

'You've been *what*? Not with *Giles*?'

'Excuse the horse pun after yesterday, but I am well and truly back in the saddle. Emma,' she sighs, 'I've come home.'

'Yes . . . but with *Giles*?'

She hesitates. 'You don't have a problem with that, do you? Oh, it's never going to be anything serious; it's just . . . he was there . . . I was there . . . we had a laugh . . . one thing led to another and – well, before I knew it, I was getting my second ride of the day,' she hoots.

'Of course I don't have a problem . . . I mean, despite appearances, Giles can be incredibly lovely. He's one of the good guys and . . . well, I know none of this is obvious, but he is a real sweetheart deep down.'

'I'd honestly forgotten how much I loved it,' she continues. 'It was like the taste of a first cigarette after abstaining for three years – only this isn't bad for me!'

'But what do you think about Giles?' I ask.

'Hmm? Oh . . . yes, he's nice. What was really surprising was how quickly I got back into the swing of things. You might have thought that after so long once would be enough, but oh no! There was no stopping me.'

'As long as you had fun.'

'I did,' she replies.

'So are you going to see him again?'

'Yeah, why not? I mean, we've texted again today and . . .

do you know, it's weird but the issue hadn't even crossed my mind.'

I'm heading back into the office, attempting to hold the cardboard tray so that I can negotiate the front door, when my phone rings. I plant the tray on the wall and pull my mobile out of my bag – and my heart does a loop the loop when I see a Manchester number.

'Is that Emma?' I'd recognise the husky tones anywhere.

'Yes. Is that—'

'Lulu McMasters. It's about the job I interviewed you for.'

Chapter 47

Handing in my notice will be weird. I don't feel anything like as elated as I should be about leaving. Okay, Perry is a nightmare and the fundamental issue of my belief that I'm in the wrong job will never go away. Yet, as I type my leaving note, I feel tearful, and this is somebody who didn't even cry at *ET*.

I began writing something straightforward and to the point, like you're meant to do. But it felt so cold, so unsatisfactory, to sum up my years here in three paragraphs. I felt the need to explain, to reminisce, to let Perry know what a massive part of my life this place has been, how much I've laughed, made friends and grown – creatively and otherwise.

'Why is it you're leaving, again?' Marianne asks when I Skype her that night.

I sniff. 'Lots of reasons. It's always been my dream to be an interior designer. It was even on the list.'

'It was your dream when you were fifteen. Dreams can change. If they didn't I'd still aspire to be Geri Halliwell.'

'But if you knew what a nightmare this place is at the moment . . .'

'Fair enough. If your boss is having a breakdown then I can understand why you wouldn't want to be part of the fallout.'

'It's not quite *that* bad.'

'You'll miss the work, though, won't you?'

'Undoubtedly.' I suddenly want to change the subject. 'Oh, I've booked my birthday party. Leaf was available – they phoned today.'

'Fantastic.'

'So, I've now completed five items on the list and am working on the others. Some, at least. You don't fancy a trip to Norway, do you?'

'Sorry – we're saving up for somewhere long haul next year. Won't Rob go with you?'

I squirm. 'It's not his idea of fun – he isn't at all outdoorsy.'

'No?'

I shake my head. 'I've been trying to persuade him to come camping with me so I can fulfil the "sleep under the stars" bit but he's having none of it. He's only been once before – when he was a boy scout. It scarred him for life.'

'It's nothing like that these days – I've got tons of good equipment over at Dad's house. You're welcome to use it. Why don't you organise to camp near somewhere really luxurious, so you can have a lovely dinner together first?'

'Hmm, I don't know. His views seem firmly entrenched. Besides, I think I may have missed the boat – it's nearly October.'

'The weather is meant to be gorgeous this weekend,' she argues. 'Oh Emma – dinner in a nice gastropub, a bit of wine and the prospect of a cuddle on a blow-up mattress . . . I'm sure he'd be persuaded.'

I bite my lip. 'I can only put it to him, I suppose.'

'I know somewhere lovely in the Lake District, if you're interested. This weekend will be your last chance, I reckon. And you could always surprise him.'

Chapter 48

'Come on – where are we going? I can't bear the tension,' Rob beams as we hurtle along the motorway in my Fiat.

'*Please* don't get too excited, Rob,' I tell him. 'You might not like it.'

'Well, *you're* clearly excited. And how could I not enjoy going away for a night? It'll be a treat.'

I grip my steering wheel and wonder when might be a good time to confess that every available inch of my boot is crammed with camping paraphernalia, none of which I'm entirely certain how to use.

'Is it Scotland?' he blurts out gleefully, as if this joyous thought has been pinging round his brain for the last twenty minutes and only just escaped. 'If it's the Turnberry Resort ... wow, Emma, I don't know what to say,' he continues breathlessly. 'I've constantly talked about wanting to go there but I never expected you to—'

'What's the Turnberry Resort?'

'A golf hotel and spa.' He pauses and scrutinises my expression, deflating like a punctured whoopee cushion. 'Oh. It's not.'

I suddenly wish I could gold-plate my response, or conjure up some tenuous similarity between the pump-up PVC mattress he'll be sleeping on and the five-star Hungarian goose down he was obviously hoping for.

'No,' I reply eventually. 'Seriously, Rob – this is not going to be luxurious. But I'm hoping it will be *lots* of fun!' I grin.

I glance over and note that his bottom lip is protruding slightly. 'I'm sure once you get your head around the idea, you'll *love* it,' I add energetically. 'This could be the start of something – we could go every weekend next summer if you like it.'

'Emma . . . where are you taking me?'

I adjust my sunglasses and pull into the services, knowing it's the last on the M6 before we turn off. 'Just stopping for a wee!'

When I return to the car, he's on the phone to someone from work and he finishes the call in such a state of agitation that his troubles dominate the conversation for the next hour. During that time, I manage to get us so comprehensively lost I almost double the journey time and inadvertently divert us into a field of leeks.

Consequently, we arrive at Crosthwaite with only twenty minutes to spare before our early dinner – which is nothing like the cautious hour and a half I'd planned for putting up the tent.

'Here we are,' I say, failing to break this news to him as I pull into the car park of the Punch Bowl Inn.

Marianne was right about this place: it's a chocolate-box pub in a spectacular location – all rolling hills and rambling hedgerows – made all the more spectacular by a glorious sunset.

He turns to look at me. 'Emma, it's *lovely*.' Then he leans over the gear stick, grabs me by the back of the neck and kisses me theatrically on the lips, before releasing me like a disengaged sink plunger.

'Um ... I'd hoped to get here earlier so we could ...' I'm about to tell him about the tent, honestly I am.

'What?' he asks, wide-eyed. 'Test-drive the bed in our room?'

'Hmm,' I mumble, looking at my watch. 'Something like that, but I think we'd better go straight in or we might lose the table.'

He smiles the broadest smile I've ever seen. 'This is perfect, Emma. A perfect night with my perfect girl.'

'Rob, I—'

But before I can finish my sentence, he flips open the car door, bounces out and is striding to the inn, breathing in fresh air.

He pushes open the door and turns to me. 'Have we got time for a drink before dinner?'

'Of course.'

He gazes round as he approaches the bar. 'This place is *gorgeous*.'

He's right. The interior is everything you could wish for from a country inn, and it's been beautifully refurbished to blend old and new to perfection. There are log fires, luxurious rugs, quirky pictures on the walls and a wine list to die for. He orders the drinks and picks up an accommodation leaflet from a display next to the bar.

'This is *such* a brilliant choice, Emma,' he gushes. I don't think I've ever seen him so excited. 'Oh listen to this: "Each of our bedrooms is individually furnished with hand-picked throws, a flat-screen TV, a spacious bathroom with Bath House toiletries ..." This room's got two baths! Two. Baths. Oh God, I hope we get that one – I can just see you and me in his 'n' her baths.' He shakes his head and gazes into my eyes. 'You're amazing.'

'Er ... thanks, but—'

He thrusts a wine glass in my hand. 'I'd like to make a toast.'

'Oh ... would you?' I croak.

'To you, Emma. The best girlfriend any man could want.'

It's this that tips me over the edge – and forces me to make a decision there and then. I don't care that the room rates start at £160 – which is £160 I haven't got. I *cannot* tell Rob that my plan involved spending the night in a sleeping bag in the adjacent field when he's expecting a room with two sodding baths.

Once I've made the decision I feel a lot better for it, a million times more relaxed. All I need to do is wait for him to go to the loo so that I can go and speak to one of the staff and covertly book us in.

There's only one problem. A problem that becomes apparent about an hour in to the dinner. Rob's waterworks appear to be capable of holding an amount of liquid comparable to that required to extinguish a factory fire.

'How about some more wine, eh?' I smile, topping up his glass. 'And water. Make sure you drink *plenty* of water, won't you?'

He frowns. 'Why?'

'Well ... we want you tipsy but not too tipsy later, don't we, eh?' I wink suggestively.

He dutifully takes a mouthful of water. I top up his glass again and offer it to him. He ignores me.

'The loos in here are *amazing*,' I enthuse. 'Honestly ... they're absolutely gorgeous. If I had my own place, that's what I'd do with my loo. You've never seen anything like them. Have you tried out the boys' yet?'

'Not yet,' he replies, picking at his dessert.

'You should. Don't miss out on those, whatever you do. You'd be missing a real treat.'

He scrunches up his nose. 'They're that good?'

'World class,' I reply, adding a small air punch to illustrate my point. 'Nothing less.'

And I should know. I've been three times since we got here, but unfortunately, given that they're in direct view of where we're sitting, this hasn't offered the opportunity for me to secretly speak to the staff yet. I decide to take matters into my own hands.

'I'm going to check on the room,' I say, pushing out my chair.

'Oh ... wait until I'm finished and we can go up together.'

I hesitate and pull the chair in again, failing to come up with an alternative idea.

'Well ...' I mumble, my mind whirring. 'I just need something from the car.'

'Don't worry – I'll get the bags once we're finished.'

I think of the tent in the boot. '*No!*' I blurt out.

He looks taken aback. 'Emma ... is something the matter?'

I compose myself and dab either side of my mouth with my napkin. 'Not at all. I'm having a lovely time. Are you?'

'Fantastic. I can't wait to get into that room,' he adds, sliding his hand across the table and running it up my arm. 'I might just go to the loo here first.'

'*Excellent!*' I squeal.

Unnerved, he pushes back his chair and heads to the toilet. I know I've got seconds. Minutes at the most. I leap up and virtually rugby tackle a passing waiter who is taking soup to two elderly ladies at a table by the window.

'I need a room,' I say urgently.

He looks at me, so shocked I'm half-convinced I inadvertently announced I needed to empty my bowels.

'Now,' I add. '*Right* now.'

He places the soup on the table and the two ladies glare at me, clearly imagining I'm running a by-the-hour type of service similar to the one that Julia Roberts ran in *Pretty Woman*.

'Er ... I'll be right with you,' he replies. 'Or, if you're in a rush, I think someone's at reception now.'

I nod like a maniac. 'Thanks. Thank you. You're a truly great man.'

I head to the front desk and am greeted by a smiley grey-haired receptionist. 'Hello,' I say breathlessly. 'I'd like a room for tonight, please.'

'I'm sorry, we're fully booked this evening,' he replies. 'I might have something available mid-week, if that's any good?'

My jaw plummets to the desk. 'Are you *serious*?'

He pauses nervously, trying to decide if this is a trick question. 'I'm afraid so.'

Panic races through me as I lean across the desk. 'I'll pay you anything,' I hiss. 'Anything you like.'

He frowns, backing away. 'I'm afraid there's nothing I can do. There are only seven rooms and they're all taken.'

I'm assaulted by a blitzkrieg of hysteria. 'Can't you tell someone there's been a mix-up? I'll pay double!'

'I'm sorry, there's really nothing I can do,' he says apologetically.

'*Please!*' I whine. I'm preparing to fall to my knees and beg for mercy, when I realise someone is behind me. I spin round and come face to face with Rob. I gulp, turn back to the gentleman at the counter and muster up the most severe expression I'm capable of – part Lady Macbeth, part Incredible Hulk. 'Well, honestly!' I huff furiously. 'I won't be coming here again, that's for sure!'

The poor gentleman looks bewildered.

'Rob – we're leaving!' I announce, spinning on my heels and grabbing him by the elbow as I drag him to the door.

'Why?' he asks, perplexed.

I shove him out of the front door, close it behind us and make sure we're out of earshot.

'You won't believe it but they haven't got a room for us!' I say, waving my arms about as if I'm conducting *La Traviata*.

'You're kidding? And you made a reservation?'

'Of *course* I made a reservation!' I laugh, marching to the car.

'Shouldn't we pay for the dinner?' he asks, scuttling behind.

'Oh God!' I reply, freezing in my tracks. I spin round again and march back to the pub. 'Wait here. Don't move. Please.'

I skulk back in, apologising profusely to the gent on reception, and then I have to endure the torture of waiting at the desk for the card machine to work, in the knowledge that half the restaurant is hoping somebody will call the police to evict me.

'Thanks!' I wave on my way out. 'Bye! Sorry! I'll make sure I recommend you to all my friends!'

For some reason he doesn't look overly thrilled at the prospect.

Chapter 49

Rob is distraught, burning up with a sense of injustice. 'This is definitely one for TripAdvisor.'

'Hmm,' I nod earnestly.

'What are we going to do now? I know – I'll look on my phone to see if there are other hotels nearby.'

He twiddles with the phone until he realises that he can't get a signal. 'Let's drive to the nearest town ... there's bound to be something there.'

I hesitate, spotting an opportunity. 'I've had too much to drink.'

His mouth opens as the full implications of this become apparent.

'Oh no! We'll have to wait in the pub drinking Diet Coke until one of us is sober enough to drive home.'

'There *is* an alternative,' I offer cautiously.

'What?'

'Well,' I begin, aware that my tone here is everything.

'Marianne ... *had* asked me ... if I would take some ... camping gear ... to her friend's house.'

Clearly, I'm fabricating this statement as I go along – hence the need for more pausing than you get with a faulty DVD player as I work out what not to say.

'*What* friend?'

I hadn't counted on questions. 'Erm ... Beyoncé,' I blurt out.

'*Beyoncé?*' he says, scrunching up his nose. 'The singer?'

'Hahahahahahahaah! Not *the* Beyoncé, *obviously*. It's a friend of hers who also happens to be called Beyoncé. That's the fashion industry for you!'

He frowns. 'Still, I've never heard of—'

'Look, it doesn't matter what her friend's called!' I snap. 'The point is, there is a friend. Who likes camping. And I'd been asked to take a load of camping equipment to that friend's – to Beyoncé's – home. In Fazakerley.'

'I see.'

'Unfortunately,' I continue, ignoring the suspicious wrinkle above his nose, 'between the guitar lessons and moving jobs and ... hooo-eee, all sorts of things that have been keeping me terribly busy, I haven't had a second to do it.'

'Do what?'

'Deliver the camping equipment.'

'I see,' he repeats, as if he's about to expose me as the killer in *Death on the Nile*. I take out my key fob.

'And so ...' I click twice and the boot springs open, displaying

enough equipment to see us through an Antarctic expedition. 'Ta-
da!'

Rob's jaw drops. And it's immediately clear that he doesn't
share my enthusiasm.

'Emma . . . did you definitely plan for us to stay in the inn?' Rob
asks as he stands watching while I breathlessly attempt to con-
struct the tent.

'Of course! These things happen.' I take off my coat to try and
reduce the torrential rate at which I'm perspiring.

'Only . . . it seems odd that you happen to have had a tent in
your car.'

I bend down and start to wrestle with a swathe of canvas. 'I
don't know what makes you say that,' I fire back. 'Could you get
that pole over here, please, and help me pull this up?'

He takes a deep breath before walking over, picking up the
pole and trudging to me. I take it from him and scrutinise both
ends. I know this jumble of metal and canvas transforms into a
four-man tent somehow, because Marianne has told me it does.
How such a phenomenon can be achieved is, at this stage, a mys-
tery on a par with the construction of Stonehenge.

It's not that I've never put up a tent before – I have.
Admittedly, there were four of us at the time, one of whom was
a practising Brown Owl. It's that, despite Marianne's claims that
this is a super-duper easy-peasy model, it emerged only after I'd
unpacked it that the instructions are in Japanese (in which I'm
distinctly rusty), and it's now dark.

I straighten my head torch, looking like I'm off for a hard day down the pits, before starting to screw together two poles. I am gratified to discover that, despite being a different length to the ones I did earlier, I am at least starting to produce something vaguely tent-shaped.

'Do you think you'll be long?'

I pause. 'I. Don't. Know.' My voice is icy enough to freeze my molars solid, but I can't help myself. And Rob clearly notices.

'Do you want me to help?' he offers begrudgingly.

'Why don't you start unloading some stuff?' I suggest, aware that if he gets started on this too he might spontaneously combust with frustration. It turns out to be a good decision – and with my focus totally on erecting the tent, it takes me only an hour and a half.

'Right, I think we're done.' I brush myself down, feeling quite proud.

Then I register that Rob is standing with a fixed, perplexed gaze, as if trying to work out the meaning behind a Damien Hirst sculpture. 'Is it supposed to look like that?'

I frown. 'Like what?'

'Well . . . with that big baggy bit in the middle. And, you know, with the roof on that side so much lower than on the other. And . . . what are these for?'

He points to three poles on the ground.

'They're spares,' I inform him confidently.

'I'm just concerned it looks a little wonky,' he adds. I take a deep breath and try to remain calm.

Technically, I can't deny that he's right. Necessity required that I made a couple of impromptu adjustments to get the thing up. We'd have been here until tomorrow otherwise – and in the light of the spots of rain, I couldn't hang about.

The result is that our accommodation, I will reluctantly admit, looks like it's been erected by King Louie from *The Jungle Book* during an acid trip.

But, hey, looks aren't everything, are they? There's no way Bear Grylls would worry about that. He'd do exactly what I've done in potential adverse weather conditions: improvise.

I usher Rob into the tent, follow him in and zip it up.

'It's a bit windy,' he grumbles. 'And that rain's picking up.'

'It just sounds heavier from inside,' I tell him as I set about briskly pumping air into the blow-up bed. 'It's cosy in here, isn't it?' I smile, stomping up and down. He throws me a look that's about as pleasant as a sewer pipe.

There's something about his sulkiness that makes me determined to enjoy this experience, whether he is or not. I mean, it genuinely isn't that bad. The wind and rain *will* pass because the weather forecast said we were in for a clear night. And, as soon as it does, I intend to go outside in my sleeping bag and fulfil this item on my list, regardless of Rob's view.

Still, I can't pretend life wouldn't be a lot easier right now if my boyfriend was smiling.

I finish pumping up the bed, put it into place, and then suggest he goes and relaxes on it while I rummage in my rucksack for the most essential equipment of the evening: a bottle of Sauvignon Blanc and two plastic glasses.

I unscrew the top and pour the wine, unconcerned that it's warm and there's a chip in the plastic. I hand a glass to Rob and give him a conciliatory smile. 'Would this cheer you up?'

He looks up, hesitates, then returns the smile sheepishly. 'What makes you think I need cheering up? I've got my gorgeous girlfriend, that's all that matters.'

'So you're not too annoyed at me for not having a room with two baths?'

He takes my glass from me and places both mine and his behind him on the ground. Then he takes my face in his hands. 'I find it impossible to ever be cross with you, Emma,' he says, kissing me on the lips.

I don't know if it's the wine, the vigorous exertion involved in blowing up the bed or the sound of raindrops on the canvas, but Rob's kiss feels suddenly very erotic.

I find myself pulling him into me, longing for his hand to venture up my top and possibly elsewhere. He senses my desire and responds by kissing me harder, moving his hands over the small of my back, my bum, between my legs.

The wind is picking up, but I don't care; I'm as warm as toast, conscious only of Rob unbuttoning my jeans and tracing his fingers across the top of my knickers. As my lips sink into his, I submit to the lovely sensation of lust swirling through my body.

I pull him in closer, as the feel of his lips across my chest leaves my skin tingling. He goes to slide his hand down inside my jeans, but there's no room, so he starts tugging at them.

'Wait,' I whisper, attempting to roll back so I can get the jeans off myself. Only, the bed is so bouncy that removing them while lying down involves several unplanned sit-ups, before I scramble to a half-standing position – the only one feasible, given that the roof is too low to take me at full height.

Rob reclines on the blow-up bed and watches me undress. His eyes are heavy with desire as they drop from my face to my hands, which are now tugging my jeans downwards. I try to do this sexily, like in an Agent Provocateur advert, but with approximately four feet in which to manoeuvre it's difficult to do anything but hop up and down in a half-stoop until both my jeans and the lacy Brazilians underneath are finally off.

With my bottom half dealt with, I plan to whip off the jumper next, a prospect Rob is physically panting over. I kneel on the ground, grab the waistband and have it round my ears, when I become aware of something.

'What was that?' I say, whipping my jumper back down. Rob looks alarmed too. And it's immediately obvious why. Within ten seconds, the wind has reached alarming levels and the tent – which looked as safe as houses twenty minutes ago – is billowing like a panto dame's knickers caught in an industrial fan.

I'm about to grab my jeans and go outside to re-secure the tent pegs when, to my alarm and astonishment, one of them – on the right side of the tent – comes loose.

This single peg, in itself no big deal, paves the way for a cataclysmic whoosh of wind to sweep through the tent with the velocity of a category nine tornado, filling the entire structure with air.

I'm vaguely aware that Rob and I are squealing as we dive to the ground, attempting to pin down the bottom of the tent with our hands. But I'm not nearly strong enough. And, before I can work out how or what has gone wrong, there is a gaping hole in the side of the tent, the poles are rattling like the bones in a decomposed corpse and the whole thing looks certain to collapse.

'Quick! Grab that side!' I yell to Rob, and he scrambles over, clutching the other side of the tent as I close my eyes against the relentless rain.

It's at that point that a bad situation gets horribly worse.

I'm not sure how the eighty per cent of the tent Rob and I are gripping ends up on the other side of the field. All I know is that one minute I have it securely in my hands; the next I'm watching in disbelief as it makes its getaway into blackness, while I stand redundantly with a tent pole in my hands, my bare bum exposed, and my hair and face being lashed with rain.

'*What the fuck are we going to do?*' Rob cries, which I must admit is a very good question.

'*Run to the car!*'

I take the one piece of canvas left on the tent and wrap it round my midriff like a hideous, mildewed sarong, before gathering up our belongings and sprinting to the car, battling against the elements. When we get there, it emerges that I've left the keys somewhere inside the tent so we're both forced to run back, fall to our knees and scramble around on the muddy ground until we find them, just in time to watch my blow-up bed disappearing across the field.

By the time I reach the car, I am too shocked, stunned and miserable to speak, and so is Rob.

So we say nothing. We curl up together on the back seat, sharing the blanket my dad always insisted would come in handy one day.

My sleep is fitful; I wake constantly through the night, with the window handle prodding my side, and shivering from cold because my hair is totally unwilling to dry. It's typical that it's only when I see the sun start to rise over the hill that I'm so dogged with tiredness, all I can do is close my eyes again and submit to the slumber.

I'm midway through a glorious dream in which I'm interior-designing a house in Miami beach and the hunkiest builder you've ever seen is hammering nails into the wall to put up a set of delightful bamboo blinds ...

Only, he carries on even when they're up – at which point I wake up with a start and realise the banging is real.

An elderly face peers through my steamed-up window, but before I wind it down I attempt to make my creaking body sit up, and pull my jumper down over my bare legs.

'Morning!' she grins. She's in her seventies, with a smart Barbour jacket and unbrushed candyfloss hair.

'Uhrrghh ... hello,' I croak.

'Might these be yours?' she asks cheerily, holding up a pair of knickers – my knickers – between the finger and thumb of her gardening gloves. 'They were stuck in my gooseberry bush and I'm about to give it a trim.'

Chapter 50

If there was a scale measuring hyperactivity, Perry Ryder Junior would spend most of his life near the top of it.

His stint in Austria – despite supposedly being a time for contemplative reflection – did little to quell this; indeed, he returned more full of beans (mad, bad beans) than you'd imagine possible for a grown man.

Yet, today, now, for the first time since I met him, he has sunk into his seat and is still, silenced.

'I'm really sorry, Perry,' I say, sitting opposite him. 'You know I've loved working here in lots of ways and . . . I'll never forget it.'

'There's nothing I could do to change your mind?' he asks, his bottom lip wobbling. 'A pay rise?'

I think for a second, then shake my head. 'I'm doing this because I believe it's for the best. It's not as if I'm going to a competitor; I'm going because I want to have a go at something completely different.'

Perry straightens his dicky bow, pulling himself together. 'Of course, I understand. And, although I'm always sorry to lose good people, it's not as if this place is going to fall apart!'

'Of course not.'

He swallows, then nods.

'I'd better get back,' I add, standing up.

'Okay.'

My eyes are glistening with tears as I walk to the door, and when I have my hand on the handle, Perry speaks again. 'Emma?'

I wipe my eyes quickly and turn round, hoping they're not red.

'I should have told you this earlier. Much earlier.' He hesitates.

'What is it, Perry?'

'You're brilliant at this job,' he says flatly. '*Really* brilliant. That's all.'

'You did it, then?' Giles huffs, when I get back to my desk.

I nod.

He shakes his head and swills his espresso round his mouth as if it's Listerine, before swallowing it. 'I'm not sure I'll ever be able to forgive you, Emma. How am I supposed to cope here alone?'

'From what I've heard you've plenty of reasons to stay cheerful outside work at least,' I reply.

He freezes, then buries his head behind his computer. Although Giles is reluctant to talk about it, I know he and Cally have seen each other twice since the polo. I'm not sure it's the start of a blossoming relationship or anything so grand. Because while I wouldn't go so far as to say my best friend is using him for sex . . . oh, sod it – I will say it. There's no other way of putting it. Still – until my resignation today – he's been like a different person. He's *happy*.

I open up the script I've been working on and scan through it, eager to tie up the loose ends. But the ring on my mobile interrupts me – and when I pick it up and glance at the front, I realise it's Asha.

'Hi, there, how are things?'

'Emma – I need to talk.'

'Is everything okay?' I ask.

'Yes. No. Look, can you do lunch? I'll meet you at the Egg café.'

The Egg is a Liverpool institution, a vegetarian bolt-hole reached via a creaky, poster-lined staircase. It's pleasantly bohemian, with brightly coloured furniture, vintage art and fantastic views over the city. We take a seat by the window and order our usual: cheese on toast with three salads.

'What's going on?' I ask.

She takes a deep breath. 'We've been spotted.'

My eyes widen. 'By his wife?'

'No, by Christina's old friend, Tara.'

I try to think of something insightful and wise to say. 'Shit.'

'We drove to a restaurant in the Wirral last night, thinking we'd be unlikely to bump into someone we knew there – most of both of our friends live on this side of the water.' She shakes her head. 'It was stupid, we were still close to home—'

'What happened?'

'We went to that lovely place in Heswall on the River Dee. We had a gorgeous dinner. It was the sort of night that underlined how much I cannot be away from this man. How much I love him. How natural and good we are and . . .' She pauses and looks at me. 'Emma, the problem when you have all those feelings is that they make what you're doing seem . . . *normal*.'

'What do you mean?'

'You convince yourself that it's acceptable for things to be the way they are, because so much feels right. Then you start behaving like normal couples in love do. Your guard is dropped.'

'What happened, Asha?' I urge.

'We were coming out of the restaurant, arm in arm, laughing . . . cuddling. Then I looked up and there was this woman. She was on her way into the restaurant with another woman who I now know was her sister. She was standing, gawping at us.'

'Did Toby say anything?'

'No – everyone was too shocked. We just doubled our pace and jumped into the car. Toby looked like he'd had a heart attack.'

'Oh God, Asha. So has this friend—'

'Tara.'

'Has she told Christina?'

'Not yet. She spoke to Toby on the phone this morning – and gave him hell. She says the only way she can possibly keep this a secret is if he dumps me immediately.'

'She's agreed to keep it a secret? From her *friend*?'

'For now – until she decides what to do. She says it's for Christina's sake and not his. And she'll only do it if he gets rid of me, instantly. Which of course he won't do – although he's not going to tell Tara that, obviously.'

I hold her hand as she fights back emotion. 'On the plus side, maybe this will bring matters to a head. Clearly, this won't happen for a little while, so the dust can settle after Christina's dad's death. It's just impossible at the moment.'

A waiter arrives with our lunch and places it in front of us. And suddenly I'm glad of an excuse not to respond.

Chapter 51

'A new job. That's a huge one to cross off your list – you must be thrilled,' says Matt, crossing his legs as he slouches on my living-room sofa with a cup of coffee.

'Yep.'

He frowns, taking in my expression. 'You're not having second thoughts, are you?'

'God, no! The job looks amazing. Did you look at the company's website?'

'I did. And you're right – it looks great. I'm sure you'll settle in immediately. It's really exciting. And there's no doubt you've got a knack for interior design. I love the way you've got this place.'

'Well ... *I try*,' I reply, mock-smug.

He laughs. 'I'm serious. Everything from the furniture to the pictures on the mantelpiece looks great.'

'Technically, I've probably got too many – but I love the pictures of us all before my mum died.'

He stands and walks to the mantelpiece, picking up a photo of my mum on the beach in Wales with Marianne and me when we were tiny. I'm wearing the gaudiest swimming costume in the world and my fringe looks as though it's been cut by someone midway through a game of pin the tail on the donkey.

'She was beautiful,' he says.

'She was, wasn't she?'

'What was she like?'

I shake my head. 'I wish I could tell you. It breaks my heart sometimes. This woman who made me, gave birth to me, loved me . . . I hardly remember a thing.'

'You must talk to your dad about her.'

'Yes, sometimes. It's not the same, though.' I'm suddenly keen to get off the subject – so I sit on the sofa and take a sip of my drink. 'So who's going to make my coffee for me with you out in bloody Iceland for a full week next month?'

He grins. 'Oh, come on, haven't you picked up anything yet? I thought the master taught you well?'

'I'm afraid not, Yoda. I had a go the other day and it tasted like liquidised rabbit droppings.'

He laughs.

'I am *so* jealous, by the way,' I tell him.

'Of what?'

'What do you mean, of what? I mean of your trip to Iceland. I mean of you seeing the Northern Lights. I mean . . . the fact that you are living one of *my* dreams and are totally blasé about the whole thing.'

'Why have you never been?'

I sigh. 'I've never really had the money. My budget for the list stretched to just under £600. With the polo and other bits and bobs, it's disappearing fast – and what's left isn't enough to fund a holiday. Plus, it's not Rob's sort of thing.'

Now that my boyfriend is speaking to me again, it's obvious that anything less than a beautiful plush hotel is simply not worth suggesting.

'Well, you should go one day. You'd love it.'

'I know,' I say glumly.

'Honestly, it'd be right up your street.'

'I know,' I add.

'You've got unbelievable countryside, amazing natural beauty. You can go snowmobiling, ride in jeeps . . .'

'Boys' stuff,' I say dismissively.

'. . . and then there's the unbeatable nightlife of Reykjavik, some beautiful hotels and restaurants . . .'

'Now you're talking my language.'

We both laugh. Then he pauses and looks at me. And, in a heartbeat, says a sentence that I'm convinced I mishear: 'Come with me.'

I carry on laughing. And laughing. Then I stop and realise he's serious.

'Matt, I couldn't.'

'Why not? I've already got a hotel room. You can have the other twin bed.' I try not to blush. 'All you'd have to do is get the flights and some spending money. Admittedly, it's not the cheapest place, but you could come just for a day or two.'

'Matt, honestly, I'd love to but I couldn't.'

'You've got time off before you start the new job, haven't you? Oh go on, it'd be fantastic. I'll be working most of the time, but you could come with me and—'

'Matt!' I snap, stopping him short. He suddenly looks embarrassed.

'Sorry . . . I just thought . . .' He shakes his head. 'Silly of me.'

'No, no it wasn't,' I insist. 'It's lovely of you to offer. Seriously, I'd love to go . . .'

'So what's stopping you?'

There is no way I could go on holiday with another man when I already have a boyfriend who loves me and is prepared to forgive me over the tent business. That would make me a hideous and horrible human being . . . and I am certain that is a category into which I do not fall. I hope not, anyway.

'It's just a bad time – I've got loads on and . . .' My voice trails off.

'No worries,' he shrugs, sipping his coffee. Then he smiles. 'You don't know what you're missing.'

Unfortunately, I think I probably do.

Chapter 52

My final three weeks at work are a flurry of deadlines, panic – and Perry flapping around so much I'm convinced that if he stands too near the window he might actually take flight, like a crazed version of Icarus just before his wings melted.

We're preparing to go to broadcast at the moment, so it's a tense and busy time, so much so that I barely get time to dwell on the fact that soon I'll no longer be doing this.

I'm so busy I hardly see or talk to anyone outside work except to know that Dad goes on two more (crap) dates, Cally and Giles seem to be stealing plenty of moments together and Toby swears to Asha *on his life* that she'll be put out of her misery soon.

On Friday, everyone at the office spills into the pub round the corner, unconcerned that I never even had time to organise a proper leaving do. It turns out to be one of those spontaneous nights that simply wouldn't be as good if it'd been planned. Everyone's been so high on adrenalin for the last week that they proceed to let their hair down so comprehensively, it's simply impossible not to enjoy it.

Of course, it helps that Perry is splashing the cash, buying bottle after bottle of champagne and demanding to know who wants to come dancing. We end up at the Krazy House, a dusk-till-dawn club full of students, blokes who look like WWE wrestlers . . . and Perry. Whose pogoing causes quite a stir.

I slip away before most of the others have left, unable to face the tearful farewells, and bump into Giles on the way out – he's apparently on his way to Cally's. Given that the time is 12.45 – when Zachary will have been tucked up in bed for at least a few hours – it has 'booty call' written all over it. Giles insists she has a plumbing emergency.

'Have fun with your pipes, then,' I say, hopping into a taxi.

I wake earlier than I'd hoped the next morning, my thoughts dominated by the idea of an entire week ahead with nothing to fill it. Actually, that's not strictly true. I'm having a double guitar lesson this week with Rob, who's concerned about my inability to progress from page four of *Guitar for the Terminally Hopeless*. I pad through to the kitchen and rewrite the mental list of things I've been meaning to do when the opportunity arises. Clean the windows. Sort out my sock drawer. Speak to a pension adviser. I couldn't be facing a less exciting week off if I'd volunteered to count the gravel on the drive.

I go to open the fridge to get out some milk and spot my list, realising I haven't yet crossed out 'Gain job as internationally renowned Interior Designer'. The 'internationally renowned' bit might have eluded me, but I think I can count this as a moral victory.

The thought that I'll be in a new job in just over a week sends a rush of exhilaration through me. I close my eyes and breathe deeply.

You're doing the right thing, Emma. You're definitely doing the right thing.

When I open my eyes I look at the list – and at what I've done so far. I'm not doing *too* badly – even if 'sleep under the stars' and 'have a one-night stand' never materialised. And I've at least got a clear idea about how to achieve most by 22 December.

I haven't started the diet yet, of course – it's only the start of November and I don't want to begin too early and risk putting all the weight back on again. I'm planning on a last-minute cabbage soup diet, which is apparently one hundred per cent effective, but does make your bowels feel like they've been attached to a centrifugal air compressor.

The only truly troublesome items now are visiting the Northern Lights and finding the man I'm going to marry, but I discounted the latter on day one anyway.

A car boot slams outside and I glance through the window to see Matt about to get into his car. He pauses and waves. I wave back. As he drives away, my mind starts imagining what it'd be like to sit on a plane next to him, to fly off to an adventure that involves seeing the Northern Lights.

I shake my head. Get a grip, Emma. Get a bloody grip.

Chapter 53

The following Wednesday, something happens in front of *One Born Every Minute*. I've never seen it before, even though Asha never misses an episode and has been trying to persuade me to watch it for weeks.

We've been sitting on Rob's sofa in front of it for forty-six minutes and I can't deny it's more than averagely gripping – even if it's had a similar psychological effect on me as *The Human Centipede* would have on my grandma.

The main protagonist is a woman in her thirties who was clear from the beginning, when she unpacked her bag of candles and whale music CDs, that she wanted *absolutely no drugs*. She's midway through having her epidural now. Ten minutes later, as the baby wriggles into the world and the camera focuses on his lovely, squished-up face, I can't help but smile.

I regret it instantly.

Because a second later I realise that Rob is looking at me. *With intent.* His glistening eyes travel my face, interpreting my expression. And I know, I *just know*, what he's thinking. I am suddenly near-telepathic, such is the clarity and volume with which his thoughts are transmitted.

That could be us one day, Emma.

'No,' I say.

He frowns. 'No what? I didn't say anything!'

I slink down into the sofa. 'Oh. Sorry.'

Rob cuddles up, his big arms round my waist, and I'm almost startled by how physically beautiful he is. From the flawless, tanned skin on his arms, to the immaculate features of his dev-astatingly handsome face. I'm very lucky, in so many ways.

Yet, as we slouch here, flicking through the channels, some-thing nags at me. Am I making too much of the camping trip, a disaster I not only should have predicted but which was caused entirely by me? I knew Rob hated that sort of thing – and the fact he's no good in a crisis hardly makes him a bad person.

But does it underline a fundamental incompatibility between us, the one that made me split up with him in the first place? Oh ... I don't know!

'Is everything all right?' He kisses me on the cheek.

'Hmmm,' I reply, forcing a smile.

'You're sure you're okay with me going away this weekend? I'd much rather be with you than on a stag weekend but he's my cousin and—'

'Rob, it's fine,' I interrupt. 'Of course I don't mind you going away. And you'll love Barcelona. It's a great city.'

He tightens his arms round me and the squeeze feels good. The thought of splitting up with him again makes my stomach knot. And yet, here I am on a normal week night ... feeling wrong. Uneasy.

'Sure you don't want a drink?' he asks, getting up for a beer.

'I'm fine, honestly.'

Rob and I have hardly said six sentences to each other in the hour since the programme finished. We've sat here – cuddling, admittedly – but singularly failing to find something interesting enough to bother mentioning. I'm twenty-nine years old and behaving with this man as if we've been together for fifty years.

'Does it bother you that we sometimes have long breaks in conversation?' I ask when he returns, flipping open his beer bottle.

'Not really,' he shrugs. 'That's normal for couples, isn't it?'

And it strikes me that even if that might be what some couples do, it's not what *I* want to do.

If I wanted to sit here in silence I'd do it by myself. The confusion and contradictions bombarding my brain suddenly overwhelm me. I feel a momentous urge to escape the claustrophobia of this room, and I don't just mean to empty my bladder.

I slink down as Rob shudders with laughter at something on TV, and I gaze out of the window, feeling my heart race.

How *bad* am I exactly – for doing what I'm about to do?

I have a feeling I already know the answer to that one.

Chapter 54

It's been a few months since I was on a plane and the experience does little to quell my unease.

'You know it's compulsory to have a G&T on Icelandair flights?' Matt tells me.

I look round. 'Nobody else is having one,' I point out.

'They must be waiting for us to kick off proceedings,' he smiles, ordering the drinks from the stewardess. She's superhumanly attractive, with a curtain of pale satin hair and ethereal skin – like a Cliniqued version of Galadriel from *The Lord of the Rings*.

'I'm really glad you decided to come, Emma,' Matt says. 'It's my mission to ensure you don't regret this.'

We clink glasses and I look out of the window into a cloudless sky, pondering how impossible that mission is.

I already regret this. I regretted it the second I hit the button to pay for the flight. And I regretted it doubly – triply – during the ominous pause on the phone after I told Rob where I was going while he was away in Barcelona.

I assured him that there was nothing going on between Matt and me, that we were just good friends and that the only reason I was going was that this was a once-in-a-lifetime opportunity to fulfil a dream I've had since I was a teenager. He told me he understood. He sounded like somebody was holding a corkscrew against his balls at the time.

Which only makes me feel worse. It would've been so much easier if he'd flown into an unreasonable jealous rage. As it is, he simply slipped into a *reasonable* sulk, one I feel so guilty about I actually considered calling the whole thing off even as I was going through Passport Control.

On the plus side, I'm literally here for just two nights. Fifty-one hours, to be precise. That's not much, is it? Particularly since Rob's in Barcelona. It's not as if I've left him at home by himself.

I *might* have got away without even mentioning it. Which clearly wasn't an option. Because that would have led to me feeling even more of a bitch than I already feel.

It's a bone-chilling minus two degrees Celsius when we step out of the airport and join a queue for the Flybus. 'I'll be glad to get into the warmth of the hotel,' I say, clapping my gloves together.

'Actually, we're having a stop-off,' he tells me, as the bus draws up.

I frown. 'What sort of stop-off?'

He grins. 'I hope you brought your swimsuit.'

*

272

The only Blue Lagoon with which I'd been familiar was the one in that racy Brooke Shields film from the early eighties. I've never watched the whole thing; I simply landed on it while channel hopping when I was about thirteen. Dad was in the room and I can remember little except making a sharp exit for a fictitious wee at the bit where they get fruity under the coconut palms. In those days (and still now, for that matter), I'd have preferred a masked gunman to burst into the living room than be confronted by the sight of a stray televisual nipple in the presence of my father. What I do recall is that the film was set in the South Pacific, which, despite my minimal geographical expertise, I'm pretty sure is hotter than here.

Matt's suggestion, therefore – that we go frolicking in swimwear *outdoors* – must be a joke. I'd need de-icer to peel off my bikini afterwards. Yet he seems one hundred per cent serious.

'Exactly how many drinks did you have on that plane?' I mutter as I follow him to the entrance of what looks like a very posh spa.

'See you in there,' he grins, heading into the men's changing rooms.

As I pull on my bikini, I get a pang of self-consciousness about the idea of Matt seeing me in a state of undress, especially since I haven't had a chance to fake-tan my legs.

That thought is obliterated entirely by another priority when I step outdoors: I can hardly catch my breath it's so cold. The chill is penetrating; my bones are virtually rigid from it. I only realise I'm not moving – frozen into inaction – when Matt grabs me by the hand and we run to the water, skipping down the steps and giggling as we sink in.

As my body submerges into the silky warmth, it's like entering the hottest, most exquisite bath of my life. I close my eyes, breathe in the clean air and feel a sense of pure, instantaneous relaxation.

'What do you think?' Matt asks.

I open my eyes and take in my dazzling surroundings properly for the first time. Encircled by snow-capped volcanic rocks, we're in a huge pool of steaming water that is totally opaque and the sort of colour you'd get if you mixed Horlicks with Blue Curaçao.

'It's . . . indescribable,' I laugh, shaking my head. 'Amazing.'

'The lagoon stays at an almost constant thirty-nine degrees,' Matt tells me. He's on his back, floating about three feet away from me, as water laps over his torso.

'I've never known anything like it.' My enthusiasm feels insufficient, but I'm in such a state of awe I can do no better.

'I'm glad you approve. Here – follow me.'

We swim to the other side of the pool, to a bank of what Matt tells me is silica mud. He picks up a handful of the creamy white goo and it oozes through his fingers.

'This stuff is meant to be good for your skin. You put it on like a face pack.'

I smirk. 'Go on, then.'

He rolls his eyes. 'I meant for *you*. Beauty treatments aren't my thing. I'm beyond help.'

I pick up a handful and pretend that I'm about to apply it to my face, but at the last second smear a great big blob on his cheek. '*There*. You'll look like Brad Pitt by the morning.'

He shakes his head, suppressing a grin as he wipes it off with mock disdain. 'Thank you *so* much, Ms Reiss. Here we are in these serene surroundings – and you're behaving like it's Splashy World.'

'Ha! Splashy World sounds like my kind of place.'

Matt and I stay in the water for hours, emerging only to cool down occasionally (which doesn't take long, as you might imagine). As we float, sipping a champagne cocktail from the swim-up bar, I can think of no other experience in my life during which I've been so simultaneously relaxed and exhilarated.

And ... something else. A feeling I'm trying hard not to submit to, but which is proving virtually impossible to resist.

When Matt takes my hand, when he guides me through the water, when his skin brushes mine ... I have an overwhelming desire to slip my arms round his neck and wrap my legs round his body. I'm drawn to him in a way that's almost magnetic, watching as he glides through the water, a vision of physical perfection.

It's not just the fact that he's nearly naked, although I can't deny that the taut stomach and bronzed arms help. It's something more than that. It's difficult to put my finger on what it is, except to say this: I'm unable to take my eyes off him.

Hours later, we finally step out of the pool and run to the doors, wrapping ourselves in the fluffy blue towels waiting inside.

As Matt and I go our separate ways to get changed, I make a con-
certed effort not to look at the ripple of muscles in his back. I
push open the changing-room door instead and compose myself.
It must be something in the water.

Chapter 55

There is a problem with the room. I'm not talking about a leaky roof or dodgy tiling. On the contrary, I suspect every room in the Hotel 101 is as gorgeous as the rest of the place. With the stripped floors, uber-cool furnishings and flickering log fires, you couldn't fault it. Except for one fact, about which Matt is mortified.

'Obviously, I'll take the floor,' he insists, slamming his hand against the lift button like he's trying to hold three cherries on a fruit machine.

He turns to me, the muscles on his neck visible. 'Emma – I had no idea they only had double beds. I'm so sorry. I was convinced the booking said it was twin. I've literally never been anywhere on one of these jobs that didn't have a twin room.'

I swallow. 'They couldn't move us?'

'There isn't a single twin room in the hotel,' he says, hitting the button again. 'I'm so embarrassed.'

I shake my head. 'Don't be. It's no big deal. And there's no way

I'm letting you take the floor – this is your room. I'm the one bunking in.'

'That's irrelevant.'

'Of course it's not. You've paid for it.'

'The company I'm working for has paid for it. Not me.' He hits the button again.

'That's beside the point. They paid for it for *you*. It's *your* room. *Your* bed. And I'm happy on the floor.'

He throws me a look. 'The floor is mine. Don't argue. Please.'

I decide not to.

The doors close and Matt and I stand next to each other in the lift with suddenly nothing to say.

The silence is oppressive as I stare hard at the door, willing the lift to have reached our floor and for it to open. I've never yearned more for a piped version of 'Mull of Kintyre'. At one point Matt starts to whistle, then becomes self-conscious and stops. So I rummage around my bag – for nothing at all.

The doors finally open and stepping out involves an odd, elaborate jig in which we try to persuade the other to go first, awkwardly clashing knees like hysterical Irish dancers.

The room is beautiful. There's a Raindance shower. A flat-screen TV. The furniture is confidently Nordic, contemporary and, hell – it's just ice cool. But next to the warmth of the wood floor it has a lovely cosiness. It's perfect.

I insist he takes the bathroom first to get ready for dinner and then go downstairs for a drink before me. That way I can chill out, do my ablutions in private and phone Rob.

At least I try. It goes straight to voicemail.

'Hi, Rob – um, sweetheart. How are things in Barcelona? Well . . . I've arrived safely. I really hope you're well. Missing you already. Well . . . hopefully we'll get a chance to speak later.'

Dinner at the hotel is lovely. The food's delicious. The service is second to none. But something's . . . well, a bit odd.

In sharp contrast to my dreamlike state in the Blue Lagoon, I feel awkward around Matt in a way I haven't since the atrocious circumstances of our first meeting. It's not only the bed situation, although that obviously doesn't help. It's something more.

And I think the problem is with me.

I am stuttering like the exhaust on a vintage Robin Reliant. I am blushing so violently it almost constitutes a pre-menopausal flush. And my flashbacks to the Blue Lagoon are causing the sort of stirrings I only thought possible with a trip to Ann Summers and four AA batteries.

There's no mistaking it. I am developing something I haven't experienced since I was a teenager. A *crush*. A proper bells-and-whistles infatuation. Which is pathetic, is it not?

Yet, I can't deny it. There are times tonight when giving in to this feels sublime, like warm brandy slipping down my throat and warming my chest.

It's only later, in my pyjamas – with Matt on the floor at the end of the bed – that I look at my mobile and see a message from Rob. A message telling me he loves me.

And I can't help thinking life would be much easier if I'd just snap out of it.

Chapter 56

Cally once told me she'd developed a foolproof trick for those occasions when she wanted to stay chaste.

'If you're going out with a man you're crazy about, but you are *determined* not to sleep with him too soon, the key is hair removal. Or non-removal, I should say.' She'd leave her legs unapologetically hirsute, her bikini line untouched and her armpits looking like one of the characters from *Fraggle Rock*.

That way, no matter what carnal urges engulfed her, the shame of her rampantly overgrown fuzz was the ultimate deterrent to going further than second base.

This morning, I wake up trying to work out a conundrum, one I know shouldn't have even entered my mind. I have one more night with these odd sleeping arrangements and there is a reprehensible part of me that doesn't want Matt to sleep on the floor.

I want something to . . . *happen*. Something that results in us wrapped round each other, cocooned in these crisp cotton sheets, his hands—

280

'We're being picked up in ten minutes,' Matt calls into the bathroom as I gaze in the mirror, razor in hand.

'O-kay,' I call brightly. Then I think of Rob. And I glance at the razor. 'Bloody harlot,' I mutter, throwing it decisively in the bin.

Today, Matt and I are heading into Iceland's countryside – completing a three-hundred-kilometre loop known as the Golden Circle – so he can take his first set of official photographs. We're going in a Super Jeep, the necessity for which is not overly comforting. I am trying not to imagine the kind of terrain that requires a vehicle with five-foot tyres.

'It'll be great,' insists Matt as we head to reception. 'I've done this a few times. Just make sure you've got plenty of layers in case we encounter problems,' he adds helpfully.

Given the lack of time and planning for this trip, I was unable to purchase an array of stylish winter gear. What I *should* be wearing is the chic get-up minor European royals swan about in on the slopes of Klosters.

Instead, I have been forced to dig out the C&A salopettes I last wore at the age of fourteen on a school ski trip – and team them with lots and lots of layers. That's *lots*. My attire must have a tog rating similar to the loft insulation they use in the Kremlin during especially harsh winters and, as a result, I am struggling to make full use of my limbs.

Our guide is an unremittingly jolly chap called Magnús and, apart from the 66 North snow gear, he looks in every other way like a Viking: tall, broad, with tufts of dark blond hair and the air of a man who, if required, could be admirably handy with an axe.

Despite it being nine a.m. when we leave Reykjavik, the city is in darkness and will remain so for some time. It's snowing heavily – and horizontally; the roads are treacherous and visibility is so bad we might as well be driving through custard.

Magnús is unfazed. 'Conditions on the glacier were like this yesterday, but we still let people to go out on the snowmobiles. We didn't lose *anybody*, not one. Yesterday was a *good day*,' he grins, giving the unnerving impression that not all days are.

En route to the glacier, we stop at frozen lakes and roaring waterfalls – and as Matt sets about taking photographs, I feel as though I'm in a David Attenborough film, in an icy wilderness that's completely removed from the real world. My real world.

The final stretch of the journey takes us deep into the heart of the country, towards the Langjökull Glacier. And the conditions here make everything else until this point feel like a trip to Disneyland. Even the massive tyres of our vehicle now struggle to grip the packed-down snow as we drive past hazard signs and press on, with nothing but bitter whiteness visible through the windows.

I'm trying hard to look calm and collected – determined to suppress my inner wimp – although it doesn't help that even the Emergency Calls Only sign on my mobile has now disappeared.

'You okay?' Matt asks, as the jeep suddenly slides down into a small ditch and I let out a whoop like a swan attempting to sing 'I Will Always Love You' on karaoke.

'Fine!'

'It's a bit scary first time, isn't it?'

'Oh, I wouldn't say that,' I say breezily, as my stomach churns with unmitigated fear.

It stops snowing briefly as we finally reach our oasis – a series of huts and hangars in the middle of pure white nowhere. In parts, the snow goes up to our waists.

My only previous experience of a snowmobile is the one owned by my Barbie. It was bubblegum pink and she had a snazzy snowsuit that matched, complete with fur-lined high heels.

This one is rather different. Like the forty or so other novice snowmobilers I'm handed a petrol-blue snowsuit – like the clobber you'd see on a Kwik Fit fitter – along with a balaclava and large black helmet.

'They're not going to fire me out of a cannon, are they?' I mutter.

Matt smiles. 'It'll be far more fun than that, I promise.'

Our snowmobile instruction takes about four minutes, which strikes me as being on the short side.

I can barely hear anything through my helmet: I just have to watch the instructor twiddling various knobs and hope they're not overly important. The only bit I do catch is this: whenever the snowmobile turns, you have to 'lift your ass off the seat and push it to the side'.

'Are you going to have a go at driving?' Matt offers, as we head to the snowmobile. 'I don't mind sitting on the back if you'd like to.'

'Oh, you know what – I'll let you do it,' I reply, as if I've given the alternative a second's consideration.

'Sure?'

I hesitate, feeling a flicker of indecision. Aren't I meant to be trying to get braver? I grit my teeth and give the only answer I'm capable of: 'I'm sure.'

We set off on the snowmobile, following the tracks in front of us, and I grip the bars on the back so hard my wrists burn.

'Remember, when we turn, you need to move your bum too, okay?' Matt shouts back at me as it begins to snow again. I drop my visor, but instantly realise it offers zero visibility, so abandon the idea.

'It'd be a lot easier if we didn't bother turning – how about that?'

He laughs. 'That would involve never going back. And there's a gin and tonic waiting for you at the hotel, remember?'

The first ten minutes involve little more on my part than burying my head into Matt's back and trying to stop the driving snow slashing my eyeballs.

There is only one moment when I'm required to do anything – and I do not cover myself in glory.

'Okay, Emma – *turn!*' Matt announces, out of the blue – at which point the instructor's words ping into my head. *My ass. I need to move my ass!* Determined that I won't approach this with the same trepidation I felt at the polo, I raise my bum with gusto and swing it to the side of the snowmobile hard and fast enough to make absolutely certain my nine-and-a-half stones in weight are contributing everything they've got.

And they would have done – if I'd swung the right way.

It's only as Matt leans confidently to the right that I realise which way I was *supposed* to go, by which stage it's too late. If luck was on my side, I'd get away with this.

Sadly, it isn't – and neither is whatever gravitational law of physics is involved as Matt, the snowmobile and I are pulled flat into the snow.

The whine of the dying engine rings in my ears as I realise we've left a shape in the snow like when Wile E. Coyote falls off a cliff.

'Sorry,' I splutter, spitting out mouthfuls of snow.

'It's all right, it happens all the time,' Matt replies, standing and pulling up the snowmobile as an instructor races to our aid.

'Is that true?' I ask, as he grabs me by the hand.

The instructor goes to check the engine, but not before slapping Matt on the back and saying, with an enormous grin, 'I *knew* that'd happen to you one day, my friend!'

For the next ten minutes the snowmobiling seems even more treacherous than before; at least, that's how it feels after my blooper.

Then something changes.

'Emma,' Matt shouts back to me. 'Open your eyes.'

'How did you know my eyes were shut?' I ask, fluttering them open.

'Just a hunch.'

I unbury my head and straighten my back. The snow has stopped and we can actually see. And it's incredible. An immense mountain rises up before us into the bluest of skies, and sunlight streams through the clouds, casting pink light on the snow.

Suddenly, my fear is gone. I feel warm. I feel elated. I feel like I'm on top of the world – and the reality is that I am, near enough.

I hear myself laughing while tears fill my eyes and an overwhelming awareness fills my head.

This is it, Emma. *This* is living.

Chapter 57

What I really want after a day that's flooded every nook and cranny of my body with adrenalin is to sit in a bar, savour my G&T, and work myself up to moving five or so steps to the restaurant over the road for dinner.

But the drink is only a stop-gap.

After a brief return to the hotel room to freshen up and refuel on bar snacks, we're going out in search of the Northern Lights. No matter how fatigued I am, I'm not going to miss this for the world. Even if I'm fully aware that I *might*.

As I'm due to fly home tomorrow, tonight is my one and only chance to see the Aurora Borealis and, although conditions are perfect, the guide tells us there's still only a fifty per cent chance they'll appear. The universe does not boast an 'on' switch for this particular phenomenon.

So we get on a bus, with fifty or so others all dressed in clothing comparable in thickness to a Sealy mattress, and we drive. And drive. Then we get out and look at the sky. But they're not there, so we get in and drive again. Then get out and look at the sky. And so on, and so on, until it is quarter to midnight, minus seven degrees and I am one thousand per cent confident that I will never regain the use of my fingers and toes.

'They'll be calling us back in soon,' Matt says, as we gaze at a sky bursting with stars, but devoid of anything that looks remotely like the Northern Lights. 'I'm afraid I don't think it's going to happen.'

Matt turns to me and gives me a nudge. 'Never mind,' he says sympathetically.

'Yeah,' I reply philosophically.

He frowns. 'You must be really disappointed.'

'Oh, don't be silly – it's been an amazing trip anyway,' I say truthfully.

'Shame about your list, though.'

'I've done things on this trip I couldn't even have dreamed about when we wrote the list.' I suddenly start shivering, a proper dramatic shiver that makes my teeth chatter as if they've been wound up.

'It's bloody freezing, isn't it?' he laughs.

'Er . . . yes.' I grin. I look up at him as he puts his arm round my shoulders and squeezes me into him. I stiffen at first, unable to work out how I'm supposed to react.

Then I can only go with how I feel. And my God, does it feel good. Heat spreads through my body and I snuggle my icy cheek into his shoulder, feeling safe and dangerous at the same time.

When the guide starts calling everyone back to the coach, we turn to look at each other.

'Guys! Come on!'

Matt doesn't move and neither do I.

Swirls of hot breath shimmer between us as our faces edge closer. I tell myself that if he kisses me I won't stop him. I haven't got it in me. I close my eyes sleepily and can feel the warmth from his mouth on my skin as everything around us falls silent.

Sightseers clambering onto coaches. Engines springing into life. Guides shouting instructions. I know they're happening but can hear none of it over the thunder of my racing heart as our lips meet – almost.

'*Guys!*'

Matt pulls away with a start. 'Look,' he says.

I gaze up at the sky and there they are. The lights aren't as bright as I know they can be, but they're definitely there: a pale green swirl dancing in the blackness like a silk scarf.

'It's beautiful.'

Matt smiles. 'Not the strongest display but ... hey, you've seen them. This trip was worth doing after all.'

'Yes,' I whisper, glancing at him. 'It was definitely worth doing.'

Chapter 58

There is only one thing to do when I get back to the room: shave my legs.

I dive into the bathroom and flip open the lid of the bin, only to realise that the maid has been in and emptied it.

'*Noooo!*' I shriek, in a way that would be justified from some-one whose village had been burned to the ground by marauding outlaws.

'Everything all right?' Matt asks through the door.

'Oh ... um – yes. I won't be long,' I cough, rifling through my cosmetic bag in desperation.

I am in luck. Sort of.

There is a razor that's been used several times already and should've been discarded long ago; it's rusting at the edges and boasts several stray hairs sprouting out of the side.

'I'll go down to the bar to get us a drink before it closes,' Matt says. It is now one thirty in the morning.

'O-kayee!' I reply, just as the door shuts.

Now, I'm not an obsessive reader of beauty pages, but I'm absolutely certain that hair removal with an implement that boasts a percentage of corrosion similar to that found in a scrap-metal yard is not recommended practice.

Every movement makes me wince. No matter how slowly I take it, this is doing my skin no good at all. So, with nothing to lose, I decide to adopt the approach recommended when removing a plaster – doing it as quickly as possible in a hope that it lessens the pain.

It doesn't. The result is that, as I tug on my skinny jeans, the limbs underneath belong in a scene from *Reservoir Dogs*.

Dinner last night was strange and I can't say tonight's nightcap is entirely normal either. But in a totally different way. I can't think of a single day I've spent in the company of another human being that I've enjoyed more.

It's as if all the best bits of the time we've ever spent together – the coffee, the play times with the kids, the barbecues – have been condensed into this perfect, distilled twenty-four hours.

So why is something so enjoyable so weird? It's weird because as I sit here laughing, chatting and having the time of my life, it's in the knowledge that I'm letting myself fall for this man, if I haven't already.

And, despite how bad and mad that is – in the light of the fact that I have a boyfriend – the experience is so intoxicating I can't stop myself.

'Will you go out again tomorrow to see if you can photograph the lights?' I ask Matt as we sit in the bar next to a flickering fire.

'Yep – they weren't really strong enough tonight, so I've got another six hours on a freezing coach. Lucky old me.'

'Ah, you'll cope,' I laugh.

'I'm sure. I'm certainly having more fun than I had last time I was here,' he says, then stops suddenly, as if he's blurted out something he shouldn't have said.

I glance at him awkwardly. 'Oh?'

He picks up the cocktail menu and scans it, clearly trying to work out how to avoid continuing. Only, now I want him to continue.

'What happened last time?'

He swallows. 'I was here with Allison. It was when we weren't getting along so well.'

I bite my lip and scan *my* cocktail menu. 'Is your divorce close yet?'

'It'll be a few months before it's finalised,' he replies.

'Sorry, I didn't mean to pry,' I mutter, trying to think of something to lighten the mood.

'It's fine ...' he says, taking a sip of his drink. 'I mean, it's fine you asking about it. It's not fine *generally*.'

I'm unable to think of anything to say. He registers my unease.

'Sorry, Emma, but ... well, as you know, I didn't want any of it to happen.'

I hesitate before asking, 'What happened, Matt? You and I have been friends for months but we've never really talked about it – apart from briefly after your barbecue.'

He takes a deep breath.

'I'm sorry, I—'

'No,' he says, putting his hand on mine. 'I want to tell you.'

I gaze into his eyes, and they've never looked more sorrowful. Then he pulls himself together and speaks calmly, almost as if he's talking about someone other than himself.

'Allison and I had been together since we were teenagers. How often do people say that these days?'

'Not often,' I concede.

'We sat next to each other in sixth form – we both studied geography. I was infatuated, but never thought for a second she'd be interested in me.' He takes a sip of wine. 'I'd had girlfriends before – a few, actually – and, laughably, had a bit of a reputation.'

'Laughably?'

He thinks for a second. 'I suppose it wasn't laughable at the time. I'd done a fair bit of . . . skirt-chasing,' he says with a grin. 'When I was *much* younger, of course.'

'Of course,' I smile sarcastically.

'The point is, the second I met Allison that changed. I was seventeen years old and haven't been with another woman since.'

'Not one?'

'I came close with you,' he smirks.

I blush furiously.

'Anyway, we fell madly in love. We went to university together, got our first house together, got married at twenty-four, had our first child at twenty-six, then followed that up with two more. All by the age of thirty. It should've been perfect. By the end . . . it was far from that.'

'What do you think went wrong?'

'Apart from the other man?'

'Sorry I—'

'No, it's a good question.' He sighs. 'I ask myself that every day and have singularly failed to come up with a satisfactory answer. Maybe we were just too young.'

'You sound as if you don't believe that.'

He shakes his head. 'Not for a minute. Not for me, anyway. Although I suppose one thing I've discovered is that Allison is different from me. I would have happily continued until we had ten kids – I *loved* it. But I think that when we had children she kind of felt . . . well, as if she lost her identity a bit.'

'In what way?'

'Don't get me wrong, she loves our children, she's a fantastic mother. But she gave up work completely and that was a mistake, with hindsight. I think part of the reason for the affair was that she needed to remind herself that she was the same Allison as before. Fun-loving, funny, desirable.'

He looks at his napkin and I realise his knuckles are white. 'I found out about Guillaume from an email on her laptop. She'd left it on and I went to check the weather forecast before a day out with the kids.'

'Oh Matt,' I say, unable to think of anything else.

'The short story is, after tears and recriminations . . . I forgave her and said I'd take her back.'

'That must have been so painful.'

'Not as much as her response,' he replies. 'She didn't *want* to come back. She wanted to stay with Guillaume.'

'Where's he from?'

'Somewhere fairly rural in France – Aquitaine, I think. But he's lived in the UK for years. Now he lives in Woolton, of course, just a few streets from her. And my children.'

I swallow. 'How horrendous for you.'

'It is. To see your kids being around another man . . .' He takes a deep breath. 'It doesn't help that they're not particularly fond of him.'

'I guess that was always going to be the case under the circumstances.'

'I guess so. Josh, in particular, hates him. I think he's scared of him. Part of me wonders whether that's why he's wetting the bed again.'

'At least they don't live together.'

'Hmm. Yet.'

He closes his eyes momentarily, as if he's about to make a confession. 'I can't help wondering if this situation is ever going to feel normal. Sometimes I wake up and expect to roll over and find Allison next to me. It's been nine months and that's still happening. I don't know when it's going to stop.'

'It will,' I assure him. I reach over to touch his hand before I can think about it and we both sit, looking at it briefly, before I take my hand away.

'I hope so,' he continues. 'I've come to accept now that she's never coming back. She's gone, out of my life . . . only not. The ghost of my wife is still there, every time I drop off the kids or she phones me about some school play. I have to look into her eyes – this woman I love so much – and try desperately to stop myself from begging her to come back.'

'You still feel like that?' I ask, realising my voice is croaking. 'After everything, you'd still have her back?'

He looks at the fire. 'She's all I've ever known, Emma. The life I had with her, with our children, that was all I've ever known – and that was how things should have been. For ever.'

We go up to the room shortly after that. I pull on my pyjamas in the bathroom, and when I emerge, Matt has stripped to his trunks and a T-shirt. He brushes his teeth and is about to crawl onto the sofa cushions on the floor, when I feel a sudden urge to reach out for his hand.

I'm not driven by the heat that's roaring through my body. I'm driven by something else: the simple need to reach out to another human being and tell him he's not alone.

He stops and hesitates, then clutches my hand tightly. For a second I don't know what will happen and neither does he. So I take matters into my own hands. I turn and lead him to the bed and we sink into it, and into each other.

My heart is still hammering as his arms wrap round my thin nightclothes and I switch off the light. His cheek presses against my neck and we lie, still and silent, holding each other in the darkness.

The Wish List

I try to empty my head of thoughts and escape into sleep. But, as he squeezes me tighter, a soft pool of his tears gathers against my skin. And I know my mind will be alive with thoughts for many hours to come.

Chapter 59

I arrive back in the UK with several facts at the forefront of my mind.

Facts that crystallised when Matt said goodbye in Iceland and I sat on the bus to the airport, thinking.

The first fact is this. I have feelings for Matt that I now can't suppress. Exactly when things changed between us is hard to pinpoint. All I know is that the growing affection I've felt for him over the last few months exploded this weekend, and I know without question that there's no going back.

I've never felt like this. About anyone. The *do-I-don't-I?* question I constantly asked myself with Rob isn't showing even the remotest signs of appearing. What people have been telling me for years – that you *just know* – has happened.

Which brings me to fact two. And this is the real bugger of the piece.

There is absolutely no doubt that this feeling is not reciprocated, for reasons Matt spelled with perfect lucidity last night.

He's still in love with Allison and he always will be. Although there were times when I thought he was attracted to me, that, really, was an optimistic interpretation – a fact underlined by him spending seven hours clutching me in bed without it leading to anything. Nothing at all.

Despite all this, despite the futility of my surge of emotion towards Matt, I know something else for certain. I hate myself for it, but it was inevitable from the day Rob and I got back together – as much as it makes despair rush through me just thinking about it.

I made a mistake, one I can't undo, one I can't turn time back to fix. But one I've got to act on.

I can't be Rob's girlfriend any more. What I feel for him isn't going to grow. It isn't going to change. As lovely as he is, I am not in love with him. It's as simple as that. And, as horrible as this is going to be, I need to end it. Now.

Chapter 60

I have the noblest of intentions regarding Rob, honestly I do. Despite my urgent need to prepare for the new career on which I'm embarking in twelve hours. Despite the desperate overhaul required for my skin, feet and hair, the latter of which looks as though I've put it on a boil-wash then attempted to tumble dry it. And despite the fact that I am so exhausted from the trip I'm considering prodding myself with a fork to avoid slipping into a coma.

My intentions remain steadfast, as I spin round the flat, depilating, plucking, fake-tanning and laying out my one and only killer work outfit (we didn't do the tailored look in kids' TV).

I'm midway through packing my bag, when my phone beeps. It's a text from Rob.

Can I come over? SO want to see my gorgeous girlfriend tonight. xxxxxx

My heart sinks.

And that very fact – that this is how I react to seeing my boyfriend after nearly three days apart – confirms what I've got to do. What any woman with an ounce of decency would do. I pick up the phone and dial his number.

'I love you!' he blurts out, as if confessing to having tried on my underwear.

'Oh! Um . . . how was Barcelona?' I ask.

He hesitates, taking in my response. 'Good. Exhausting. We didn't take in much art.'

I laugh.

'How was your trip?'

'Lovely,' I reply. 'Really good. Yep.'

He pauses, clearly waiting for me to expand on this.

'Can I come over?'

I swallow. 'Oh . . . I'm shattered. And I've got to get ready for tomorrow. I'm as nervous as hell and—'

'I could give you one of my massages. You *loved* the last one.'

The last sentence drips with innuendo, and I can feel myself physically cringing. Not that I can deny it – I *did* enjoy it. There was a point, before things became so complicated, when I was more than happy to let a gorgeous bloke strip from the waist down and get to work with enough strawberry oil to leave me whiffing of Müller Light.

But things have changed. It would be much easier if they hadn't, but they have – and there's nothing I can do except take the bull by the horns.

I take a deep breath, focus and attempt to muster the words required.

'How about I give you a shout tomorrow?'

I wonder if I'll ever stop being such a wimp.

Chapter 61

You know how, when you start a new job, you're always *really* nervous – but certain you'll be fine once you get there? That's exactly what I told myself as I caught the train to Manchester for my first day at Loop Interiors.

I'm not convinced I was right.

'Hi!'

I look up from my desk and Dee, who sits opposite, has a bright smile as she peers over her computer.

Dee has a perfect snub nose, flawless (if slightly overdone) make-up, and is impeccably turned out in the most painfully sublime outfit I've ever set eyes on.

For five hours, she's sat finishing-school-straight at her desk, tapping away delicately at her keyboard and studiously refusing to recognise my presence, apart from when she's ready for a cup of tea. And getting it is apparently my job.

'I think it's tea time!' she trills, handing over a bone-china cup. 'Less milk this time, if you don't mind.'

'Sure. No problem.' I take it from her and stand up.

The worst thing is, I'm glad to be making tea. Making tea is the most excitement I've had all day. Compared with any other task I've undertaken, filling the kettle is as thrilling as a trip on the Orient Express followed by a scuba-diving session in the Great Barrier Reef.

Because it involves *doing something*. Admittedly, it's not interior design, but it's significantly better than the brain-deadening boredom I've experienced sitting in front of a computer for which nobody has given me a login yet.

I go to the kitchen and flick on the kettle, savouring the moment as I choose the tea bags, for I know this flurry of decision-making will be the equivalent of an intense morning of debate at the Hague – and as demanding as work will get for the next few hours.

I take a deep breath and force myself not to be negative.

No. I need to be something quite different from negative. I need to be pro-active. That's what you're meant to be if you want to get on in life these days, isn't it? *Pro*-active. The alternative, presumably, is sitting on your arse all day waiting for something to do, then grumbling vociferously when it actually arrives.

Well, that's not going to be me. In fact, it *isn't* me. I'm used to an office that's buzzing with creativity, one where people dash about trying to hit deadlines and, when things get really stressful, each other.

I strain the tea bags and take the cups through to the office. I wish I could say the problem was only with Dee, who appears to have been born with a rod shoved so tightly up her backside it's a wonder she ever learned to walk. But I suspect it isn't.

What I was too flustered to notice on the day I came for my interview was that this office has about as much atmosphere as the cold chamber of a morgue.

There is no banter. There is no joke-cracking. And as I discovered the first time I was sent to make the tea, there are definitely no Hobnobs. This is because – with the staff's encouragement – an office-wide prohibition on all foodstuffs containing more than 1.5g of fat was apparently implemented last year. Dee told me this, before removing a celery stick from her bag and taking a dainty nibble.

I walk back to the desks, suppressing an almost overwhelming urge to pluck one of the strings on the harp just to see what everyone does. Then I place Dee's cup on her desk. She pauses from typing and examines it, checking it has the optimum level of milkiness – something I've so far consistently failed to achieve.

After a few seconds she looks back at her computer. 'Thanks,' she mutters, and the sense of triumph I experience is simultaneously uplifting and soul-crushing.

'So ... do you enjoy working here?' I ask, taking a seat and hoping to engage her in conversation.

Except Dee doesn't answer. You'd think I hadn't even spoken. I glance round, wondering self-consciously if I'd only imagined voicing the words aloud.

'Um ... do you enjoy working here?' I repeat, louder this time.

Dee says nothing at first then looks up, startled. 'Oh! Were you talking to me?' She scrunches up her nose so there's a tiny, barely discernible line at the top.

'I was wondering if you enjoy working here?'

She stares at me momentarily, then purses her lips into a funny little half-pout. 'I'm sorry, but I've got a report to finish. I can't stop and talk.'

At which point, she looks down and starts tapping again.

I search my desk, looking for paper clips to tidy, when the door bursts open and Lulu marches in. She heads straight towards me and I grin enthusiastically, eager to show eagerness. To tell her I'm raring to go. To demonstrate how willing and able and—

She sails right past me and swans into her office, slamming the door shut.

I bite my lip and decide to try to muster up some courage. I stand and head towards her door, knocking on it gently.

'*Come in!*'

It is apparent from the second I enter that Lulu doesn't want me there.

'Yes?' she asks. But not in a nice way.

'Hi,' I reply, determined not to be intimidated. 'I was just wondering . . . well, is there anything you'd like me to do?'

She pauses from rifling papers on her desk and looks up. Then frowns. Then smiles.

'Oh, this must be so frustrating for you!' she says. 'I'd hoped to have had some work lined up for you by now but I've been so busy on some pitches I've been putting together there hasn't been time.'

'Can I help?' I offer eagerly.

She glances at her folder. Then looks up at me.

'I think probably best not for the moment. Until you've had a chance to learn the ropes.'

'Will there be an opportunity to start doing that soon?' I ask.

'Of course!' she smiles. 'I've got a packed diary this week and it'd be lovely if you could accompany me on some meetings.'

'That would be fantastic,' I say, relieved. 'Are there any today?'

She turns to her online diary and starts flicking through it, considering each appointment, before dismissing it. 'There's one on Thursday that'd be ideal.'

'Thursday. Okay,' I say brightly. 'So ... what do I do until then?'

'Oh, I'm sure you'll think of something,' she says breezily. 'I really haven't got time to sit down and start spoon-feeding you.'

'No, I didn't expect—'

'Aha! I've got just the thing,' she grins. She picks up a cup and offers it to me. 'Tea. No sugar. And not too milky.'

To be fair to Lulu, I get to accompany her on a client meeting before she'd expected me to – when Thursday's appointment is moved to the Tuesday afternoon. The visit is to a humungous pile of a house near Alderley Edge in Cheshire owned by the boss of a company that supplies Jacuzzis.

You can tell. Because if there's one thing this place has got, it's Jacuzzis. In virtually every room. It's like Rhyl Sun Centre, without the slides. Unfortunately, what they have in spa appliances is not matched in taste.

Which is fine, obviously – that's why we're here.

As I walk through the door behind Lulu, my mind is bursting with ideas for the place; I'm thinking of soft furnishings, colour schemes, gorgeous quirky touches that would really bring it alive.

But what's clear within a minute of me setting foot in here – from the fact that I'm not even introduced to the client – is that I have one purpose and one purpose only. To make Lulu look important.

Which I don't mind. I mean, not at all – she's the boss.

Only, in between my hovering around and carrying her pencil case, I somehow drop what's clearly a major clanger.

It happens when they're discussing tiles in the kitchen. 'They have some beautiful ones in Fired Earth,' I pipe up. 'They have a slight shimmer and I think they'd look amazing with the work surfaces you're considering.'

Both Lulu and her client turn to look at me incredulously – their expressions so utterly disbelieving you'd think a passing Arabian camel had just knocked and offered to do the dishes.

Then they return to their conversation, clearly deciding it'd be best to pretend I either hadn't spoken at all or, even better, didn't actually exist.

That evening, as I find a seat on the train – desperate, for the second night on the run, to get home as quickly as possible – my phone rings and when I answer it I'm so grateful to hear Giles's voice I almost tell him I love him.

'Does Cally like the Yorkshire Dales?' he says, thankfully before I have a chance.

'Hmmm ... everyone likes the Yorkshire Dales, don't they?'

'S'pose. Bit hilly for me, personally.'

'How are things at work?' I ask.

'Oh, you know ... Perry's off his sodding head, we're on the verge of missing another deadline for Channel 6 and the whole place is in danger of going tits up at any given moment. Why, do you miss us?' he asks sarcastically.

And for once I can't bring myself to answer.

Chapter 62

Part of my mission to complete the list involved giving my work and love life a shake-up. So the irony that neither is remotely on track isn't lost on me.

'At least you've seen the Northern Lights,' Cally offers, when I stop at her house on the way home from the station.

'True. It's just my emotional and vocational lives that are a complete mess,' I say, rolling my eyes.

Zachary bounces in from the living room and climbs onto a bar stool, catching his foot against a fraying piece of fabric. Cally's house has changed dramatically since pre-Zachary days. She moved into it because she fell in love with the original tiling on the hall walls, the same tiling that's now rarely without chocolate smeared all over it.

I have seen at first hand that maintaining even the most basic household standards is a battle with Zachary around. Trying to get the house to look like, say, that of an average childless couple would be a full-time job.

And Cally's got one of those – a fairly demanding one at that. So there's only one option: not to bother. The result isn't exactly a scene of total devastation; it's probably best described as a minor natural disaster on the scale of, for example, the eruption of Mount St Helens.

'I can do magic!' he announces proudly.

I put down my tea and feign surprise. 'You can't!' I challenge him.

'Can – look,' he says with a grin, then he holds out two clasped – and clearly already empty – fists. 'Choose one.'

'Um . . . that one!' I say, touching his left hand.

'Ta-da!' he replies triumphantly, and I pull a pretend 'shucks' face as he runs back into the living room.

I notice Cally is frowning at me.

'What is it?'

She shakes her head and smirks. 'Nothing. Look, let's take one thing at a time. What's wrong with the job?'

'Oh . . . nothing, seriously. It's been two days. I need to give it time, that's all.'

'Something's obviously bothering you.'

I hesitate. 'I *thought* I was taking a position as a trainee interior designer. Only, so far I've done no interior-designing and no training – and there appears to be none on the horizon either. I have absolutely no problem with starting at the bottom, by the way. I have no problem with making the tea. I'd just like to do something as well as that.'

Cally thinks for a second. 'It *is* early days. It might grow on you. I mean, if the people are okay . . . That's why I love my job. It's not just the number-crunching, believe it or not—'

'The people are bitchy,' I leap in. 'And boring.'

'Bitchy *and* boring? It sounds like the *Big Brother* house.'

I put my head in my hands. 'They have celery instead of Hobnobs. Hobnobs are a banned substance.'

It's clear that the Hobnobs are a defining factor – she is momentarily silenced.

'Give it a couple of weeks. You might get used to it. And, bugger it – take in some Hobnobs. Start a revolution. It's a breach of European legislation to stop you. It's *your* sodding cellulite so you can do what you want to it.'

'You're totally right. It'll all be fine. I've made the right decision. No doubt about it. Even if there are times when I'd give anything to hear Giles whinging again.'

I look up and realise what I've said. 'Not that Giles is a whinger,' I mutter. 'Not much, anyway. He's got lots of other lovely qualities.'

Cally laughs. 'It's all right, it's not as though it's going anywhere between me and him.'

'Isn't it?'

'Oh no!' she hoots, pouring some milk into a glass for Zachary. 'Don't get me wrong, he's great fun. I mean, he really is. I haven't had this much fun with a guy since . . . well, a long time.'

'Zachary's dad?' I offer.

She shrugs. 'I guess so.'

I bite my lip. 'Do you ever think about trying to trace him?' I ask.

'Zachary's dad?' She takes a deep breath. 'You know I thought about it when I found out I was pregnant,' she replies, although the truth is I don't think she thought very hard. 'These days, it'd be impossible. I don't even know his surname. Obviously, if I knew the guy I'd tell him about Zachary, even though it'd complicate things. Zachary's growing up in a stable and loving environment and I'm doing the best I can by him. Things aren't easy, but my mum's started baby-sitting more regularly and . . . I'm not sure how much good it would do anyone.'

'Have you thought about introducing Giles to him?'

She looks at me as if I've taken leave of my senses. 'God, no!'

'Why are you so certain it wouldn't work out?'

'You know I've always preferred blonds,' she winks and takes the milk through to Zachary in the living room.

When she returns, she's determined to steer the conversation to *my* love life. 'So what's going on with the gorgeous Rob?'

I swallow. 'I'm going to dump him.'

'*Again?*'

I tut. 'I've only done it once before! You make me sound like a serial offender.'

'Once, Emma, was plenty.'

'What do you mean?'

'I *mean*, the second you dumped him, you were consumed by what a big mistake you thought you'd made.'

313

'But it's not working.'

'You said that last time. Before you said you missed him terribly and wished you hadn't done it.'

I cringe. 'Did I?' I ask feebly, knowing full well I did.

'Look, don't get me wrong, *you're* the one who's got to sleep with him. You're the one who's got to put up with him proclaiming his undying love for you. You're the one who's got to go through the *hell* of being treated like a princess and—'

'Are you telling me I *shouldn't* break up with him?'

'Of course not. If you've no longer got feelings for him, then that's settled. You need to do it, no question. I'm simply reminding you what happened last time. If you dump him again, Emma, that *really* needs to be it. You can't keep bouncing in and out of someone's life like that – it's totally unfair. And Rob's lovely, he doesn't deserve it.'

I sigh. 'I know you're right . . . it's just . . .'

'What?'

'You know the trip to Iceland? And Matt? And . . .'

She stares at me as the penny drops slowly. 'You've got the hots for Matt!'

I nod.

'Oh, well, that puts a whole different perspective on things,' she grins. 'I can *totally* see you two together. Of course, the fact that he's got three kids might not make you an ideal match but . . . the point is, he is gorgeous! So what happened in Iceland?'

'Nothing,' I reply, although attempting to stop Cally is like trying to put the brakes on a recently launched ballistic missile. 'It's complicated.'

'Why? Did you flirt with him? You must have. Come on, what happened?'

I hesitate. 'I did flirt with him. I did . . . hope something would happen, awful as that makes me.'

'And?'

'He told me he's still in love with his wife.'

Cally's grin vanishes instantly, as if she's wiped it off with white spirit, leaving a sour pout in its place.

'Do you have to look like that?'

'Sorry, it's just not the happy ending I was expecting to that little short story.'

'Me neither!'

She looks at me sternly. 'Emma . . . what is *the* fundamental rule of falling in love?'

I shake my head blankly. 'That it conquers all?'

'It's *never waste time on men who aren't interested in you*. Because lots of others will be.'

I bite my lip. 'I think he fancies me a little—'

'Of course he does – you're attractive and he's a man. But Emma, he's told you – he's told you to your face – that he's in love with another woman. Forget him. This isn't some challenge you've got to win. You *can't* win. Stick to men who recognise you as the goddess you are.'

I blow my nose. 'You mean Rob?'

'Not necessarily. But *maybe*,' she shrugs. 'Don't fall into the classic trap, as so many women do, of finding men who are unattainable the most attractive. There's a minimum requirement you should expect the man in your life to meet, Emma.'

'What's that?'

'That he thinks *you're* the best woman on earth.'

'Oh . . . why are you making this so hard on me?'

'*Sorree*. If it's any consolation, at least you haven't got things as bad as poor Asha.'

'Why, what's going on?'

'You need to talk to her, Emma. She never listens to me. She needs to get rid of that guy, and quickly.'

Chapter 63

It has now been over a week since I saw Rob and it's starting to become obvious that my excuses are just that. I've simply got to go and see him, to do the right thing once and for all. I only wish I could accurately determine what *the right thing* is after the gargantuan spanner Cally threw in the works.

She was right about one thing, though – my predicament isn't as bad as Asha's.

So, I've arranged to go to Rob's at eight thirty, but stop off first to see how Asha's feeling.

She answers the door like she's trying to pull it off its hinges with her bare hands. 'Come in.'

'Is everything okay?' I ask tentatively, following her to the kitchen, where she picks up a knife and begins to bludgeon some basil leaves.

'I *used* to be a feminist. What the hell happened to that? How did a woman who grew up reading Betty Friedan and listening to Ani DiFranco end up ... a ... a mistress?'

She spits the word out, like salt on her tongue.

'Asha,' I say, touching her arm. 'Come and sit down.'

'I need to make something to eat,' she replies, going at the basil again so violently she ends up with a slimy splodge on the chopping board, like in that scene from *Ghostbusters*.

'Don't take it out on your dinner.' I take the knife from her and lead her to the kitchen table.

'What's brought this on?'

'Absolutely nothing.' She looks up at me. 'I *mean*, he's still done absolutely nothing about leaving Christina. As terrified as I was, part of me thought that when her friend saw us, that might prompt him into action. He keeps saying he needs more time. And I feel like the bitch from hell for even asking him to act. But if he *is* going to do it, surely he needs to get on with it. I mean, I understood about Christina's dad but that was ages ago and . . .'

She slumps back into her seat.

And for the first time since Toby came into her life, my thoughts on him are totally clear. She might love him. She might never love anyone like him. But, no matter how difficult Toby's predicament is, one thing is certain: this is doing her no good at all.

It doesn't matter that Toby is trying to do the best by everyone. He's failing miserably. And if Asha allows it, this could go on for ever.

'If it means anything, things aren't simple between Rob and me either,' I say. I don't know why I feel the need to tell her about what's going on with Rob. But when I've finished, her take is different to Cally's.

'You know what I think, Emma? I think Rob is absolutely gorgeous. If I had a boyfriend like him, I'd never want to let him go. He's funny and sweet ... I'll be brutally honest: he's fantastic.'

'So you think I should stay with him?' I say numbly.

'No, Emma. You either feel it or you don't. And if you don't feel it, you can't beat yourself up about it – you've just got to put everyone out of their misery.'

I sigh. 'Asha, I think we both know what we need to do, don't we?'

She snorts bitterly. 'Are you suggesting we do a double dumping? An *I'll-do-it-if-you-will* type of thing?'

I laugh, but I'm not feeling at all blithe. She continues before I get the chance to reply.

'I don't know about you, Emma – but my decision's made.'

'Are you doing it, Asha?'

She nods, her jaw tensing. 'I've got to.'

I look out of the window as rain pelts against it. 'Me too.'

Chapter 64

Rob will cry. There is no question about it. And I'm dreading it.

As I drive over to his flat, my stomach in knots, all I can think is: I hate this, for more reasons than I can possibly list. I hate it because he'll be excited about seeing me after days apart and, instead of a romantic reunion, he'll get a big metaphorical slap across the face. I hate it because I don't *want* to be a bad person, but feel like Darth Vader poised to slaughter Bambi with his light sabre. And finally I'll hate it because, despite being sure I'm doing the right thing, there's every chance I'll regret it the second the words are out of my mouth.

I pad to his door and ring the bell, half wondering if he's going to be expecting this. I mean, you would, wouldn't you? I've been on holiday with another man (about which I've admittedly spent a long time protesting the innocence) and haven't even seen my own boyfriend since I returned. I don't know how I can sleep at night.

He's smiling as he answers the door, and the words going

through my head are: 'Rob, please don't cry. Please, *please* don't cry!'

His expression changes instantly.

'Emma … why are you crying?' As he guides me into the flat I realise fat, salty tears are sliding down my face, stinging my skin. 'What is it?' He wraps his arms round me as I try to form my words, to pull myself together. But all I can do is snivel fervently, while my nose heats up and my skin pebble-dashes with red.

'Emma … what's the matter with my gorgeous girl?' He lifts up my chin. 'What's happened?'

We sit on the sofa and he hands me a tissue. When I blow my nose it feels like a lump of hot dough expanding in an airing cupboard.

Then I look into his eyes and know that this is it. The moment I'm going to do the awful deed, once and for all. All I can do is stay strong.

'Emma, can I say something?'

'Yes?'

He hesitates, searching my face. 'You need to … um …'

'What is it, Rob?' I ask, emotion swelling up inside me.

'You need to wipe your nose again. You've got a … a bogey.'

I grab another tissue and suffer the indignity of frantically removing stray snot from my face, uncertain, after the procedure is complete, whether or not I've even removed all traces.

'That's better.' He smiles, leaning in to kiss me.

I pull back. 'Rob, don't.'

Suddenly, I don't need to say anything. All the protestations

I'd planned about what a wonderful guy he is and how I'm certain he'll meet someone who's right for him and I know I'll miss him like mad . . . they're about to become pointless.

Because he knows. I'm already breaking his heart for the second time. And I've never felt worse.

Chapter 65

I don't stay at Rob's for long afterwards. He's upset, I'm upset, and there is little point in analysing something that isn't going to change. The fact that he wants to stay friends is about the only consolation in a situation that makes me lie awake all night – thinking about him, then Matt, then me, the last of these being a person I really don't like. Not tonight.

The following day continues in the same vein: staring at a redundant computer with intermittent Assam tea runs for Dee.

When I return to Liverpool that night and drive home from the station, I pull up to the house feeling like my brain has been turned inside out. Matt is outside, heading into his flat. When he spots me, he's clearly about to come over. So I grab my mobile and start talking into it as I open the car door, pretending to be engaged in a conversation comparable in importance to the Middle East peace talks.

'Oh *absolutely*!' I whoop enthusiastically, as I step out and give Matt a cursory wave. 'You're *so* right. Totally. Hmmm.' I nod a couple of times. 'Gosh, that's terrible. Oh I think so. I definitely think so.'

He watches as I head into the house, continuing my fictitious conflab, then I close the door.

My head feels swollen with thoughts as I slump on the sofa and lie down, shutting my eyes.

The darkness doesn't help. It only sharpens my guilt about Rob and my misery about work tomorrow.

Then my mind drifts to thoughts of Iceland.

To my indecent desire as I gazed at Matt's muscular back while he swam through the Blue Lagoon. To my thudding heart as he embraced me in bed. And to the pain in his eyes when he spoke about Allison ...

My eyes jerk open.

All I can do is put thoughts like that *right* out of my mind. I decide to try a relaxation technique, but only tense and release my muscles twice before the doorbell rings. I drag myself from the sofa and head to the door.

Even before I open it, I suspect it'll be Matt, but I'm still not prepared for the dance my heart breaks into as I set eyes on his moonlit features.

'You forgot something,' he smiles, holding out my cardigan. 'You left it behind in the hotel room – I presumed it wasn't a gift for the maid.'

'Ah, thanks.'

'So, how's the job?'

I scrunch up my nose.

'You're not enjoying it?'

'I'm sure things will improve. Besides, that's the least of my worries.'

He pauses, waiting for me to explain.

'Rob and I have split up.'

He hesitates. 'I'm sorry to hear that, Emma. Are you okay?'

His dark eyes dart across my face, and I pray he doesn't try to do something nice, like hug me. I can't bear the thought of a friendly cuddle from him. I had a friendly cuddle that lasted all night when we were in Iceland and waking from that – unkissed – was not a good feeling.

'I'm fine,' I reply firmly. 'Right, I've got loads to do before work tomorrow so . . .'

'Of course.' He takes a step backwards. 'We'll catch up at the weekend.'

'Goodnight.'

He skips down the steps, brushing against the leaves on the birch tree and leaving them swishing in the cold air. The second I shut the door, I want him back, this man for whom my feelings are totally unrequited.

It is that thought – the horrible imbalance in our affections – that inflames the rims of my eyes with tears, reducing me to a mess again . . . just as the doorbell rings for the second time, a minute later.

I wipe my eyes and go back to the hall, returning to the spot where I stood only a moment ago. A volcano erupts inside me when it's him again.

He is silent for a second. It is enough time for my heart to react to the sight of his parted lips under the soft rays of silver light.

'I shouldn't do this ... you've only just split up with someone ...'

'What?' I frown.

His eyes lock with mine. 'I forgot something else, Emma.'

At first he doesn't move; neither of us does. Then he steps forward, bending towards me slowly, sweeping his arm round my back. His mouth draws near as my eyelids dreamily flicker shut. We float into the kiss, brushing lips with a feather touch while my insides blaze and my blood feels like molten lava.

It's a long, long kiss – as sweet as a first kiss, as strong as a last.

In my case, it's neither.

It's simply the best.

Chapter 66

A strange thing happens over the next few days. Technically, my life should be about as cheerful as an *EastEnders* Christmas special. It always has been when work isn't going well.But very little dampens my mood.

Not Lulu telling me I won't get internet access until I've reached a certain (unspecified) level of seniority. Not Dee asking me to refrain from eating an orange because being four feet from the zest irritates her sinuses. Not the anaesthetising boredom, the abominable rudeness of my colleagues, nor the fact that the closest I get to interior design involves buying batteries for the office smoke alarm.

Because something amazing has happened. His name is Matt.

When I'm at work, I spend hours thinking about him.

When I'm not at work, largely, I'm with him. We spend all weekend together. We go to the cinema together. We cook a huge family dinner on Saturday, followed by several games of

Twister (both when the kids are there and – ahem – after they're in bed).

In the five days following that blissful kiss, everything changes. Minor irritations go unnoticed, major catastrophes feel like no big deal.

Obviously, life on Planet Emma isn't entirely perfect.

My guilt about Rob simmers underneath this euphoria, almost constantly. I keep wondering if he'll make contact again – or indeed if I should text or call him. But I don't want to give him hope when there is absolutely none.

I'm meeting Asha for a run on a cold Tuesday evening, and on the way one of the (many) wonders I'm pondering about this unexpected situation is how comfortable I feel around Matt's sons. It's a new and strange feeling, one that puts a smile on my face as I think about it.

Still, I resolve not to be too cheerful when I meet Asha, who I know will have had a difficult week. Not least because breaking up with Toby coincided with a chaotic time at work – her only response to my text enquiring how it went was:

Up the wall right now – I'll fill you in on Tuesday x

But as we set off for our run, it becomes apparent that there is little to fill me in on.

'Let me get this straight, you *haven't* dumped Toby?'

'No. I haven't,' she replies defiantly, as if it was never on the agenda.

'What happened to "I used to be a feminist"?'

She deliberately speeds up, and my thighs are on fire as I try to catch her.

She shakes her head. 'If you just knew what it was like.'

'But you said—'

'I know what I said, Emma. Oh, you don't understand.'

We run along in silence for a minute, before her phone rings and we stop as she takes it out of the holder on her running pants.

'Hi.' I can tell from the way she answers that it's Toby. 'Okay. Yep. I'll phone at ten tomorrow. Speak to you then.'

As she slips the phone into its holder, something occurs to me. 'Have you got a new phone?'

'This is a temporary one. To phone Toby on,' she confesses reluctantly.

'What?'

She sighs. 'Christina found his phone bill and started quizzing him about why my number appeared so many times. So he bought me this one.' She glances at my expression. 'Oh don't look at me like that, Emma.'

I shake my head, too stunned to answer.

'You don't understand,' she repeats.

And it strikes me that she might be right. I've been finding it increasingly hard to comprehend the situation the longer it's gone on.

'He's like a drug to me. There's no point in me trying to defend this. It's indefensible. But I can't keep away from him.'

'Did you *try* to dump him?'

'Yes,' she huffs, her face crumpling. 'I ended up sleeping with him.'

She pauses at the top of the hill, exhausted more by the conversation than the run, and leans forward with her hands on her knees as she catches her breath.

'What a *loser* I am,' she spits eventually, straightening up. 'I know it. Go on, Emma. Tell me that's what I am – I deserve it.'

'Asha, I don't think you're a loser. I just don't think this is good for you. In fact, I think it's terrible for you – and everyone else involved. I want the best for you. That's all.'

Tears gather in pools in her eyes and the self-hatred that consumes her breaks my heart.

'Oh, Asha,' I tut, reaching over to embrace her.

She squeezes me tightly and closes her eyes. 'Thanks, Emma. You're such a good friend. If it means anything ... he really *will* do it eventually. I just have to be patient. Don't you think?'

She starts to look up but I pull her gently towards me again, before answering in the only honest way I can: 'I don't know, Asha. I genuinely don't know.'

Chapter 67

Watching crap telly has never been so stimulating. I am lying on my sofa on Wednesday night, my eyes fixed in the direction of the television, and every nerve ending in my body is buzzing.

The show is the kind of reality tripe that makes it hard to believe whoever devised it invested more than six minutes of their life and the back of a packet of Silk Cut.

I say this, of course, and I am still watching it. Although that's largely because the only thing I'm concentrating on as I lie on Matt's chest is the touch of his hand as he strokes my hair, twirling strands round his fingers as my heart thuds in my ears. I close my eyes and breathe in his neck – then the TV volume explodes.

'WHOOOOAAAAAAAAH!'

I stiffen and focus on the source of the interruption – a woman leaping from a plane at twelve thousand feet. It prompts the sort of response in my stomach that most people would feel only as a consequence of a violent bout of gastroenteritis during a particularly hairy cross-Channel ferry trip.

'That's on my list,' I mutter. 'At least, it *was*.'

'Oh yes – skydiving,' Matt replies. 'I remember you mentioning that. I didn't think I'd seen it on the list pinned on your fridge, though.'

'That would be because I cut it off the bottom.'

He bursts into laughter. 'Why don't you do it?' he asks, as if we're talking about something as straightforward as clipping my toenails.

'I don't think I could, Matt. Genuinely. I decided early on that that's one I'll be sitting out.'

'Well, it's not something anyone can be persuaded to do,' he concedes. 'You've got to really want to do it.'

I narrow my eyes. 'Have *you* done it?'

He nods. 'I did it for charity a few years ago, just after Mum had breast cancer.'

'I didn't know she'd had cancer.'

'She's had the all-clear for a number of years now, although it was scary at the time. Anyway, I raised quite a lot of money. I loved it.'

'Seriously?'

He laughs. 'Is that such a surprise?'

'I'm in awe, that's all. The reason I cut it off the bottom of my list is because I know I'd get up in the plane and refuse to jump out.'

'You *wouldn't*,' he tells me with total confidence. 'No matter how tempted you are to bottle out, you'd go through with it.'

He shakes his head determinedly, then grins and switches it to a nod. 'Very.'

I giggle as he pulls me towards him and brushes my lips with his, making me flutter with lust.

'The boys aren't coming this weekend. They're visiting their grandparents in Worcester. I thought maybe, if you're around, we could go for a drive in the country. Have lunch and maybe a walk afterwards.'

I try not to grin. 'I'm around.'

He hesitates, gazing at me with hot eyes as he focuses on my lips. I reach up, just one degree, and kiss him, my insides swirling with desire. His tongue is gentle against mine at first, until the urgency in both of us takes over and I hunger for his hands on my body.

Matt pulls away momentarily to reach for the remote, mute the television and switch off the lamp on the table next to us.

He plants butterfly kisses on my collarbone, moving his hands to the buttons on my shirt as I throb with longing. I watch as he prises open each button, giggling as he grapples with the last one.

The shirt is discarded. My bra is next. And after slowly constructing a mountain of clothes, we make love for hours, our skin bathed in flickering celluloid light.

Chapter 68

The following evening I pop in to see Dad in the shop. He and Deb are staying late tonight to reorganise the riser-recliners or something – and I can't resist asking for an update on how his date went last night. He was *very* optimistic, so certain it was going to go well, that I was half expecting to be introduced to my new stepmother by the end of the week. Which can only mean one thing.

'She wasn't really my cup of tea,' he says apologetically.

'What was the matter with her?'

He ponders for a second, vexed about the idea of saying something unpleasant. 'She was terribly bossy. And *mean* to the waiters. And ... well ...'

'Not her feet?'

He frowns, clearly disappointed with himself for reaching a verdict that's anything other than kind. 'She had a funny face.'

'Funny?'

'That sounds cruel, doesn't it? I don't mean to be. It's just . . . follow me.'

We enter the back of the shop and he logs onto Facebook on his computer. He only has twenty-seven friends because he hardly uses it, except to randomly and inadvertently 'poke' everyone in his acquaintance each time he's on.

I scrutinise his date's profile pic and come to the conclusion that 'funny' barely covers it. She's had more surgery than a run-over cat.

'How old is she?'

He glances at me. 'She said . . . forty-three.'

I start coughing. She looks closer to seventy-three, even after her skin's been stretched tighter than a Latin American snare drum.

'Here we go!' announces Deb, appearing from the kitchen carrying two cups of tea.

Deb has the best legs of anyone I know – pale and shapely, with a slender ankle that she knows how to show off to spectacular effect. Today she's wearing a wool dress that reaches just below the knee, with opaque tights. It's perfectly nice by itself, but teamed with her red Wizard of Oz heels, it's a show-stopper.

'Emma – when did you arrive, love? Let me make you a cup too.'

'Deb, don't worry. I can't stay long.'

She glances at the computer screen, then catches my eye.

'I've told your dad he can do better than that. Lots of women out there'd snap him up. And he needs to change his username to GeorgeClooneyAlike. I checked on Match.com and it's still available.'

Dad and I burst out laughing. 'Wouldn't that breach some sort of trades descriptions act?' I suggest.

She scrunches up her nose. 'But he *does* look like him,' she protests. 'Don't you think? He's the spitting image.'

Despite the fact that my dad is about as close to being George Clooney's doppelganger as I am to Marge Simpson's, Deb appears entirely serious.

'I'm not *that* bothered anyway,' Dad shrugs. 'I'm happy as I am, all in all. I can't complain.'

'How is *your* dating going, Deb?' I ask.

She sips her tea. 'You always get highs and lows with these things, Emma. And I'll be honest, I've been at no risk of vertigo for quite some time. Some men on those websites are after only one thing – and it's not my knowledge of orthopaedic chairs.'

Dad guffaws. 'At this rate, you and I will have dated so many of those people on Match.com there'll only be the two of us left!'

Deb takes an awkward sip and smiles. 'God help us!'

I get home late and, with Matt working, make do with a ready meal in front of the television, fluttering with excitement about tomorrow. I decide to get an early night and am in bed reading when my phone beeps. I pick it up and register that it's an email – from Rob.

At the top of the email is a link. I click on it and instantly recognise the music it takes me to. It's 'Always On My Mind' by Elvis. The song we danced to when he first said 'I love you' at his cousin's wedding. The song is beautiful, the voice haunting, and, as the music dies, I scroll down to see four words at the bottom of the email:

I miss you, Emma
xxxxxxxxxxxxxxxx

I don't sleep well.

I spend the night tossing and turning, cogitating over what I should do about Rob. The thought that he's hurting, and that I'm the cause, is unbearable. All he's ever been is good to me.

Yet, there's no way to resolve this issue.

The only thing that would make him happy is getting back together with me. But even if things *hadn't* developed between Matt and me, no relationship guru would recommend going out with someone because you feel sorry for them.

The next morning I'm still in two minds – no, about seven minds – about how to respond. After more drafts than the Magna Carta, I compose an email. I have no idea if this is the right thing to do, but it's the only thing I *can* do.

Rob, I miss you too. You're a fantastic person. But you and I aren't meant to be together and I haven't changed my mind.

I'm sorry. That doesn't mean I don't think the world of you,
because I do. Take care and have a wonderful weekend.
Emma x

Every word of that is true. Yet that fact – and the absence of
an alternative plan – doesn't make me feel even slightly better.

Chapter 69

I know it's possible to look forward to something too much. I'm aware that some eagerly anticipated experiences turn out to be about as enjoyable as discovering a verruca. But not this one.

'Have you been to the Trough of Bowland before?' Matt asks as we dart along winding lanes with sunlight sparkling through the trees.

'I visited it for a wedding five years ago. My friend Grace got married in a place called the Inn at Whitewell.'

'Well, someone recommended the pub we're heading to but I've no idea if it'll be any good.'

'I'm sure it'll be lovely.'

He reaches over the gear stick and touches my hand, making my chest flutter. No man has ever had the capacity to do this to me. Not ever. The physical effect of Matt's skin against mine is sometimes enough to leave me speechless.

'Here we are,' he says, removing his hand and changing gear as he pulls into a car park.

We're going for our walk first, to build up an appetite for dinner, so set off over rolling fells and stunning moorland. The place is beautiful, a world away from city life, with forests, hills, rivers and stretching sky. Matt can't resist taking photos – some of which I manage to persuade him *not* to include me in.

After the walk, we eat an early evening dinner in the pub then, given that it's unseasonably mild for late autumn, head to the terrace overlooking the valley to finish our drinks.

'So what's left on the famous list?' he asks.

'Well, I've got the job as an interior designer. I might not be interior-designing anything, but for technical purposes, that one's a tick. I've learned to play the guitar, even if my lessons came to an abrupt end.'

'Ah. That was Rob's job?'

I nod and decide not to say anything more about that. 'I've done the polo ... I'm growing my hair ... the Michelin-starred restaurant ... the snogging somebody famous—'

'Disgraceful.'

'Apparently I *didn't* do the one-night stand – but I'll have to learn to live with that one.'

He smirks. 'Sorry.'

'I also haven't jumped out of a plane and am unlikely to do so. But that doesn't count because I ripped it off the bottom of the list.'

'Cheat.'

'Nor have I slept under the stars, which, given that we're now heading into winter, is *never* going to happen either.'

'So what was the last one? I thought there were twelve.'

I gaze up at him, embarrassed.

'I'm right, aren't I?'

'Yes, all right, Poirot. It was "find the man you're going to marry".'

His mouth twitches. 'I see.'

'But, obviously, that one's been crossed off. Mentally, at least. Who needs that pressure? I'd prefer to be single than spend my life with the wrong person.'

'Quite right. Marriage isn't all that bad, though, you know. I largely enjoyed mine. Until it went hideously wrong, of course.'

He says this as if it's a quip, but there's no fooling either of us. 'Sorry, I didn't mean to . . . That was a silly thing to say,' he adds.

'It's fine,' I reply, too brightly. As an awkward silence lingers, a malignant thought grows in my brain.

I'm not the jealous kind. I never have been. But I'm sitting here falling irrevocably in love with a man who I strongly suspect still adores his ex-wife. One question rampages through my head as I gaze at the setting sun: what am I letting myself in for?

'So, sleeping under the stars,' he says, and I'm glad of the change of subject. 'What makes you sure that one's a dead loss?'

I raise my eyebrows. 'Because it's nearly winter and we don't live in the Seychelles.'

'Hmm.'

'What does "hmm" mean?'

He turns to look at me. 'I've got a bit of a surprise. But I'm not entirely sure how much you'll like it.'

I start to feel uneasy. 'What is it?'

'Exactly how adventurous are you feeling, Emma?'

When I first heard the term 'glamping' I assumed it was something to do with parking in the wrong place – a bit like how Dad thought *TOWIE* was a gadget you heated up in the microwave to keep your feet warm.

Furthermore, after my experience with Rob, I vowed never to go near a tent again, glamorous or otherwise.

Matt has other ideas, despite this not being the conventional time of year for this sort of thing – a fact that makes our host at Walnut Hill Farm chuckle like he's having his toes tickled as he shows us to our yurt.

Mercifully, our accommodation for the evening is much more than a tent; it has a wooden floor, Moroccan rugs, futon beds and a massive wood-burning stove.

'You two are brave!' he grins. 'It's safe to say you're my last booking of the season. I just hope you've got something warm to wear – I've given you all the duvets I've got.'

As darkness falls over the valley, Matt and I – fully dressed in gear similar to that we wore in Iceland – cuddle up in a feather bed directly underneath a big, round skylight.

I have no idea what the temperature is outside, but I've never been warmer. We kiss for most of the night, under a canopy of stars, and by morning one thing becomes crystal clear.

Whatever happens between Matt and me, I know one thing for certain: I'm a gonner.

Chapter 70

Although my obsession with Matt is taking my mind off minor irritations in my life, there's only so much it can do. Because work, frankly, is getting ridiculous.

I turn up on Monday to discover that my chair has relocated to a meeting room in advance of a pitch that Dee's giving at ten thirty. I look round the office to see if there are any spares. Every one is currently firmly occupied by the peach-perfect arses of Loop's other employees.

'Don't suppose you know if there's anywhere else I can sit?' I ask as Dee taps away on her keyboard, like one of those creepy Victorian dolls after an Estée Lauder makeover.

'Hmm?' She fails to remove her eyes from the screen.

'I just wondered ... where do I sit?'

She frowns at her computer screen then drags her eyes to me, pursing her glacial lips. 'I have no idea. I have other things to worry about. This pitch is worth thousands.'

'Is there anything I can help with?'

She pulls another strange face, as if my absurd suggestion has the same effect on the lining of her nostrils as the zest of citrus fruit.

'I don't think so.'

I know some people spend most of their working life on their feet. If I was a trainee shoe-shop assistant, gymnastics instructor, or mortuary manager I'd have no gripes whatsoever.

But I'm not. I'm a trainee interior designer. And not only do I now have nothing to interior design, I also have nothing to put my bum on while I'm not doing it. Even when I plead to keep my seat until ten fifteen, Dee insists that the meeting-room layout can't be disturbed. So I hover redundantly next to my desk while pondering alternatives and realise that there is but one. I head to Lulu's office and knock.

'Come in!'

She holds up her hands before I've opened my mouth. 'I know what you're going to say!'

I hesitate. 'Do you?'

'Yes! I have work for you, honestly. I've got a job that's perfect for you. Tomorrow.'

'Oh,' I say, my spirits rising.

'It's a restaurant – you'll learn lots.'

'Oh ... oh, that's brilliant,' I gush, perching on the edge of the seat opposite her. '*Thank you*, Lulu. I know I'm starting at the bottom and, seriously, I'll do anything at all. I'm not precious. I just want to ... you know, get going. On something. Anything.'

She smiles and links her supremely manicured hands together. 'I know.'

'Is there any preparation I can do? Anything at all? I could research the client, gather some background, come up with ideas . . .'

She drums her nails on a folder, then picks it up and looks at it anxiously. She starts to give it to me. She actually stretches out her arm, poised to grant me temporary possession.

I hold my breath as I reach out and am literally millimetres from it, when she swallows and snatches it back. My hand is left hovering in the air as if I'm practising moves to 'The Robot'.

She places the folder on the desk and smiles, picking up her tea cup. 'Not too milky this time. Okay?'

I meet Giles for lunch in Pret a Manger. Which is a phenomenon I never, ever thought I'd see. He never used to leave the office – I was convinced at one point he was living out of the filing cabinet – and here he is coming all the way to Manchester to see me.

'How do you do this journey every day?' he asks, downing his triple espresso as I unwrap my crayfish salad.

'It'd be fine if the job was okay—'

'I need to talk to you about Cally.'

'Oh. And here was I thinking you wanted to catch up with your old friend.'

He looks at me, momentarily unsettled. 'Yeah, that too . . . but I need your advice. Urgently.'

I can see he does too. He's virtually twitching. There are almost sparks coming off him. 'What is it?'

As he takes a deep breath and looks out of the window, it strikes me how well he brushes up these days. He's wearing after-shave – a pleasant one. And, despite the metal T-shirt, the recent explosion of grooming means he looks, well, *nice*. 'Am I wasting my time with her?'

I can't resist sitting back with a little smile and crossing my arms. 'What?' he asks.

I shake my head. 'I never thought I'd see the day you asked *me* for romantic advice.'

He frowns.

'I'm simply saying,' I continue, 'that whenever I attempted that with you, your advice never deviated from: "He sounds like a dick. Dump him." You never wavered. I could've been dating Daniel Craig and you'd have said the same.'

'I'm sure I offered more insight than that.'

'No. No, you didn't.'

'Fine. I wish I hadn't said anything.'

'Oh, Giles … I'm kidding. I'm sorry. What was the question again?'

'It doesn't matter,' he sniffs, opening his sandwich.

'I'll tell you anything you need to know. I was only jok—'

'I'm in love with her.'

I pause and look at him, realising he means it. And, although in some ways I shouldn't be shocked after the way he's been acting, that, I'm afraid, is exactly what I am.

*

Giles has got it bad. And the fact that he's shaving regularly is but one sign.

I should be delighted for them. He and Cally are two of my best friends and, as unlikely a couple as they once seemed, the idea of them getting together makes me feel warm and fuzzy inside.

Only, there's a problem. He knows it and I know it.

'I'm worried she's using me for sex,' he says earnestly.

'Oh . . .' I try to think of a way of protesting with conviction, but fail abysmally. 'Really?'

'It's obvious.'

'Is it?' The truth is, it couldn't be more obvious if it was a poisonous wart at the end of his nose. 'Some men would be happy with that set-up,' I suggest.

He looks offended. 'I'm not *some men*. And she's not *some woman*. And, like I say—'

'You're in love, I know,' I finish, feeling suddenly very sorry for him – and regretting my flippancy earlier.

'She doesn't want to do things that normal couples do. Apart from *one* thing' – he raises a meaningful eyebrow – 'and she wants to do that *a lot*.'

'What sort of things did you have in mind?'

He shrugs. 'I want to take her away for the weekend. To meet her family. I just want to *be* with her. All the sodding time. Do you know what that feels like, Emma?'

'I think I might.'

'So what do I do? I have overwhelming feelings of love and

affection for this woman ... I'd do anything for her ... and all she wants is my—'

'I've got the picture,' I interrupt, suddenly going off my crayfish salad.

He looks out of the window despondently and I reach over and clasp his hand.

'The difficulty is, there's nothing you can *do*, Giles, not really. People feel how they feel ... that's that.'

'You're not saying I should cut my losses and stop seeing her?' he gasps, horrified.

'Of course not. You need to ... play it by ear, I guess. To see if things develop, see if her *feelings* develop. She *does* really like you. At the end of the day, you're the first man in her life for a very long time. And that counts for a lot.'

'Hmm. But probably not enough.'

I offer to walk with Giles to the station as it's on the way to the office and, as we leave the café, an email arrives on my phone. I can see from the catch-line that it's from Rob – which has the sudden and profound effect of inducing a migraine.

Emma, Aunt Jemima has died and the funeral is on
Wednesday. I know it's over between us, but you got on so
well with her, I thought you'd like to know. I hope you're
okay.
Rob x

'Oh no,' I groan.

'What is it?' Giles asks as we continue walking.

I met Rob's aunt Jemima a few times and she was lovely. I'm sure he's upset, but is attending the funeral of your ex-boyfriend's aunt the done thing? There's no entry in Debrett's for that one. I reread the email and decide to put it in my too-difficult box, for now at least.

'Nothing. Hey, we haven't had a chance to talk about work.'

'I know, sorry. My woes have dominated proceedings,' he says as we arrive at the station. 'Things are pretty intense at work.'

'More than usual?'

'The big pitch for the renewal of our contract with Channel 6 is in just over two weeks. Nobody's very optimistic. The whole team has been working on the proposals, with me and your replacement, Mathilda, responsible for storylines.'

'How's that going?'

He looks at me ominously. 'It isn't.'

'Really?'

He shakes his head. 'God knows what's going to happen. We haven't got a set of scripts ready. We haven't got anything *like* a set of scripts ready. In all honesty, we should be doing a pilot, but nothing seems to be coming together.'

'What's the problem? You and I have produced scores of these over the years.'

He shrugs. 'Maybe it's what's going on with Cally ... maybe it's Perry going into meltdown. .... maybe it's because I've given up smoking.'

'Oh yes! Well done – what prompted that?'

'Well, with Cally's little boy it's not very nice for her to have to go home smelling of smoke, is it?'

'Oh Giles.'

'Actually, it's not that either. I know exactly what it is. It's because your replacement, Emma, is the spawn of Lucifer's loins.'

'She can't be that bad.'

'She talks *all day* and never manages to utter a single mildly interesting thing. She has a degree in child psychology and won't countenance anything in the script that doesn't fit with national curriculum guidelines. I had a week of this before saying to her, "What about *fun*? That's what this is supposed to be about. Is there nothing to be said for *fun*?"'

'What did she say?'

'She pulled a face like I'd started picking my nose and flicking it at the wall in the shape of a swastika. She banged on about how *learning* was fun – and if kids wanted to have *fun* they shouldn't be in front of the television.'

'She might grow on you.'

'Yes, like scabies. Anyway, she's the least of my work worries. I can't see Perry winning this pitch to Channel 6 on the basis of what he's got to show them. It's not that people aren't putting in the work – it's just not being pulled together. It's a mess.'

I frown. 'What's the company going to do if its one and only TV programme no longer has a channel that wants to air it?'

He looks me in the eyes. 'I think we both know the answer to that one.'

Chapter 71

The singing of hymns can be a depressingly lacklustre affair. The composer of 'O Lord My God, When I in Awesome Wonder' may have imagined a soul-stirring delivery, but the reality is often far feebler, an unconvincing cacophony of tuneless, grating tonsils.

As I stand at the front of St Mary's Church, I'm aware of the wobbly off-key drone, and I fully admit my part in producing it. I'm aware of it, but that's not what I'm concentrating on. It's difficult to concentrate on anything with Rob standing next to me and taking an *entirely* different approach from the rest of us.

Clearly, these are not the circumstances in which to give any form of critical appraisal of someone's vocal techniques, particularly since I'm not exactly Leona Lewis myself. But Rob's projection is so loud and enthusiastic you'd think he was attempting to make contact with someone in the afterlife using the power of song alone.

'HOW GREAT THOU ARRRRRRRT! HOW GREAT ... THOU ART!'

If you turned the volume down on today's proceedings, you'd never guess he was making such a racket. He sings straight backed, open jawed, head swaying at the emotional bits.

When the song is over I rub my ear to attempt to delay the onset of tinnitus and sit down as the vicar invites Rob's uncle to the lectern for the eulogy.

Rob looks down at the floor and I feel a swell of affection for him. I reach over and squeeze his hand and he turns to me and sniffs gratefully.

'Mummy ...' says the five-year-old boy behind us. 'This is boring. When does the fun bit start?'

I'd hoped to not make it to the 'fun bit', assuming that Aunt Jemima's wake was what the little boy was referring to.

But as Rob and I leave the church I get swept up in a tidal wave of relatives, friends, family ... the cast of people to whom, in the eight months we were together, he was always so proud to introduce me.

'You don't have to come if you don't want to,' he tells me, gazing into my eyes. 'I'm just so glad you came at all.'

'I wouldn't have missed it for the world,' I say awkwardly, wondering how I've managed to make this sound like a Christmas party.

'Emma, love! It's been *ages*,' says Rob's mum, touching me on the arm. 'I can't wait to have a good chinwag.'

It becomes very difficult to duck out and, as the only alternative is getting on the train to Manchester to go to work, staying at a funeral becomes an oddly attractive proposition.

So I go to the wake and it's that strange combination of merry reminiscing, heartbreaking sorrow, and unnatural amounts of Victoria sponge and brandy.

It becomes apparent early on that Rob hasn't told any of his relatives that we're no longer together.

For some reason this doesn't surprise me, but I don't embarrass him by challenging anyone about it. Besides, I feel weirdly comfortable going along with the lie. Because I miss his family. I miss being a part of them, and Rob clearly misses me being there too.

We leave together and he walks me to the car park as leaves gently weave through a pink sky. When we reach my car, we gaze at each other, trying to work out the appropriate thing to do.

'I'm really grateful you came,' he says.

I look down at my shoes, because I'm worried that if I look into his eyes they'll be full of hurt. 'I know,' I whisper.

Only, when I look up, they're not full of hurt. They look green and lovely and it strikes me for the umpteenth time what a beautiful person Rob is, inside and out. He smiles. 'I'll never forget you, you know.'

And suddenly the statement scares me. 'Why would you have to forget me? We're going to stay friends, aren't we?'

He swallows. 'I don't know, Emma.'

I search his face, waiting for an explanation. Because I don't want Rob not to be in my life. I really don't. If today has underlined one thing, it's that.

He reaches over and holds my hand. 'You know I'd have you back in an instant. You know what I feel about you. But I know it's not going to happen. And . . . today just reminded me how much I miss having you as my girlfriend. This might sound selfish or silly or, well . . . I don't know what. But I'm not sure I can be just friends.'

'But it was you who wanted that,' I protest weakly. 'You'll come to my birthday party, won't you? I'd love you to be there. It's at Leaf on my birthday itself. The twenty-second of December. Please come.'

He looks down. 'I think we need to say our goodbyes.'

I know I have to get out of here. I stand on my tiptoes and kiss his cold cheek, leaving a salty tear on his skin.

Then I get into the car and drive away, glancing in the mirror to see him touching his face. I turn on the radio, seeking distraction, and the song playing is 'Jar of Hearts' by Christina Perri.

'Who do you think you are . . . running round leaving scars . . . tearing love apart.'

As I pull up at the traffic lights it strikes me as a very good question.

Who do I think I am?

Chapter 72

There's a thing I've noticed about being around children. No matter what's going on in your life – good or bad – they have an undeniable ability to take your mind off everything. And, after today's funeral, the distraction of a trip to the cinema is very welcome. Even if, in the event, Joshua falls asleep, Jack goes to the loo six times and Ollie spends much of the film complaining that he wanted to see *Resident Evil* instead.

Afterwards, I suggest a bite to eat – insisting that it'll be my treat, even though I know I'll have to arm-wrestle Matt for the bill until my face is the shade of a ripe Victoria plum. We end up in a pizza place and the kids are in a giddy mood. It's as if the dark, quiet conditions in the cinema have propagated their energy levels, which have now rocketed to a state of hyperactivity and giggles. There is no naughtiness, just excitement. Okay, possibly overexcitement.

Ollie's knife and fork are play-fighting while he provides commentary in an impressive array of voices, while poor

Josh's three-year-old body is doubled up with laughter at Jack's jokes.

It's only when Josh has lost the ability to speak for giggling that I register disquiet on a table adjacent to ours. The couple, in their late fifties, are simmering with disapproval, clearly having hoped that their consumption of a Pizza Margherita in a self-declared family-friendly restaurant would be as serene a dining experience as they'd have in Claridge's.

I glance up just as the woman mutters 'Terrible!' at her husband. Matt notices too – and tells the boys to quieten down. Which they do. At least, they try to.

Unfortunately, not being androids, they don't come with an 'off' switch. Which means that over the next hour, every time one of them dares to laugh, the tutting and head-shaking at the adjacent table gets worse. It's deliberate, it's obvious – and it's oppressive.

'Should we say something?' I whisper to Matt, halfway through. 'The boys aren't even doing anything wrong!'

Matt shakes his head. 'Just ignore them. Don't let it get to you. The kids haven't even noticed.'

'*I've* noticed. You couldn't not.'

By the time the bill arrives, Matt has won the battle to pay and I've offered to watch the kids while he pops to the Gents.

While he's gone, the woman's furious complaining reaches a whole new level. 'Well, thank *God* they're going,' she says loudly, her scrunched-up face like mouldy suet.

I take a deep breath and remember what Matt said, determined to concentrate on the people that matter: the boys. So I laugh at Jack's joke. And I tell Ollie his picture is lovely. It's only when little Josh gets carried away and asks Jack to show him how to make his armpit fart that I forget myself and laugh too – frankly, it's impossible not to.

'*Shhhhh!* Bloody animals!'

Indignation bubbles up inside me. Even in the days when I was terrified of children, I'd never have felt like that, let alone acted on it in such an obnoxious way.

When Matt returns, we gather our belongings to leave. Matt is clearly less bothered about the situation than I am, but all I can think about is how a lovely dinner – the one *I'd* suggested – has been dominated by someone with about as much charm as a picked scab.

I know I'm too much of a wimp to challenge her. So I follow the gang, pretending to ignore her – until she spits out two words after us. 'Good. Riddance.'

As the boys scuttle ahead with Matt, I realise my feet have stopped walking. Instead, I spin round and seem to be marching up to her.

'Hello,' I say politely. 'I'm sorry you've been offended by the children, but this *is* a family-friendly restaurant. They really weren't doing anything wrong; they weren't behaving badly. They were just having a nice time.'

She blushes furiously, her head clearly spinning with comeback lines, arguments, philosophical posturing – until she settles on but three words. 'Just piss off.'

I'll admit, I'm genuinely taken aback by this. 'Pardon?'

'*Piss. Off,*' she hisses.

'Not again, Eileen,' her husband whispers, looking as though he'd like to crawl under the table and die.

I decide this really isn't worth the battle. 'Sure. I'll do that,' I shrug, calmly walking away. Then I hesitate, turn round and address her again. 'Just one last thing.'

I shove my hand under my T-shirt and, recalling the exact technique I used at the age of nine, conjure up the most spectacular armpit fart I possibly can – a loud, resonant and realistic one, the sort that makes heroes of schoolgirls. The woman's eyes look as though they're about to pop out and become a pizza topping.

'Enjoy your meal,' I add sweetly, spinning on my heel and going to join the boys, who look as if they may just explode with pride.

'Sorry if I was a bad influence,' I tell Matt after they've gone to bed. 'She deserved it, though.'

'I can't deny that. Or that the boys think you're the most wonderful woman they've ever met.'

I grin. 'Really?'

He smirks. 'Really. But please don't get any ideas. Promise me you won't be going round armed with a whoopee cushion and water pistol, ready to employ them on anyone who annoys you.'

'Now you're putting ideas in my head.'

He laughs and glances down at his phone distractedly.

'Everything all right?'

'It's playing up, that's all,' he says, shoving it decisively into his back pocket and putting his arms round me instead.

Every kiss between Matt and me seems to get better – just when I think I can't desire him any more, my longing reaches the next level. We slip onto the sofa and the fact that we can't make love because the children are in the house only makes our desire more all-consuming.

I can feel how hard he is, how much he wants me. And as he runs his hands across my buttocks and his mouth explores mine, I've never wanted anyone more in my life.

I leave the house at ten thirty with a whirlwind of lust gathering in my stomach, one that leaves me tossing and turning all night, and continues the next day all through work, going to the supermarket, and a call from Marianne telling me that Brian can't make it to my birthday party.

At just after eight, my doorbell rings and it's Matt again. It's been nearly twenty-four hours since I saw him. Neither of us needs to say anything. We simply stumble backwards into my flat and are quickly naked, wrapped round each other and likely to stay that way for the rest of the night.

Chapter 73

It's only on the train, as I'm reliving the more glorious parts of the previous night, that I start to get a gnawing feeling; my stomach feels like
I've eaten too many Easter eggs, but without any of the actual fun.

As I gaze through the window watching the world pass by, the
occasional thing that Matt said or did starts to sit uneasily with
me. He didn't seem himself.

I take out my phone to text him, but stop myself. Don't start
looking needy, Emma, for God's sake. He hasn't put a foot wrong.
So don't text him. Under any circumstances.

I take out my phone and compose a message.

Hey – how are things? What are you up to tonight? xxx

The problem with situations like these is that something that
shouldn't be an issue becomes one. Before, I never thought twice
if it'd been three hours since he texted; now, I'm consumed with
the issue all morning.

Still, today, for only the second time since I started at Loop, I have something to do. It might be no more than holding Lulu's pencil case while she swans around looking important, but it is at least something. And I am determined to be the best damn pencil-case holder in the north of England.

It has got to the stage when I will do anything to try to persuade Lulu to give me some responsibility and see my potential. So, while I'm conscious not to be too pushy, I've been researching restaurants in the same target market as the one we've been commissioned by, the Quay, and have a notebook bursting with ideas as we drive there in her white Mercedes.

'Lulu, may I ask you something?'

'Of course, what is it?'

'Would it be okay if I played a slightly more *active* role in today's proceedings?'

Her pale-grey leather gloves squeak as she grips the steering wheel silently, not removing her eyes from the road. 'In what way, Emma?'

'Well, I've got lots of ideas for this place.'

'You haven't even seen it yet,' she smiles icily.

'I know, but I've researched other venues, plus I read an interview with the managing director of the company in which he talked about his favourite restaurants around the world. He mentioned Gastro Park in Sydney ... Capizzi in New York. I've got printouts of their interiors and thought—'

'We don't copy!' she trills. 'At Loop we *never* copy! We are originals.'

'Of course. I thought it could help, that's all.'

She purses her lips as I return the copies to my file and look out of the window.

'Oh all right!' she blurts out. 'Add some thoughts, but for God's sake not too many. No offence, but we're charging this lot top dollar for *me*. The boss. They've turned to us relatively late because the company they were using let them down. So we *have* to be good. If they think they're being fobbed off with a trainee, it won't do.'

'I understand,' I reply, too overwhelmed with gratitude to care that my effort would represent a 'fobbing off'.

She sighs. 'By all means, if you come up with something brilliant, go for it. I'm sure it'll be fine. Absolutely fine. No problem at all.' Then she glances at me uneasily, as if gazing upon an unexploded Molotov cocktail.

David H. Jones is sophisticated, successful and – although I'd guess in his mid-fifties – he remains very good-looking.

I know from reading up on him that Jones is known for a number of things: a superhuman ability to turn around failing businesses, a nose for an opportunity and (this one I've worked out without any reading material) the capacity to make Lulu almost wet her knickers on sight.

'It's such an honour to finally meet you, Mr Jones!' she blathers, half giggly schoolgirl, half Playboy bunny. 'Your reputation precedes you! I can't thank you enough for giving us this opportunity! I'm absolutely certain you'll be confident you've made the right choice.'

He smiles, clearly taken aback at the way Lulu is gushing.

'Yes, I'm sure too. I've heard good things about Loop.'

'*Have* you?' she replies orgasmically. 'Oh . . . wow! Well, that is good to know. Gosh!'

Then the three of us stand awkwardly in the entrance of what will soon be a restaurant, and a silence descends.

'So, where do we start?' He claps his hands together.

'Of course!' Lulu starts rifling through her files, thrusting her pencil case at me. 'Perhaps you could show us round first?'

I do a double take as she does this funny curtsey-type thing, like one of the toddler bridesmaids at a royal wedding.

'Sure. Follow me.'

He takes us into the lobby first and there's no doubt it's going to be impressive. At the moment, though, it's little more than an empty shell, one in which builders are hammering away and electricians twiddling with things (as you can see, I'm already learning the technical jargon).

Lulu does not stop talking . . . actually, that's not the right word. *Wittering* is more like it. Yet, strangely, she's so nervous, she's not just failing to say anything that sounds impressive, she's failing to make sense. She simply flits from corner to corner, talking utter, unremitting, bollocks.

The unfortunate effect of this is that, while David H. Jones is as cool as a cucumber ice-pop, Lulu's mood is rubbing off on me. And, having had a head full of ideas on the way here, all I can do is scurry behind, nodding and murmuring my agreement of what, frankly, he'd achieve with more success from a trip to MFI. I've also dropped the pencil case twice, so I'm becoming convinced that I'm not even worthy of that job.

'Where were you thinking of taking inspiration from?' David H. Jones asks coolly.

Lulu swallows. 'Um ... Capizzi in Sydney.'

'New York,' I hiss.

She glares at me. 'That's right! Whoops! I was thinking of Castro Park in Sydney.'

'Gastro,' I cough. 'Gastro Park.'

She gulps. 'Gastro Park.'

He looks at us both, clearly having come to the firm conclusion that he's hired a couple of imbeciles. I glance at Lulu and a dainty bead of sweat trickles down her Botoxed brow.

And despite the fact that I can't honestly say Lulu's my favourite person, I know there and then that I've got to save this woman.

'Any ideas about colour?' he goes on, but by this stage Lulu has clearly lost the ability to speak and turned a peculiar shade that, on her colour chart, would be described as Hint of Puke. We all stand there, willing her to speak, before it becomes painfully evident she isn't going to.

'I have just the thing!' I step in, and Lulu stares incredulously. 'I was thinking blues ...'

'Blue's overdone,' he replies.

'Or maybe greens ...'

He pulls a face. 'Not for us.'

I swallow. 'Reds?'

'Too porno.'

'Pinks?'

'Too twee.'

'Maybe black and white ...'

'Too eighties.'

'Or a yellow ...'

He pauses and thinks. 'Yellow. I could go for a yellow. What's your best shade?'

I rustle around in my folder and produce the ideal colour – a colour I've loved since the moment I saw it. 'Here,' I declare proudly. 'Lemon Turd.'

Lulu's knees buckle.

'What?' David H. Jones says.

'I mean curd. Lemon *Curd* ... Why, what did I say?' I splutter.

'You said ... Oh, forget it,' David H. Jones replies, barely stopping himself from rolling his eyes. 'Listen, why don't you ladies spend some time looking round – we can review things when you've had a chance to put something together in a couple of weeks. Pete!'

He starts waving, beckoning over a guy in a suit and hard hat on the other side of the room. Pete, whoever he is, jogs over, clearly taking the term loyal servant to a new level.

I'm in the process of trying to sort out my folder when Pete appears at our side and his boss asks him to show us round. So it's only when I'm finally done and he asks us to follow him upstairs that I get a proper look at him.

At first, his floppy blond hair and slightly gawky smile look only vaguely familiar. But something about him gnaws at my mind until I come to a realisation: I *know* this guy.

'Have we met before?'

He turns and looks at me, but his expression is blank. 'I don't think so. Unless you live in Chorlton?'

'No,' I reply, shaking my head.

'I've obviously got a common-looking face,' he grins.

Lulu relaxes slightly while we complete the tour, taking notes. She's still hyper enough to single-handedly power half the electricity in this place, but it's an improvement on how she was earlier.

As Pete sees us out, he hands business cards to both Lulu and me, then we shake hands and head back to the Merc.

The second she closes the door, her smile disappears, like gumdrop lips dropped into boiling tar.

'*That* was an unqualified disaster.' She glares at me.

I frown. 'Um . . . I'm not sure – I—'

'You're not sure? Where exactly do you buy this shade of *Lemon Turd* from, eh? The Shit Shop?'

I swallow and look out of the window, saying nothing. After a while a text arrives on my phone. It's from Cally.

Fancy popping round for a catch-up tonight? Zachary's due
an early night. xx

I'm about to respond when something hits me. I take out the business card from my bag and look at the name. The last time I saw Pete Hammond might have been three years ago. But I'd recognise him anywhere.

He's Zachary's father.

Chapter 74

Cally is defiant. 'It can't have been him. You've got it wrong, Em.'

She takes a sip of tea then puts her cup down, unwilling to discuss this further.

'Cally – I'm certain. It is the guy you slept with that night. It is Zachary's dad.'

'Shhh! Keep your voice down.' She throws her eyes up to the ceiling; Zachary sleeps in the room above.

'Sorry,' I whisper, cringing. I take a deep breath and start again – quietly. 'Why are you so sure it isn't him? You didn't see him – and I'm *positive*. I don't understand.'

She waves her hand dismissively. 'Zachary's dad could be anyone. I was a one-woman Club 18–30 resort in those days.'

'You never slept with anyone without using protection. You always said that that night was the only slip-up you ever had.'

She stirs her tea so violently it spills out from the sides of the cup.

'I've got his business card. You could call him up and—'

'I could call him up?' she interrupts furiously, rolling her eyes. 'Just like that? And say: "Hi, you won't remember me but we slept together three years ago. Great night. Would you like to meet *your son?*"'

'I know it wouldn't be easy. But you always said that if you knew who he was you'd tell him. There's got to be a way—'

'It's *not* a good idea, Emma.'

I lower my eyes and dig out the business card, before holding it out to her. She doesn't take it, so I place it on the table in front of her.

She hesitates, picks it up and reluctantly stuffs it in her jeans pocket. 'I'm sorry, Em,' she sighs, rubbing her forehead. 'I didn't mean to snap. Can we change the subject?'

'Of course. Think about it, though, won't you?'

She nods.

'So . . . how are things with Giles?'

She shrugs, then smiles. 'Aw, he's great fun. A gem.'

This lifts my spirits immensely.

She thinks for a second. 'I've been wondering if I should go on one of those dating websites. You know, now I've got back into the swing of things.'

I open my mouth, horrified. 'What about Giles?'

'Giles and I aren't serious, Emma,' she says, clearly believing this wholeheartedly. 'Ask him – he'd burst a lung laughing at the thought.'

I am about to contradict her, when I decide against it. I have a feeling that alerting Cally to Giles's real feelings wouldn't help him one bit.

'Although,' she muses, 'you're probably right. I won't go online – that's tacky when I'm, you know . . . physical with someone else. And, I'll give Giles one thing, he knows how to show a girl a good time. He's great.'

I try to muster a smile. 'He is, Cally. He really is.'

Cally's situation – with Giles, with Pete – isn't the only thing that puts me on edge when I leave her house. It's Matt. As I get into the car to drive home, I check my phone, noting that he hasn't responded to the text I sent at nine o'clock this morning. I remind myself that his phone had been playing up and that *that* could be the reason.

Except this stupid, and probably insignificant, thing causes me to drive home with a head full of thoughts. Of the new low I hit at work today. Of Cally. Of Giles. But most of all of Matt. And how he's never chosen not to reply before.

By the time I've got home – noticing all the lights to his flat are off – and I'm Skyping Marianne, I have considered a vast array of reasons, including one particularly grim possibility.

'Exactly how put-off do you think a man would be if you'd *let yourself go* in the bikini-line department?'

Marianne stares blankly out of my laptop screen. 'I love these deep and meaningful philosophical discussions.'

'I'm serious – what do you reckon? Would you get away with a week's worth of extraneous growth . . . a week and a half maybe?'

My sister looks at me as if I am a small child who has asked whether the moon is made out of Dairylea.

'I would say that if a man had got that far into your knickers he wouldn't be overly bothered about how coiffured you were down there. Should I even ask why you're deliberating over this?'

I scrunch up my nose. 'Probably not. So what else is new?'

'Brian's had a meeting with a TV producer. They're really interested in his script.'

'Brilliant.'

'Of course, you know how competitive these things are so we just don't know what'll happen. But it's really encouraging.'

'Good for him. Sounds like he deserves a break.' I take a deep breath. 'Hey, listen, can I ask you about something – in confidence?'

'Of course.'

'It's about Cally.'

I tell her about my day, about Pete, about my certainty that he's Zachary's father – and, the real issue I want her advice on: Cally's reaction.

'You know what I think, Emma? I think you should just leave it.'

'*Really?*' I say, taken aback. 'Don't you think there's some sort of moral obligation to—'

'No, I don't.'

'Even if—'

'Drop it, Emma. This is Cally's decision. She's Zachary's mother. It's nothing to do with you.'

As I log off and check my phone for the umpteenth time, I can't help wishing that people would stop surprising me.

Matt gets round to texting me at 11.15 p.m. I feel a tingle of indignation. I mean, I could be in bed, blissfully asleep, only to be unnecessarily roused by a man who has failed to make contact for fourteen hours.

I know this is hardly Apollo trying to reassure the chaps in Houston, but that's not the point. Nor is the fact that I've *actually* sat up feeling sorry for myself because the only person who's been in touch is Iain, from Totally Money, asking me if I want advice on ISAs.

Em – so sorry I haven't been in touch. Are you around at lunchtime tomorrow? xxxxx

I bristle, wondering for a split second if I should compose a text saying: 'Sorry, I'm busy.' But the idea of not seeing him is too much to bear, so I buckle under pressure and type:

Yes! Whenever you like! Been anywhere nice? x

'A will of iron, Emma,' I mutter, pressing Send and trying not to analyse what this could be the start of. I never experienced this with Rob, not even a sniff of it. He was the perfect boyfriend in many ways – constantly in touch, constantly attentive.

Perfect apart from the small matter of me not being in love

with him. Something that's categorically the case with Matt. Because despite – or maybe because of – these ripples of anxiety, there's simply no doubting what I feel for him.

It's only at the moment his next text arrives that I realise exactly how potentially catastrophic this situation is. I pick up my phone with trembling hands and read the message with incredulity.

Can't really explain via text – can we talk tomorrow?

It's not that part of the text that worries me – nay, stabs me in the chest repeatedly with a rusty pitch fork. It's the next bit:

I'm over at Allison's x

Chapter 75

I've been meaning to write and send my birthday party invitations for weeks. But I hadn't counted on doing it at six in the morning, after only twenty minutes of sleep all night. I'm dogged with tiredness but buzzing with anxiety as I place each one in an envelope and slam the stamp on it with my fist, like I'm Tom Cruise in the courtroom scenes of *A Few Good Men*.

Eventually, I dress and tackle some chores, before deciding to go out to post the invitations. I'm standing at the letter box on the corner of Aigburth Road, when I hear someone calling my name.

'Emma!'

I spin round and focus on a figure that looks like it's recently climbed out of a skip, shoplifted a designer suit and – judging by the wobbling – lost all use of the muscular tissue in its thighs.

When Marianne and Johnny were dating he was one of the most naturally handsome men you could meet. Until the last two times I've seen him, he's never been less than immaculate.

However, as he runs haphazardly across the road to reach me, he looks anything but.

'Hey, you!' he grins, squinting through red and sore eyes that look as if someone's rubbed salt in them.

'Johnny . . . hi.' I try my best not to look alarmed.

'Excuse the state of me – I've been home for a friend's birthday and it turned into a big one. He was thirty – we had to help him celebrate in style.'

'I can appreciate that – I'm thirty myself soon,' I reply awkwardly. 'I'm just posting my invitations.'

'So how's your sister?' he says, diving straight to the only subject he's ever interested in.

'Fine. She seems to be enjoying Edinburgh and—'

'I miss her like *hell*, you know,' he says dramatically.

'Oh,' I reply, taken aback.

'What's this guy like? The one she's seeing?'

'Brian. I don't know him well. He seems nice enough. She likes him.'

He looks at his hands, swaying. 'I'm still in love with her.'

I open my mouth to speak, but fail to come up with anything appropriate.

'Hey, where are you having your party?' He focuses on the invitations.

'Oh . . . Leaf.'

'*Great* choice. I might pop along if I'm home. When is it?'

'December the twenty-second. But—'

'I'd better go,' he says, and as he leans over to kiss me on the cheek I'm assaulted by a lungful of such powerful alcoholic fumes that if I struck a match I think he'd turn into a human fireball. 'Great to see you, Em. Miss ya lots!'

And, at that, he spins on his heels and bounces down the street, leaving me with a sincere hope that he's too drunk to remember this conversation.

An hour later I'm back home and the bell rings. I answer the door as nonchalantly as is possible for a woman who has been torturing herself all night about what the man she loves has got up to with his ex-wife.

The second I register Matt's face, two things hit me: firstly, how deeply and passionately I feel for this man.

Secondly, how certain I am that my worst fears are coming true. His expression says everything without him having to say a word. The only man I've ever loved is leaving me for his exwife.

'Hi.' Cold beads of sweat prick on my forehead.

'Hi, Emma. Can I come in?'

I nod, determined not to fall to pieces outwardly, no matter what's going on inside. 'Of course.' With a pounding heart, I invite him into the kitchen. 'Coffee?'

'I'd love one.'

Things are instantly weird between us. The tension in the air is acute. The difference from a week ago – when he'd rush in, throw his arms round me, and smother me with kisses – is like a knife twisting in my stomach.

I set about making coffee, searching for a sentence, any sentence. But small talk escapes us both.

'Emma.'

I turn to look at him, but briefly – before snatching away my eyes and taking out two cups.

'Emma, we need to talk.'

The coffee is almost done and I have nothing to do except stare at the machine, my arms crossed. 'You don't need to explain. I understand.'

'I don't think you do. Emma – I was with Allison all last night. We were talking. Some things have changed.'

'I understand, Matt. Honestly,' I reply, hearing my voice wobble.

I pour coffee into a cup and hand it to him, refusing to look at his face. 'It's not as if you haven't made things clear from the beginning. She's the love of your life.'

He pauses for a second. 'I know what I said back then in the summer. It's different now … but – what's this got to do with anything?'

It strikes me that he looks on me – he's always looked on me – in the same way that Cally looks on Giles. I've been a bit of fun. Light relief. Allison's the woman he can't live without. The woman he's loved for ever. The woman who can effectively click her fingers and he'll drop what he and I have and—

'She's moving to France.'

I pause, taking in his words, my head swimming. 'What?'

He looks at his hands. 'I was at the house for hours yesterday, trying to persuade her not to go.'

'But . . . why *is* she going?'

'Things are serious between her and Guillaume. She's decided she wants to make a go of it with him – to start a new life there.'

I abandon the coffee and walk to him, sitting on the chair next to his and holding his hands. They're shaking, cold. My head is suddenly bursting with thoughts – but there's one that smashes the others into oblivion.

'But what about the boys?'

It's then that I see one of the worst sights of my life. Matt starts to cry. This big, strong, beautiful man, spilling out his heart, his life ripped in two. I wrap my arms round him, pulling him towards me, hugging him, desperate to stop his pain. Eventually, he pulls back and wipes his eyes with the back of his hand, then he shakes his head and replies to my question.

'They're going with her.'

'But they *can't*.'

'They can,' he whispers. 'They can.'

'But how would that work? You'd hardly ever see them. Not unless . . .'

My words trail off as my mind burns with emotion and he looks up at me with red eyes.

He needs to say nothing. Nothing at all. And, although it's me who says it, I also know that it's his only option.

'You're going too.'

He swallows, then nods once, before leaning in and wrapping his arms round me, squeezing me tightly.

I feel like I'm never going to breathe again.

Chapter 76

The loathsomeness of work was bearable when I had Matt as a distraction.

Now, all I can think of is him, a man I adore, moving to another country. Which is typical, isn't it? I wait almost thirty years to experience this feeling, this overwhelming emotion everyone goes on about. And as soon as I get a sniff of it – with my next-door neighbour – he has to move to the other side of the English Channel.

I am consumed with unhappiness throughout Monday, unable to think of anything except a future without Matt. That and dreaming up imaginary scenarios that could keep him here: everything from Allison developing an allergy to baguettes to her being denied entry to France for a hitherto clandestine drugs trafficking conviction.

Even the fact that Lulu has finally given me something remotely interior designy to look at does nothing to cheer me up.

She's asked me to source fabric for the curtains in a posh gastro pub in the Lake District, the sort of thing I'd once thought would be interesting. But, as I've quickly come to discover, once you've seen one champagne-silk dupion you've seen them all.

'Emma! We're out of Duchy Originals,' Lulu cries, popping her head round her office door.

I muster a smile. 'I'll get right on it.'

'And I'd like you to pop back to the Quay today.'

'Oh.' My spirits lift. 'Which part of the project will I be working on?'

She turns up her nose, momentarily bemused. 'I left my umbrella there.'

When I arrive at the site, it's quieter than last time; half the workers are on lunch. I tentatively open the door, like one of those teenagers in a dodgy eighties horror film, and wonder where I'm going to start looking for Lulu's sodding Marc Jacobs umbrella.

'Hello!' I call out, as footsteps approach.

Suddenly there he is, in front of me. Pete Hammond. Zachary's father.

The resemblance isn't overwhelming – not to the same extent as Zachary looks like Cally. But the more I look at him, the more I can see it. The blue eyes, the blond hair, the slightly turned-up nose.

'Hi, again. Can I help?' he asks.

'My boss left her umbrella here the other day.'

'Oh. Any idea where?'

'Upstairs, she thinks.'

'I'll have to come with you – it's still a state up there.'

I follow Pete up the stairs with an acute sense that, just by uttering one sentence, I could change his life for ever. When we reach the top, his phone rings and he stops to answer it.

'I'm with someone, sweetheart. Yep, I'll get some on my way home. It's the SMA White, isn't it? Okay – got to go. Bye. Love you too.'

'Sorry,' he grins, ending the call. 'That was my wife. I'm on the baby-milk run tonight.'

'Oh,' I smile.

'There it is.' He points to the umbrella on the other side of the room and marches towards it.

'Thanks,' I reply, and as he hands it to me I'm unable to take my eyes off his face.

'Anything else I can help with?'

I hesitate, as he tucks his phone into his inside pocket again.

'No.' I shake my head. 'That was all. Thanks.'

It's a ten-minute walk to catch a tram back to the office and I reach a shelter just before the heavens open. I sit, as damp and cold as a used tea bag, watching the rain fall in sheets, feeling empty inside.

The tram arrives and I'm about to step onto it when I realise I've forgotten to buy a ticket. 'Shit,' I mutter, scratching around in my purse and realising I've got seventy-three pence to my name.

'Oh God . . .'

I step back from the tram and watch as the doors close and it disappears. I gaze at my suede shoes. This morning they were a shade called Oyster. Now, they are more Regurgitated Kipper.

With my hair sodden, I put up the umbrella and begin traipsing in the direction of the office, a forty-minute walk away. It is the most miserable journey of my life, one that involves relentless battles with traffic and slimy splashes from the gutter, and leaves my toes feeling as if they've been through a mincing machine.

When I arrive at the door of Loop and stand in the lift, a grey pool of water gathers under my shoes. I enter the office squelching like a toilet plunger. For the first time since I started work here, every person in the office turns to look at me.

Lulu marches over furiously and snatches her umbrella. 'Where have you been? I've got a meeting at three and have been standing here waiting.'

She strides off, shaking the umbrella and grabbing her coat. I trudge to my seat, wondering how I'm going to dry out without an industrial dehumidifier, and drop my bag on the desk.

'Do you mind?'

I look up and Dee is pulling one of her septic faces. It appears that the strap from my bag has encroached on her desk – by an inch. I calmly remove it and smile sweetly, to conceal the fact that I'd like to stab her with a sharp pencil until she screeches like a mutilated pterodactyl.

I glance at the clock. I have two hours and sixteen minutes of this working day left and the thought makes me want to cry. In fact, I think I'm going to. In fact ...

It is as I sit with tears teetering on the rims of my eyes, that I hear my phone ringing. I hastily compose myself, sniffing back tears, rain and snot, before answering.

'Hello?'

'Emma, it's Perry. Got time for a chat?'

Chapter 77

When Matt and I make love that night it's as if we're in a bubble, one in which nobody can ruin things, where everything is so right that it's impossible to imagine anything else.

I am on top, our faces inches apart as my thighs squeeze his hips and I gaze into his eyes. He is beautiful to me, there's no other way of saying it.

I sink my lips into his, tasting him, drinking him in. I kiss the sweet skin on his neck and I inch my hips upwards until I'm poised in that heavenly and unbearable position where he's almost, but not quite, inside me. His hands slide up my body as we become one and I groan with pleasure as his fingers run through my hair.

We make love into the night and it isn't only lust that makes me want him so badly. I need to be with him, as close as it's humanly possible to be. Because otherwise I'm overcome with one terrible fact about Matt and me.

That this great thing we've got has suddenly become horribly finite.

*

It is three a.m. and even though I have to be at my desk in Manchester in six hours, I can't bring myself to turn off the light.

'You're going to be exhausted at work,' Matt tells me, brushing hair away from my face.

'I'm beyond caring.'

He tuts. 'I really feel for you having to work for people like that. If you'd gone to another interior-design company it could've been completely different.'

'Maybe. The company certainly hasn't helped. But, if I'm honest, it's more straightforward than that. Interior design isn't for me – not as a career. I love making my home look lovely, but doing it as work – when I *get* to do it – removes all the fun. I took my old job for granted.'

'We've all been guilty of that. It's easy to get so used to something being there that it's only when it's gone you realise how much you wanted it.'

I swallow, momentarily silenced. 'Has Allison set a date for when they're leaving yet?' I ask, leaning up on my elbow.

He hesitates before answering. 'Yes, actually. She told me today. It's the twenty-second of December.'

The contentment I've been experiencing all night disintegrates. I nod and clench my jaw. 'My birthday.'

He lowers his eyes. Neither of us can bring ourselves to comment on that little gem. 'I guess you'll have to look for work out there soon?'

'I started this afternoon. One of my old friends, Patrick, has contacts over there. He put me in touch with a magazine and they commissioned something for an edition in a few months. I've started to do some social media work in French and sent my portfolio out.'

'Good,' I force myself to say, though it sounds as though someone's stretched an elastic band round my tonsils. 'What are you going to do about your flat?'

'I'll try renting it out first, though it's inevitable that I'll have to sell it. It pains me to think about putting it on the market when I haven't owned it for even six months yet.'

He kisses me softly on the lips. 'Emma, I'm going to be here for your birthday. I was intending to go on the same day as Allison but, in the light of the date, I'll postpone it until the next morning. I'd stay even later but I can't miss doing something with the kids over Christmas ... even if it's going to be very different from last year. The point is, I'll be there for your party. I wouldn't miss it for the world.'

I close my eyes tightly, trying to force back the tears, before opening them again and realising I can't.

'Matt.' I squeeze his hand, unable to look at him. 'I hope you understand why I'm saying this but I think it'd be better if you just went when you were intending to.'

Saying goodbye to my twenties on the evening of 22 December is one thing; saying goodbye to the love of my life as well would be unbearable.

'Is that how you'd prefer it?'

I nod. 'It is.'

Chapter 78

If I'd hoped, before I met Perry at a restaurant near work, that he'd become any less mad in the month since I saw him, I'd have been disappointed. His outfit looks as though it was raided from the archives of the V&A and he's gesticulating so wildly our fellow diners would be forgiven for thinking he's attempting to start an aerobics class.

'The scripts,' Perry says, wide-eyed, 'they're *almost* there. Almost. But they're missing a sprinkle of magic. I've made a few suggestions but nobody seems overly keen. And—'

'Perry.'

Perry's mouth slams shut and he looks at his father.

Being in the presence of Perry Ryder Snr is like sitting in front of the Godfather – except I suspect the most violent he's ever got is threatening his son with instant removal of his teddy bear collection.

He is almost totally bald, but for two or three straggly grey hairs clinging to the top of his head, and despite his age he remains a big, strong-looking man. His milky-blue eyes are compelling, partly because I know that behind them is a mind that has enchanted millions of children with some of the most brilliant and original stories ever written.

I'm in the presence of a legend. A genius. A man whose work I watched when I was a little girl and who has inspired every single creative thing I have done since (this is in spite of the fact that the last time we both worked for Little Blue Bus – before he retired and in the early years of my career – I was too in awe to ever speak directly to him).

'Emma, I'll get straight to the point,' he says, putting down his knife and fork. '*Bingbah* has been incredibly successful but, as you know, every major television channel is constantly reviewing things. And we are up for review. The fact that it's been successful in the past isn't enough.'

'Of course.'

'That's particularly the case given the influx of competitors recently. Other production companies, especially overseas ones, can do things more cheaply, often more quickly.'

'But can they do them as well?'

'We can't afford to be complacent. Ratings are unsteady, Emma – and that makes everyone nervous. Factors have combined against us this year. The loss of Sarah McIntyre and probably – if Perry's entirely honest – some lack of direction.'

Perry pulls a face as if he's been sent to his room without supper. 'I was only trying to come up with something different ...'

'You see, Emma,' Perry Snr says, rescuing Perry from himself, 'the thing I've explained to my son is that when Little Blue Bus was at the height of its success, when we were blazing a trail in the industry ... it was a team effort. We had the best working for us. And every one of those people had a clear idea of our aims. That's how we were a success. And that's how we'll be a success again.'

'I see.' I twist my napkin. 'So ... what's your role in all this, if you don't mind me asking?'

'The presentation to Channel 6 takes place a week today. Which makes this one of the most critical weeks in the history of the company. If we don't win this, there *is* no company. I'm the major shareholder in Little Blue Bus Productions, Emma, and although I've taken a back seat, there are times when I have to do what I think is best for the company. My intention is to come out of retirement for limited and fixed period of time. To prepare for the presentation and – if it goes the way we want – to get the next series off the ground. At the same time, I intend to launch the process of trying to find our next big hit, something I propose we dedicate a significant amount of time and resources to. All being well, I will step down at that point.'

'I wish you luck. Little Blue Bus is a brilliant company and it deserves to thrive.'

'I'm glad you think so. Because there was a reason we wanted to see you today, and it wasn't just for a chat. I wanted to ask you what we could do to persuade you to come back.'

At that moment, I think of the hell I've been enduring under Lulu and I want to leap over the table and smother him with kisses. I manage to restrain myself. And instead simply manage: 'Well, it's really flattering—'

'Before you refuse,' he interrupts, 'I should tell you that it's not your old job we're offering you. It's Creative Director. You'd be in charge, Emma.'

My jaw drops so rapidly it almost lands in my starter. 'Me?'

I look up at Perry Jnr and he throws me a wobbly smile. 'It's nothing less than you deserve.'

'Of course, there's a lot riding on the pitch – I can't pretend otherwise,' Perry Snr continues. 'If we don't succeed in persuading Channel 6 to take the next series, everything is up in the air. I hope you think it's a risk worth taking.'

In the history of resignations, nobody has ever done it as fast as me. I quit this job faster than a Serengeti wildebeest on the run from a cheetah, faster than Superman pulls on his tights and, if not faster than the speed of light, then certainly fast enough to break some law of physics.

The only thing faster is the speed with which Lulu accepts it.

'This has been an interesting experiment for both of us,' she smiles, as we skip to the door after I've handed in my notice, precisely twenty minutes after I left the two Perrys.

'Do I need to put this in writing?'

She races back to her desk, rips off a bit of scrap paper from her desk pad and hands it to me. 'Scrawl something on that – it'll do.'

'How would you feel about me leaving early?' I try.

She grins. 'Go for it!'

I grin. 'Thanks!'

And after I've scribbled an official cheerio on a piece of paper, told Dee that she can shove her request for a not-too-milky tea up her perfect jacksy (not really, that was in my dreams), I've grabbed my coat, my bag, and am striding out of the door of this dystopian hell, ecstatic at the end of a not-so-beautiful relationship.

Chapter 79

'Well, I'm very glad,' Dad concludes, duster in hand as he attempts to put such a shine on the mantelpiece that it'd be capable of causing instantaneous optic-nerve damage. 'You've got to feel passionate about what you do. It was obvious that that was the last thing you felt in that place.'

'Do *you* feel passionate about what you do?'

He spins round. 'Of course! Show me another mobility specialist offering seventeen different brands of bath lifts. You don't achieve that unless you do it with passion. Your mum was the same. She approached everything with one hundred per cent commitment, not least raising you girls.'

I smile.

'She used to read to you for hours, you know – even when you were tiny,' he continues. 'She'd recite *The House at Pooh Corner* endlessly when you were still ages off being able to speak. You were a bit of a slow starter, admittedly.'

I pretend I haven't heard the last bit. 'I wish I could remember that sort of stuff.'

'You were very small, Emma.'

'I wish I could remember *anything*,' I say, sipping tea. 'I can't tell you how much it frustrates me that all this information is missing.'

Dad puts down the duster and looks at me, as if the possibility that I feel like this has never occurred to him. He sits on the armchair opposite mine.

'Do you really feel like that?'

I nod, suddenly overwhelmed by how much I do.

'You can ask me anything you want about her – at any time.'

I think for a second, barely knowing where to start. 'What was she like when she was my age?'

Dad looks out of the window and smiles. 'She was beautiful and bold.' He turns back to me. 'Just like you. She loved dancing. And Roxy Music. And gingerbread. And bright red lipstick. And she loved being a mum.'

I smile hesitantly. Because knowing she loved gingerbread and Roxy Music and bright red lipstick still doesn't feel enough. I want to know what she'd advise me to do about Matt. And Cally. And I wonder if she'd think I'd done the right thing about work. I want to know how she spoke, her way of thinking. Was her personality like mine?

'You know, thinking too much about this can get you into a real spin, Emma,' Dad says. 'None of it will bring her back. If *thinking* about someone could do that, I'd have managed it long ago. You have to get on with life. It's too upsetting otherwise.'

'But it's good to think about someone important to you every so often, don't you think? Even if it is upsetting.'

Dad looks at his hands and says nothing. Then he looks up again. 'Not long now until the big day, hey?'

I frown. 'What big day?'

'Your birthday! The big three-oh!'

'Oh . . . yes. Two-and-a-half weeks.'

'How many people are coming to your party?'

'About fifty or so.'

Dad frowns. 'You don't look overly excited. When you were seven you didn't sleep for three nights then almost fell asleep on your own birthday cake. Your hair would've been like a fireball if Aunt Sheila hadn't had reflexes like the Karate Kid.'

'I am excited, Dad, honestly. And it's *so* good of you to pay for this. You really don't have to.'

'All I ask is that you have fantastic time.'

'I will,' I promise, determined not to let him down – even if this suddenly feels like the worst birthday of my life.

Every moment Matt and I spend together now is a moment to savour. Every small thing we do – from going to the park with the children, to cooking dinner – is precious. Because the moment I hit thirty, he'll be gone.

'Any more dating news, by the way?' I ask.

Dad rolls his eyes. 'I'm giving up.'

'Oh.' I feel surprisingly disappointed. 'Have you met someone else who was no good?'

'I wouldn't say that. She looked like Jerry Hall.'

'So what was the problem?'

'I don't look like Mick Jagger.'

Chapter 80

The night before my return to Little Blue Bus Productions, I have a dream about walking in there.

My reception is comparable to that of the Duke of Wellington when he came back from Waterloo – all back-slapping, cheering and cries of how much I've been missed. I pull into the car park with 'Take Me Home, Country Roads' on the radio, then push through the door to be greeted by Carolyn, the receptionist.

'Morning, Em!'

'Morning!' I grin. 'God, it's nice to be back.'

'Ooh, I'm just back from Turkey myself – we must have been on our hols at the same time. Been anywhere nice?'

Giles is already in the office when I open the door and head to my old desk – Mathilda apparently decided to take advantage of another free desk last week, a move Giles is both baffled and delighted by. As creative director, I'll apparently get a new one, although it won't be ready for a while. Not that I care – because I'm astonished to see that the office has been spruced up. It's been decorated *and* cleaned. It actually smells of *Cif*, that joyful whiff of chemicals that's been absent for so very long.

'You won't believe what that imbecile's done to my script.'

I raise an eyebrow.

'He wants me to rework it. I've already told him I've reworked it. How many times *can* you rework something? If I rework it any more it'll go up in smoke.'

He throws an espresso down his neck and I silently switch on my computer.

'And another thing.'

'Yes?'

He smiles. 'I'm so glad you're back.'

In some ways, work is a blessed relief from my personal life over the next couple of days. It's still pandemonium, of course – a frenzy of stress, turmoil and creative wrangles capable of resulting in GBH charges.

Despite this, working at Little Blue Bus is more enjoyable than I ever remembered. It's as if the sheer joy of the job has returned tenfold – and is every bit as exhilarating as in the early days. Despite Giles's warning, I even got on with Mathilda, before she went off sick with stress and handed in her notice.

I can't deny I'm feeling the pressure too. As creative director, the buck stops with me. I've never even had a buck before. This is the most scared I've been since a power cut during *The Woman In Black*, when I screamed like I was undergoing open-heart surgery with Germolene as the anaesthetic.

Yet, I love it. I love it so much that I have to remind myself how serious our situation is. If we don't win the pitch next week, I and everyone else could be out of here faster than we can pocket our P45s and ask directions to the Job Centre.

Of course, the one issue that's constantly at the back of my mind – the thing from which I need a distraction – is Matt.

Every moment of my spare time is spent with him and even when he's doing something as mundane as watering the plants on his kitchen windowsill, I can barely keep my hands off him. Not in a sexual way, you understand. Well, okay, *sometimes* in a sexual way. The point is, for the first time in my life I find myself constantly needing to kiss someone's skin, or feel his hand clutching mine, or stroke his cheek or ear or . . . just about everywhere, if I'm honest. It's as if my hands have a life of their own and are making the most of every inch of him before they're unable to touch him again.

On Sunday afternoon, he is packing all his worldly goods into the boxes from which they came less than six months ago. I spend the morning helping, but when Marianne – who's home for the weekend – phones to ask me to the cinema with the girls that afternoon, Matt insists that I leave the dirty work to him. Clearly, he wants to save my poor, reddened eyes from further torture.

Woolton Picture House is tucked away in a side street of what is unquestionably Liverpool's prettiest village – a conservation area of beautifully preserved terraces, with a Victorian swimming pool and lovely old-fashioned pubs.

I've loved coming to this cinema ever since Dad brought Marianne and me to see a rerun of the *Wizard of Oz* when we were little. It's how cinemas used to be – an art deco palace complete with retro music at the start and an ice-cream lady in the interval (yes, there's one of those too).

We're here for one of their classic film afternoons, even though I'm not normally an enthusiast – anything pre-*Dirty Dancing* leaves me a little cold. However, my sister's suggestion, Hitchcock's 1940s version of *Rebecca*, is brilliant. It's one of the most chilling and compelling movies I've seen.

Afterwards, we drive to a pub next to the river to grab a quick drink before heading home.

'That was an exceptionally good way to spend a Sunday afternoon,' says Asha as we step out of the car.

'Wasn't Olivier something special?' agrees Marianne. 'They don't make stars like they used to.'

'People might say that about Justin Bieber one day,' I reply, only, as I turn to Asha, I realise I've lost her. I mean, really lost her. She dropped back several steps ago and is frozen to the spot, gazing at the opposite side of the large car park.

'What is it, Asha?' asks Cally, at which point Asha ducks behind a car, as if instigating the first game of cat and mouse we've played since the days when we wore gingham every day. 'Get down,' she hisses.

We all look at each other, bemused, before crouching behind her.

'Look,' she says in a choked whisper.

I peep round the car and focus on what's caught her attention.

It's Toby. And he's not alone. The love of Asha's life has a little boy on his shoulders. Next to him is a woman I recognise as his wife, Christina, holding hands with a small girl. They're a bundle of giggles, chatter, swinging hands – like real-life Boden models, a deliriously gorgeous representation of family life.

It's a vision that's so far removed from the description of domestic misery Asha has described it's almost impossible to believe these are the same people.

'Shit,' mutters Cally.

I turn to look at Asha and it's immediately apparent that this image isn't one she expected either. Her face has turned an insipid shade, the sort of tone no skin should have while its owner is still breathing.

Asha can't bring herself to speak – and I'm pondering what I can say to break the silence when Toby lifts the boy down from his shoulders and places his arm round his wife, stroking her belly and smiling tenderly as she says something.

He takes out his keys and unlocks the car, kissing her on the lips then gathering up the children and piling them into the back. They are gone before Asha has caught her breath.

It's a snapshot, of course. It's feasible that we've caught them at an exceptional moment. They could have just won the lottery and put down a deposit on a starter villa in St Lucia for all we know. It doesn't matter. This fleeting moment has smashed into a million pieces the picture Toby painted Asha; the one she painted us.

'Oh Asha,' Cally says, placing her hand on our friend's shoulder. Asha's face is a picture of dejection, her eyes dull with confusion and unfolding realisation. 'Sweetheart, you always knew he had a family,' she adds softly.

She nods, fixing her gaze on the middle distance, her jaw clenched.

'I'm sorry,' Marianne adds.

I put my arm round her, her hunched shoulders trembling under my touch as she covers her face with her hands. It's a terrible sight. My beautiful, brave friend – former teen peace activist and the tough-as-nails linchpin of a centre that's helped thousands of women – reduced to this.

It's obvious none of us know quite what to say or do, not yet. We all know it'll be the start of an evening of tears and consolation, one that'll involve wine, recriminations and enough slagging off to leave Toby's ears in flames.

But, for now, it's hard to know what to say.

'Asha, I'm so sor—'

Before my words have escaped, something changes. Her back straightens. She fills her lungs with cold sea air, wipes salty tears from her cheeks and turns to us with burning eyes.

'So am I. Truly.'

She opens her bag and produces a mobile phone, the one Toby bought her. Sniffing back tears, she sets about composing a text with shaking hands as she marches to the railings of the promenade, wind whipping back her tears. Cally and I follow and reach her side as she presses Send.

'Are you okay?' Cally asks.

Asha looks at the phone and nods, her expression giving away nothing. Then she leans back with her arm stretched out behind her, in the stance of the teenage athlete she once was. When she lets go of the mobile, it hurtles through the air like a torpedo – until it crashes into the water and sinks, gone for ever.

'What did your text say?' I ask.

She replies through quivering lips. '"It's over."'

And, for the first time, I'm actually convinced it is.

Chapter 81

'I really feel for Asha,' says Cally, slumping on her kitchen chair. Asha insisted on being alone for a little while. So Marianne and I dropped her off at home before driving over to Cally's place to say hello to Cally's mum, who'd taken Zachary for a pizza while we were out. Now that she's left – and Zachary's in bed – one subject dominates the conversation. 'I know I've given her a hard time about Toby, but today was awful.'

'I think she needed to see that, horrendous as it was,' Marianne points outs.

'And at least she's done the right thing,' I add. 'I think he's out of her life now – his poor wife doesn't have that luxury.'

Marianne pushes out her chair and stands up. 'Cally, can I use your loo?'

'Of course. You know where it is.'

As Marianne disappears upstairs, I take the opportunity to bring up a subject that's been on my mind since the start of the week. 'I saw Pete again.'

Cally freezes. 'You didn't say anything, did you?'

'Of course not. I suppose . . . I wondered if you'd put any more thought into it?'

She gets up and goes to fill the kettle. 'Em, can we drop this? It's more complicated than you think.'

I look at my hands. 'Obviously, it's your call. You're probably right. But I need to tell you, Cally, that I was with Dad the other day, talking about my mum. There are a million things I want to know about her that I can't know because she's gone. Tiny things, from the perfume she wore to whether she liked *Gone with the Wind*. The idea that Zachary's not going to know about his own father when potentially he *could*—'

I hear a rustle and realise Marianne is at the door. I stop talking instantly, looking as guilty as if I were a vegetarian clutching a bacon roll at two in the morning, and glance at Cally, expecting her to change the subject. She simply stares at Marianne.

'Shall I tell her?' Cally asks my sister.

'Tell me what?' I look between the two of them.

Marianne sits down and nods. Cally joins her. And it's patently obvious that they both know something I don't.

'Zachary's father, Emma . . . it's not Pete,' Cally tells me.

I frown. 'So who is it?'

She takes a deep breath and her jaw tenses as she looks at Marianne. 'It's Johnny.'

I'd always considered myself a good judge of character. Now I'm starting to think my people radar is about as effective as candyfloss toothpaste.

I glance at Marianne incredulously. 'Johnny cheated? With *Cally?*' I turn to Cally furiously.

'I didn't cheat,' she protests as I feel rising indignation on Marianne's behalf. 'It wasn't like that. It was—'

'She *didn't*,' Marianne interrupts. 'Zachary was conceived while Johnny and I weren't together. That three months we had apart in the summer of 2009.'

'I'm not proud of it, Emma, believe me,' Cally protests, rubbing her head. 'It happened when I bumped into Johnny one Friday night in Liverpool while I was out with work. He was home for the weekend and we stumbled across each other in a bar in Slater Street. I was drunk. And I convinced myself it was okay because he and Marianne had split up a couple of months earlier. I didn't know they were going to get back together.'

I say nothing, but feel anger rising inside me. The fact that Marianne and Johnny had technically broken up might be a relevant factor – but doesn't let Cally off the hook entirely as far as I'm concerned.

'You must've known there was a chance they'd get back together,' I point out. Cally drops her eyes.

'Don't give her a hard time, Emma,' Marianne tells me. 'She and I went through all this twelve months ago. I don't feel resentful, I promise you.'

'What happened twelve months ago?' I ask.

Marianne takes a deep breath. 'That was when I found out.'

'Before then I'd told no one who Zachary's father was,' Cally tells me. 'There were two reasons for that. The first was because

Johnny convinced me not to. He wanted nothing to do with our baby from the beginning, particularly given that he and Marianne had just got back together when I found out I was pregnant. The second was precisely *because* they were a couple again. As much as I thought Johnny was a tosser for wanting nothing to do with me or the baby, I didn't want to ruin things for Marianne.'

'What happened last December?' I repeat.

Cally looks at her hands. 'As time went on, I made several attempts to contact Johnny, to change his mind about seeing Zachary – about even recognising his existence. He ignored them all. Then, in the run-up to Christmas, I started to feel a real sense of injustice. It wasn't even about any maintenance I was entitled to – which I've never had. But Zachary *did* exist, whether Johnny liked it or not.'

'What did you do?'

'I thought if I could go and speak to him face to face, it would help. I took the day off work while Zachary was at nursery and got the train to London, to his flat. I had no idea if he'd be in or not. It turned out he was in.'

'What happened?'

Cally looks at my sister.

'I walked in on a blazing row,' Marianne says. 'As the story unfolded, the Johnny standing before me just became horrible, a bully – someone who wanted nothing to do with his own child. I was in shock, of course. But it was more than the revelations. I was looking at this man and I realised I didn't love him any more. I didn't even like him. I hadn't liked him for a long time.'

'What do you mean?' I ask.

'Johnny wasn't the dream boy you thought he was, Emma,' Marianne tells me. 'At least not by the end. I've never said anything because, frankly, I was no dream girl either. All those parties ... the decadence ... there was a dark side to it.'

I frown. 'In what way?'

'Johnny was ... *is* being destroyed by cocaine. He's a mess. He's totally dependent and is spending a fortune. If I'm entirely honest, there was one time when I could see myself going the same way.'

My jaw drops.

'It was Johnny who introduced me to it. His circle of friends became my circle of friends. Except they weren't real friends. It was amazing fun to begin with. There's nothing like your first experience of coke. And that's the problem. It's never as good after that, so you take more.'

She swallows. 'That time we split up – the summer of 2009 – was after I'd collapsed one day and been rushed to hospital. Emma, I felt like I was lucky to be alive. Unfortunately, Johnny didn't even come to collect me. He was out with his friends and I virtually crawled home to recuperate. That was when I dumped him – the first time. I still loved him, but I also hated him. It was then that Cally met him and—'

'I'm sorry, Marianne,' Cally whispers, lowering her eyes.

'You didn't know we were going to get back together,' Marianne reassures her. 'I never should have. And after we did, it never worked – I refused to touch any drugs after what had happened. Johnny, on the other hand, couldn't get enough. We'd become different people.'

'But why did the fact that Johnny is Zachary's dad remain secret after last Christmas? Once Marianne knew, why couldn't everyone know?'

'That was Cally's choice,' Marianne replies, looking at her.

Cally suddenly looks like every ounce of energy has drained from her body. 'I have no idea whether I've done the right thing. I have no idea whether I'm *still* doing the right thing. And maybe things will change in the future. But I thought this: do I want my son growing up knowing that there's a father out there who's actively chosen to have nothing to do with him? Or is it better to think his dad is someone we could simply never track down?'

'I see what you mean.'

'I may change my mind as time goes on, I don't know,' Cally continues. 'But, after Marianne left him, Johnny's attitude was almost *worse*. It was like he blamed Zachary for it. As far as he's concerned, he wishes that Zachary had never been born.' Tears swim in her eyes as she looks up at me and I reach over and clutch her hand. 'And I don't want my baby boy growing up knowing that. I really don't.'

Chapter 82

It's gone ten when I arrive home, and I'm aching to feel Matt's arms round me. I leap out of the car and am on my way to his flat when the door opens and he steps out.

His smile is the loveliest sight in the world, dissolving my worries instantly.

'I was on my way to see you,' I say.

'My place or yours?' he laughs.

'Mine's as good as anywhere,' I shrug.

Inside, he takes me in his arms and kisses me while the rest of the world melts into nothing. I am swollen with desire as he runs his hands down my back, his mouth on my neck.

We stumble into my bedroom and fall into bed. My body is alive with lust ... but not only that. Three words light up in my head, one by one, like tiny fireworks exploding.

I.

LOVE.

YOU.

I repeat them internally over and over again, for no other reason than I can't help it. This isn't about the sex. This is about a man I love, so passionately and wholly, that I can barely think about anything else.

A man who's leaving.

'What's up?' Matt lifts up my chin and kisses my cheeks.

'Nothing. It's been a difficult week.'

And I sink my lips gently into his, because this is not a conversation I can have.

Chapter 83

The following day is when we put the final touches to the most significant presentation in Little Blue Bus's history. We haven't managed to do a pilot like we should have done, in my opinion (and I'm allowed one of those now I'm creative director). But we have put together some seriously brilliant original scripts – and, courtesy of the talented animators with whom we work, will be presenting the concepts in a way only a corpse could fail to be excited by.

It's a true team effort – one in which the business side of things is just as important as the creative side, hence my requirement to nod as if I know what I'm talking about when our producer, Julian, gets out his spreadsheets. I hadn't thought it'd be easy. Although I admit I'd hoped I might be home before midnight after working so hard that my eyeballs feel as though they've been scrubbed.

'Good work, everyone,' Perry Snr says as we bid each other goodnight and head to the car park. I'm about to respond when he explodes into a coughing fit, like his lungs have gone on a sudden campaign of strike action.

'Are you okay?' I ask.

He nods stoically. 'Bad chest, that's all.'

I think nothing of it until the next morning, when I am attempting to remove a foundation splodge from my blouse at 7.25 a.m. and a text arrives from his son.

> Dad's poorly, so it's just you and me today, kiddo! I'll do the
> bits in the presentation he was meant to!!!! We'll be
> FINE!!!!!!!

'Oh *shit*,' I groan, wondering how many exclamation marks a man has to use before the state recognises him as clinically insane.

Have you ever had one of those mornings when, despite having prepared everything, nothing goes your way?

After abandoning the blouse and finding another one, I try to curl my hair, but my tongs fizzle and die halfway through. I decide to attempt a stylish up-do instead, like one I saw in *Glamour* on Penelope Cruz. Except, despite scouring the flat like a demented sniffer dog, I can find no Kirby grips.

All I *can* find, at the bottom of a drawer, is the item I won in a Christmas cracker: a plastic hair clip with pink feathers and lights that haven't ceased flashing in the two years since I won it. I throw it on the floor, stamp on it violently to halt the flashing – then pluck out the feathers as if it's something I'm about to fill with sage-and-onion stuffing and roast at 180 degrees Celsius.

I then position it carefully – hiding the offensive parts (i.e. all of it) behind a mass of hair – and spray on enough Extreme Hold hairspray to support a set of shelves.

This turns out to be just the start. The tights I left out last night develop the sort of ladder you could use if you were cleaning windows upstairs, I sneeze when applying mascara and, worse than that, half of my 'lucky' underwear goes inexplicably missing, meaning that – having not unloaded the washing machine yesterday – I'm forced to wear a crap bra with my Elle Macpherson Intimates knickers.

Predictably, I'm late when I arrive at the Channel 6 offices. And after leaping over the barrier in the car park, sprinting to the office and announcing myself to the receptionist, I finally meet Perry *just* as he's being shown to the presentation room and clearly in a lather as regards my whereabouts.

'Here she is!' he grins.

'Great,' says one of the three executives he's with. 'We'll do the introductions in a minute. After you.'

'Thank you,' I reply coolly, heading into the room. I have taken but two steps when I feel Perry's hand on my shoulder, tugging something from the back of my collar like a magician pulling a set of hankies from his sleeve.

'Emma,' he hisses, thrusting something in my hand. 'Is this yours?'

I unclench my fist and examine the item.

I appear to have found my Elle Macpherson bra after all.

*

The presentation is due to last for two hours and there is so much adrenalin pumping through my body I feel ill. As I'm introduced to the panel one by one, their titles seem to get ever more intimidating: Creative Executive Producer ... Commissioning Editor ... and the head honcho himself: Controller. I'm trembling as I shake hands, and the overriding thought dominating my brain is this: we are *not* going to win this without Perry Snr. It's just not possible.

The fact that proceedings began with my underwear flopping out of the back of my suit – and that the main event involves Perry Jnr jumping up and down like there's a hopscotch grid underfoot – don't help.

'Thanks for coming, both of you,' begins Mark McNally, the Controller. He's in his early forties, has a formidable reputation in the industry, and, since he won the top job at Channel 6 last year, he has made sweeping changes.

'I should start by saying that the team has stressed how much they've loved working with you for the last few years. *Bingbah* has been a great success. But, as you know, ratings are slipping. Our young viewers – and advertisers – want something new. You'll already know that the competition from overseas is strong. All those factors meant we had no choice but to throw open this tender.'

He clasps his hands. 'We don't want to make changes for the sake of it. However, you're the last company we're seeing and, I'll be honest, some of the other presentations have ... *excited* us. A lot. If we're to commission another series of *Bingbah*, you need to be very persuasive.'

He looks at Perry, who, thirty seconds ago, was leaping about hyperactively but is now sitting as though cryogenically frozen, like one of those people in *Awakenings*. I dig him in the ribs.

'Of course!' he splutters.

Mark McNally smiles and opens his arms. 'Well, would you like to show us what you've got?'

I glance at Perry. This is his part of the pitch, but he's immobile again. Just his lips are moving – slightly; he is muttering. The next few seconds are excruciating. I feel like a teacher waiting in the wings during the school nativity play, trying not to prompt anyone's lines, determined to let them have a go at getting it right themselves.

Only, Perry's not going to get it right. It's obvious. And there's nothing else for it. I'm going to have to wing it.

'Of course,' I say, reaching over to the laptop to start the presentation. 'Um ... where do I start ...'

Perry's hand is suddenly on mine. I glance up and he smiles. 'I've got this, Emma,' he says.

'Sure?' I whisper.

He nods.

Reluctantly, I remove my hand and sit back, wondering how far exactly the power of prayer can get you.

Chapter 84

The next couple of days at work are strange. We're in limbo, with no idea whether our future is secure, yet with no other option but to do as the fridge magnets advise: keep calm and carry on.

Giles has bombarded me with questions about how the pitch went, but the honest answer to that is that I don't know.

All I know is that Perry surprised me. He was manic, of course. And I spent most of the time trying to rein him in – something that had limited success given the number of times he kept returning to an idea he'd had about a group of gardening implements that come to life.

Aside from that, he was surprisingly good. As – I think – was I. And the presentation, complete with some brilliant work from the animators, was genuinely spine-tingling. Yet, am I certain we convinced Mark McNally that we were capable of achieving everything he wanted? Far from it.

'Couldn't you work out anything from their body language?' Giles asks, shoving an entire Hobnob in his mouth. I resist the temptation to enquire what his next trick is.

'I was at a pitch – not on a date. The truth is, I don't know. I suppose I'm . . . quietly confident.'

The second the words are out of my mouth I regret them. I have literally no idea if they're true – and now I've made Giles sit back in his seat, relieved, when frankly he's in no position to be.

Still, we potter away on what turns out to be some of the best work of the series – simply because there's nothing else to do to take our mind off the pitch. And, of course, the other thing that's burning me up – Matt.

There are now eight days until my birthday – and the day Matt leaves, a thought that makes my stomach clench every time I think it.

I turn to my computer and realise I've got two last-minute replies to my birthday invitations. Neither is from Rob, who is obviously sticking to his guns on the idea of not being friends. Just before I leave work – at five p.m. for the first time in ages – I compose a short email.

Hi Rob,
Just wondered if you'd got the invitation to my birthday party? Hope you're well. x

Then I log onto Facebook and send another – to Johnny.

Hi there, I know I mentioned my birthday party when I saw
you, but I'm afraid I've had to be really strict with the
numbers – and I'd be grateful if you didn't come.
Thanks,
Emma.

I know it's brutally short and to the point. I can't bring myself
to feel he deserves anything more.

Matt's kids are with their mum tonight and we've arranged to go
to dinner in Lark Lane. I stop off at the supermarket on the way
home to get some shampoo, and I'm waiting to pay, when I hear
a blood-curdling shriek from behind.

'Arrgh!'

'Little fuck—'

The initial scream made me jump. The language – and the
ferocity with which it's delivered – forces a gasp from me.

I spin round and register a little boy being hoisted up by the
collar and smacked hard on the back of the legs by a large
snarling bloke doing a good impression of the sort of dogs that are
seized by the local council.

A fellow shopper steps in and tells the big guy to 'take it easy',
but he just shrugs him off and marches away, dragging the little
boy. It's at that point that I realise who the little boy is. 'Joshua!'
I fling the shampoo on the conveyor belt and march over, as
instinct overtakes rational thought.

'What the hell's going on?' I blurt out, my neck burning.

'*Emma!*' squeals Joshua, as he wriggles away and runs to me, clutching my leg.

'It's okay, sweetie.' I stroke his hair as he sobs into my side.

'And who are you?' The strong French accent is dripping with contempt. I don't need to ask the same question of him.

'I'm Emma,' I reply, trying to keep my voice level. 'I'm Joshua's neighbour and a ... friend of the family.'

He looks at me blankly, unimpressed. 'Yeah. Nice to meet you,' he says sarcastically. 'Joshua – 'ere.' He jerks his head, ordering him back like a disobedient animal.

Joshua doesn't move.

'*'Ere!*'

Guillaume reaches over and drags Joshua towards him with such force that the little boy almost falls over again. He stands quivering next to Guillaume while my mouth falls open in shock.

'We're going.' He flings down the shopping, turns and grabs Joshua by the arm, and begins marching him away.

Joshua's tiny legs struggle to keep up, as my mind starts spinning. Shoppers look on uncomfortably, assuming that Guillaume is his father, but still wondering if he's crossed a line sufficiently to be challenged. Suddenly, something inside me snaps.

'*Hey! Wait!*'

Guillaume stops and looks at me.

I grab my phone and start dialling Matt's number, simply because I don't know what else to do.

'I think Joshua ought to come with me,' I ramble, as my phone starts ringing.

'Yes! I'm going with Emma!' Joshua cries, attempting to run to me – until he's dragged back.

Guillaume glares at me. '*I've* been put in charge of him. By his mother.'

'Mummy's not back till later.'

Guillaume slaps Joshua around the ear, sharp and hard.

'*Stop hitting him!*' I hiss furiously – as Matt's phone goes straight to messages and a lady next to me tells her friend that she's going to get a security guard.

'Matt. Will you ring me back, please? I need to talk to you. Urgently.'

As I finish the call, Guillaume turns on me. 'Who the 'ell do you think you are, crazy woman? This is not *your* kid. You are a neighbour. You are *nothing*.'

'Well, *you* are not allowed to hit him,' I say firmly.

He leans in and whispers, 'I'll do what the fuck I want.'

'And stop using language like that – he's *four*, for God's sake.'

Joshua dives towards me and tries to escape, the sight of which makes Guillaume explode. 'Little shit. You do as you're told. Now *get 'ere.*'

He drags the little boy into the car park, while passers-by look on, assuming Josh has been naughty but still horrified, and with no more idea of what to do than I have. I mean, this man has been left in charge of Joshua by his mother. He hasn't kidnapped him.

Joshua is sobbing as he's strapped into his car seat and I watch helplessly.

'When is his mother back?' I demand.

Guillaume turns to look at me, appalled. 'In 'alf an 'our, if you must know. Although it's nothing to do with you.'

He slams the car door as a security guard finally appears at my side and Joshua, weeping in the darkness, is driven into the night.

Chapter 85

Every inch of colour leaves Matt's face as he listens silently. I'm trying not to be dramatic, but it's difficult to play this down. For a second, I even wonder if telling him is the right thing to do. He is distraught.

'He actually *hit* him?' He is incredulous as he sinks onto a stool in his kitchen.

'I'm really sorry, Matt. I didn't know what to do. Should I have tried to bring him here with me? God, I should, shouldn't I?'

'How? The guy's huge, Emma. You couldn't have stood up to him, unless you've got a black belt in something you haven't told me about.'

I sigh. 'You must've wondered what my message was all about.'

'What message? My phone broke this morning – it's being fixed at the shop so I'm using a replacement.'

'I phoned you to ask what I should do. I was in a total panic.'

He stands up and wraps his arms round me, squeezing me into

him. 'Emma, you did everything you could.' He pulls back. 'I need to go and speak to Allison.'

'Do you think she knows what Guillaume's capable of?'

'No. I don't,' he says firmly. 'Say what you want about my ex-wife, but the one thing I'm certain of is that she adores her children. If she had even an inkling that Guillaume – anyone – wasn't treating the boys right, she'd be devastated. She won't stand for it, I know it.'

'Do you want me to come with you?' I offer.

'I don't want to drag you into this.' Then he hesitates. 'Although, perhaps if Guillaume denies it . . .'

We hardly say anything on the way there. Matt stares silently ahead, concentrating on the road, as an avalanche of hideous thoughts tumbles through my head.

The house is an attractive Victorian semi, surrounded by neatly manicured lawns and unnaturally square hedges. There are two cars on the drive; I recognise the expensive one as Guillaume's. Matt rings the bell and waits, crossing his arms and tapping his fingers impatiently.

As an internal door is unlocked there is a burst of music and laughter, followed by footsteps. Then the main door opens and Allison is there, in jeans and a cashmere jumper, her auburn hair tumbling over her shoulders. She looks at me first, then glances at Matt. 'What's going on?'

'I need to talk to you, Allie,' he says urgently.

Allison looks at me again, presumably wondering who I am.

'This is—'

'Emma,' she finishes. 'I know. The kids talk about her.'

Matt shifts uncomfortably, then glances into the house behind her. 'Where are they?'

'Inside,' she shrugs.

'With Guillaume?'

She folds her arms. 'Of *course* with Guillaume.'

Matt slows his breathing deliberately. 'Allie – it's him I need to talk to you about. Emma saw something at the supermarket this evening that was ... very disturbing.'

She narrows her eyes defensively. 'What?'

'He *hit* Joshua.'

Allison turns to me. 'He'd never do that.'

'He *would*,' Matt says firmly. 'She saw the whole thing.'

Allison snorts incredulously. 'Ollie, Jack and I came home ten minutes ago – and found Guillaume and Joshua having a wonderful time together! Look.' She pushes open the door and Guillaume is at the kitchen table as Joshua and Jack play snakes and ladders.

Her boyfriend isn't exactly behaving like Mary Poppins – in truth there's little evidence of any interaction at all. But he's a long way from smacking anyone around the head and legs, like I saw earlier.

'I don't care what they're doing *now*,' Matt says, standing firm. 'Guillaume shouted at him in the supermarket – and, more importantly, he hit him.'

Allison sighs and looks at me like I'm terminally befuddled. 'There's no way that would've happened, Matt. It's been a misunderstanding. Joshua was simply told off after he tried to steal something – I heard about this ten minutes ago.'

'He wouldn't do that,' Matt insists.

'Actually, he did it at nursery the other day too,' Allison replies, entirely satisfied with the explanation. 'I *told* Guillaume to make sure he chastised him if he did it again.'

'Daddy!' At that moment Jack comes running towards us and hurls himself into Matt's arms.

'Can I come in and see Joshua, please?' Matt asks, squeezing Jack back.

Allison hesitates. 'Fine. Come and say hello, but then you need to leave. I don't want them overexcited before bed.'

As Matt and I enter the kitchen a flicker of unease crosses Guillaume's face, but disintegrates instantly. 'Hello again,' he says coolly.

'Hello,' I reply, feeling my heart race.

'Guillaume, there's been a misunderstanding about what happened in the supermarket,' Allison begins, matter-of-factly. 'There is some suggestion that you *hit* Joshua.'

Guillaume stands up next to Allison and pulls an expression as if this is as fanciful as something I'd written for *Bingbah*. 'He was throwing a tantrum so I held his arm. For his own safety.' He puts his arm round Allison's waist affectionately and squeezes her into him.

'That isn't how I remember it,' I reply, glancing at Joshua, who's playing with the dice with such intensity it's clear he wishes this isn't happening.

Allison pulls away from Guillaume and walks up to Joshua, crouching next to him. 'Sweetheart, when you were in the supermarket ... you know Guillaume only told you off because you were naughty, don't you?'

The little boy glances at Guillaume, clearly terrified.

'When grown-ups are looking after you, if you don't do as you're asked, you're told off,' she continues. 'You know that, don't you?'

Joshua looks down and nods.

'He swore at him,' Matt says, pure hatred oozing from every pore as he looks at Guillaume.

'No,' replies Guillaume calmly. 'You misheard me. I told him off, that's all.'

'I heard and saw the whole thing clearly,' I say, as sweat pricks on my brow.

'This is ridiculous,' Allison interrupts furiously, before levelling her voice. She takes Joshua's little hands in hers. 'Darling, you can tell Mummy.'

She kisses him on the head and brushes hair away from his face, gazing at him in such a way that it's obvious Matt is right. She loves these children, more than anything. She looks up at Guillaume and gestures for him to leave the room. He leaves, closing the door behind him.

Allison sits next to Joshua and pulls him onto her knee. 'Tell Mummy. Did Guillaume hit you?'

Joshua swallows hard and looks at the door. He glances briefly at me, then focuses on his hands again.

'No,' he whispers.

Chapter 86

There's nothing more to do but leave. Only, leaving isn't that smooth an operation. Allison and Matt's bickering begins in the hallway, spills onto the drive and continues as he marches to the car, trying to end the conversation before things get out of hand.

'I don't know *what* you're playing at, Matt,' she hisses, pulling the door behind her. 'I thought we'd agreed to do this amicably. How is this helping?'

He tries to stay calm. 'Allison, Joshua is terrified of Guillaume. *That's* why he said it never happened.'

She rolls her eyes. 'How could he have been terrified when Guillaume was in the other room?'

'What does *that* matter? He still knows he's going to have to live with the guy.'

'We're not living together,' she corrects him. 'Not yet.'

Matt tries to collect himself. 'Please. Just promise me you won't leave *any* of the kids alone with him again. Come on, humour me.'

She breathes out. 'Fine. Okay.'

He hesitates and closes his eyes, clearly trying to think of a diplomatic way of addressing what's really on his mind. He fails. 'Look, about moving to France . . .'

'*That's* what this is about, isn't it?'

'No. Well, maybe. Obviously, I'm worried sick about you moving to another country with a bloke who hit my youngest son—'

'We have established that he didn't do anything other than chastise him!' she leaps in, speaking through gritted teeth.

I can't listen any longer without interrupting. 'I'm afraid he did.'

She throws me a filthy look. Then she turns to Matt again. 'You *know* me. Those children are my world. I'd never do anything to put them in a situation that endangered or upset them. And I'm totally confident that this isn't one.'

He shakes his head. 'Unfortunately, I'm not.'

Uttering this sentence is like lighting a touch paper. 'I *know* what this is all about, Matt, let's not keep pretending,' Allison explodes.

'*What* is it all about?'

'It's about you trying to stop me from going to France. It's about you trying to prove that Guillaume isn't the man for me. It's about the reconciliation you're still determined to get. Matt!' she says, grabbing both of his arms and glaring in his eyes. '*It. Isn't. Going. To. Happen.*'

I look at my shoes. Suddenly, there doesn't seem to be

anywhere else to look. Partly because all three of us know she's right.

He doesn't want her to go to France. He doesn't want her to be with Guillaume. And, most importantly, this man whom I adore so pointlessly always made clear who he really wants to be with. Allison.

'You're wrong.'

I look up as she lets go of his arms.

'Oh, come on, you spent months after I left trying to persuade me to return. All you've done is tell me you still love me.'

Matt replies calmly, 'Things have changed, Allison. Yes, I wanted you back at first. I never wanted you to tear our family apart – and certainly not because you'd met another man. I *was* in love with you. There's no doubt about it . . .'

The sky swims in and out of my vision as I wish I wasn't here to hear this. I can't bear to hear this.

'. . . but I'm *not* any more. Not even a tiny bit.'

She takes a step back, as if she's been punched in the stomach.

'There's no turning back time – even if that's what I wanted,' he says. 'Which I don't. All I want now is for you and me to be friends. To bring up our children as best we can.'

Allison is almost speechless. 'So . . . so your feelings have done a complete about-turn? You feel *nothing* for me? Am I supposed to believe that?'

'We had some wonderful times, Allison. But they're over.'

'You feel *nothing*?' she repeats furiously.

'I'm not in love with you, Allison. I'm in love with somebody else.'

He glances at me briefly, then looks back at her. Allison glares at me.

'I don't want us to fight,' he continues.

She sniffs and crosses her arms. Then she shakes her head. 'Neither do I.'

'I'm going to go.' He opens the car door. 'Just watch out for the kids for me, won't you?'

She wrinkles her nose and her eyes fill with tears. 'Of course I will. You know I will.'

He gets into the car. And as we drive home through floodlight streets I wonder what it'll take for my head to stop spinning.

Chapter 87

Matt can't relax when he gets home; he paces up and down the living room as he talks.

'The one consolation is that I *think* she'll stay true to her word and not leave him alone with them. I know she's acting like she believes he's Walt Disney and Pa Walton all rolled into one, but hopefully we've put some doubt in her mind, enough to keep her alert to any repeats of tonight. At least in the near future.' He frowns and slumps on his sofa. 'If this is a long-term thing, though ... I can't bear the idea of my children being around him. He sounds like a psychopath.'

I sit down and put my arm round him, feeling the tension in his shoulders.

'I've never liked him,' he mutters through gritted teeth.

'That's understandable. He ran off with your wife.'

He stops and looks at me, his face softening.

'There are some things I should probably say to you, Emma.'

'You don't have to ... I understand why you said what you said. You needed to demolish Allison's argument.'

He hesitates and looks at his hands, the sinews in his neck tensing as he reaches for mine. 'It wasn't to win an argument. I meant it.'

My heart is hammering so fast it's almost all I can hear. Almost. Because as the next words slip off his tongue, I don't know whether to laugh or cry.

'I love you, Emma.' My heart erupts with a thousand emotions, the sheer joy and pain of the situation nearly unbearable. 'I'm *totally* in love with you. Every bone in my body feels it.' He glances away furiously. 'And now I've got to leave you and move to another bloody country.'

All rational argument leaves my brain and I squeeze his hands as tears prick my eyes. 'Matt, I love you too. And ... *sod it*.'

'What?'

I sniff back tears determinedly. 'I don't care what people say about long-distance relationships. We can make it work, don't you think? Or ... I'll move to France.'

He gazes at me, his eyes full of hope. 'Do you *want* to move to France?'

I open my mouth to respond, but words escape me as the implications of the suggestion dawn on me.

I am a scriptwriter for children's television. As the interior-design fiasco proved, this is what I do, it is the only thing I'm qualified to do, and it is the only thing I *can* do.

Even if I could speak French, there are no jobs for kids' TV scriptwriters in the deeply rural part of the country where Matt is going. When I Googled the region last week I discovered it's so far in the middle of nowhere they could've set *Return of the Jedi* there.

Despite all this, I can think of nothing else to say, except: 'I want to be with you.'

His eyes are full of sorrow as he leans in to kiss me, aware as he is of the impracticality of the suggestion. We both know that this isn't the answer. So what the hell is?

Chapter 88

I know you're supposed to make 'lifestyle changes' these days rather than go on crash diets, but I'm too fond of the part of my life that involves Chunky KitKats to relinquish those for long. I'd prefer a short period of intensive, focused dieting to achieve the item on my list that says: 'Fit perfectly into a size ten dress.'

Of course, when I told myself to do this six months ago, I probably had in mind that my 'short period' would be longer than seven days. Still, I like a challenge. And this is one.

'Have you tried the Fast Slim diet?' Cally asks on the phone on Saturday morning. 'It works. You feel ready to collapse from malnutrition and your stomach grumbles like it's auditioning for *The Voice*. But it does work.'

'Even I'm capable of sticking to a diet for seven days,' I reply confidently. Although, as I say it, it strikes me that there's only one guaranteed way of boosting my will-power enough to tick this one off – and that's to actually *buy* a size ten dress for the party.

That way, unless I stick to my guns – and celery – I will have simply nothing to wear. I know my wardrobe is groaning with the weight of worn-once items, but there's no way I can stoop to wearing those on my thirtieth.

I head to the city centre at lunchtime and know 'the' dress the second I set eyes on it. It's in Karen Millen. It's a size ten. It's also three times my budget, but given that it'll be a decade before I have another birthday this big, what does that matter?

The nice shop assistant shows me into a cubicle and I try on the dress. Which makes the exercise sound simple and straight-forward, doesn't it?

It's neither.

Passers-by would be forgiven for thinking that Houdini was locked in a straitjacket and chains behind the curtain, such is the variety of elaborate contortions needed for me to squeeze into the dress. Pulling up the zip is a quasi-gymnastic experience, leaving me red-faced, sweaty and panting like a hyena that's been locked in a car on a hot day.

Finally, I straighten up, tensing my stomach muscles, and fling back the curtain. I make my way to the mirror, an exercise so badly hampered by the tightness of the skirt that anyone watching would think I'd suffered a major trampolining injury and had only recently come out of traction.

'Would you like some heels?' suggests the assistant, producing a beautiful pair of emerald stilettos.

I take them from her and look at them. Then I look at my feet. I contemplate the logistics required to make my upper body descend sufficiently low to bring the two into contact – and just thinking about it makes my eyes become bloodshot.

I lean a degree to one side and lower the shoes as far as I can to the floor, which proves to be not very far. So I drop them, thinking I'll simply manoeuvre them into place with my toes, then slip them on.

Sadly, the heel of one lands directly on my little toe, which achieves the same effect as the techniques employed by Vlad the Impaler in the fifteenth century, and leaves me hopping about while wondering whether the toe might regain any feeling before the end of the year.

I chase the other shoe round in circles, attempting to get it on my foot solely with the aid of my big toe. The mesmerised assistant finally steps in, kneels on the floor and bulldozes it onto my size six foot in a way that makes me think she was taught by an ugly sister.

'It's ... definitely you,' she smiles hesitantly. The 'definitely' isn't as definite as I'd have liked. 'Have you thought about ... a twelve?'

I glare at her – and she instantly realises her error.

'Not because I'm saying you necessarily *need* it,' she adds hastily. 'I thought it could be an option. Some people like a size bigger, just to leave them ... the option.'

The option of *what* – I can't help but think. Eating loads of cakes?

'I know it's a bit of a squeeze, but I'm sure it'll be fine by the party.'

'Oh, you're on a diet?' she asks, relieved.

'Not yet, but I will be.'

'Lovely,' she smiles, returning with me to the cubicle. 'So when's your party?'

'Saturday.'

She freezes. '*Next* Saturday?'

'Yes,' I reply defiantly.

She opens her mouth, but manages to say nothing, clearly thinking that the only way my wish will be granted is via a violent bout of dysentery.

Chapter 89

On Monday afternoon, I'm called into Perry Jnr's office, where he and his father are looking very worried indeed.

'It's all over, Emma,' says Perry Jnr, leaping from his desk to gaze dramatically out of the window.

'I thought we weren't due to find out until the end of the week?' I ask.

'We weren't,' he replies, his lip wobbling like a school-canteen blancmange. 'But I've had an email.'

I glance at Perry Snr and suddenly become convinced that this is more than the usual theatricals from his son.

'Come and sit down, Emma,' he says solemnly. 'We'd appreciate it if you didn't tell the rest of the staff. Nothing's official yet.'

Perry Jnr sniffs back tears. 'I emailed Mark McNally – twice – to ask if they were close to making a decision. I know I shouldn't have done, but not knowing was *torture*! I couldn't sleep! My Night Nurse was powerless. I found myself up at three a.m. watching the subtitled version of something called *Loose Women*,' he says, with wide-eyed air quotes. '*This* is the sort of hell I've been going through, Emma.'

Perry Snr looks away, clearly believing this move to have been as well-judged as packing an inflatable doll in your honeymoon suitcase.

Perry Jnr continues, 'He replied to say that the decision-making process was ongoing, but that an announcement would be made on Friday and he'll write then officially. He added ... well, let me read it to you.'

He opens up his email and begins quoting: '"Off the record, however, I can say, in strict confidence, that it was felt that your proposals for the next series on the Bingbahs may not be enough for our requirements."'

'Oh no,' I reply under my breath.

He swallows and looks at his father, then back at me. 'We're stuffed, Emma. Comprehensively stuffed.'

Chapter 90

Maybe losing the Channel 6 contract was meant to happen.

Unemployment is the one thing that frees me up to go and live in France with Matt. I have a dream to that effect on Monday night – one in which I move to rural France, certain that I'm doing the right thing.

In the event, the only gainful employment I can find is as a goatherd, a job that involves skipping over hills dressed as Little Bo Peep, complete with gravity-defying pigtails and freckles the size of Cadbury's chocolate buttons.

I wake up at the moment I realise I've managed to lose every one of my charges – and acquired several hundred mutant frogs in their place.

'Are you okay?' Matt whispers into my hair, stroking my arm. 'You sounded like you were having a funny dream.'

'Was I ribbiting?'

He laughs gently. 'I don't think so.'

I curl into his chest. 'Sorry if I woke you.'

'You didn't. I couldn't sleep.'

I kiss him on his lips, glad that the dim light hides the glistening of tears in my eyes. 'You've got a lot on your mind, I'll bet.'

He hesitates. 'Yes.'

'What time is it?' I ask.

He leans over to pick up his mobile, fumbling with it furiously to find the clock. 'I hate this phone.'

'When's yours ready?'

'Saturday.'

The mere mention of that day sends a wave of misery through me.

'What time will you have to set off?'

'Late afternoon is about the latest I'll get away with, if I'm to catch the ferry.'

I suddenly bitterly regret the fact that I persuaded him it was okay to miss my party. I swallow and look at him, overwhelmed with emotion.

'I love you, Matt.'

His face crumples with pain as he closes his eyes and shakes his head, clutching my hand. 'We've both got to snap out of this, Emma. It's no good . . .' He kisses me on the head and sniffs. 'Are you excited about your birthday?' he asks, changing the subject.

'I suppose so. Part of me doesn't feel grown-up enough to be thirty.'

'You've done virtually everything on your list, haven't you?'

'I've knocked off most of it. Although the skydiving eluded me. And the one-night stand.'

'I wouldn't worry too much about those.'

'And ... there was that other one. About finding love. Finding the man I'm going to marry.'

'Oh, yes.'

I rest my head on his shoulder and gaze at the wall, contemplating a hideous but all-too-pertinent question: will it be another thirty years before I feel anything like this about someone again?

Chapter 91

Friday is an odd day. The whole company is aware that this is when the Channel 6 announcement is due, but only the two Perrys and I know the verdict already. It feels like waiting for the firing squad when everyone else is poised with party poppers and champagne.

Giles – who's blissfully ignorant of what I know – is tense but optimistic, a state it's so unbearable to be around that I suggest a trip to the pub at lunchtime.

I rarely do this – daytime drinking and I generally don't mix. After even just half a pint of lager, I return to my desk unable to focus on the screen and proceed to write scripts that are comparable to some of Hunter S. Thompson's work when he was riddled with psychedelic drugs (and are inevitably destroyed the following morning).

We go to a bar round the corner from work, so Giles can buy me a pre-birthday drink. It isn't *entirely* the merry experience it sounds.

'God, I hope we get this contract,' he sighs, glugging Guinness like a man who's trekked across the Sahara and is so dehydrated he can't see straight. 'I don't know why – I have a good feeling about this.'

'Do you?' I whimper.

'Yep. And I tell you: I need some good news at the moment.'

'Oh. Why?'

He shrugs. 'This situation with Cally has been getting to me lately. And you know me; I never usually look on anything other than the bright side of life.'

I take a sip of my drink to prevent myself from commenting.

'Maybe this is what being in our thirties is going to be like,' he proffers. 'Maybe we just have to get used to this sort of shit.'

'What do you mean?'

'You know ... relationship woes.'

'Oh.'

'It's *you* I feel sorry for,' he continues generously. 'I've got it bad enough with Cally. *You* on the other hand are going into your thirties and the one bloke you've *ever* felt anything for is emigrating. You must feel like *crap*. A great big bag of crap. A great big bag of crap that's been thrown into a hand blender, turned on high, and liquidised into an even crappier bag of crap. You must wish—'

'—that you'd *shut up*.'

He pauses, shocked – and I suddenly feel the need to get some things off my chest.

'You know what, Giles? You're right. Things haven't turned

out perfectly, for you or me. And they might continue not to for the foreseeable. *Maybe* we won't get the Channel 6 contract' – he frowns defensively – 'but we'll find new jobs. I'm sure of it. We're bloody good at what we do and we're survivors.'

He straightens his back, liking this description.

'As for Cally ... and Matt ... and love ...' I swallow. 'Things might not have worked out as we'd hoped. But, Giles, you and I need to hold onto this thought: we had something special. We *felt* something that not everybody feels.'

He closes his mouth.

'And, okay ... so Cally isn't in love with you. Does that mean you wish you'd never met her? If you'd never met her you'd never have felt the pleasure and pain and sheer intensity that love means.'

He says nothing, just nods.

'I'd gone through thirty years of my life and never felt anything like I've felt with Matt. And yes, I'm going to lose him,' I say, my voice breaking. 'Frankly, that thought is killing me. But at least I *had* it. At least I *felt* it. My thirty-year wait has been worth every minute. Even knowing it's going to end.'

He goes to speak, but I interrupt him again. 'I read a quote once, Giles: "Don't cry because it's over, smile because it happened." That's how I'm going to look at this.'

'Who said that?'

I squirm. 'Dr Seuss. It was on someone's fridge.'

'It doesn't have to, though ... does it?' Giles points out. 'You could always ...'

'The goatherder option,' I mutter, staring through the window.

'What?' He scrunches up his nose.

'You mean I should go with him, don't you? To France?'

He hesitates. 'How remote is it, exactly?'

'I'm starting to think that maybe I should find out.'

By the time I've walked back to the office I've replayed my Little Bo Peep dream so many times, it's involved six outfit changes – like I'm Lady Gaga on tour – none of which sets off the pigtails any better. As we walk into reception, Perry bursts out of his office like a man looking for two buckets of water after his feet have caught fire.

'*Emma!* Get in here . . . *Quickly!*'

I enter his office and Giles follows, uninvited but unapologetic, as Perry leaps into the seat behind his desk.

'I need you both to tell me I'm not having some sort of . . . *trip!* I took one too many of my beta blockers on top of three Lemsips this morning and have felt a bit iffy since then.'

I perch on a chair in front of his desk. 'Is this about the decision?'

'Yes! It's an email. *The* email. From Mark McNally.'

He starts blathering away – that's the only term – reading bits and pieces of the email, until Giles and I walk round his desk and read it ourselves.

'Blah, blah,' Giles begins. '"You'll recall that I mentioned our requirements went above and beyond another series of *Bingbah*."'

We all look at each other. 'That wasn't quite what he said,' Perry says, scrunching up his nose.

Giles continues: "'The team would like you to work up a proposal based on the brief ideas you mentioned about the talking garden implements. In the meantime, I would like to confirm officially that Channel 6 will be commissioning the next series of *Bingbah* and add how delighted we are to be working with you and your team again.'"

'Wait – it goes on,' Giles says. "'May I add that the decision to promote Emma Reiss to Creative Director on the show was inspired – and I have no doubt will ensure that the next series of *Bingbah* is the best yet.'"

Perry looks at Giles, then at me. '*We did it! We plonking well did it!*'

He starts leaping up down – literally – undertaking one grand jeté after another, before almost pirouetting out of the window.

Giles and I burst into laughter. '*You* did it, Perry. You deserve this. You were great at the pitch.' I turn to Giles. 'I told you he was great.'

Giles is shaking his head, grinning as he leans in to shake our boss's hand. 'Perry, mate, well done.'

Perry shakes his head and pauses, leaping to his computer again. 'I couldn't have done it without ...' Then he rereads the email, his face contorting with incredulity. '*They liked my idea.*'

'I know.' I grin, slightly taken aback myself. We've spent so long being bombarded with Perry's crap ideas that when he finally came up with a good one I barely noticed.

'Emma, Giles,' he says triumphantly, 'the next series is going to be *amazing*. Nothing less. And with Emma as creative director, this company is once again going to be right where it should be: at the very top.'

I laugh nervously. 'Oh, I'm sure you'd manage it whether I was creative director or not.'

Perry shakes his head, grinning as he throws his arms round me. 'We need you, Emma. I need you. Giles needs you. The whole company needs you. I'm going to make you never want to leave.'

Chapter 92

It's my last night with Matt and neither of us can bear spending the evening surrounded by boxes in his flat, so we simply get a takeaway and eat it in my living room, which is even more crowded since I put up the Christmas tree.

'How are the kids feeling about moving?' I ask.

'Distinctly unhappy, Josh in particular. But glad I'm going with them. At least I can keep an eye on things.'

'Oh bugger!' I gasp, poised with a forkful of Chinese food. 'I forgot I'm meant to be on a diet.'

Matt scrunches up his nose. 'Why are you on a diet? You're perfect.'

'I'm glad you think so, you poor deluded fool,' I reply, rolling my eyes. 'Unfortunately, the size ten dress I've got for tomorrow night indicates the opposite.'

He puts down his fork and leans over to kiss me on the cheek, before looking down, embarrassed.

'What was that for?' I ask.

'Being you.' He shakes his head. 'God, that's corny,' he laughs.

I swallow and force myself not to well up again. I fail totally. 'Sorry. I didn't mean to ... I don't want to ruin our last night together.'

'You know what I think?' he says decisively. 'I think we should make tonight a little pre-birthday celebration. A celebration of what we had. You and me.'

I nod, as tears slip down my face. He squeezes my hand, then picks up his wine glass.

'Here's to you and me, Emma. It was brilliant. Almost.'

I'm crying now, I just can't help it, but manage to lift up my glass and ping it against his, before collapsing in a weeping heap.

'Come on, now,' he whispers, pulling me into him and stroking my head. 'None of this can be helped, can it?'

I look up. 'I could—' I'm about to tell him again that I'll come with him, when he puts his finger to my mouth and shakes his head.

I realise that I need to pull myself together. This is so much worse for him. He's the one having to move to a different country. He's the one whose kids will be living with a man who's a complete bastard. The fact that I'm not going with him is probably neither here nor there.

It doesn't stop me thinking one thing, though. One thing that keeps me awake all through the night, long after the clock clicks on midnight and I officially turn thirty.

This hurts like hell.

Chapter 93

Am I supposed to feel different? More grown-up? More responsible? More comfortable in my skin? That's what the celebs say when they hit thirty, isn't it? As if skin becomes something to compare with a nice pair of Hush Puppies.

Still, I understand the sentiment and I'm determined to embrace it. I'm going to be a fabulous thirty-something – a Cameron Diaz-style thirty-something, with glowy skin, young admirers and, courtesy of the diet I'm certain I'll feel motivated to embark on now I'm older and wiser, a stomach you could dry your laundry on.

I wake up before Matt and pad to the bathroom, trying to convince myself that – no matter what's happening in my love life – this is the start of a new era.

For lots of reasons, I should be optimistic. My job is amazing, something it's taken a raft of experimentation and trauma to recognise. I have a wonderful family and friends. I'm generally happy, generally fulfilled. And the fact that I've done all bar a couple of the things on my list is something I feel good about, thanks very much.

So I'm not going to be negative today, no matter what my instinct tells me. I've done all my crying; I will weep no longer. Instead, I will look on the bright side – at how much I've achieved, how much I've lived and how much the last six months has changed me for the better.

Besides, one thing's for sure – at least I'm not fifteen again.

I flush the toilet and go to the sink to wash my hands, and as I look in the mirror I am confronted by a zit the size of Mount Olympus.

Chapter 94

Matt and I spend the day together and it's lovely. He finished packing yesterday and although there are loose ends to deal with, the morning is largely for the two of us.

We eat lunch in Lark Lane then wrap up and stroll to the Palm House, arm in arm, to listen to the carol singers. To passers-by, we'd look like a couple with a lifetime ahead of us. We are anything but.

We've promised to stay in touch, but we both know that the only sensible way to deal with this situation is to get on with our lives. It's a thought that rips me in two and for that reason I don't even think about it, not today. I simply enjoy my birthday.

'Would you like your present?' Matt asks as shards of winter sunlight ripple through the glass.

'Oh . . . I thought you'd forgotten!' I jest.

He rolls his eyes. 'Yes, because you've hardly mentioned this birthday since I met you . . .'

I nudge him in the ribs as he produces an instantly recognisable turquoise bag – from Tiffany's. I unwrap it carefully, my heart pounding as I gently pull each white ribbon, before I remove the lid and have to stop myself from gasping.

It's a bracelet, the most exquisite bracelet I've seen in my life – a string of tiny silver beads with a single heart-shaped charm.

'Matt, it's absolutely beautiful.'

'Really?' he asks, and I realise he's been nervous about his choice.

'Seriously. I don't know what to say.'

'Well, that's your first present. The second you can't open until a month today.' He removes an envelope from his coat pocket and hands it to me.

I frown. 'Why? My birthday's today.'

'That's the deal. Promise me.'

'Okay! Fine! You didn't need to get me two, though.'

'I wanted to.'

Then he reaches out to hold my face in his hands, and as he leans in to kiss me my mind flashes back to the very first time this happened.

'Hey,' he says, pulling away. 'No tears. It's your birthday.'

I smile as he stands and takes me by the hand towards the car, to face the inevitable.

I see the children only briefly to say goodbye, when Allison stops at the house with them to pick up something of Joshua's that he wants for the ferry. I'm glad she did as I'd bought them all a variety of books and stickers for their journey, a small selection to add to the Christmas presents I'll be sending along with Matt.

'Are you all excited about your trip?' I ask as I peer at them in her people carrier.

Jack frowns and crosses his arms. 'No. It's rubbish. I don't want to go to France. I'm fed up.'

Which just about sums up the situation, really.

Matt and I go our separate ways at two thirty, like we'd agreed, before he locks up his flat and drives south to the ferry.

Our final kiss is on his gravel driveway and it feels like a fitting end: in front of the house that holds so many memories created in such a short space of time.

I give it everything I've got not to cry.

I want him to remember me as the woman he shared six months of fun with, not some puffy-faced wreck.

'I'm sorry,' I mutter, as he pulls me into him, a move that leaves me assaulted by thoughts that are so horrific I lose the ability to speak.

This is the last time I will feel my cheek against his neck.

The last time his lips will melt into mine.

The last time I will hear him say my name.

The last time I will feel those hands in mine.

The last time . . .

'You'd better go,' I tell him, unable to bear it.

He nods. Then he backs away, and I watch him go into the house and close the door behind him. For the last time.

I look into the sky and feel the strength leave my body.

I'm thirty years old today.

It's the most perfect and the most awful birthday of my life.

Chapter 95

Dad offers to give me a lift to the party and arrives while I'm in sweat pants and a hoodie, putting the finishing touches to my make-up.

I've been doing so while carefully avoiding the opportunity to look out of the window to see if Matt's car has disappeared.

'Happy birthday!' Dad staggers in carrying such a mountain of presents it looks as though he's stood at the end of the *Generation Game* conveyor belt and wrapped everything that came off it.

He struggles past and I go to shut the door. I hesitate with my hand on the latch, and the temptation to pop out to examine Matt's drive is too much. The car has gone.

'I might have gone a bit overboard!' Dad shouts from the living room.

I shut the door, composing myself, before joining him.

'I've kept all the receipts if you want to take anything back,' he says, thrusting a parcel at me. 'Although Deb helped me pick some out and she's snazzier than me, as you know.'

I tear off the paper until the first gift is revealed.

'It's a pogo stick,' Dad announces. 'They're making a comeback. You can burn over a thousand calories a minute apparently.'

I don't question the plausibility of this statistic.

I wouldn't describe the pogo stick as the highlight of my gifts, but it's fair to say that it's a mixed bunch. Still, the T-shirt Deb chose is really nice, and I'm sure I'll find some use for the 'Slanket' – a fleece blanket with sleeves – which is so huge I'm convinced it only needs its own bathroom and it could accommodate a family of five.

'You didn't need to get all this, but thank you, it's all lovely.' I give him a massive hug. 'Right – I'm just going to get my dress on and we can go whenever you're ready.'

'Er ... Emma.'

'Yes?'

He hesitates. 'There's something else. I need to pop to the car.'

He disappears while I put the gifts in my bedroom and I return to find him sitting on the sofa holding a small cardboard box. I say a fleeting prayer that he hasn't bought me a guinea pig.

But when I sit next to him I realise that it's a box full of envelopes. Tons of them.

'What are they?'

'They're for you, sweetheart. They're from your mother.'

There's a letter for every birthday between the age of seven and thirty – and dozens more, apparently, going right up to the age of a hundred, if you can believe that.

'Your mum said that if you made it past then, the last thing you'd need was her wittering to keep you going,' Dad smiles.

'But ... why are you giving them to me only now?'

Dad looks at his hands and shakes his head. 'Your mum wrote letters for both you and Marianne – there is another set for your sister too. The year after she died, I gave Marianne the first one. Emma, she was devastated – unbelievably upset. I couldn't bear it. It was all just too traumatic. So I packed away both sets of letters and promised myself that only when the time was right would I get them out again. But, it never did seem right. Until now.'

'Oh Dad.' I clutch the letters, mesmerised by the handwriting.

He smiles. 'It was when we had the chat about how you wished you knew more about her ... well, it became obvious that I'd made the wrong decision all those years ago. I'm sorry, Emma.'

I squeeze his hand. 'I'm just glad you didn't throw them away.'

'Oh heck, no! And there's more where they came from!'

I run my fingers over the faded envelopes. 'I want to read them all. Every one. Right now.'

Dad looks at his watch.

'Your party starts in forty-five minutes. Why don't you start by opening the one she intended for today?'

I feel my breath quicken as I flick through the envelopes and find the one marked: 'For Emma, on your thirtieth birthday.'

My heart is racing as I pick it up, imagining my own mum sealing this envelope with her hands so many years ago.

I prise it open and slip out the letter. It's still crisp, a single page of my mother's beautiful cursive writing, in indigo fountain-pen ink.

To my darling Emma

I begin by reading out loud so Dad can hear too, but after a sentence that becomes impossible. I simply want to read. To hear the message my mum sent to me for this very day, today. As I scan the words, the soft tones of her voice come back to me, as if she's sitting here.

It's supposed to be hard for a mother to imagine what her little girl will grow up to be like. But somehow I'm finding it easy. The six-year-old Emma I knew was bright, beautiful, loving, smart, sensible and full of spirit. It's impossible to imagine a thirty-year-old Emma who isn't the same.

Thirty is a funny year, isn't it? I can imagine exactly what you're thinking, if you're anything like me when I said goodbye to my twenties: Oh God . . . I've got to grow up now! I've got to be responsible and careful and all those things you're meant to be when you hit this milestone.

Well, here's my advice to you, my darling daughter: don't grow up. Be fearless. I never had the chance to experience my thirties, but I have a feeling about you, Emma, call it intuition. This is your time to shine.

By now you've learned how strong you are, how much you're capable of. Grasp that knowledge with both hands and run with it. Take risks. Have fun. And – if you're fortunate enough to have met someone – love him. With every bone in your body, if he's the right one for you.

The Wish List

You've had these letters every year now, but, given that it's a special birthday, I thought I ought to mark this one as such, at least in a small way. So please find enclosed my gift to you, darling girl: the thing you loved so much when you were small. I hope it's been worth the wait.

Happy birthday, Emma.

Until next year,

Your loving Mum

xxxx

With trembling hands, I put down the letter and look in the envelope again. At the bottom is a small, folded piece of tissue paper. I take it out and unwrap it, even though I've guessed exactly what's inside. The second I see my mother's diamond necklace – the one in that picture I love so much – tears spill down my face, and I pick it up and clasp it tightly.

It's the best birthday present I could ever have wanted.

Chapter 96

After a week of lacklustre dieting, there's plenty more room in the dress than when I tried it on. By which I mean approximately half a millimetre, possibly less. Still, there's no way I'm ticking off all those things on my list and failing on this one – technically the most straightforward.

'I think I may be pushing my luck,' I mumble to Asha, examining my creaking zip. I have come to the conclusion that if it survives the night under such colossal pressure, Karen Millen should consider a side line in the production of mountaineering clips.

We're in the Ladies in Leaf before everyone arrives. And I mean everyone. The fifty-odd people I know and love best are coming – university friends, work colleagues, favourite relatives. Which means Perry will be rubbing shoulders with the likes of Aunt Sheila and Uncle Dave, producing a social mix that couldn't be more eclectic if the staff of *Kerrang!* gatecrashed the *Vogue* Christmas party.

'You look gorgeous,' Asha reassures me, topping up her mascara. 'Besides, the tailored look is in this season, isn't it?'

'This isn't tailored, Asha. This risks puncturing my vital organs.'

She smiles softly, but her eyes betray how sad she really is. Yet, despite Toby's persistent phone calls, she's stuck to her guns – and is determined to never see him again.

'How are you doing, sweetheart?' I ask.

'I'm doing fine. Yesterday was a challenge, I must admit.'

'What happened?'

She puts her mascara back in her bag and takes a deep breath. 'Christina is pregnant.'

'Oh Asha.' I don't know what else to say.

'Quite an achievement considering that, allegedly, they weren't having sex, don't you think? I only know because he emailed me a long letter saying he'd finally got the message. He admitted defeat, and said he understood why I didn't want anything to do with him any longer. The bit about the new baby was almost a postscript.'

I sigh and lean in to hug her.

'It's fine,' she says. 'I'm thirty years old. I'm a grown woman. Worse things happen, eh?'

'You'll find someone, Asha, I know you will.'

She smiles. 'It's odd, but part of me feels almost relieved, believe it or not. As well as feeling completely and utterly shit, obviously. But I've got my friends. I've got my family. And I've finally got my self-respect – which is something I haven't been acquainted with for a long time.'

'I'm proud of you, Asha.'

'The feeling's mutual. Happy birthday, lovely!' She smiles again, squeezing my arm. 'You'd better get out there before your guests arrive.'

By nine thirty the place is packed. I feel like I'm at my own wedding; the only thing missing is a groom – and, given the events of the last six months, it seems unlikely there'll ever be one.

'Emma. . . . Emma . . . *Emma!*'

I glance down and Zachary is standing next to me, tugging my skirt. 'Here's your present. It's a book called *Riders*.'

I bend down and take it from him as Cally appears behind him. 'Sweetheart, it was meant to be a surprise.'

'That's okay,' I insist. 'Thank you *so* much, Zachary.'

He leans in and gives me a hug, squeezing me as tightly as his podgy arms can manage, before darting away again to 'fix' a speaker by thumping it with his plastic hammer.

I can't help smiling.

'I really hope you don't mind me bringing him,' Cally says. 'Mum's away this weekend so I had no childcare.'

'It's lovely to see him here. Besides, I've seen him dance to the Black Eyed Peas and I'll need someone to deflect attention from Dad. Besides . . . he's a lot mellower these days, isn't he?'

She shrugs. 'Well, all two-year-olds go through a bit of a wild patch, but yes, he's changed. As have you,' she smiles.

'Drinks, ladies.' Giles appears and presents us both with a gin and tonic, clinking his glass against mine. 'Happy birthday again, Em. You deserve a fantastic one.'

'Oops ... Zachary!' Cally shrieks as he begins scaling sofas. '*Spiderman* was on this afternoon and ... *Zachary!*' She thrusts her drink in my hand with her usual lightning reflexes and goes to rein him in. Except someone beats her to it. Before anybody can argue, Giles is on the other side of the room, coaxing the little boy down. He instantly captures his attention, presumably with one of his jokes about flatulence, underpants or burping – these, he assured me the other day, were the only things anyone who wished to bond with a small male child needed to remember.

'Is this the first time they've met?'

Cally nods. 'I introduced them today.'

'They seem to be getting on well,' I point out, as Giles launches into a coin trick that has the little boy enthralled.

'Yeah. Don't they?' she grins. 'They've talked a lot about farting, admittedly, but I can't complain about that. So, how are you feeling?'

'Happy that I've ticked off so many things on my list. Happy to be surrounded by most of the people I love. Happy about the letter from my mum,' I add, touching my necklace.

'But sad about Matt?'

I nod, feeling my throat tighten. 'You know, Mum said something in her letter about being fearless. About loving with every bone in my body.'

She frowns.

'Cally ... I need to do something about this.'

There's an urgency in my voice as adrenalin rushes through me. 'I need to do something big.'

She looks alarmed. 'You don't mean go after him? To France?'

The hint of a thought that's been gathering pace for days explodes in my brain and is suddenly perfectly clear, perfectly lucid. 'Is that so crazy, when you're in love with someone? I need to be with this man, Cally. It's as simple as that.'

She shakes her head, clearly unconvinced, but before I can argue there's a tap on my shoulder and it's James, the animator at work. I'm swept up in a bustle of chatting, drinks, gift-giving. Yet my mind is firmly on one thing. And what's going on around me only confirms it.

This should be the night of my life. But something's missing. Something is on his way to France right this minute. And I should be with him.

'Emma.'

I recognise the voice before I spin round and set eyes on Rob. He's wearing a checked shirt, slim jeans and has left a trail of my younger cousins swooning in his path. 'Thanks for inviting me,' he says awkwardly.

I smile, at first leaning in to kiss him, then deciding to turn it into a hug. 'Rob, it's so lovely to see you.'

He smiles shyly. 'Are you enjoying yourself?'

'I am,' I shrug. 'Being thirty isn't bad, after all.'

'So have you given up on the guitar?'

'I'm not sure I'm a natural. What do you think?'

He laughs. 'You just didn't practise enough. I may have a new student, by the way. I spoke to Asha earlier – did you know she's thinking of taking it up?'

'Seriously?'

'Yeah,' he grins. 'She's nice, Asha, isn't she?'

I smile, as an idea infiltrates my head. 'She is, Rob. She really is.'

Marianne has never looked so beautiful – or happy. My sister is dressed in a simple, floral, River Island dress but it's enough to dazzle everyone in her path – including Brian.

'We meet at last!' I go to kiss him, but he nearly sweeps me off my feet with a hug instead. I hadn't appreciated, from our brief online conversations, how tall he is – at least six foot three – with an athletic physique and a smile that is warm, genuine. Unlike the last time I saw him, he's dressed impeccably and has lost the woolly mammoth look from his chin.

'I know I wasn't meant to be here tonight – but they agreed to let me have the day off from work and I couldn't think of a better way of celebrating.'

'You're celebrating?' I ask.

'Brian's script has been bought by a production company,' Marianne says, clearly bursting with pride.

'You're kidding me? That's unbelievable! Do you know how hard that is? Of course you do . . .'

He laughs. 'Well, there's a long way to go before I collect my Bafta, but it's all going in the right direction.'

I glance at Marianne, at her beaming smile. 'Yes,' I say. 'I can see it is.'

It's ten thirty when Dad makes his big speech and I'm not nearly drunk enough. It's not that he says anything awful – although I could have done without the reference to the school nativity play when I was so stage struck I vomited into the manger.

'Many of you know that Emma's been learning the guitar. She's been very secretive, but that's all going to change,' he beams, as I shift anxiously from foot to foot. 'She told me ages ago that one of the songs she's learned – the one she'll be playing tonight – is one of her favourite songs by the Lone Roses.'

My throat suddenly feels in urgent need of hydration. And while I vaguely remember my ambition to play something by the Stone Roses tonight, that was during the blissfully ignorant first stage of my lessons – before I worked out that my musical capabilities stretched only to shattering ear drums.

'Come on, birthday girl, don't be shy!' grins Dad – as Deb hands him my guitar. I don't move anything but my head – and that I *really* move, shaking it from side to side, my eyes wide with blood-curdling terror.

'Emma! Come on now!'

Cally – one of the select few who've heard my guitar playing – winces as if someone's squirted petrol in her eye.

But with the rest – the poor, ignorant rest – cheering, I can do little except move reluctantly to the stage and start to negotiate the steps, a manoeuvre which, courtesy of my dress, gives the impression that I've been recently mummified.

'Um ... thanks, Dad,' I mumble as he hands me the guitar and shoves me in front of the microphone. 'At least I'm among friends.'

Everyone laughs riotously, as if I'm joking. Which of course I am. A little. There's something about being on stage, having an audience, that gives my confidence a slight boost. I mean, I know I'm no Susanna Hoffs but I'm not *that* bad. Not really.

'Here we are,' says Dad eagerly, thrusting a stand in front of me, complete with my guitar book.

It's open at the song I was determined to play: 'I Am the Resurrection'. The opening chords are strumming through my mind as the crowd looks on expectantly.

I close my eyes and breathe in the atmosphere, electricity buzzing through my veins. I suddenly know I don't need the sheet music – no more than John Squire needed it when he stood before thirty thousand enraptured fans at Spike Island.

So I step away from it and gaze at the audience, anticipating the performance of my life. Then I strum. And I sing. And they recognise the lyrics instantly ...

'*Kum-ba-ya, my lord . . . kum-ba-yaaahhhh. . . .*'

Half an hour later, the dance floor is so packed you'd think it was at the centre of a magnetic field. Giles is teaching Zachary 'The Time Warp' as Cally giggles uncontrollably. Brian is swinging Marianne round like he's trying to start a fire with the soles of her shoes. And Deb is giving Dad detailed instructions on how to master the pelvic thrust without risking trauma to his dodgy hip.

The party is roaring, everyone is having a blast, and I feel a swell of gratitude to be surrounded by friends and family like these. The cast of people that make up my life; the people I love.

I untangle myself from Uncle Trevor – assuring him Aunt June would be a better partner for his *Dirty Dancing* routine – and stand breathlessly at the bar as the room throbs with noise. As music rushes through me, I reach up and touch Mum's necklace, twirling the tiny diamond between my fingertips. My future – my choice – is the only thing on my mind.

France is wrong for me in every way. I have no job there. I'll have severe difficulty in ever getting one, given that I'd be living in the middle of the countryside. None of my friends and family are there. And that's before we get onto the fact that the only French I can remember from school is: '*J'ai douze ans*' – which became defunct in 1994. Moving there would be the biggest risk of my life – and, I'll be honest, it's one of which I can see only one benefit: Matt's there. And that's why it's so completely right. Being with him is the only thing that counts.

I put down my drink and rush to the cloakroom to find my phone. Only, as I pull it out and glance at the screen, I freeze.

There are four missed calls, all made in the last hour. All from Matt. I weave through guests in the main room and head outside to get a signal so that I can phone him.

It's freezing, yet I'm red hot, my breath swirling in the darkness as I frantically dial his number. I get an engaged tone the first time, then the second. I'm about to repeat the exercise when footsteps distract me.

'Hey! How's the birthday girl?'

It's Johnny. Looking better than he did the last time – but then he'd probably consider this early compared to some of the twenty-four-hour binges Marianne has told me about.

'Um ... hi, Johnny. Didn't you get my Facebook message?' I ask.

'Hardly use it, Em. Had a good birthday?'

'Johnny, I know about you and Cally. And Zachary. Your son.'

He pauses, taking in the information. 'I see.' He takes a deep breath and looks me in the eyes. 'I suppose you think I'm an arse, do you?'

I hesitate. 'Something like that, Johnny.'

His jaw tenses with anger. 'When I become a father, Emma, it's not going to be the result of a one-night stand with some slut.'

'Johnny, you already *are* a father,' I find myself saying. 'That's the case whether you like it or not. Cally is no slut. And, by the way, your son is amazing.'

He shakes his head furiously. 'Emma, I'm in love with your sister and I always will be. She's the one I should've had kids with. I'm paying for one mistake ... one stupid bloody mistake that never should've happened – and I'll be paying for the rest of my life.'

'Johnny, Marianne fell out of love with you long before you

fathered a child with Cally. The way you've acted over that has sealed the deal. You have a beautiful, healthy, funny little boy. He's yours. Your flesh and blood, Johnny. Look.'

I grab him by the hand and pull him to the window, where I wipe clean a section and peer in. 'Look,' I repeat.

He glances at me reluctantly then leans his face towards the window, focusing on the corner of the room. Zachary is on Giles's knee, giggling as he's being tickled.

'That's your boy, Johnny. Isn't he lovely?'

I stand up straight, wondering if it's possible for him to alter his position on Zachary now he's seen him. I have my answer sooner than I imagined.

He looks at me briefly, then turns his back and walks away. From his son. From his past. And from his son's future.

I am about to turn my attention to the phone again, when it rings. I recognise the number immediately and answer so fast I almost drop it.

'Emma.'

'Matt,' I reply. 'What is it? I missed a load of calls.'

He doesn't answer at first. I can hear nothing through my handset except footsteps. They're faint to begin with, but then get louder and louder until I become woozily aware that they're in surround sound.

'Matt?'

I head to the side of the building, following the sound that's identical to what I'm hearing in my phone, and I have my answer. His eyes say everything and nothing as he stands before me, looking almost as disbelieving as I am.

'I'm here,' he laughs.

And we fall into each other's arms, hysterically kissing each other so urgently it's as if we're afraid one of us will disappear in a cloud of smoke.

Chapter 97

'What are you doing here?' I ask incredulously, pulling away as he strokes the hair from my face.

'I hate to miss a good party.'

The emotion in his expression is hard to describe or comprehend. He looks like a man who's had the best and the worst days of his life all in one.

'You postponed your trip for twenty-four-hours?'

He hesitates. 'I postponed my trip indefinitely.'

He squeezes me into him and when he finally releases me, he suppresses a smile, shaking his head. 'Sorry. I just never thought I was going to get to do that again.'

'Matt, what's going on?'

'I owe you a favour, Emma. I owe you the biggest favour of my life. You phoned me from the supermarket last week, when Guillaume was shouting at Joshua. And you left a message. One I only picked up today when I got my phone back.'

I frown. 'But it didn't say anything more than I'd already told you.'

'Not initially. Only ... you forgot to end the call. The message recorded everything. Every last horrible bit of it.'

My jaw drops. 'So you heard what Guillaume said, what he did?'

'Everything.'

'That must've been horrific.'

'Horrific for me – and horrific for Allison. She could do nothing but believe you about Guillaume, about what happened. She heard it for herself. She was devastated. And furious.'

'So what did she do?'

'I've been looking after the kids tonight – at their house – while she and Guillaume thrashed things out.'

'And are things ... thrashed?'

He swallows, emotion washing over his face as he speaks. 'They're not going to France with Guillaume any more. They're staying right here.'

I suddenly feel as though I've lost my voice, but I find it from somewhere. 'Does that mean *you're* staying too?'

He holds my face in his hands and leans in to kiss me. His warm lips melt into mine and the world falls silent.

He pulls back and nods. 'I am.'

Chapter 98

As I open the door to Leaf I'm hit by a wave of music, heat and laughter. It's clear that I hadn't been missed.

I weave through the throng, clutching Matt's hand, pausing briefly to say hello and introduce him to friends and family in various stages of inebriation.

'Are you going to dance with me on my birthday?' I ask, as we find refuge by the bar.

'Was it ever in any doubt?'

With elation running through me, we hit the dance floor – just in time for me to spot Dad next to the window with Deb. At first glance, I think nothing of the ambiguous look in their eyes. Only, when I glance down, I see something that redefines their relationship in a way I should've recognised a long time ago: they're holding hands.

Exactly when Deb and Dad got together I have no idea. It could've been months ago – it could've been minutes.

'Is everything all right?' Matt asks.

I smile, reach up to his face and kiss him firmly on the lips. 'Everything's *brilliant*.'

The rhythm of the music changes and I feel a tap on my back.

'This one's for you, Em,' Cally grins as she slips her arm round me, drags me from Matt – and Marianne and Asha appear.

My sister, my friends and I swing our hips to 'Groove is in the Heart', just like we did as teenagers – only, this time I manage not to break my ankle.

Today I'm thirty years old.

And this is my time.

Epilogue

24 January, 10.43 a.m.:
one month and two days later.

I wonder if I should worry about the fact my darling boyfriend bought me a birthday present that has the potential to cause instant death, hideous mutilation or – if I'm lucky – just bring me out in the sort of sweat that rots armpits.

I told him I'd try not to hold it against him. That was before I got into the plane.

Now that I'm in it, making my twelve-thousand-foot ascent into the heavens, I'm hyperventilating like I'm trying to break the world record in carbon dioxide production.

There are a million questions firing through my brain – everything from 'What happens if the parachute doesn't work?' (I know the answer to that one) to 'What if I wet myself?' (I know the answer to that too – and the six-foot-tall Scottish instructor I'll be strapped to doesn't come out well).

There is so much adrenalin in my body I feel drunk with it. I don't need to look in a mirror to know that my complexion is the colour of the Jolly Green Giant.

'How are you feeling, Emma?' grins Ricky. He's the Scot.

'Like I'm about to die.'

He laughs and slaps me on the shoulder. 'Ah . . . you'll love it. I guarantee.'

'Why do I not believe you?'

The truth is, it's only now I'm up here that I realise how much I want to do this. How much I *need* to do this, even though my deadline for the list has well and truly passed.

Yet I also know Matt's right about what he's been telling me since yesterday: I shouldn't beat myself up if I don't make this leap. I should only do it *if I want to*. I'm not a failure if I don't. And I certainly shouldn't let it alter my perspective on everything else in my life.

My life. Which is unbelievably show-stoppingly great. If the rest of my thirties are like the first month, then bring 'em on.

Work has been fantastic since we won the pitch – and, as well as Perry's mad/genius (I still can't decide which) idea about garden implements, I've been asked as creative director to put together firmer plans for one idea Giles and I came up with – about an ice-skating princess – a year ago. Perry Snr is so excited that we're making a pilot for Channel 6 – and have a meeting with them in six weeks' time. I can't pretend Perry is any less mad, but since his father insisted on the appointment of a deputy CEO – and persuaded Sarah McIntyre back from Australia –

we're not at the mercy of his lunacy to anything like the same extent.

Not that it'd bother Giles if we were. Well, not much. The point is, Giles is happy. Very, very happy. Something that can largely be attributed to the shift in Cally's attitude since my party; it's as if that night she saw a new dimension to him. The fact that Zachary adores Giles is an added bonus – and the feeling's mutual. Giles talks about his new little friend so much there are times when I almost wish he'd start moaning again.

Asha told me last week that Rob has asked her on a date. Ridiculously, she seemed nervous about it, concerned I had lingering feelings about him. I reassured her that I'm over the moon – and suggested she never, ever takes him camping.

I've been waiting for weeks for Dad to mention what's going on with Deb – and had started to think I'll still be waiting when the Queen begins to compose her hundredth-birthday telegram to him. So I came out asked him. There was so much stuttering you'd think Paul van Dyk had remixed his vocal chords. Eventually, when I pointed out I'd seen them holding hands at my party, he was forced to confess that she'd sent him an email via Match.com.

'She was the best of the bunch by a long, long way,' he said sheepishly. 'Don't you mind?'

He'd been worried Marianne and I wouldn't like the idea of him dating Deb, given that Mum knew her. But Mum would've approved, I know it. Just as I'm sure she'd have approved of Matt.

Reading her letters – and the ones she sent to Marianne – has given me a unique insight, one that makes an element of my life finally feel complete. She was so wise, funny, clever, brave. Everything I want to be.

Not that I'm feeling overly brave right now. I'm so paralysed with fear I'm not sure I can actually move towards the door. Despite that, I feel different these days. Maybe it's being in love with someone who loves me back. Maybe it's being in my thirties. Maybe it's all just coincidence.

All I know is this.

As I perch next to the open door with a deafening heartbeat, I am delirious with fear. I have lost the ability to speak. My stomach is turning over at the rate of approximately four hundred revolutions a minute.

Ricky checks if I'm okay. At least, I think that's what he does. I can't hear him properly and I hesitate and close my eyes, wondering if I can really go through with this.

He repeats his question, more clearly: 'Emma, are you ready?'

The sound in my brain fades to nothing but I can hear two words, words that have somehow left my mouth, despite the fact that I haven't taken a breath in at least a minute. 'I am.'

Then I breathe. I smile. And I leap.

Jane Costello

All the Single Ladies

**Samantha Brooks' boyfriend has made a mistake.
One his friends, family, and Sam herself know
he'll live to regret.**

Jamie has announced he's leaving, out of the blue.
Jamie is loving, intelligent and, while he isn't perfect,
he's perfect for her – in every way except one: he's a
free spirit. And after six years in one place, doing a job
he despises, he is compelled to do something that
will tear apart his relationship with Sam:
book a one-way flight to South America.

But Sam isn't giving up without a fight. With Jamie still
totally in love with her, and torn about whether to stay or
go, she has five months to persuade him to do the right
thing. So with the help of her friends Ellie and Jen, she
hatches a plan to make him realise what he's giving
up. A plan that involves dirty tricks, plotting,
and a single aim: to win him back.

But by the time the tortured Jamie finally wakes up to what
he's lost, a gorgeous new pretender has entered Sam's life.
Which begs the question . . . does she still want him back?

'Close the doors, open a bottle of wine, get out the
chocs and enjoy this wonderfully witty read.
Jane Costello at her best' Milly Johnson

ISBN 978-0-85720-553-7
PRICE £7.99

Jane Costello
Girl on the Run

He's a real catch ... if only she could catch him up

Abby Rogers has been on health kicks before – they
involve eating one blueberry muffin for breakfast
instead of two. But since starting her own business,
after watching one too many episodes of *The Apprentice*,
the 28-year-old's waistline has taken even more of
a back seat than her long-neglected love life.

When Abby is encouraged to join her sporty best friend's
running club – by none other than its gorgeous new
captain – she finds a mysterious compulsion to exercise.

Sadly, her first session doesn't go to plan. Between the
obscenely unflattering pink leggings, and the fact that
her lungs feel as though they've been set on fire,
she vows never to return.

Then her colleague Heidi turns up at work and makes
a devastating announcement, one that will change
her life – and Abby's – forever.

ISBN 978-1-84739-626-6
PRICE £7.99

Little Black Dress®

Win a £1,000 wardrobe from LittleBlackDress.co.uk!

To celebrate the launch of Jane Costello's THE WISH LIST, Little Black Dress is offering Simon & Schuster readers the chance to win £1,000 worth of its best designer dresses, accessories and jewellery.

Little Black Dress is home to the world's largest and finest collection of LBDs, party dresses and accessories to complete your going out look. Shop the site for unique dresses, shoes, bags and jewellery from designer, high street and independent fashion brands, and keep ahead with the latest fashion news, trends and advice with LBD's Daily Style magazine.

To enter and for full terms and conditions, visit
http://pages.simonandschuster.co.uk/competitions/littleblackdress

Follow us on Twitter: **@teamLBD**
Like us: **Facebook.com/yourlittleblackdress**

www.littleblackdress.co.uk

EXCLUSIVE OFFER
10% OFF
USE CODE WISHLIST10 AT LITTLEBLACKDRESS.CO.UK

CBS●drama

Whether you love the glamour of Dallas, the feisty exploits of Bad Girls, the courtroom drama of Boston Legal or the forensic challenges of the world's most watched drama CSI: Crime Scene Investigation, CBS Drama is bursting with colourful characters, compelling cliff-hangers, love stories, break-ups and happy endings.

Autumn's line-up includes Patricia Arquette in supernatural series Medium, big hair and bitch fights in Dallas and new Happy Hour strand daily from 6pm with a doublemeasure from everyone's favourite Boston bar Cheers.

Also at CBS Drama you're just one 'like' closer to your on screen heroes. Regular exclusive celebrity interviews and behind the scenes news is hosted on Facebook and Twitter page. Recent contributors include Dallas' Bobby Ewing (Patrick Duffy), CSI's Catherine Willows (Marg Helgenberger) and Cheers' Sam Malone (Ted Danson).

www.cbsdrama.co.uk

f facebook.com/cbsdrama

𝕏 twitter.com/cbsdrama

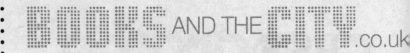